2001

Praise for

SUTURE

and MARY DA

Bed-and-Break

"Delightful"
Kansas City Star

"Skillfully takes a satiric scalpel to the hospital
industry . . . There are funny twists aplenty . . . [and]
telling jabs at modern hospital care as the novel
scampers to its zany conclusion. The other inmates of
Good Cheer Hospital—staff and patients alike—are so
wacky that every ward seems like a psychiatric unit."
Portland Oregonian

"Like Joan Hess' Maggody series, Daheim's bed-and-
breakfast mysteries show a funny and often stinging
insight into people's relationships and behavior.
SUTURE SELF is less about solving a crime than
about the too-real-not-to-be-funny personalities of the
people involved."
Houston Chronicle

"Daheim fans will relish the witty and revealing
interactions between familiar characters."
Publishers Weekly

"[A] screwball crime novel . . . The banter . . . is
choice . . . And Good Cheer Hospital does live up to
its name in the warped sense that it malfunctions even
more blatantly than a real-life hospital."
Newark Star-Ledger

Other Bed-and-Breakfast Mysteries by Mary Daheim

MARY DAHEIM

SUTURE SELF

AVON BOOKS
An Imprint of HarperCollinsPublishers

This is a work of fiction. Names, characters, places, and incidents are products of the author's imagination or are used fictitiously and are not to be construed as real. Any resemblance to actual events, locales, organizations, or persons, living or dead, is entirely coincidental.

AVON BOOKS
An Imprint of HarperCollins*Publishers*
10 East 53rd Street
New York, New York 10022-5299

Copyright © 2001 by Mary Daheim
Excerpt from *Silver Scream* copyright © 2002 by Mary Daheim
ISBN: 0-380-81561-3
www.avonbooks.com

First Avon Books paperback printing: January 2002
First William Morrow hardcover printing: February 2001

Avon Trademark Reg. U.S. Pat. Off. and in Other Countries,
Marca Registrada, Hecho en U.S.A.
HarperCollins ® is a trademark of HarperCollins Publishers Inc.

Printed in the U.S.A.

10 9 8 7 6 5 4 3 2 1

SUTURE
SELF

ONE

JUDITH GROVER MCMONIGLE Flynn took one look at the newspaper headline, released the brake on her wheelchair, and rolled into the kitchen.

"I'm not sure it's safe to go into the hospital," she said to her husband, Joe Flynn. "Look at this."

Joe, who had just come in through the back door, hung his all-weather jacket on a peg in the hallway and stared at the big, bold front-page headline.

ACTRESS DIES FOLLOWING ROUTINE SURGERY
John Fremont Succumbs After Minor Foot Operation

"Who's John Fremont?" Joe asked after kissing his wife on the cheek. "The explorer? No wonder he wrecked his feet, going over all those mountains. Huh. I thought he was already dead."

"He's been dead for over a hundred years," Judith replied. "It's a—"

"A shame the local newspaper doesn't jump on those stories faster," Joe interrupted. "What's Queen Victoria up to this week?"

Judith made a face at Joe. "It's a typo," she said in a testy voice. "It's supposed to be Joan Fremont. See, there it is in the lead. You know who she is—

we've seen her in several local stage productions. She is—was—a wonderful actress."

Joe frowned as he read deeper into the story. "Jeez, don't these people proofread anymore?"

"That's not my point," Judith asserted. "That's the second well-known person in three weeks to peg out at Good Cheer Hospital. I'm getting scared to go in next Monday for my hip replacement."

Joe opened the cupboard and got out a bottle of Scotch. "You mean Somosa, the pitcher? That's no mystery. He was probably full of amphetamines." With an air of apology, Joe gestured with the bottle. "Sorry, I hate to drink in front of you, but I spent ten hours sitting on my butt for that damned insurance stakeout."

"Never mind." Judith sighed with a martyred air that would have made her Aunt Deb proud. "I'm used to sacrifice and self-denial. After a month in this stupid wheelchair and taking all those pain pills, I suppose I should be looking forward to surgery and getting back to a normal life. How'd the stakeout go?"

"It didn't," Joe replied, dumping ice cubes into a glass. "The guy didn't budge from his sofa except to go to the can. Then he used a walker. Maybe he's legit. The insurance company expected him to play a set of tennis or jump over high hurdles or do the rumba. I hate these alleged insurance-fraud assignments."

"They pay well," Judith pointed out, giving the amber liquid in Joe's glass a longing look.

"Oh, yeah," Joe agreed, sitting down at the kitchen table. "We can use the money with the B&B shut down for five weeks. I'm expensive to keep, and you're not delivering."

Teasing or not, the comment nettled Judith. Just after Christmas, her right hip had deteriorated to the point that she'd been confined to a wheelchair. With the help of Joe and their neighbors, Carl and Arlene Rankers, Judith had managed to keep Hillside Manor running smoothly through the holidays. But Carl and Arlene had left the day after New Year's for a vacation in Palm Desert. And even though Joe was retired from the police force, his part-time private investigations had become almost a full-time job. It had been a difficult decision for Judith, but she had been forced to cancel all reservations for the first ten days of January, until the Rankerses' return. Her only consolation was that the days in question were the slowest time of the year for the Bed-and-Breakfast industry.

"We've lost at least four grand," Judith said in a morose tone.

Joe gave a slight shake of his head. "Dubious. The weather around here this winter isn't exactly enticing to visitors."

Judith glanced up at the window over the kitchen sink. It was raining. It seemed to have been raining for months. Fifty degrees and raining. No sun breaks, no snow, just relentless rain and gloomy, glowering skies. Day after day of gray, gray, and grayer. Even a Pacific Northwest native like Judith had an occasional hankering for a patch of blue sky.

"People still visit people," Judith said, unwilling to let herself be cheered.

Joe gave a solemn shake of his head. "Not in January. Everybody's broke."

"Including us," Judith said. "Because of me. Renie and Bill are broke, too," she added, referring to her cousin and her cousin's husband. "Renie can't work with her bad shoulder. This is the busiest time of year for her, with all the annual reports. She usually designs at least a half-dozen, which means big bucks. She's out of commission until March."

"When's her surgery?" Joe inquired.

"A week after mine," Judith replied. "We'll be like ships passing in the night. Or should I say sinking?" Judith emitted another heavy sigh as she rolled over to the sink and took a Percocet. Then she took another Percocet. It couldn't hurt. Besides, she ached twice as much as she had the day before.

As a distraction, Judith read the rest of the story about Joan Fremont. The actress had been admitted to Good Cheer Hospital the previous day. Her surgery, pronounced successful, had been performed that afternoon. But at ten-thirty this morning, Joan had died suddenly and without warning. She left behind two grown children and her husband, Addison Kirby, the city hall reporter for the evening newspaper.

"No wonder her name got misspelled," Judith remarked. "Joan's husband works for the paper. The staff must be shaken by her death."

"Oh?" Joe raised rust-colored eyebrows above the sports section. "Kirby, huh? I've run into him a few times at city hall. Nice guy, but strictly business."

Judith put the newspaper's front section down on the table. "They'll investigate, I assume?"

"Oh, sure," Joe responded, his gaze back on the sports page. "They did with Joaquin Somosa, they will with Joan Fremont. It's automatic when someone relatively young and in otherwise good health dies in a hospital. The county medical examiner has jurisdiction."

"That makes sense," Judith said as she rolled to the stove. "I made beef-noodle bake. It's almost done. I've fixed a salad and there are some rolls I'll heat up. Then you can take Mother's portion out to the toolshed."

Joe grimaced. "Can't I phone it in to her?"

"Joe . . ." Judith stopped. Serving Gertrude's meals was a bone of contention since Judith had become wheelchair-bound. Joe Flynn and Gertrude Grover didn't get along. An understatement, Judith thought. How else to put it? If duels were still legal, they would have skewered each other by the birdbath a long time ago.

The phone rang just as Judith slipped the foil-wrapped rolls into the oven. Fumbling a bit, she pulled the cordless receiver out of the gingham pocket on her wheelchair.

"Coz?" said Renie, who sounded excited. "Guess what."

"What? Make it quick, I've got my head in the oven."

"Coz!" Renie cried. "Nothing's that bad! Hang in there, you're only a few days away from surgery. You'll be fine."

"I mean I'm trying to put dinner together," Judith said, sounding cross. Her usual easygoing manner had begun to fray in recent weeks.

"Oh." Renie paused. "Good. I mean . . . Never mind. I called to tell you that Dr. Ming's office just phoned to say that they'd had a surgery cancellation on Monday and I can go in a whole week early. Isn't that great? We'll be in the hospital together."

Judith brightened. "Really? That's wonderful." She paused. "I think."

"You think?" Now Renie sounded annoyed. "We could share a room. We could encourage each other's recovery. We could make fun of the hospital staff and the other patients. We could have some laughs."

"Yes, yes, of course," Judith said as she closed the

oven door. "It's just that . . . Have you seen tonight's paper?"

"Ours hasn't come yet," Renie replied. "You know we always have a later delivery on this side of Heraldsgate Hill."

"Well," Judith began, then caught Joe's warning glance. "It's nothing, really. You can see for yourself when the paper comes."

"Coz." Renie sounded stern. "Tell me now or I'll have to hit you with my good arm. You can't run away from me, remember?"

Judith sighed. "There's been another unexpected death at Good Cheer Hospital. Joan Fremont, the actress."

"Joan Fremont!" Renie shrieked. "Oh, no! Wait till I tell Bill. I think he's always had a crush on her. What happened?"

Ignoring Joe's baleful look, Judith picked up the front section of the paper and read the story to Renie.

"That's terrible," Renie responded in a shocked voice. "She was so talented. And young. Well— younger than we are. A little bit, anyway. She'd probably had work done, being an actress."

"That's two deaths in three weeks," Judith noted.

"Joaquin Somosa," Renie murmured. "Younger still. Elbow surgery. Supposed to be healed by the All-Star break."

"Won't," Judith said, suddenly feeling light-headed. "Dead instead."

"This is scary," Renie declared. "Do you suppose we should ask Dr. Ming and Dr. Alfonso to operate on us in the privacy of our own automobiles?"

Judith started to respond, but just then the back door banged open. Gertrude Grover stood in the hallway, leaning on her walker and wearing a very old and slightly shabby wool coat over her head. Worse yet, Judith saw two of her. Maybe she should have taken only one Percocet.

"Where's my supper?" Gertrude demanded, thumping the walker on the floor for emphasis.

Judith spoke into the phone. "Gotta go. Mother's here." She rang off. "I'm heating the rolls," Judith said with a feeble smile, trying not to slur her words. "Mother, you shouldn't come out in the rain. You'll catch cold."

"And die?" Gertrude's small eyes darted in the direction of Joe's back. "Wouldn't that suit Dumbo here?"

"Mother," Judith said with a frown, accidentally ramming the wheelchair into the stove. "Oops! 'Course not. You know better." She tried to ignore the puzzled expression on her husband's face. "Hasn't Joe taken good care of you while I've been laid out? I mean, laid up."

"It's part of his plan," Gertrude said, scowling at Joe, who was still turned away from his mother-in-law. "He's waiting until you go into the hospital. Then, when I'm supposed to be lulled into . . . something-or-other, he'll strike!" Gertrude slammed the walker again. "He knows the ropes, he used to be a cop. They'll never catch him, and he'll make off with all my candy."

"Mother . . ." Judith wished she didn't feel so muddled. She wished she could walk. She wished her mother wouldn't insist on wearing a coat that was at least twenty years old. She wished Gertrude would shut up. She wished she didn't have two mothers, standing side by side.

Joe had finally risen from the chair. "I don't eat

candy," he said in his most casual manner. "You got any jewels stashed out there in the toolshed, Mrs. G.?"

"Ha!" Gertrude exclaimed. "Wouldn't you like to know?" It was one of those rare occasions when Gertrude addressed Joe directly. As a rule, she spoke of him in the third person.

Clumsily, Judith opened the oven. "Here, your dinner's ready. Joe can help dish it up for you, Mother."

"I'm watching his every move," Gertrude said, narrowing her eyes. "He might slip something into my food. I should have Sweetums eat it first, but that ornery cat's too danged finicky."

Joe got the salad out of the refrigerator and removed the beef-noodle bake from the oven. He filled Gertrude's plate with a flourish, added a roll, and started for the back door. "At your service," he called over his shoulder. "Let me help you out."

"Out?" Gertrude snapped. "Out where? Out of this world?"

She was still hurling invective as the two of them went outside. It was a conflict of long standing, a personal Thirty Years War between Joe Flynn and Gertrude Grover. When Joe had first courted Judith, Gertrude had announced that she didn't like him. He was a cop. They made rotten husbands. He was Irish. They always drank too much. He had no respect for his elders. He wouldn't kowtow to Gertrude.

Judith and Joe had gotten engaged anyway. And then disaster struck. Joe had gotten drunk, not because he was Irish but because he was a cop, and had come upon two teenagers who had overdosed on drugs. Putting a couple of fifteen-year-olds in body bags had sent him off to a bar—and into the arms of the sultry singer at the piano. Vivian, or Herself, as

Judith usually called her, had shanghaied the oblivious Joe to Las Vegas and a justice of the peace. The engagement was broken, and so was Judith's heart.

Judith was still dwelling on the past when Joe returned to the kitchen. "She's still alive," he announced, then looked more closely at his wife. "What's wrong? You look sort of sickly."

"Nozzing," Judith replied, trying to smile. "I mean, nothing—except Mudder. *Mother.* It bothers me when she's so mean to you."

Joe shrugged. "I'm used to it. In fact, I get kind of a kick out of it. Face it, Jude-girl, at her age she doesn't have much pleasure in life. If it amuses her to needle me, so what?"

Judith rested her head against Joe's hip. "You're such a decent person, Joe. I love you."

"The feeling is eternally mutual," he said, hugging her shoulders. "How many pain pills did you take?"

"Umm . . ." Judith considered fibbing. She was very good at it. When she could think straight. "Two."

Joe sighed. "Let's eat. Food might straighten you out a bit."

"Wouldn't you think," Judith said halfway through the meal when she had begun to feel more lucid, "that when you and I finally got married after your divorce and Dan's death, Mother would have been happy for us?"

Joe shook his head. "Never. You're an only child, and your father died fairly young. You're all your mother has, and she'll never completely let go. The same's true with Renie. Look how your Aunt Deb pulls Renie around like she's on a string."

"True," Judith allowed. "What I meant was that even if Mother resented you at first, after I married Dan on the rebound, and he turned out to be such a . . . flop, you'd figure that Mother would be glad to see me married to somebody with a real job and a sense of responsibility and a girth considerably less than fifty-four inches. Dan's pants looked like the sails on the *Britannia*."

Joe grinned and the gold flecks danced in his green eyes. "Your mother didn't want a replacement or an improvement. She wanted *you,* back home, under her wing."

"She got it," Judith said with a rueful laugh. "After Dan died, Mike and I couldn't go on living in that rental dump out on Thurlow Street. The rats were so big they were setting traps for *us*."

It was only a slight exaggeration. After losing one house to the IRS for back taxes, defaulting on another, and getting evicted twice, Judith, Dan, and Mike had ended up, as Grandpa Grover would have put it, "in Queer Street." Dan had stopped working altogether by then, and Judith's two jobs barely paid for the basics.

The Thurlow rental was a wreck, the neighborhood disreputable. After Dan died, Judith and her only son moved back into the family home on Heraldsgate Hill. Her mother had protested at first when Judith came up with her scheme to turn the big house into a B&B. Eventually, Gertrude had given in, if only because she and Judith and Mike had to eat. But when Joe reappeared in Judith's life during the homicide investigation of a guest, the old lady had balked. If Judith married Joe, Gertrude announced, she wouldn't live under the same roof with him. Thus, the toolshed had been converted into a small apartment, and Gertrude took her belongings and her umbrage out to the backyard.

She complained constantly, but refused to budge.

Judith pictured her mother in the old brown mohair chair, eating her "supper," watching TV, and cursing Joe Flynn. Gertrude would never change her mind about her son-in-law, not even now in her dotage. But at least some sort of truce was in effect, which made life a little easier at Hillside Manor.

Shortly after seven, Judith called Renie back to get the details on her cousin's surgery. Neither of them knew exactly what time their operations would be scheduled and wouldn't find out until Friday afternoon. Judith hunkered down and tried to be patient. It wasn't easy: Even in the wheelchair, she experienced a considerable amount of pain and, due to the recent news reports, it was accompanied by an unexpected apprehension. Still, Judith could do little more than wait.

The tedium was broken Friday morning when Mike called from his current posting as a forest ranger up on the close-in mountain pass.

"Guess what," he said in his most cheerful voice.

"What?" Judith asked.

"Guess."

The first thing that came to mind was that Mike had been promoted. Which, she thought with plunging spirits, might mean a transfer to anywhere in the fifty states.

"Don't keep me in suspense," Judith said. "I'm an invalid, remember?"

"Mom . . ." Mike chuckled. "It's only temporary. Which is good, because you're going to have to be up and running by the time your next grandchild gets here around the Fourth of July."

"Oh!" Judith's smile was huge and satisfying. "That's terrific! How is Kristin feeling?"

"Great," Mike replied. "You know my girl, she's a hardy honey."

"Hardy" wasn't quite the word Judith would have chosen. "Robust," perhaps, or even "brawny." Kristin McMonigle was a Viking, or maybe a Valkyrie. Mike's wife was big, blonde, and beautiful. She was also constrained, conscientious, and capable. Almost too capable, it seemed to Judith. Kristin could repair a transmission, build a cabinet, bake a Viennese torte, shingle a roof, and balance a checkbook to the penny. Indeed, Judith sometimes found her daughter-in-law intimidating.

"I'm so thrilled," Judith enthused. "I can't wait to tell Joe. And Granny."

"That reminds me," Mike said, "could you call Grandma Effie, too? I don't like making out-of-state calls on the phone in the office. I'd call her from the cabin tonight, but I'm putting on a slide show for some zoologists."

"Of course," Judith said with only a slight hesitation. "I'll call right now."

"Thanks, Mom. Got to run. By the way, good luck Monday if I don't talk to you before you go to the hospital."

Judith clicked the phone off and reached for her address book on the kitchen counter. She ought to know Effie McMonigle's number by heart, but she didn't. Ever since Dan's death eleven years earlier, Judith had called his mother once a month. But somehow the number wouldn't stick in her brain. Maybe it was like Gertrude not speaking directly to Joe; maybe Judith hoped that if she kept forgetting Effie's number, her former mother-in-law would go away, too, and take all the unhappy memories of Dan with her.

Effie was home. She usually was. A nurse by profession, she resided in a retirement community outside Phoenix. In the nineteen years that Judith and Dan had been married, Effie had visited only three times once for the wedding, once when Mike was born, and once for Dan's funeral. Effie was a sun-worshiper. She couldn't stand the Pacific Northwest's gray skies and rainy days. She claimed to become depressed. But Judith felt Effie was always depressed—and depressing. Sunshine didn't seem to improve her pessimistic attitude.

"Another baby?" Effie exclaimed when Judith relayed the news. "So soon? Oh, what bad planning!"

"But Mac will be two in June," Judith put in. "The children will be close enough in age to be playmates and companions."

"They'll fight," Effie declared in her mournful voice. "Especially if it's another boy."

"Siblings always fight," Judith countered. "I guess." She had to admit to herself that she really didn't know. Judith and Renie had both been only children, and while they occasionally quarreled in their youth, they had grown to be as close, if not closer, than sisters.

"When are they coming to see me?" Effie demanded. "Mike and Kristy have only been here twice since Mac was born."

"It's Kristin," Judith said wearily. "I'm not sure when they'll be able to travel. With the new baby on the way, they'll probably wait."

"Oh, sure." Effie emitted a sour snort. "I haven't had a new picture of Mac in ages. I'm not even sure what he looks like these days."

"I thought Mike and Kristin sent you a picture of the whole family at Christmastime."

"They did?" Effie paused. "Oh, *that* picture. It wasn't very good of any of them. I can't see the slightest resemblance to my darling Dan in either Mike or Mac. If they both didn't have my red hair, I'd have to wonder."

As well you might, Judith thought, and was ashamed of the spite she felt inside. "Mac doesn't look like me, either," she said in an attempt to make amends.

"When are you coming down to see me?" Effie queried.

"Not for a while," Judith admitted. Indeed, she was ashamed of herself for not having paid Effie a visit since the year after Dan died. "It's so hard for me to get away with the B&B, and now I'm facing surgery Monday."

"For what?" Effie sounded very cross.

"A hip replacement," Judith said, gritting her teeth. "I told you about it on the phone a couple of weeks ago. I wrote it in my Christmas letter. I think I mentioned it in my Thanksgiving card."

"Oh, *that* hip replacement," Effie sniffed. "I thought you'd already had it. What's taking you so long?"

"It's the surgery scheduling," Judith responded patiently. "They have to book so far ahead. You know how it is. You used to work in a hospital."

"Hunh. It was different then. Doctors didn't try to squeeze in so many procedures or squeeze so much money out of their patients," Effie asserted. "Medical practice today is a scandal. You'll be lucky if you get out alive."

Judith glanced at the morning paper on the kitchen table. It contained a brief item about an autopsy being performed on Joan Fremont. In the sports section, there was a story about possible trades to replace the

Seafarers' ace pitcher, Joaquin Somosa. At last Effie McMonigle had said something that Judith didn't feel like contradicting.

Some people weren't lucky. They didn't get out of the hospital alive.

All Judith could hope was that she and Renie wouldn't be among the unlucky ones.

TWO

JUDITH'S SURGERY WAS scheduled for eight-thirty on Monday. Renie's was set for nine-fifteen. Joe and Bill delivered their wives to admitting at the same time. The cousins had worn out the phone lines over the weekend encouraging each other and trying to make light of any potential dangers.

Their husbands chimed in. "Hey, Bill," Joe said, "we could have hurried this up by driving together and dumping the old, crippled broads from a speeding car."

"You already called the girls?" Bill said with a straight face.

"You bet," Joe replied. "Chesty and Miss Bottoms. They're rarin' to go."

"Not funny," Judith muttered.

"Nothing's funny this early in the morning," snarled Renie, who usually didn't get up until ten o'clock.

Nor did Good Cheer Hospital's forbidding exterior live up to its name. Built shortly after the turn of the last century, the large, dark redbrick edifice with its looming dome and wrought-iron fences looked more like a medieval castle than a haven for healing. Judith half expected to wait for a drawbridge to come down before driving over a moat into the patient drop-off area.

Renie, who was bundled up in a purple hooded coat, shuddered as she got out of the Joneses' Toyota Camry. "Why couldn't we go to our HMO's hospital? This place looks like a morgue."

"Don't say that," Judith retorted as Joe helped her into the wheelchair. To make matters worse, it was a damp, dark morning with the rain coming down in straight, steady sheets. "You know why we're here. Our HMO doesn't do orthopedic surgeries anymore. All the hospitals are consolidating their services to save money."

"Yeah, yeah," Renie said with an ominous glance at the double doors that automatically opened upon their approach. "It just looks so gloomy. And bleak."

"It's still a Catholic hospital," Bill Jones pointed out as he helped Renie through the entrance. "That should be some consolation."

"Why?" Renie shot back. "The pope's not going to operate on my shoulder."

Bill wore his familiar beleaguered expression when dealing with his sometimes unreasonable wife, but said nothing as they waited for Joe to wheel Judith inside. The hospital's interior looked almost as old as its exterior. Over the years, the Sisters of Good Cheer had put all their money into equipment and staff. As long as the building was structurally sound and hygienically safe, the nuns saw no reason to waste funds on cosmetic improvements. Thus, great lengths of pipes were exposed, door frames were the original solid stained wood, and though the walls had been repainted many times, the color remained the same institutional shade of bilious green that long-dead patients and staff had endured almost a hundred years before.

There was no one around to meet the Flynns and the Joneses. A wooden sign with flaking gold lettering and an arrow pointed to admitting, on their right. They turned the corner and almost collided with a robot that was sending off loud beeping signals.

"That's new," Judith remarked. "I wonder what it does."

"My name is Robbie," the robot said in a mechanical voice. One metal arm reached out as if to snatch Renie's big black handbag.

"Watch it, Robbie, or I'll FedEx you to the scrap heap," Renie threatened.

"My name is Robbie," the robot repeated. The steel creature kept moving, giving and asking no quarter.

"I hope he's not one of the surgeons," Judith said.

"We should ask if he's covered for malpractice," Joe said as they approached the admitting desk.

A nurse in traditional uniform and white cap sat next to a nun in a modified habit that consisted of a navy blue suit, white blouse, and navy and white veil and coif. The Sisters of Good Cheer were relatively conservative in their attitude toward apparel. As long as they wore habits, the nurses who worked for them would wear uniforms. "May we help you?" the nurse inquired with a strained smile.

"Let's hope so," Joe replied. "We're checking our wives in." He gestured at Judith and Renie.

"Jones," said Bill. "Serena. Rotator cuff surgery." He pointed to the carefully lettered yellow Post-it note on Renie's sweater. Overcautious as ever, Bill had written, "Serena Jones, right shoulder, allergic to nuts, peanuts, and morphine, inclined to complain."

"Flynn," said Joe. "Judith. Right-hip replacement." He cast a worried look at Judith's side. Maybe, she thought, he was wishing he'd stuck a note on her, too.

Renie nudged Judith. "I guess we checked our voices at the door."

The nun looked at a computer screen. "They're right," she said to the nurse. "Jones and Flynn, Drs. Ming and Alfonso."

"Whew," Renie said facetiously. "I'm sure glad we're the right people."

Bill poked her in the ribs. "Don't say anything. Let them do their jobs."

Renie scowled at Bill. "I was only trying to lighten the—"

Bill poked her again, and Renie shut up.

The nurse handed several forms to Joe and Bill. "Have your wives fill these out over in the reception area. We'll call their names when the doctors are ready."

"What are these?" Renie asked, despite the glower from Bill.

"Medical information," the nurse responded. "Consent forms. Releases."

"Release from what?" Renie inquired, resisting Bill's efforts to propel her away from the desk.

"Consent to the procedure," the nurse said, looking impatient. "Releasing the hospital from responsibility in case you expire."

"Expire?" Renie blanched. "As in . . . croak?"

"Let's go," Bill muttered, his jaw set.

Joe had already wheeled Judith into the waiting area. "Did Renie say 'croak'?" she asked her husband.

"It sounded like 'croak,'" Joe answered in his breeziest manner. "Of course, it might have been 'joke' or 'Coke' or 'cloak.'"

Judith looked down at the forms that Joe had put in her lap. "She said 'croak.' If I croak, it's not their fault.

I wonder how Joaquin Somosa and Joan Fremont feel about that? I mean, I wonder how their families feel?"

"Glum," Joe replied. "Just fill the damned things out and let's get on with it."

"Aren't you and Bill being a bit callous?" Judith demanded.

"No," Joe asserted. "Those were flukes. Didn't the newspaper hint that Joan Fremont had been doing some drugs? She was an actress, Somosa was an athlete. I once worked in Vice. I know how that goes. It's all show biz, and a lot of those people get involved in drugs, both legal and otherwise."

Judith wasn't reassured, but she stopped arguing. Renie had also gone silent, laboriously trying to sign the forms with her crippled right arm. The cousins had just finished when they were joined by a tall, handsome, middle-aged man and a wispy blonde woman about the same age. The man looked vaguely familiar to Judith.

Bill, who had an excellent memory for faces, caught her curious glance. "Bob Randall," he said in a low voice. "Former Sea Auk quarterback."

"Ramblin' Randall," Joe murmured, with an admiring glance for the three-time all-pro. "I'll be damned. Maybe I'll shake his—"

"Judith Flynn?" a plump young nurse called out.

"Here," Judith responded. "I think."

"We're ready for you." The nurse smiled, then nodded at Joe. "Is this Mr. Flynn? He can come along, if he likes."

"He does," Judith said firmly.

Joe lingered. "Can I catch up with you in a minute? I'd like to introduce myself to—"

"Joe!" Judith cried as the nurse began wheeling her away. "I really need you!"

Reluctantly, Joe trudged after his wife. Judith arrived at a large room with several curtained partitions. It looked like a busy day at Good Cheer. At least four other patients were already being prepared for surgery. Directly across the way from Judith's cubicle, an elderly woman was making her confession to an equally elderly priest. Judith's spirits plunged.

"I should have had Father Hoyle anoint me or something," she murmured. "Is it too late?"

"You mean before that old duffer keels over?" Joe responded with a nod in the priest's direction. "I don't know. He could go at any minute."

Judith scowled at Joe. "I'm serious. Go ask him to come here when he's done with that woman's confession."

The nurse began to take Judith's vital signs. Another nurse arrived to draw her blood. A third nurse showed up with a hospital gown, a paper hat, and a pair of socks with treads on the bottom. The first nurse asked Judith if she had voided.

"Voided?" Judith echoed in alarm. "Voided what?"

"Have you gone to the bathroom recently?" the nurse inquired with a gentle smile.

"Oh. Yes, just before I left home."

Judith tried to relax, but it wasn't easy with all the poking and probing. She had just put on the gown, the hat, and the socks when the anesthesiologist arrived.

"I'm Dr. Bunn," said the young man, who looked too young to be on his own without his mother. "Here's what we're going to do . . ."

The curtains had been opened again after Judith changed. She could see Joe strolling casually up and down the floor, still waiting for the elderly woman to finish her confession. Judith wondered if the old girl was recounting every sin since childhood. Finally the priest appeared to be giving absolution. Judith sighed with relief.

At that moment, Bob Randall entered, supporting the wispy woman with his famous right arm. His wife, Judith thought vaguely. The poor woman looked as if she were about to meet the Grim Reaper. Maybe she was. Judith said a quick prayer for Mrs. Randall.

Dr. Bunn had finished his explanation, which Judith had only half heard. The priest was standing up. Well, Judith noted, at least he was *trying* to stand up. The poor man looked very unsteady.

Judith turned to see if Joe had noticed. He was nowhere in sight. Then, on the other side of the curtain, she heard her husband's voice.

"Bob," said Joe, sounding unusually hearty, "excuse me, but I want to thank you for all the years of pleasure and excitement you gave us when you quarterbacked the . . ."

The priest was tottering away. Judith heard Bob Randall's booming voice in reply: "Flynn, eh? Great to meet you. After fifteen years out of the league, you sometimes think nobody remembers . . ."

Dr. Bunn had stepped aside as one of the nurses began an IV in Judith's left hand. "Doctor," Judith said in a plaintive voice, "could you get my husband from the next cubicle?"

"Hold on there," Dr. Bunn said in a soothing voice. "He'll be right along. At the moment, he'd be in the way."

"But I wanted to . . ." Judith began, then heard Joe bidding Bob Randall good-bye.

"Good luck with the knee," Joe said, and suddenly appeared from the other side of the curtain. "Hey,

Jude-girl, Bob Randall's having knee surgery this morning. You know how it is with quarterbacks. The knees always seem to give out. He's a really great guy."

Judith felt for Joe's hand. "I thought his wife was the one who . . ." Judith felt drowsy. "Joe, can you find that . . ."

Judith felt nothing.

She awoke nearly seven hours later in the recovery room, staring at Renie. "Coz," Judith said thickly. "Hi."

"Unh," Renie replied and blinked twice.

"We're . . . alive," Judith said, her voice sounding very strange.

"So far," Renie replied, also unlike herself.

Judith's eyes came into focus. Her gaze traveled to the end of the bed. Joe was standing there, along with a nurse Judith didn't recognize.

"Hi," Joe said. He sounded different, too, almost shy. Judith concentrated harder on his face. He looked pale. She looked in Renie's direction. Bill was by her bed, also looking pale. Both Joe and Bill had ruddy complexions. Could they actually have been worried about their wives?

"How do you feel, Mrs. Flynn?" the gray-haired nurse inquired.

"Okay," Judith replied, despite the fact that she was too woozy to know. "Hi, Joe."

With a quick glance at the nurse, Joe came around to the side of the bed, almost bumping into Bill. "You're going to be fine," he said, taking her hand. "I've already seen Dr. Alfonso."

"Good," Judith sighed, wishing she could feel relieved, but not feeling much of anything.

Across the aisle, Dr. Ming was hovering over Renie. Judith tried to hear what he was saying, but couldn't. A moment later, Renie was being rolled out of the recovery room, with Bill trailing an orderly, a nurse, and Dr. Ming.

"Where's she gone?" Judith asked in alarm.

"To her room," Joe replied. "Renie's surgery was only three and a half hours. Yours was almost six, plus it was after nine before they actually started."

"Ohmigod!" Judith shut her eyes. "What time is it?"

"Does it matter?" Joe smiled. "It's going on four o'clock. Here." He proffered a plastic cup. "Drink some water."

Judith had trouble getting her lips around the straw. "It's hard," she moaned.

Dr. Alfonso, looking as exhausted as Judith, approached the bed. Or was it a gurney? Judith couldn't tell; didn't care.

"You'll be up and dancing soon," he said with the hint of a twinkle in his dark eyes.

"Hunh," said Judith.

"I've talked to your husband and given him all the details," Dr. Alfonso went on, pushing a swatch of silver hair under the shower-cap-like hat he still wore. His blue scrubs were spattered with blood; Judith involuntarily shuddered when she realized the stains probably came from her. "I'm taking a lunch break now," the doctor said, "but I'll be in to see you before I go off duty." Dr. Alfonso jabbed at the plastic cup. "Keep drinking as much as you can. You need plenty of fluids to keep from becoming dehydrated."

Dr. Alfonso had no sooner padded away than Judith began to feel pain. She tried to crane her head to look at the IV source, but her head wouldn't move, her neck wouldn't swivel.

"Joe, get a nurse," Judith said, wincing slightly. "I think I'm running out of pain medication."

"The anesthesia's probably wearing off," Joe said. "Hang on, I'll find the nurse who was here a few minutes ago."

The next half hour was taken up with the nurse's attempts to make Judith more comfortable, with Joe pressing fluids upon her, and with Judith thinking that maybe she *would* be better off dead. At last the pain began to ease a bit as a result of the increased morphine dosage. Judith felt more aware, but less content.

"We're going to move you to your room now," the nurse said smiling. "Once we get you in bed, you'll feel better."

"No, I won't," Judith muttered. "I feel like bird poop."

"You can sleep," the nurse said. "It'll be quieter there."

Judith had been vaguely aware of the comings and goings in the recovery area. The surgeons must have been busy that day, since at least a half-dozen patients had been wheeled in or out while she emerged from her anesthetic cocoon. The noise hadn't really bothered her, but she'd be glad for some peace and privacy.

"I saw Bob Randall after his knee surgery," Joe said as Judith was being trundled down the hall. "He seemed in pretty good spirits. But then he always was a warrior."

"I . . . didn't . . . know . . . you . . . were . . . such . . . a . . . fan," Judith gasped as every buckle and bump in the hallway floor seemed to set her teeth on edge.

"Randall played fourteen years for the Auks," Joe said, hurrying to keep up. "Those were the years I was married to Herself. Watching Randall pass for a first down on third and eight was a lot more fun than watching Vivian pass out over an empty fifth."

"Yes." It was all Judith could manage to say as they turned a corner on what felt like two wheels. The lingering odor of food and antiseptic seemed to chase her down the hall like a stale wind.

A sort of shrieking reached Judith's ears as the gurney slowed. Judith frowned but couldn't quite manage to lift her head. "What's that?" she asked as the noise grew louder.

The nurse and the orderly didn't reply but kept moving closer to the source.

"Joe?" Judith asked as a series of obscenities assailed her ears.

The gurney was steered through a doorway. The obscenities grew in volume and ferocity. "Joe?" Judith repeated.

They had arrived in a two-bed room on the third floor. The curses emanated from the other side of a pale blue curtain. Joe didn't respond. He didn't have to. Judith recognized the voice.

"Hi, Renie," he finally said as Judith was flipped and flopped onto an ancient hospital bed with a black iron bedstead. "How're you doing?"

Renie's answer was unprintable.

Judith and Renie had requested sharing a room, but the staff had made no promises. Good Cheer wasn't a hotel or a summer camp—it was a hospital.

"May I?" Joe asked in an unusually meek voice as he gave the blue curtain a twitch.

"Why not?" Renie snapped. "You can set fire to the whole damned place as far as I'm concerned."

Judith moved just enough to see Renie, propped up

on pillows with her right arm in a blue sling and her shoulder sporting a bloody dressing.

"Hi, coz," Renie said in a more normal tone. "How are you?" She didn't wait for an answer, but let out a bloodcurdling scream.

"What's wrong?" Judith asked in alarm.

"It's the only way to get attention around here," Renie said, then screamed again.

"Stop that!" Judith exclaimed. "It makes my head throb!"

"I throb everywhere," Renie shot back. "They dumped me in here almost an hour ago, and I haven't seen anybody since." She slapped with her left hand at what appeared to be a buzzer button extending from a thick rubber cord. "I've poked this stupid thing so often I think I burned the light out over the damned door. Now I'm getting hoarse from yelling."

"Where's Bill?" Joe inquired.

"He left," Renie replied after taking a deep sip of water. "He had to run some errands and then have dinner. He'll be back this evening."

Judith looked at Joe. "You ought to go, too. It's been a long day."

Joe seemed torn. "Shouldn't I wait until Dr. Alfonso comes in?"

Judith gave a faint shake of her head. "You've already talked to him. You have to tell Mother I'm okay and let Mike know I survived. Frankly, you look beat. I'll be fine, as long as Screaming Mimi over there shuts up. I might be able to sleep a bit."

"Well . . ." Joe's green-eyed gaze roamed around the room. "I suppose I should head home."

"Of course you should," Judith said, also taking in her surroundings. The walls were painted a dreary

beige that hadn't been freshened in years. A crucifix
hung over each of the beds and the only other furnish-
ings were a pair of visitors' chairs, a commode, and the
nightstands. A TV was mounted high on the far wall,
flanked by a small statue of Jesus revealing the Sacred
Heart and, on the other side, Mary holding the infant
Jesus. Two old-fashioned sash windows on Renie's
side of the room looked out over one of the city's residential areas. The roofs were gray, the houses were
gray, the skies were gray. Even the trees looked gray
on this late-January afternoon.

With a reluctant sigh, Joe leaned down to kiss Judith's forehead. "Okay, I'll check in at the B&B to
make sure that Carl and Arlene are getting along all
right. I'll see you this evening."

Despite her brave words, Judith kept her dark eyes
on Joe until he was out of the room. Indeed, he was
practically run over by a disheveled young man carrying a balloon bouquet in one hand and an almost life-
sized cutout of a football player in the other.

"For Bob Randall," Judith remarked, daring to gaze
at Renie.

"The ex-quarterback?" Renie snorted. "I swear, the
only time I ever watched him play, he always threw an
interception or got sacked." She paused, then made a
futile attempt to snap the fingers of her left hand.
"That's it! Ramblin' Randall is getting all the attention
while we suffer and starve. I timed myself. I screamed
for eleven minutes nonstop. Nobody came. I think I'll
set fire to the bed."

"Coz—" Judith began to plead, but was interrupted
by a tall, handsome nun in an exceptionally well-tailored
modified habit.

"Mrs. Jones? Mrs. Flynn?" the nun said, standing on

the threshold. "Which of you has been requesting help?"

If not embarrassed, Renie at least had the grace to look slightly abashed. "Yes . . . that would be me." She offered the nun a toothy smile. "I'm having quite a bit of pain."

You're being quite a pain, Judith thought, but kept silent.

The nun glanced at the IV. "I'll see what I can do," she said in her crisp, no-nonsense voice. "By the way, I'm Sister Jacqueline, the hospital administrator. I should point out that our staff is extremely busy this week. The surgery floor is full, and as usual, we're a bit shorthanded. The economics of medicine aren't what they used to be." She gave the cousins a tight little smile.

"I understand," Judith said. "It's a terrible problem that nobody seems able to solve."

"It's those damned insurance companies," Renie asserted, lifting her head a few inches from the pillow. "Let's not even talk about the greedy jackasses who run the pharmaceutical industry. What about the patient? I'm lying here in misery and half starved while a bunch of bumbling morons in Washington, D.C., try to figure out whether their pants get pulled up over their fat butts or go down over their empty heads. Or maybe they aren't wearing any pants at all. Furthermore, if anybody had an ounce of—"

Sister Jacqueline cleared her throat rather loudly. "Mrs. Jones. Ranting will do you no good. I suggest that you exercise the virtue of patience instead."

"I *am* the freaking patient!" Renie cried. "And I'm not a patient patient."

"I gather not," Sister Jacqueline said mildly, then

turned to Judith and spoke almost in a whisper. "If someone is discharged tomorrow, we might be able to move you to a different room."

Judith tried to smile. "It's fine, Sister. Honestly. I'm used to her. She's my cousin."

The nun drew back as if Judith had poked her. "Really!" She glanced from Judith to Renie and back again. "Then patience must be one of your outstanding virtues."

Judith looked sheepish. "Well . . . Many things in life have taught me patience. In fact, my cousin really doesn't—"

A tall, thin middle-aged man who looked vaguely familiar tapped diffidently on the open door. "Sister?" he said in an uncertain voice.

The nun stepped away from Judith's bed. "Yes?"

"I'm worried," the man said, removing his thick glasses and putting them back on in a nervous manner. "My brother isn't getting any rest. There are way too many visitors and deliveries and I don't know what all. I thought since Margie volunteers at the hospital, she'd keep things under control."

"I haven't seen Mrs. Randall since Mr. Randall was in the recovery room," Sister Jacqueline replied. "Even though the post-op news was very good, she seemed downcast. Perhaps she went home to rest."

"I hope not." The man who appeared to be Bob Randall's brother gave a shake of his head. "There's supposed to be a big snowstorm moving in. She might get stuck at the house." He uttered a heavy sigh. "Poor Margie. She's always downcast. I guess it's just her nature."

The nun turned back to Judith, but avoided looking at Renie, who wore a mutinous expression. "Excuse me, I must get things straightened out. Keep drinking those liquids, both of you. Come along, Mr. Randall. Jim, is it?" She put a firm hand on Jim Randall's elbow and steered him out into the hall. "I agree, too much excitement isn't good for . . ."

Her voice faded as they moved down the hall. Renie picked up a tiny digital clock from her nightstand. "It's going on five. I haven't eaten since last night. When do they serve around here?"

"I thought you hurt so much," Judith remarked, plucking listlessly at the white linen sheet. "Good Cheer Hospital" had been stitched in blue on the hem, but the letters had worn away to leave only "Goo . . h . er Ho . p . . ."

"I do," Renie said, "but that doesn't mean I can't be hungry."

Before Judith could respond, Dr. Alfonso reappeared, now dressed in blue jeans, a denim shirt, and a black leather jacket. "You're looking a bit brighter, Mrs. Flynn," he said, though his own voice was weary. "Let's take a peek at that dressing."

"When do we eat?" Renie asked in a petulant tone.

"After a bit," the surgeon replied without taking his eyes off the loose bandage. "We'll get the nurse to change that. How's the pain?"

"Awful," Renie broke in. "Whatever happened to Demerol?"

"It's bearable," Judith responded bravely. "Though it hurts quite a bit to make even the slightest move."

"We'll take care of that, too," Dr. Alfonso said with a tired smile. "Now let's talk about your rehab—"

"How can a person rehab," Renie demanded, "when his or her arm feels like it fell off? In fact, I think it did. Do you want to check the floor for me?"

"We'll have you try to sit up tomorrow," the doctor said to Judith. "Maybe later in the day, we'll see if you can take a few steps."

"That sounds next to impossible right now," Judith said, though her weak smile tried to convey courage. "I'll do my best."

"I'll do my worst if somebody doesn't put something besides corn syrup in this IV," Renie snarled.

With shoulders slumped, Dr. Alfonso started to turn away from Judith. "I'll be by in the morning to—"

His words were cut short by screams and a large thud from nearby. Judith stiffened in the narrow bed and Renie's expression went from grumpy to curious. Dr. Alfonso picked up his step, but was met by a petite Asian nurse in a fresh white uniform and cap.

"Come, please, Doctor," the nurse urged in an anxious voice. "Something's happened to Mr. Randall."

"Randall?" Dr. Alfonso echoed, following the nurse out into the hall. "Dr. Garnett's patient?"

Judith's jaw dropped. Surely not another local celebrity had succumbed at Good Cheer Hospital. She pricked up her ears, trying to catch the nurse's fading reply.

"Not Bob Randall," she said. "It's his brother, Jim. He suddenly collapsed and is unconscious."

Renie made an airy gesture of dismissal with her left hand. "Maybe he's dead. Can anybody around here tell the difference?"

Judith stared incredulously at her cousin. "That's not funny."

Renie's face fell as she realized the enormity of what she had just said. "No," she agreed, a hand to her head. "It's not."

THREE

IT WAS ALMOST a quarter of an hour before the cousins learned what had happened to Jim Randall. A simple faint, it seemed, according to the Asian nurse, whose name tag identified her as "Chinn, Heather, R.N."

"He's so different from his brother, the football player," Heather Chinn said as she adjusted Renie's IV. "They look alike, sort of, but they don't act like brothers, let alone twins."

"Twins?" Judith said, comparing the gaunt, pale Jim Randall with the robust, suntanned Bob. "As in identical?"

Heather shrugged and smiled. She had matching dimples in a perfect heart-shaped face. "I don't know about that. Their mannerisms are really at opposite ends, too. Mr. Jim is so shy and doesn't seem to have much self-esteem. Mr. Bob is full of life and confidence. He'll be out of here in no time."

"What made Mr. Jim pass out?" Judith inquired as the nurse added more painkiller to her IV.

Heather shrugged again. "Stress, maybe. Worrying about his brother. Though I don't think Mr. Jim is very well. He's had several tests to determine what's wrong, but . . ." She finished with the IV and grimaced. "I shouldn't gossip like that. It's unprofessional, and I'm merely speculating."

The pain was beginning to ebb. Judith moved in the bed, her gaze following Heather Chinn as she tried to make Renie more comfortable.

"You'd have more room," Heather said in a pleasant, reasonable voice, "if you'd put some of these . . . items in the drawers of your nightstand." Her slim fingers pointed to the paperback book, two magazines, pack of gum, roll of breath mints, several spring fashion catalogues, and a small grinning doll with an equally small suitcase.

"Don't touch Archie," Renie warned as Heather started to move the doll. "He stays with me. My husband got him as a good luck charm. Archie loves hospitals." Renie grasped Archie's tiny hand. "Don't you, Archie? See how cheerful he is? Archie always looks cheerful."

While Judith was accustomed to Renie and Bill's proclivity for talking to inanimate objects, including their car, Heather Chinn wasn't. The nurse looked askance.

Judith decided to intervene before Heather recommended committing Renie to the mental health wing. "I don't suppose," Judith said in a manner that only suggested a question, "you had either Joan Fremont or Joaquin Somosa as patients."

"The actress?" Heather responded, looking at Judith over Renie's tousled head. "No. But the other one—was he some kind of ballplayer, too? I was on duty when he flat-lined."

Renie jerked around to look at the monitor beside her bed. "Flat-lined? Is that what you call it? All those funny squiggly marks are good, then?"

"Yes." Heather smiled, revealing her dimples. "You're doing fine, Mrs. Jones. In fact, we've noticed that you're unusually . . . resilient."

Loud, Judith figured was what Nurse Heather meant. And maybe nuts. "Mr. Somosa . . . flat-lined for no apparent reason?"

"Not at the time," Heather replied, checking Renie's IV. "I believe there was something in the postmortem that indicated otherwise."

"Drugs?" Renie put in. "I heard that might have been the case with Joan Fremont."

"I really can't discuss it," Heather asserted, the dimples now invisible and the brown eyes on the silent TV set. "Would you like to watch the news? There's a button on each of your beds."

"No," Renie said.

"Yes," Judith replied. "I never get to see the early news at home. I'm always working."

"I almost never watch the news," Renie said crossly, "unless it's sports." She pulled herself up in the bed and addressed Heather Chinn. "Are you saying Somosa did drugs? I don't believe it. For one thing, the Seafarers have a tough stand on drugs. So does major league baseball in general. Not only that, but until he blew out his elbow, Somosa had a 2.4 ERA and averaged ten strikeouts a game. How do you explain that?"

"I can't," Heather replied with the ghost of a smile. "I have no idea what you're talking about. I don't follow sports. I only know about Mr. Randall—Mr. Bob—because somebody said he'd played professional football."

"Hunh," snorted Renie, and fell back against the pillows.

Heather had refilled the cousins' water carafes, replacing them on the old wooden bedside stands that matched the room's much-varnished door and window frames. "Remember to keep drinking fluids. Dinner will be along shortly," she added as she exited the room.

"It better be," Renie muttered after taking a big sip of fresh water. "Really, coz, I doubt that Somosa did drugs. Or Joan Fremont, either. They didn't call her the First Lady of the local theater for nothing. She was a lady, in every way."

"Good Cheer is undoubtedly dodging a couple of huge malpractice suits," Judith said, clicking on the TV. "Can you imagine? Not only the survivors, but maybe Le Repertoire Theatre and the Seafarers' ownership."

Renie was silent for a moment as KINE-TV's anchorpersons radiated their own type of good cheer by rehashing humankind's latest tragedies. "At least turn down the sound," she said crossly. "It's Mavis Lean-Brodie doing the news and she's never liked me."

Years ago, Mavis had been involved in a homicide that had occurred in Judith's dining room. Since then, Judith had encountered her a few times, including a recent run-in during a murder investigation at an apartment house on Heraldsgate Hill. Mavis had featured Judith in a well-intentioned TV interview that had come off as awkward and inaccurate. Still, Judith held no grudge.

"Mavis is okay," Judith allowed, hitting the mute button as the screen switched to a close-up of the governor in front of the state capitol. "She's just aggressive. It comes with the job description."

Dinner was brought in by a solemn young orderly. Wordlessly, he set up Judith's tray first. There were two covered dishes, a plastic container, a plastic cup, packets of salt and pepper, silverware, and a napkin. A whole-wheat roll wrapped in plastic rested on a plate with a butter pat.

The orderly moved to Renie's bed. "What the hell is this crap?" she yelled, removing the metal cover from the larger of the two dishes. "It looks like cat spit!"

The orderly, who sported a mustache, a shaved head, and a gold stud in one ear, didn't respond. Without speaking, he left the room.

"I think," Judith said warily, "it's mutton."

Renie's brown eyes widened in horror. "No Grover since our grandfather has ever eaten mutton, and he only did it because he was English. I think I'm going to be sick."

"It's not very good," Judith allowed. "In fact, it's tasteless. I tried salting the gravy, but that doesn't help much. There's a green salad, though." She searched around on the tray. "It's under the other covered dish, but I don't see any dressing."

"Rice," Renie said, holding her head. "How can you ruin rice? And why is it sort of beige?"

"Brown rice?" Judith suggested, taking a bite. "No, maybe not."

"This isn't even wholesome," Renie complained. "Mutton is fatty. I'm going to call Bill."

"What for?" Judith asked. "He's not with the Department of Health."

"No, but he can swing by Art Huey's and pick us up some Chinese. What do you want?"

Judith's attention, however, had been caught by the TV screen. Sister Jacqueline was in living color, speaking in front of Good Cheer Hospital. Judith turned the sound back on.

". . . to clear our reputation," Sister Jacqueline was saying. "The general public doesn't realize that every time a person goes into surgery under a general anesthetic, they risk death. It's simply a fact, which is why hospitals require signed waivers before any procedure. Sometimes, of course, there are extenuating circumstances."

Mavis's male coanchor reappeared, looking solemn. "Statistically, the number of otherwise healthy patients who die within a week of a surgical procedure is very small. Good Cheer Hospital's most recent deaths have been local celebrities, thus bringing the long-time institution under scrutiny. It should also be pointed out that Good Cheer is the only local hospital where orthopedic surgeries are performed. As chief of surgery Dr. Peter Garnett said earlier, the statistics are bound to be skewed when each hospital has its own specialties."

The camera angle expanded to include Mavis. "Thanks, Paul," she said with a grim smile. "I guess I'll think twice before I get those bone spurs removed." Paul dutifully chuckled. Mavis announced they were cutting to a commercial break.

"Face-lift," Renie said. "She's had two already. Pretty soon her ears are going to be sticking out from the top of her head."

"The hospital had to expect some bad publicity," Judith remarked, ignoring Renie's comment and muting the TV again. "I'm surprised there hasn't been more about it in the newspapers."

"So am I," Renie said, dumping her entire tray in the wastebasket beside her bed. "I wonder if the *Times* has muzzled Addison Kirby. You know, Joan Fremont's husband who covers city hall."

"You think so?" Judith remarked, then realized that Renie had hung up the phone without speaking to Bill. "Hey, what about your Chinese order?"

Renie let out an exasperated little sigh. "The anesthesia must have affected my brain. I'm told it can, especially your memory. I forgot that Bill never answers the phone, especially around the dinner hour. Why don't you call Joe?"

Judith hesitated. Joe had plenty of responsibilities on his shoulders now that Judith was completely incapacitated. "I kind of hate to. We don't live as close to Art Huey's as you and Bill do."

"Okay." Renie picked up the phone again. "Art Huey's Restaurant," she said. "Yes, you can dial it for me."

"You're going to have them deliver our dinner?" Judith asked, taken aback. "Is that allowed?"

"Who knows? Who cares? I'm paying for it. Yes, this is Mrs. Jones, and I'd like to order the prawn chow yuk, the wonton soup, the . . ." Renie listed another half-dozen items, then gave some special instructions: "Tell the people at the front desk you're visiting Mrs. Jones. Put the stuff in a plain cardboard box and throw one of those plastic geraniums on top. There's a big tip in it for you if the food arrives hot."

"*If* the food arrives at all," Judith remarked as Renie hung up. "Do you think whoever brings it can get past the desk?"

"Yes," Renie declared, clicking on the old-fashioned gooseneck lamp next to the bed. "Now dump that crap off your tray and settle back. I should have ordered a couple of drinks while I was at it."

"We can't drink," Judith said, taking yet another sip from her plastic water glass, "except for stuff like this. We're on pain medication."

"We are?" Renie harrumphed. "You couldn't prove it by me."

The food did indeed arrive, along with Joe, Bill, and the delivery boy. Renie had already managed to get out her checkbook, though it was a struggle to write with her left hand.

"Let me," Bill sighed, tearing up the check. "This looks as if you'd written it with your lips."

"I should try that," Renie murmured, struggling to open the cartons. "Here, pass some of this to my roommate."

Joe and Bill had come to the hospital together. The guests were settled in, Carl and Arlene had things well in hand, and Gertrude was spending the evening inside Hillside Manor playing three-handed pinochle with Judith's stand-ins.

"They're so good to her," Judith said, referring to the Rankerses. "I try to ignore Arlene's threats to move. I couldn't bear it if they weren't next door."

Taking a bite of Judith's marinated steak, Joe agreed. "By the way, I've accepted a new case."

"You have?" Judith was surprised. "But you're already overloaded."

"I'm okay, I got most of the loose ends tied up before your surgery," Joe said, sampling a sweet-and-sour prawn. "But this is one I don't feel I can refuse. There was a call from FOPP waiting for me when I got home from the hospital this afternoon."

Judith's forehead wrinkled. "FOPP? What's that?"

"Friends of Powerless People, advocates for the homeless," Joe replied, eyeing another of Judith's prawns. "It seems that a couple of street residents have been killed in the last month. Not that it's unusual in itself, but these weren't the typical murders. You know, a couple of the poor devils get into it, one brains the other with an empty bottle of Old Horsecollar. Or smart-ass kids hassle the homeless until it gets out of hand. According to Steve Moeller at FOPP, the two most recent killings appeared to be deliberate and were committed out of sight. Both stabbings, maybe by the same knife. I'll get more details tomorrow."

"What about the police?" Judith inquired. "Aren't they trying to find the killers?"

Joe gave a slight shrug. "Sure, but you know how it is. Even when I was still on the job, if Woody and I got a case that was more high-profile, then our homeless homicide got put at the bottom of the pile. That's why FOPP has decided to hire a private investigator."

Judith frowned. She'd always had a sense of security during the years that Woodrow Wilson Price had been Joe's partner. A solid man of African-American descent with a walrus mustache and deceptively soulful eyes that could wring a confession out of the most hardened criminals, Woody had never let Joe down. And vice versa. But that was then and this was now. "It sounds dangerous. Furthermore, you don't have Woody for a partner anymore."

Joe shook his head and grinned. "I'll manage. The worst of it is trying to make sense of what the witnesses will say. *If* I can find any witnesses."

"Take someone with you," Judith urged. "Bill, for instance. He can tell who's crazy and who isn't."

Joe made a face at Judith. "Bill has plenty to do, too. He still sees some of his private patients and consults at the university. Besides, on these investigations, I like to work solo."

Judith started to argue, but she was too worn out and knew she'd lose. At the other bedside, the Joneses *were* arguing, something about the assignments of their three children while Renie was in the hospital.

"Why," Renie was demanding, "should Tom wash the windows in January? He needs time to work on his Ph.D. thesis."

"That doesn't mean the windows aren't dirty," Bill pointed out. "Besides, he's been in graduate school for eight years. I don't see that he's in any rush."

"He has deadlines," Renie countered. "You know that, you've been through it."

"Not in Babylonian history," Bill pointed out, his voice growing more heated. "What's he going to do with that degree when he gets it? How many recruiters are out there looking for an expert on the Mushkenu social class?"

"He can teach," Renie retorted.

"He doesn't want to teach," Bill asserted. "He wants to stay in graduate school, live in our house, eat our food, and wait until we're carried out feetfirst, just like his brother and his sister are doing."

Joe, who had been fidgeting, stood up. "Hey, Bill, maybe we should head on out. It may snow tonight."

Bill all but flew out of his visitor's chair. "Good idea. Heraldsgate Hill has some pretty mean streets in bad weather."

Joe and Bill kissed their wives and fled.

"Do you really think they have girls lined up?" Judith asked.

"No," Renie answered. "They have basketball games, though. Pro and college. Besides, we're boring."

"Joe ate half my dinner," Judith said in dismay.

"Bill didn't try to touch any of mine," Renie said. "He knows better."

Judith checked her watch, which was lying on the bedside stand. "It's almost eight. I could use some more painkillers."

"Me, too," said Renie. "You buzz. They hate me."

Judith pushed the button. "I have to admit, they aren't exactly killing us with kindness. Excuse the phrase."

But Heather Chinn appeared almost immediately. "Sorry," she apologized. "It's been so busy on this floor tonight. I'm behind in taking vitals."

"How about victuals?" Renie said, indicating the empty white boxes on her tray. "Could you get rid of these for us?"

Heather hadn't noticed the small cartons. "Oh, dear! Did you two . . . ? Really, that's not allowed. Lately, our patients seem to think they can consume just about anything they like. That's not so. You have to keep to a hospital diet while you're with us. If we hadn't been so caught up with other patients, we'd never have permitted this."

"Those aren't ours," Renie said, feigning shock. "Our husbands brought their own dinner. We'll both speak severely to them about doing it again."

Frowning, Heather removed the boxes, then began taking Judith's pulse and temperature. "What happened with Jim Randall?" Judith inquired after the paper thermometer had been removed.

"Oh," Heather said, wrapping the blood pressure cuff around Judith's arm, "he went home. I guess he was upset about his brother."

"Mr. Bob's recovering nicely?" Judith asked.

Heather didn't answer right away. She was listening to the stethoscope and looking at the gauge attached to the cuff. "Yes," she finally said as she made entries on

Judith's chart, "he's doing fine, though I don't think he'll like being on a walker and then a cane for some time. He strikes me as a very active person." Heather moved to Renie's bed. "Here, Mrs. Jones, let's see how you're getting along."

"I could have eaten more fried wontons," Renie said. "I think they shorted us on the sweet-and-sour prawns."

Heather shook her head in a disapproving manner, then became involved in taking Renie's vital signs. Judith watched until a wispy figure appeared in the doorway. It was Mrs. Randall, looking morose.

"Nurse Chinn?" she called in a soft, tentative voice. "I'm leaving now, but I'll be on duty at nine tomorrow."

Heather Chinn finished taking Renie's pulse, then turned to the newcomer. "That's fine, Mrs. Randall. You must be very pleased with your husband's successful surgery."

Margie Randall hung her head. "Dr. Van Boeck says I should be, but you never know. All sorts of things can happen—pneumonia, a blood clot, an aneurysm. I've seen it before, here in this very hospital, and recently, too. I don't think I'll be able to sleep tonight."

"You need your rest," Heather said, now working with the blood pressure cuff on Renie. "You put in such long days volunteering for us."

"It's such a source of comfort for me," Margie sighed, though she looked quite desolate. "It's such a blessing to be able to offer consolation to patients and their families. Why, this very morning, while Bob was in surgery, I counseled a family who had just lost an elderly father. They'd been practically immobilized with grief until I began telling them how soon any one of them could be called to join him. A brief, deadly illness. An auto accident. Getting caught in the gunfire of a drive-by shooting. They suddenly became energized and all but ran out of the hospital."

"Lovely," Heather said absently. "Good night, Mrs Randall."

Margie Randall drifted away. Judith leaned slightly toward the nurse. "I was wondering, who operated on Joaquin Somosa and Joan Fremont? Do you recall?"

Heather removed the blood pressure cuff from Renie's arm and looked at Judith. "It was Dr. Garnett, the same surgeon who performed Mr. Randall's surgery. I remember, because it's sort of unusual. Surgeons specialize, like Dr. Alfonso for hips and Dr. Ming for shoulders. But Dr. Garnett is the second in command at Good Cheer, under Dr. Van Boeck, and he likes to stay diversified."

"I see," said Judith, who wasn't exactly sure what Heather meant in terms of medical skill, hospital privilege, or professional hierarchy.

"The good stuff," Renie put in, using her left elbow to point to the IV. "Make me feel good. Or at least tolerable."

Heather finished dispensing medication, a short, stout woman with a blonde Dutch-boy bob drew their blood, and, finally, the priest Judith had seen that morning came by to visit.

"I'm Father McConnaught," he said in a voice that indicated he wasn't quite sure. "God bless you, Mrs. Flynn. An Irish lass, perhaps?"

"No, actually I'm—"

He nodded at Renie. "And Mrs. Jones. Welsh, you'd be, eh?"

"No, I'm pretty much the same as my—"

"Well, now." Father McConnaught's faded blue eyes

crinkled at the corners. He was almost bald, except for a few strands of white hair that stood up on his head like little wisps of smoke. "Let's say a prayer of thanksgiving that you both came through, eh?"

Judith and Renie dutifully said the Our Father and the Hail Mary along with the priest, which was a good thing because he seemed to forget some of the words along the way.

"Now," the priest said, smiling even wider, "how many will this be, Mrs. Flynn?"

"How many what?" Judith asked, puzzled.

"And you, Mrs. Jones?" he inquired of Renie.

"Since I've only got one other arm—" Renie began.

Father McConnaught put up an arthritic hand. "Never mind now, the Good Lord always provides extra hands. Will we be seeing you both again next year with another wee one?"

"I doubt it," Judith said, finally enlightened and smiling gently. "Ten's quite a few, Father."

The priest looked skeptical. "Twelve, and the archbishop himself will baptize the babe."

"Will he raise the kid, too?" Renie asked.

Father McConnaught put his hand behind his ear. "Eh?"

"Never mind," Judith said kindly. "Thank you for coming, Father. We'll keep you in our prayers."

"And so shall I with you and all the wee ones." He made a small, painful bow and departed.

"Deaf *and* blind," Renie remarked after Father McConnaught had gone. "When are we going to get some younger priests around here?"

"We should pray more for vocations," Judith said. "Nuns as well as priests. I'll bet very few members of the nursing staff are from the Sisters of Good Cheer."

"It's like the teaching orders," Renie said, then stared at Judith. "Say—when you were talking to Nurse Heather about who operated on Joan Fremont and Joaquin Somosa, were you sleuthing?"

"What?" Judith feigned disbelief.

"You heard me," Renie said. "Are you suspicious about the cause of their deaths?"

"Well . . . you have to wonder."

"*You* do," Renie retorted, turning off the light by her bed. "I don't. In fact, I'm going to try to get some sleep."

"That's a good idea," Judith agreed. "Frankly, I'm exhausted." She, too, clicked off her light. "I guess I was just curious."

"Oh."

"I mean, it's got to be a coincidence, right?"

"Right."

"If they hadn't been well known, we'd probably never have heard about their deaths."

"Shut up."

Judith obeyed, but couldn't get comfortable. "I still hurt like hell. This bed's too narrow. I'll never be able to sleep."

"Count sheep. Count Chinese food cartons. Count all those imaginary kids you told Father McConnaught you had."

"I'll try."

Judith slept, but her dreams were disquieting in the extreme. Joaquin Somosa appeared on the pitcher's mound, where an army of fried wontons marched onto the field and savagely attacked him with chopsticks. Joan Fremont, as Lady Macbeth, was wringing her hands when Birnam Wood, in the form of towering bok choy leaves, invaded the castle and crushed her to the ground. Finally, Judith saw a third form, more shadowy than the others, wearing what looked like a cape and pacing anxiously as a band of deep-fried prawns lay in wait with a cauldron of boiling sweet-and-sour sauce.

Judith woke up with a muffled gasp, but saw only Renie, clutching Archie the cheerful doll, and snoring softly.

FOUR

No one had died by morning. Judith awoke after a fitful night, not only of pain and discomfort and nightmares caused by an overdose of Chinese food, but of constant disturbances by nurses taking more vital signs. Not only didn't Judith feel rested, but she was very stiff and sore. The weakness she had suffered as a result of the surgery was still there, leaving her limp and lifeless.

Breakfast turned out to be more palatable than the previous meal. The cousins ate oatmeal, toast, scrambled eggs, and bacon. There was apple juice and coffee. Even Renie didn't complain. Much.

"You get to go home in a couple of days," Judith said, pushing her tray aside. She'd eaten only half the food; her appetite seemed to have shrunk. "Dr. Alfonso said I'd be in here for almost a week."

Renie was standing up, scratching various parts of her anatomy with her left hand and trying to adjust the sling on her right arm so that it didn't tug at her neck.

"I have the feeling that if we were in any other hospital," Renie declared, finally managing to loosen the sling an inch or so, "I'd be headed home this morning. Good Cheer has held fairly firm in al-

lowing longer patient stays. Maybe it's got something
to do with the hospital being run by a religious order."

"In other words, by people who have good sense?"
Judith said.

"Exactly." Somewhat unsteadily, Renie went into
the bathroom and closed the door.

Judith felt envious. Her cousin was mobile; it would
be weeks before Judith would be able to get around
with ease. She'd be stuck using a bedpan or the commode. Doctors and nurses bragged of success stories
about eighty-year-olds who danced the fandango six
weeks after surgery. But Judith knew those tales were
the exception to the rule. Besides, she'd never known
how to dance the fandango with two good hips.

Renie emerged from the bathroom, a big grin on her
face. "That must be the original toilet," she said, moving cautiously toward her bed. "It's the old-fashioned
chain type. It's so high off the floor that my feet didn't
touch. By the way, we're sharing."

"We are?" Judith said. "With whom? Robbie the
Robot?"

Renie shook her head. "No, Robbie the Pro Quarterback. There's a door on the other side. I could hear him
talking on the phone. He was thanking somebody
named Taylor for something or other. No doubt some
special treatment he's getting that we are not."

"Bob Randall's famous," Judith said. "He's used to
five-star treatment. We are not famous, thus we are not
entitled to special treatment."

"Doesn't infamous count?" Renie retorted. "I'm
working on that one."

Judith sighed. "So you are. And with great success,
I might add."

Dr. Alfonso arrived on his rounds shortly before ten

o'clock. He was full of encouragement for Judith, though she remained skeptical. With the help of a willowy redheaded nurse named Appleby, he managed to get Judith into a sitting position. She confessed she felt dizzy, almost nauseous, and had to put her head down. The faded linoleum floor swam before her eyes.

"Perfectly normal," Dr. Alfonso assured her. "By tomorrow, you'll hardly feel dizzy at all."

After the surgeon had gone, Corinne Appleby informed Judith that they'd have her on her feet by late afternoon. "You'll be surprised," the nurse said, a tired smile on her long, freckled face. Like Heather Chinn, Nurse Appleby wore a crisply starched white uniform, spotless white rubber-soled shoes, and a perky cap with a single black band. "You may feel weak now," Corinne went on, "but little by little, you'll get your strength back."

"I hope so," Judith said, trying to block out Renie's latest complaints to an orderly who was attempting to straighten her bed and apparently had attempted to molest Archie the doll. Maybe it was a good thing that her cousin would go home first. When Renie was in a drawn-out bad mood, she could be nerve-racking.

"Did you bring a book?" Judith asked after the orderly had managed to flee.

"Yes, but it sucks scissors," Renie declared. "I started it last night, somewhere between the vital signs and the nurses' argument over who ate the last package of M&M's."

"Oh." Judith glanced at the paperback on her bedside stand. "I couldn't even try to read last night, but maybe I will now. Unless you want to watch TV."

"During the day?" Renie was aghast. "There's nothing on except the Weather Channel."

"There's CNN," Judith said meekly.

"That's just news, and it won't be good," Renie asserted. "I'd rather read. Maybe if I started this book from the end and read it backwards, it'd be more interesting."

"I brought a deck of cards," Judith said, brightening. "If you could sit by my bed, we could play cribbage."

"I haven't played cribbage in years," Renie said. "I don't know how anymore."

"I could teach you," Judith said. "I play with Mother all the time. She usually beats me."

Raised voices and a sudden scurrying in the hallway diverted the cousins' attention.

"What's that?" Renie asked, sitting up in bed.

Judith leaned forward as far as she could, which was only a few inches. "I can't tell. A couple of people—I think Nurse Appleby was one of them—just ran by."

"Code blue!" someone shouted.

"What was that?" Renie asked, clumsily getting out of bed and trailing her IV stand behind her.

"It sounded like 'code blue.' I don't think that's a positive phrase in a hospital."

Renie padded across the floor in her baggy hospital gown and brown-treaded bed socks. "I thought they said *'cordon bleu.'* I thought it sounded like something good."

"I think maybe it means . . . dead," Judith said, gulping.

"Oh." Renie sounded dismayed, but kept moving until she was in the doorway. After a few seconds, she turned back to Judith. "Whatever it is seems to be happening in Bob Randall's room next door."

"No!" Judith's hands flew to her cheeks. "It can't be! Maybe I'm wrong about what the code means."

A large bald-headed man in a white coat came striding down the hall. He saw Renie halfway out of the door and barked at her to get back. Startled, she took a single step but remained on watch.

"Dr. Van Boeck," Renie said over her shoulder to Judith. "I heard somebody say his name."

"Who else do you see?" Judith asked, wishing she could join Renie at the door. But just thinking about it made her feel vaguely light-headed.

"I see the patient from across the hall looking at me," Renie said. "He's a man." She waved. "Hi, I'm Serena Jones."

"Hello," Judith heard the man reply in a chipper voice. "I'm Mumford Needles. Call me Mr. Mummy. Everybody else does."

"Sure, Mr. Mummy," Renie said. "What's happening?"

"I don't know," Mr. Mummy said. "I don't think it's anything good, though."

Judith had to strain to hear the last part of Mr. Mummy's sentence. "Do you see anybody else?" she asked Renie.

"Umm . . . Here comes Margie Randall. Can you hear her?"

Judith could, as Margie uttered a series of keening noises that sounded like mourners at an Irish wake. "That's awful," Judith said, putting her hands over her ears.

"There must be a bunch of people in the room," Renie said, cautiously taking a couple of steps farther into the hallway.

But suddenly, except for Margie Randall's shrieks, the commotion seemed to subside. Renie informed Judith that there were a handful of staffers milling about, with anxious, curious expressions on their faces.

"Here comes Sister Jacqueline," Renie said. "She's with some guy who looks like Ronald Colman on a bad day. What was that movie he made where he was drunk all the time?"

"Never mind," Judith responded. "What does the guy look like? A doctor? Security? A wizard?"

"A doctor, he's wearing a white coat," Renie answered as the man quickly passed by. "He looks very grim. So does Sister Jacqueline."

For several minutes, nothing seemed to happen, at least nothing that Renie could tell. Then, quietly and somberly, several of the people who had been in Bob Randall's room came back into the hallway. They spoke in hushed tones, shaking their heads and placing hands on each other's arms, as if to give comfort. Margie Randall had finally stopped shrieking, though she was nowhere in sight.

Mr. Mummy gave a sad shake of his head. "I don't like the looks of this, do you, Mrs. Jones? Or may I call you Serena?"

"Mrs. Jones is fine. What did you do to your leg?"

"I broke it in several places," Mr. Mummy said. "A nasty fall off a ladder while I was taking down Christmas lights. I had surgery in the community hospital out where I live, then they transferred me in here today. It's a very small town and a very small hospital, with only one surgeon. Excuse me, I must lie down. Perhaps I'll see you again?"

"Probably," Renie said in mild surprise. Mr. Mummy returned to his room.

"Is Mr. Mummy going to ask you out?" Judith inquired with a quirky little smile.

"I hope not. He's almost as old as I am, bald except for two tufts of hair sticking straight up, glasses, and about a fifty-inch waist. Cute in a way, but not my type." Renie spotted Corinne Appleby. "Nurse?" she asked, trying to sound humble but not succeeding. "What's wrong?"

Corinne's face was very pale under her freckles. "There's been a . . . problem. An emergency. Don't worry, everything's under control."

"It doesn't seem like it to me," Renie shot back. "Come on, we have a right to know. Whatever it is, it happened right next door."

With trembling fingers, Corinne tucked a red curl under her cap. "Sadly, Mr. Randall expired. Excuse me, I must get back to the desk."

If pain and posture had permitted, Judith would have fallen out of the bed. Instead, she stared at Renie, who had turned back into the room. "Bob Randall's *dead?*"

Renie gave a helpless shrug. "As a dodo, I gather."

Awkwardly, Judith fell against the pillows. "I should have known."

And then she wondered why she'd already guessed.

Renie's job as sentry wasn't easy, but she remained propped up at the door, clutching the pole that held her IV, and keeping Judith apprised of what was going on in the next room.

"I can hear Margie sobbing," Renie reported, "but at least she's not yelling her head off."

"Can you ask somebody what happened to Bob Randall?" Judith urged, feeling supremely frustrated. The room seemed to be closing in on her; the windows were shrinking and the walls were shriveling. Judith felt as if she were in a cage instead of a bed.

Renie glared at Judith. "If I draw any more attention

to myself, they'll probably make me go back inside and close the door."

Her cousin had a point. Judith tried to relax. She could hear the distorted sounds of the hospital loud-speaker, summoning certain parties to specific places. "Okay," Judith inquired, "who do you think is in Randall's room besides Margie and Dr. Van Boeck and the other guy?"

"A couple of nurses, maybe," Renie said. "What's her name? Appleby? Oh, and Sister Jacqueline, but she just came out and is headed"—Renie paused—"right past me. She's going to the nurses' station."

The doctor who had reminded Renie of Ronald Colman came back into the hallway. He caught Renie's eye and scowled.

"Would you mind stepping back into your own room, please?" he said in a cold, cultured voice.

"I kind of would," Renie replied. "What about the patient's right to know?"

"Know?" snapped the physician, his fine silvery mustache quivering with outrage. "What do you *need* to know? Please go back inside and close your door."

"Okay," Renie said, but didn't budge. Apparently the doctor wasn't used to being disobeyed, since he didn't look back, but resumed his quick pace down the corridor.

"Back to the play-by-play," said Renie. "Coming in out of the bullpen and onto the mound, otherwise known as Bob Randall's room, is Peter Garnett, chief of surgery." She relayed the information she'd gotten off the man's name tag. "His ERA, otherwise known as Good Cheer's mortality rate, is way up. No wonder he looks so bad."

A moment later, two orderlies bodily carried Margie

Randall out of her husband's room. She looked as if she'd fainted. The little group moved off in the opposite direction. Then, before Renie could recount what had happened, two more orderlies appeared, on the run.

"More action on the field," Renie said. "Margie struck out—as in out cold—and another pair of orderlies have been called in from the dugout." She'd barely finished speaking when the orderlies reappeared, pushing what looked like Bob Randall on a gurney. His face was covered with a sheet, and Renie let out a little squawk as the entourage all but flew down the hall, then disappeared into an elevator that must have been waiting for them.

"Oh, dear." Renie gulped and crossed herself. "I think Bob's just been taken out of the game."

"What's the rush?" Judith asked. "Maybe he's not really dead."

But Renie sounded dubious. "He looked pretty dead to me." She lingered in the doorway, but events seemed to have come to a standstill. Several staff members were still talking in groups of twos and threes, but the high-pitched excitement of the past few minutes had dwindled into muffled voices and slumped shoulders. Robbie the Robot scooted down the hall, blinking and beeping to announce his passage.

"Call for the nurse, any nurse," Renie said, finally returning to her bed. "They'll come for you. Whoa." She collapsed, still clinging to her IV stand. "I'm not ready for prime time. I feel all wobbly."

Judith pressed the button. "I could use a dose of painkiller," she said. "It's been a while."

But it was almost half an hour before Corinne Appleby appeared, her face flushed and her manner still agitated. "I'm supposed to be off duty at eleven," she said with a quick glance at her watch, "but as you probably know, we have had an emergency. I have to stay a bit longer. I'll take your vitals now and then get some more pain medication."

The nurse's fingers fumbled with the thermometer; she gave herself a good shake. "Sorry. It's been an upsetting morning."

"What caused Mr. Randall to die so suddenly?" Judith asked.

Corinne didn't look at Judith. "I don't know. He seemed to be doing quite well."

"Why did they rush his body down the hall after he died?" Judith queried. "I mean, he was already beyond help, wasn't he?"

Corinne gave a curt nod. "Yes. He must have been an organ donor. The same procedure was followed with Mr. Somosa and Ms. Fremont."

Judith pressed on before Corinne could put the thermometer in her mouth. "Will they perform an autopsy on Mr. Randall?"

"Yes, it's required in such cases." The nurse still avoided Judith's gaze as she began the pulse routine.

Renie had managed to get herself back under the covers. "But how can they do an autopsy if he's donating his organs? That doesn't make sense."

"They can take the corneas," Corinne replied. "Eyes aren't part of a routine autopsy."

"So they did autopsies on Fremont and Somosa?" Renie asked, filling in for her cousin, who now had the thermometer in her mouth.

"Yes." Corinne kept focused on her watch. "As I said, they have to when a patient dies unexpectedly. The county automatically assumes jurisdiction in such cases."

"What did they find out with the first two?" Renie inquired.

"I couldn't say," Corinne replied, removing the thermometer from Judith's lips. "There, now let's take your blood pressure."

"Couldn't?" Judith smiled. "Or can't?"

"Won't." Corinne wound the cuff around Judith's arm. "The hospital has made its public statement."

" 'Extenuating circumstances'?" Renie quoted from what she'd read in the newspaper. "As in, not the hospital's fault?"

Corinne shrugged, but said nothing. Judith couldn't resist goading the nurse. "I saw the news last night on TV. Good Cheer is being sued, I gathered." It was only an assumption, given the brief news bit the cousins had seen, but it seemed a logical conclusion.

Corinne made no response of any kind, but removed the cuff, made some entries on a chart, and started working with Renie.

"Nope," Renie said, rolling over away from the nurse as far as she could. "I'm bored with vital signs. You aren't any fun, Appleby. Why don't they let Robbie the Robot do this stuff?"

"Please, Mrs. Jones," Corinne said severely, "don't act childish."

"But I *am* childish," Renie replied. "Often immature and a downright brat. Come on, lawsuits are a matter of public record."

Corinne took a deep breath. "I really don't know. There have been some rumors."

Renie didn't budge. "There were other rumors, too, about Fremont and Somosa being drug abusers. Is that the hospital's defense?"

Corinne Appleby made an angry gesture, her face so

flushed that the freckles disappeared. "None of that's any of your business. If you won't let me take your vitals, that's fine. But I intend to enter your lack of cooperation on the chart."

"Be my guest," Renie shot back as the nurse headed for the door. "I'll file a complaint. I'll call you a big drip."

Corinne was almost out of the room when a deep, angry voice could be heard from the hallway.

"Don't tell me who I can talk to and who I can't!" the man shouted. "I'm sick of this runaround! Where the hell is Dr. Garnett?"

Startled, Corinne scooted away and closed the door behind her.

"Drat!" Judith exclaimed. "She can't do that! Coz, could you . . . ?"

"Aargh," groaned Renie. "I guess." She struggled to get out of bed again. "Who do you suppose that is?"

"I don't know," Judith replied. "I could only hear, not see, him."

Renie opened the door just in time to see the man, who had a dark beard, accost two young people. "Look, I'm sorry," he said, "but I want to help. Let's go somewhere else so we can talk in private."

Trying to get a better look at the newcomers, Renie stepped farther out into the hall. From the bed, Judith could see only Renie's backside and the IV stand. She gave a little jump when her cousin stumbled into the room, propelled by the firm hands of Sister Jacqueline.

"We simply cannot have patients interfering or getting involved with hospital routine this morning, Mrs. Jones," the nun said in an emphatic tone. "Please remain in your room, and we'd prefer you to keep your door shut. Remember, it's for your own sakes as well. You need to rest in order to make a quick recovery."

Perhaps it was all those years in parochial school, but even Renie could comply with the wishes of a nun. "I know that bearded man," she said, back-pedaling in a clumsy manner. "That's Addison Kirby, the newspaper reporter. He was married to Joan Fremont."

Sister Jacqueline merely gave a slight nod. "Please get back in bed, Mrs. Jones."

"Who are those two young people?" Renie persisted. "Are they the Kirby kids?"

The nun started to turn away, then paused. "No. They're Mr. Randall's son and daughter. They came to the hospital to be with their mother."

"How is Margie Randall doing?" Judith asked with genuine sympathy.

Sister Jacqueline had reached the doorway. "Not well, I'm afraid. She's a very emotional woman. Excuse me, I must go."

Judith gazed at Renie. "It cannot be a coincidence for three well-known people to die unexpectedly after routine surgery in Good Cheer Hospital."

Renie looked pained. "I never like encouraging you to track down murderers, but I have to admit, this is pretty weird."

"More than weird," Judith responded, remembering to take another sip of water. "But what's the connection? One actress. Two sports stars. One active, one retired. From different sports, too. Who could possibly want all three of them out of the way?"

Staring out through the windows with their faded muslin curtains, Judith grew thoughtful. It was another gray day, with heavy, dark clouds hovering over the city. Maybe it would snow. But the weather was the least of Judith's worries.

"There's got to be a police investigation that hasn't

been made public," Judith said after a long pause. "Maybe Joe can find out from Woody."

Lunch arrived, brought by a small Filipino woman with silver streaks in her short, dark hair. Making each of the cousins a little bow, she introduced herself as Maya. Sitting up in bed, Renie bowed back.

"Such a morning!" Maya exclaimed in little more than a whisper. "Did you hear about Mr. Randall? What next, I wonder?"

Judith had an impulsive urge to hug the little woman. At last, there was somebody on the floor who wasn't tongue-tied. "It's terrible," Judith said, putting on her most sympathetic face. "It must be so hard for the people like you who work here, Maya."

Maya set Judith's tray in place, then put a hand on her breast. "It's terrible," she said, rolling her dark eyes and then crossing herself. "All these deaths. Fine people, too, each one very nice."

"You were on duty when all three of them died?" Judith queried, trying to contain her own excitement.

"Yes." Maya uttered the word like a victory chant. It was obvious to Judith that she reveled in high drama. "Can you imagine? Every time, the same thing, the same way. They do fine, getting better, then . . ." She held up her small hands. "Poof! They go to heaven."

"It must be very sad for you," Judith said, "to see these people and their families and then to have them die so unexpectedly. I suppose all their loved ones were extremely shocked. Did anybody say what might have happened?"

Maya waved a hand in a vexed gesture. "They say too little and too much. The doctors, they don't understand what happens. Not their fault, they say. Can't explain. Maybe patient have unknown sickness or take bad medicine. The families, they cry, they make threats, they blame doctors, nurses, everybody in hospital. Why, right now, Mr. Kirby, the husband of the actress, he's here again, making the big fuss." Maya shook her head. "What is fame, what is riches, if you die too soon? So sad, so very sad."

"Mr. Somosa left a wife, but no children, I believe," put in Renie as Maya delivered her tray. "The Kirby children are grown, and I guess the Randall kids are, too."

Maya nodded several times. "Yes. Mrs. Somosa, so pretty, so young, she had to be put in the hospital herself, she was so filled with grief. Now she has gone back to her homeland, the Dominican Republic, I believe. Mr. Somosa was buried there, with his ancestors. The Kirby children I never saw, they live far away, but they must have come for the funeral, yes? And now Mr. Randall . . . Oh, my! Mrs. Randall, she will be in the hospital, too, if she doesn't stop crying so."

"Maybe the children can help," Judith said. "I understand they're at the hospital now."

Maya's dark eyes flashed. "That's so." She put a finger to her lips. "Know what? They are with Mr. Kirby. Why do you think?"

"I don't know," Judith said.

"I do," Maya said with an emphatic nod. "They talk of a cabal."

Judith stared. "A cabal? What sort of cabal?"

"A plot to kill these poor souls," Maya declared with a swift glance over her shoulder to make sure the door was firmly shut. "What else?"

Judith made an extra effort to look impressed. "Who would do such a thing?"

Maya waved her hand again. "The riffraff. The rabble. The kind of people who hate the rich and famous. Communists, no doubt. It's what you call a vendetta." She clenched a fist and made stabbing motions, as if she held a dagger.

The door opened suddenly and Heather Chinn appeared, looking suspicious. "Your lunch cart is outside, Maya," said the nurse. "Is everything all right in here?"

"Yes, yes," Maya said, smiling, her compact little figure all but bouncing toward the doorway. "These fine ladies, they need what you call the pep talk. You know Maya, she can give the good pep talk."

Heather stepped aside as Maya made her exit. "I hope she wasn't pestering you," Heather said to the cousins, a faintly wary expression lingering on her face. "Maya's quite a talker."

"She's interesting," Judith said.

"Yes," Heather agreed, turning to leave, "but don't pay much attention to her. She likes to hear herself talk."

The nurse departed, closing the door behind her. "Well?" Judith said. "How much of Maya's spiel do you believe?"

"None of it," Renie replied, lifting lids and looking dismayed. "It seems we have bath sponge for lunch."

Judith also examined the meal. Everything was a pale yellow, including the lettuce leaves in the salad. "It might be some kind of creamed chicken on . . . something. Toast?" Judith prodded the gelatinous mass with her fork. "Hunh. Whatever. We also have pears, more apple juice, and a big, fat, unattractive cookie with jaundice-yellow frosting. No wonder I don't have much appetite."

"That makes two of us." Renie sighed. "I was starved last night, but Art Huey's food is always terrific. Today, I feel sort of . . . blah."

"That's not like you," Judith remarked. Renie's appetite was usually boundless. "I suppose it's natural. We've been through a lot."

"True," Renie said as someone knocked on the door but entered before either cousin could respond.

"Mrs. Flynn and Mrs. Jones?" The man who spoke was Addison Kirby, who closed the door behind him and immediately introduced himself. He was hatless, and wearing a classic trench coat over dark slacks, a tweed jacket, and a light-brown flannel shirt. "May I?"

"You want to see us?" Judith asked in surprise.

The newspaper reporter gave a curt nod. "It'll only take a minute."

"Okay," Judith said, puzzled. "Have a seat."

Addison started to sit down in Judith's visitor's chair, then hesitated. "Are you sure?" he asked, his penetrating hazel eyes darting from cousin to cousin.

"Positive," Renie said, draining her apple juice. "I recognized you out in the hall. Let me say right off, I'm terribly sorry about your loss. Your wife was a wonderful actress, and I've heard she was a fine person as well. She always seemed active in helping raise money for charity."

Briefly, Addison hung his head. He was going bald, but there were only a few strands of gray in his well-kept beard. "She was terrific in every way," he said, looking up. "On top of it, we managed to raise three children who are now off and on their own. We have two grandchildren, charming little twins. Joan was so fond of them. We'd visit when Le Repertoire wasn't . . ." He stopped abruptly and bit his full lower lip. "Sorry. I'm not here to talk about that."

"That's okay," Judith said with sympathy. "Go ahead, tell us whatever you want to."

"No, no," Addison replied, now very businesslike. "I have just a couple of questions." Again, he paused, this time to clear his throat. "This morning, before Bob Randall died, did either of you see or hear anything unusual?"

Judith and Renie exchanged quick glances. "No," Judith finally said. "I don't recall anything."

"You're sure?" Addison Kirby looked disappointed.

Renie's expression was uncharacteristically diffident. "I did hear Randall talking on the phone this morning while I was in there." She gestured at the darkly stained wooden door to the bathroom. "He was talking about somebody named Taylor, or to somebody named Taylor. I couldn't catch much of it, though."

Addison looked puzzled. "The only Taylor I know was Joan's eye doctor. But it's a common name. That's all you heard?"

"I'm afraid so," Judith responded with an apologetic expression. "Why do you ask?"

Kirby shook his head. "I'm paranoid," he said. "Obsessed. Nuts."

"Who isn't?" Renie offered.

Standing up, Kirby replaced the visitor's chair and jammed his hands into the pockets of his trench coat. "I had an appointment this morning to meet with Dr. Garnett, the chief of surgery. I've got a lot of unanswered questions about Joan's death. Garnett had been stalling me, figuring, I suppose, that anything he said would be on page one of the *Times*'s next edition. But he finally gave in, and we'd just gotten started when he was summoned to this floor. I could tell it was urgent, so I followed him, and learned that Bob Randall had died. I didn't really know Bob, but I've seen him around town over the years. Anyway, it seemed damned peculiar, with Joan dying so suddenly and Joaquin Somosa, the same way."

"It's incredible," Judith declared.

"You bet it is," Addison asserted, the hazel eyes sparking. "I was already suspicious, that's why I wanted to see Garnett. If nothing else, I wanted to clear Joan's reputation."

"In what way?" Judith asked.

Addison had turned to the door, but now he faced the cousins again. "Because," he said angrily, "the results of the autopsy indicated she'd ingested a large quantity of Rohypnol—one of those date-rape drugs—which caused her death. That's bull, Joan never did drugs in her life. Even if she had, why in the world would she take that one?" His voice dropped and his eyes sent off more sparks. "It doesn't make sense, which is why I think my wife was murdered."

FIVE

JUDITH WASN'T SURPRISED by Addison Kirby's declaration. It only confirmed her suspicions about the three deaths.

"So you think there may be something fishy about Somosa and Randall as well?" she asked.

Addison shrugged. "Maybe. I can't speak for Somosa, because I didn't know him. But I heard through my county sources that the autopsy indicated he'd overdosed on some kind of street drug. Ecstasy, I think. As for Randall—we don't know yet, do we?"

Their visitor paced back and forth in front of Judith's iron bedstead. He seemed to be arguing with himself. "I just spoke with Randall's son, Bob Jr., and his daughter, Nancy. They caught snatches of conversation among the staff that indicated suicide."

"What?" Judith couldn't believe her ears.

"That's right," Addison said, nodding gravely. "I can't get to Mrs. Randall—she's had some kind of emotional collapse."

"What about his brother, Jim?" Judith asked. "Has he been notified?"

"Jim?" Addison blinked several times. "I didn't realize Bob Randall had a brother. Is he around?"

"He was here last night," Renie put in. "He was fussing because Bob had too many visitors and so much hubbub going on in his room."

"Interesting," Addison remarked. "I'll try to get hold of him."

"Say," Renie said, adjusting her sling and leaning forward in the bed, "why haven't you gone public with any of the stuff about your wife and Somosa? I haven't seen a word about it in the *Times*."

The journalist gave Renie a twisted little smile. "You don't understand the politics of publishing, Mrs. . . . Jones, right? My superiors don't want me ruffling feathers. Blanche Van Boeck is a powerful figure in this community."

Renie slapped at her head with her good hand. "Of course! I didn't make the connection with Dr. Jan Van Boeck. That's his wife, right? She's on the city council and just about everywhere on the map in this town. Oh, my."

Addison's smile became wry. "She certainly is. Rumor has it she may run for mayor. She has powerful friends in powerful places. Of course, she has enemies, too."

Renie was suddenly wearing what Judith called her "boardroom face," the no-nonsense sharpening of her features that she presented to corporate clients in her graphic design business.

"Blanche has made some big waves in the past few years," Renie said. "She's always struck me as putting Blanche at the head of her agenda, rather than the social and political programs she espouses."

Addison nodded. "That's what many people would say, which is why I have to dance all around her in print. Which also means I have to dance around Good Cheer Hospital, because her husband runs the place."

"But Good Cheer was on the news last night," Judith pointed out. "We missed the first part of the story. What was that all about?"

"The Seafarers are calling for an investigation into Somosa's death," Addison replied. "Apparently, they think something's wrong, too. I intend to meet with Tubby Turnbull, the team's general manager, this afternoon."

Judith was shaking her head. "So I wasn't wrong," she said faintly.

At the door, Addison frowned at Judith. "Wrong about what?"

"About these deaths being linked," Judith said. "Frankly, the deaths of your wife and Somosa struck me as more than a coincidence right from the start. Now, with Randall's passing, the situation seems downright ominous."

Addison's expression was frankly curious. "Why does it interest you so much, Mrs. Flynn?"

Judith felt the color rise in her cheeks. "Oh . . . You might say that my hobby is snooping." She uttered a lame little laugh.

Addison now looked puzzled. "Snooping?" he said.

"It'd be more accurate," Renie said, "to say that her hobby is murder."

"And to think," Renie mused after Addison Kirby had departed, "I wondered how we'd pass the time during our hospital stay."

"I don't think the deaths of those poor people were intended to keep us occupied," Judith said, feeling glum and staring up at the mottled plaster ceiling.

The uncommunicative orderly of the previous day came in to remove the cousins' luncheon trays. If he noticed that neither of them had eaten much, he made no comment, but stoically left the room without a word.

"Can he talk?" Renie asked, getting up and heading for the bathroom. "Or does he consider us unworthy?"

"The latter, I suspect," Judith responded. "Maybe if you didn't trash your bed so much, we'd get more respect. Where did that Falstaff's grocery bag come from?"

"Falstaff's," Renie replied, turning around at the bathroom door. "It's my back-up food supply. Fruit, cheese, crackers, Pepsi, popcorn. We'll share when I come back to bed. Now I'm hungry."

"How did you fit that thing into your purse?" Judith asked.

"Easy," Renie replied. "I have a huge purse." She went inside the bathroom and shut the door.

The outer door opened almost simultaneously as Heather Chinn entered. "Time to get you on your feet," she said in a cheerful voice. "How do you feel, Mrs. Flynn?"

"Not like I want to get on my feet," Judith said. "I thought we'd do this later in the afternoon."

"It's almost two," Heather said. "The more you lie there, the weaker you'll become. Here, let me help you swing around to the edge of the bed."

It took Judith a few moments to sit up straight. Then, slowly and unsteadily, she let Heather help her move her legs. Pain spread out from her hip to envelop her entire body. "I feel dizzy already," Judith asserted.

"You're doing fine," Heather soothed. "Now lean on me and try to stand up."

Judith could both feel and hear the artificial hip move. She was frightened. "Is that . . . ?" she gulped, still dizzy.

"That's fine, keep coming. You've got all your weight on your good leg," Heather coached. "Now put just a little on the other leg, okay?"

The worn linoleum was rising up toward Judith in tired, wrinkled waves. She felt as if she were falling overboard, into a murky yellow sea. Suddenly her world went dark, except for shooting stars and trailing comets.

"Coz!" Renie had just come out of the bathroom. Moving as quickly as she could, she went to Judith, who had, fortunately, fallen backwards onto the bed. Heather was looking more annoyed than frightened as she took Judith by the hands.

"It's nothing," the nurse said to Renie. "Maybe she isn't quite ready to stand. Still, if she doesn't try . . ."

"If she doesn't try, she won't pass out," Renie cut in tersely. "Let me get somebody to help you put her back to bed."

Though Heather was stronger than she looked, she didn't turn down the offer. The nurse was a short, slim size four; Judith was a statuesque size fourteen. Another strong body was needed for the task. Renie found the silent orderly just outside the door, stacking trays onto the meal cart.

Judith's eyelids fluttered open as the nurse and the orderly got her back into bed. "Oh . . . What happened?" she asked, her mouth dry and her eyes unfocused.

"You had a little setback," Heather said, tucking the covers around Judith. "We'll try that again later." The nurse began taking vital signs.

Renie was standing by the windows. "Damn," she breathed, "I think it may snow. I wish Bill and Joe would get here soon, while it's still daylight."

"Joe said he'd be by around three," Judith said. "Bill's coming with him, I think." She took a deep breath before Heather popped the thermometer in her mouth.

"Right, there's no point in taking two cars," Renie said, looking down at the hospital entrance's graceful landscaping and the adjacent parking lot. "Boy, it looks really cold out there. I can feel the chill through the windows."

Judith couldn't respond with the thermometer in her mouth. The dizziness had passed, but she felt weak as a newborn lamb. The idea of trying to stand up later in the day sounded impossible.

"I need some water," she said in a thick voice after Heather had removed the thermometer. "I'm so dry."

"You mustn't get dehydrated," Heather warned, proffering the plastic glass. "Remember how we've told you to keep taking in fluids."

"Hey," Renie said, "I see Addison Kirby heading for the parking lot. I wonder if he's off to see Tubby Turnbull at the . . . Look out!" She shuddered as her good arm reached out toward the window in a pleading motion. "Ohmigod!"

"What?" Judith sputtered, choking on the water.

Horror-stricken, Renie staggered around to stare at Judith and Heather. "It's awful," she gasped, leaning against the window embrasure for support. "A car just came from out of nowhere and ran over Addison Kirby!"

Heather Chinn ran off to get help. Renie stood rooted by the window. "The car took off," she said in a shaky voice. "Poor Addison's lying there in a heap."

Judith had rolled over onto her side, though she

couldn't get a better view of what was happening beyond the window. "Is he . . . ?" she asked in a fearful
voice.

"No, he's moving," Renie said. "Sort of."

"Damn!" Feebly, Judith swung a fist in frustration.
"I feel so helpless!"

"Here comes a guy in a white coat and another guy in
some kind of uniform." Renie was trying to open the
window with her good hand, but it wouldn't budge.
"The white coat may be a doctor. Yes, I think it's what's-
his-name—Garnett, the second in command. The guy in
uniform may be security. Here comes somebody else, in
civvies. He looks sort of familiar." She gave up trying to
open the window and flexed the muscles of her left arm
before rapping loudly on the wavery old glass. "Hey,
he's looking up. It's Jim Randall," Renie said, breathless. "Here come some more people with a gurney."

"Double damn," Judith muttered. "I feel like an
idiot. Why couldn't I at least be in a wheelchair?"

"You will be," Renie responded. "Huh. They seem to
be paying special attention to Addison's left leg.
Maybe it's broken. Poor guy."

"Where's the car that ran him over?" Judith asked.

"I don't know. It hit Addison and kept going, toward
the parking lot." Renie paused, staring down below.
"Dr. Garnett and one of the others are hovering over
the gurney. Jim Randall is walking away. The security
guy is wandering around, like he's looking for someone or something."

"The car, I suppose," Judith said. "You'll have to tell
him you saw it. What color and make was it?"

"It was sort of beige," Renie said, "fairly new, but
from up here on three, I couldn't guess what make. All
I could see was the roof."

"Do you remember if there's an outlet from the parking lot?" Judith inquired.

"No, of course not," Renie answered. "We pulled into the patient admitting area on the opposite side of the entrance."

"Oh." Judith rolled over onto her back. "I forgot. That anesthesia has muddled my brain."

"It does that," Renie allowed. "They're all going inside now, including the uniform." She waited a moment, then went back to her bed. "Shall I phone security and tell them I saw it?"

"Sure," Judith said. "They'll need a witness. Insurance, and all that."

Renie picked up the phone, dialed zero, and asked to be connected to security. She was informed that security was out. "He's it?" she said after leaving her name and room number.

"Probably not, at least not at night," Judith replied.

Renie began hauling food out of the Falstaff's bag. "Let's eat something before the nurses come around with all their paraphernalia. I don't want them confiscating my stash."

"I might nibble on an apple," Judith said.

"Red Delicious, Golden Delicious, Granny Smith, Gala?" Renie offered.

"Red Delicious," Judith said, gazing at the sack with its Falstaff logo. "How much stuff have you got in there?"

"Plenty," Renie replied, using her left hand to toss Judith a shiny red apple. It was a surprisingly accurate throw, considering that Renie was normally right-handed. "Hey," she said with a grin, "maybe I could've been a southpaw pitcher. Cheese? There's Monterey jack, Havarti, Brie, and a really nice Gouda." She produced a small knife and held it up.

"The apple's fine," Judith said with a slight shake of her head. "I don't see how you got all that stuff in your purse, big as it is."

"That's because I took everything else out and put it in my overnight bag," Renie said. "Food first; the rest is a distant second."

The phone rang. Judith thought it must be security, calling Renie back. But Renie gave a brief shake of her head. It wasn't her phone. Judith wrestled with the receiver, and finally managed to say hello.

"Hi, Mom," Mike said, sounding vaguely apprehensive. "How are you getting along? Joe told me the surgery went fine."

"It did," Judith replied with a big smile on her face. "I'm getting along just great."

"That's a huge relief," Mike said, and Judith knew he meant it. Her son was a worrier. "Kristin and Mac and I'd like to come into town tonight to see you, but it's snowing like crazy up here at the pass. I think they're going to close the highway pretty soon. It's a regular blizzard."

In her mind's eye, Judith could picture the U.S. Forest Service cabin that Mike and Kristin called home. It was small but cozy, and with a magnificent view of the surrounding mountains and forest. At least when they could see through the snow.

"Don't even think of coming down until I get home," Judith said. "I'm not going to be here forever."

"I know, but I'd still like to pay a visit before the weekend," Mike said. "Didn't they figure you'd be home about Saturday?"

"They didn't make any promises," Judith said. "How's Kristin? What's little Mac up to?"

"They're fine," Mike said. "Kristin still has the queasies sometimes, but basically, she feels strong."

Like a fifty-foot Douglas fir, Judith thought, picturing her daughter-in-law.

"Mac wants to go back outside to play in the snow," Mike went on, "but it's blowing too hard. Kristin took him out there a while ago, and the wind knocked him over. He made a perfect snow angel when he fell, though. Thanks again for the snowsuit you gave him for Christmas." He paused, and Judith could hear Mac jabbering in the background. "Tomorrow, little fella, okay? Say," Mike said into the phone again, "I wasn't going to mention this until I saw you, but now that I think about it, you're probably pretty bored, huh?"

"Well . . ." Judith glanced at Renie, who was gobbling cheese and pear slices. "Not exactly, but I may be later."

"We're going to put Mac in preschool this fall," Mike said, sounding like a typical proud papa. "There's a really good one about twenty miles down the highway. Kristin's been filling out the forms, and one thing they'd like to have is a family tree. Then, when the kid enters on the first day, there's his picture on this cutout of a tree, with information about all of his ancestors. Cute, huh?"

"Cute," Judith agreed, though her voice had gone flat. "So you want me to put together a family tree." She caught Renie's gaze; Renie choked on her pear.

"If you could," Mike said. "Nothing fancy; I gather the teachers do the artwork and arranging. No real rush, either, though they'd like to have all this stuff by the end of the month."

"The end of the month?" Judith frowned into the phone. "Why so soon? Mac won't start school until fall."

"The teachers have to make the trees for about sixty

kids," Mike said reasonably. "Of course, they have to decide if they'll accept Mac in the first place. But the earlier we get all this stuff done, the more likely he'll get into Little Einsteins."

"That's the name of the school?" Judith gulped.

"Right. They don't take just any kid," Mike said, pride still evident in his voice. "Of course, it's not cheap, but we can swing it. Education's so important these days. I mean, it's not like when I was a kid, and you sent me to Ethel Bump's place. All we did was string beads and finger-paint her furniture and roll around on our rugs."

"That was day care, Mike," Judith said over Renie's loud coughing fit. *You were there so I could work two jobs while Dan laid on the couch, starting his day with an entire bottle of blackberry brandy and working his way up to his first vodka at eleven in the morning.* "You did more than just play at Ethel's," Judith continued. "You learned your numbers."

"Not all of them," Mike responded. "I always left out nine."

"True." Judith hung her head. "Okay, I'll see what I can do."

"Great, Mom. Got to go. There's a message coming in on my fax. Love you." He hung up.

"Family tree, huh?" Renie said, having conquered her choking.

Judith grimaced. "I've dreaded this for years."

Renie offered her cousin a sympathetic smile. "Don't you think Mike knows that Dan wasn't his real father?"

"Define 'real,' " Judith said with a frown.

"I meant natural father," Renie responded, eating a piece of Havarti cheese. "Yes, I certainly know that

Dan raised Mike, that in spite of being a lousy husband, he was a pretty good dad. I also know that Mike has always felt that Dan really was his dad. But a year or so ago, I got the impression that Mike had figured it out. Do you remember? We were all having our pictures taken with little Mac, and Mike suddenly looked from the baby's red hair to Joe's, and since Mike himself has red hair and Dan was very dark, I got the impression that Mike finally realized the truth."

"He's never said a word," Judith asserted. "Not to me, not to Joe. But you're right, I think he must know, deep down. How much denial could he possibly have? I wanted to broach the subject with him then, but I kept putting it off. We'd already had one big conversation a couple of years ago, and it became clear to me that the truth would have altered his memory of Dan."

"He was younger then," Renie pointed out. "That was before he got married, wasn't it?"

"I can't remember," Judith admitted. "I know, I tend to bury things, hoping they'll go away. But they don't."

The phone rang again, this time on Renie's line. She responded in monosyllables, then hung up. "Security. His name is Torchy Magee. He'll be up in a few minutes, along with a cop."

"If Joe had never been a cop," Judith sighed, "and never gotten drunk that night in the bar with Herself, I wouldn't be in this quandary now."

"Nonsense," Renie retorted, cutting another slice of cheese and popping it in her mouth.

Judith didn't say anything for a few moments. She was reliving that terrible time when Joe had suddenly disappeared just weeks before their wedding. She'd only heard secondhand that he'd been shanghaied to Vegas by Vivian, and that, while he was still in a drunken stupor, the pair had gotten married in a casino wedding chapel. It wasn't until many years later that Judith had found out he'd tried to call her later that same day. Gertrude had intercepted the call and never told Judith about it. Not hearing back, and feeling compelled to honor his commitment to Vivian, Joe had stayed married to Vivian for over twenty years. He'd felt sorry for Herself, he explained to Judith after they were finally reunited. She'd had two unhappy marriages already, and was trying to raise two small boys on her own. Then Vivian had given birth to their own daughter, Caitlin. Joe felt stuck, and he knew that Judith had married Dan McMonigle on the rebound. It was only after the children were raised and Herself had grown more passionate about Jim Beam than Joe Flynn that he had finally decided to make a break. There had been no need for an annulment. In the eyes of the Catholic Church, Joe's marriage to Herself had never been valid. Taking vows while not in his sane and sober mind was only part of it; the Church didn't recognize the union because Vivian was still the wife of another man.

Meanwhile, Judith had lived a lie, at least as far as Mike was concerned. Joe didn't know that she was pregnant when he ran off with Herself. Judith had never told him, not until almost a quarter of a century later. Dan had raised Mike as his own, and perhaps his often antagonistic attitude toward Judith was a form of punishment for bearing another man's child. Whatever the cause, Judith had suffered a great deal during the nineteen years that she was married to Dan.

"But he was a good father." She repeated the phrase so often that it was like a mantra. She could never make Dan happy, but she could honor his memory, especially in Mike's eyes.

"Yes, yes," Renie said testily. "But Mike's a grown man now, he can handle the truth. It's not fair to Joe. It never has been, and I'll bet my last five bucks he resents it, deep down."

Judith heaved a big sigh. "Yes, I know he does. I guess I'll have to bite the bullet."

"It's about time," Renie said, still testy. "Your problem, coz, is that you hate making decisions, you can't stand rocking the boat, you're absolutely terrified of change. Go ahead, make out that family tree, and fill in all of Joe's family. His brothers, his parents, the whole damned clan."

"I never knew his mother," Judith said, as if her early death might give some excuse for abandoning the project.

"Do it," Renie barked. "I'll help."

Before Judith could respond, a burly, uniformed man in his late fifties poked his head in the door. "Mrs. Jones?" he said in a gravelly voice.

"Here," said Renie, raising her left hand. "You're Torchy Magee?"

"Yes, ma'am," the security guard responded as another, much younger man in a patrolman's uniform followed him into the room. "This is Johnny Boxx, that's with two *xx*'s, right, Johnny?"

"Right," replied the young officer with a tight little smile.

"He's fairly new to the force," Magee said, swaggering a bit as he nodded at Judith and approached Renie's bed. "Me, I was a cop for over twenty-five years before I retired a while back. Arson, vice, larceny, assault—I did it all, and have the scars to show for it." He chuckled and gave Johnny Boxx a hearty slap on the back. "Yessir, see this?" He pointed to a long, thin scar on his right cheek. "Attacked by a knife there." Magee rolled up his left sleeve to reveal another scar. "Shotgun, just below the elbow. Hurt like hell. I was wounded three times, here, in the shoulder, and just above my ear. Got a plate in my head to prove it."

"My," Renie said, keeping a straight face, though Judith could tell it was an effort, "you've had some bad luck."

"Just doing my job," Magee responded. "That's not all, either. I got my nickname, Torchy, when I was in arson. Look, no eyebrows."

Sure enough, Magee's forehead stretched from his eyes to the bald spot on top of his head. "What happened?" Judith asked.

"Let's put it this way," Torchy Magee responded with a chuckle and a wink, "when you're investigating an arson case, you should make sure the fire is out first." He chuckled some more, a grating sound, then turned to Renie. "Okay, little lady, let's hear all about what you saw from this third-story window."

" 'Little lady'?" Renie curled her lip.

"Well . . ." Torchy shrugged. "In a manner of speaking." He rested one foot on Renie's bed frame. "So what'd you see?"

"I was standing by the window," Renie began, eyeing Torchy's foot with annoyance, "when I saw Mr. Kirby leave through the front entrance."

Officer Boxx held up a hand. "How did you know it was Mr. Kirby?"

"I'd just met him," Renie replied. "He was wearing a trench coat, he had a beard, it wasn't that hard to identify him three floors up."

"Sounds right to me," Torchy said. "Go on, Mrs. J."

"Mrs. *Jones*," Renie said with emphasis. "Anyway,

he'd just started toward the parking lot when a beige car, a mid-sized sedan, came from out of nowhere and struck Mr. Kirby down."

"Heh, heh." Torchy chuckled. "Now, Mrs. . . . Jones, a car can't come out of nowhere. Which direction?"

Renie looked exasperated. "I was watching Mr. Kirby. You know damned well a car can come from three directions out there—the parking lot, the main drive into the hospital, and the ambulance and staff area off to the right of the main entrance. That is, my right, from my point of view, through my window."

Torchy's expression had grown serious. "Through this window."

"Yes." Renie's patience appeared to be wearing thin.

"Tell us about the car," Officer Boxx inquired. "It was a beige medium-sized sedan. Any idea how old or what make?"

"Very clean," Renie answered, "so I thought it was fairly new. It was shaped like so many cars these days, especially the Japanese imports. Bill and I have a Toyota, about the same color as the car I saw. In fact, our car looks like every other car these days. Sometimes I get mixed up in a parking lot and try to get into the wrong one. My husband and I call our Toyota Cammy. Except Bill says Cammy is a boy. I don't agree. Cammy's a girl."

"Can't you tell by looking underneath?" Torchy laughed aloud at his joke.

"I never thought of that," Renie said with a straight face and a flashing eye.

"License plate," Boxx put in. "Did you get any kind of look?"

"Ah . . ." Renie bit her lip. "I didn't notice."

The young policeman frowned. "Do you remember if it had in-state plates?"

Her eyes half closed, Renie seemed to be concentrating. "Yes, I think so. I can see it from the rear as it headed toward the parking lot. I'm a very visual person."

"Huh?" said Torchy.

"I'm a designer, an artist by trade," Renie explained. "I see more than most people do, but sometimes I don't realize it until later."

"But you didn't see any letters or numbers," the policeman prompted.

"No." Renie looked chagrined.

"So this car went where after hitting Mr. Kirby?" Torchy inquired.

"Toward the parking lot," Renie replied. "You can't see much of the lot because of those evergreen trees and shrubs. Anyway, I was riveted on Mr. Kirby."

"How is he?" Judith broke in.

"Kirby?" Torchy turned around. "Broken leg, bruises and so forth. Kid stuff." The security guard touched his head, presumably where he'd been shot. "He'll live."

"That's more than his wife did," Renie declared. "She never got out of this place alive."

"Now, now," Torchy said in a soothing tone. "That was a different matter."

"How different?" Judith asked.

"Well," Torchy began, then paused and scratched his bald spot, "she had an operation. And then . . . well, maybe she was taking some stuff on the side. You know." He winked again.

"Actually," Renie said, "we don't know. Mr. Kirby doesn't think his wife was taking 'stuff on the side.' Have you talked to him, Security Officer Magee?"

Torchy gave a little jump. "Me? Why, sure. That's

my job. But what do husbands know about what wives do when they're not with the old man?" He winked a third time. "Or the other way around, for that matter. Besides, she was an actress. You know what those theater people are like."

Renie held up a hand. "If you wink again, I'll have to kill you. Yes, I know something about theater people. But the real question is, what do you know about the untimely deaths of three well-known local residents in this very hospital? Isn't that your business?"

Johnny Boxx had strolled to the door, maybe, Judith thought, in an effort to disassociate himself from Torchy Magee. "If you think of anything else," Boxx said to Renie in a courteous voice, "let us know." It was clear he meant the police, not security.

"I will," Renie promised.

Torchy lingered after Officer Boxx went out into the hall. "Let me know first," he said to Renie, his jocular manner evaporating.

"Sure," Renie said, her brown eyes wide with innocence.

Judith pushed herself up on the pillows. "Drugs, huh?" she said in a conspiratorial tone. "Fremont and Somosa both, I heard. And Bob Randall committed suicide. How horrible."

Torchy's close-set gray eyes narrowed. "Where'd you hear all that?"

Judith shrugged. "Hospital scuttlebutt. You know how people like to gossip."

The security man, who had been midway to the door, stopped at the foot of Judith's bed. "Don't pay attention to what you hear. Of course," he went on, lightly caressing the iron bedstead rail, "sometimes truth has a way of getting out." Once again, Torchy winked.

"That's so," Judith said, smirking a bit and ignoring Renie, who was making threatening gestures at Torchy with her cheese knife. "It's hard to imagine why Bob Randall would kill himself. It's even harder to imagine how he did it." She gave a little shudder, which wasn't entirely feigned.

Torchy frowned. "I'm not sure I know yet. That is, I couldn't say if I did, of course. That'd be telling tales out of school." Torchy gave the bedstead a quick slap. "Gotta go. No rest for the wicked."

The security man left. The cousins stared at each other.

"What do you think?" Renie inquired.

"I think," Judith said slowly as her eyelids began to droop, "that no matter how Bob Randall died, it wasn't suicide. I'm willing to bet that it was . . ."

She fell asleep before she could finish the sentence.

SIX

JOE AND BILL arrived shortly after three o'clock. Both had already heard about Bob Randall's sudden death. Joe was wild; Bill was thoughtful.

"I don't get it," Joe raged, pacing up and down the small room. "There's nowhere you can go in this entire world and not run into a dead body. If I shot myself right now with my trusty thirty-eight, and you entered a cloistered nunnery tomorrow, the first thing you'd find is the Mother Superior's corpse, carved up like a damned chicken!"

"Joe," Judith pleaded, "you know I was apprehensive even before . . ."

"Post-op anxiety, depression, fear—it could play out that way," Bill was saying quietly to Renie, "but I doubt it. On the other hand . . ."

"I'll have you moved," Joe said, suddenly stopping between the cousins' beds. "To some rehab place; I think there's one connected to our HMO . . ."

". . . Bob Randall may have been overcome with family difficulties," Bill continued. "Maybe, when he signed that release before surgery, he envisioned his own mortality and . . ."

"No, what am I thinking of?" Joe said, catching

himself. "There'd still be a damned body somewhere. It's hopeless, it's beyond comprehension, it's . . ."

". . . given his other problems, Randall felt his life was unbearable." Bill turned his palms up in a helpless gesture.

Judith turned toward Bill. "What did you say? About Bob Randall's family problems?"

Bill gave Judith a vaguely apologetic look. "Sorry. I shouldn't have mentioned it. You see, I've been treating Margie Randall for some time."

"What?" Both cousins shrieked at Bill.

"Good God almighty!" Joe exclaimed under his breath and fell into Judith's visitor's chair.

"You never mentioned Bob Randall's wife as a patient," Renie said in an accusing tone.

"Of course not," Bill replied calmly. "I don't disclose my patients' identities to you unless it's someone you've never heard of and the name is meaningless. In fact, I often make up the names."

"Patient confidentiality," Renie scoffed. "How come you didn't speak to Margie Randall in the waiting room yesterday morning?"

"Because it would have frightened and embarrassed her," Bill said. "Besides, I don't think she saw me. Which is understandable. Part of her problem is that she's completely locked into herself."

"So what awful problems—other than Margie—did Bob Randall have with his family?" Judith asked, trying to ignore Joe's angry glare.

Bill sighed. "Honestly, I shouldn't say. But we may be involved in a homicide here, and eventually, the media will get hold of all the details. Besides, Margie canceled her last two appointments and may not still consider me her psychologist; I can allow that the two

Randall children are deeply troubled. In fact, they're a big, fat mess."

"That's clinical enough," Renie said, her annoyance fading. "How so?"

As was his wont, Bill took his time to answer. "Really, I can't betray a patient's trust. Nancy, the daughter, and Bob Jr., the son, both have what you might consider life-threatening problems. Let's leave it at that."

"You're no fun," Renie said. "I want a divorce."

"You can't have one," Bill responded. "But I can assure you that life on the home front wasn't all highlight reels. Bob might have had good reasons to do himself in."

"No such luck," Joe said glumly with a dirty look at his wife. "I'll bet my old classic MG that he got himself killed. I should be so lucky to have my charming bride run into a plain old suicide."

Judith felt too tired to carry the fight any further. "Knock it off, Joe, please." She gave him her most winsome look. "Be reasonable. I had to have this surgery, Good Cheer is the only hospital in town that does it, I'm incapacitated, and it's not—and never has been—my fault that I keep running into dead people. I'm just an ordinary wife, mother, and innkeeper."

"You'd run into fewer dead people if you were a coroner," Joe muttered. "Okay, okay, your usual logic has made a slight impression. For now. Here," he said, reaching down to the shopping bag he'd placed on the floor. "I got you some books and magazines."

Bill, meanwhile, had given Renie another Falstaff's grocery bag. A veteran of his wife's foraging, he stepped back as wrappers ripped, paper flew, and liquid spilled from an unknown source. Renie removed sandwiches, peeled carrots, sliced cantaloupe, potato chips, two packages of cookies, a box of graham crackers, and more Pepsi, the beverage she claimed inspired her graphic designs.

"Great," Renie enthused, opening one of the sandwiches, which was on a small baguette. "Lunch was inedible." She leaned toward Judith. "Ham or chicken?"

"I'm not that hungry," Judith admitted.

Joe was concerned, so Judith reluctantly related her experience in trying to stand up. "I've got to do it again this afternoon. I don't suppose you could stick around until they make me try it?"

Joe grimaced. "I can't, Jude-girl. I'm really sorry. I have to get back on this homeless homicide investigation. I finished the background this morning. Now I'm going to check out the sites where the bodies were found. Both of the murders occurred in the same area, not far from here, under the freeway."

Judith knew the area that Joe was talking about. Many homeless people tucked their whole world beneath the city's major north-south arteries. It wasn't as aesthetic as the local parks, but citizens and police alike were less apt to hassle them. Still, their ragtag little neighborhoods were occasionally sent packing, a caravan of bundles, bags, and grocery carts. And people. The thought made Judith sad.

But she wasn't naïve. "Be careful, Joe. I don't like this assignment any more than you like me encountering murder." She paused, a fond expression on her face. "Joe, we have to talk." Judith paused and swallowed hard. "About Mike. He wants a family tree made up for little Mac's preschool."

"Oh?" Joe's face was blank.

Judith nodded. "He called just a while ago. I told him I'd do it."

"Preschool?" The word seemed to strike Joe as an afterthought. "Good God, the kid's only a baby. He's still wetting his pants."

"They teach them to stop in preschool," Judith responded with a glance for Renie and Bill, who suddenly, discreetly, seemed to be absorbed in their own conversation. "Mac's not going to enter until the fall. He'll be two this summer. Anyway, that's not the point. Don't you want Mike to know the truth? The last time we discussed this seriously, you seemed crushed because I wasn't ready to tell him."

Joe sighed and scratched at his thinning red hair. "It almost seems like it's too late."

"What do you mean, too late?" Judith was taken aback. "Mike's over thirty, he's matured, he ought to know because you and he have never had that father-son intimacy. You've been buddies, period."

"That's what I mean," Joe said, ducking his head. "He's a grown man. He doesn't need a father."

"Oh, Joe!" Judith put her hands over her mouth and stared wide-eyed at her husband. "I was still in my teens when my dad died, and I miss him every day. Your father lived much longer, until you were—what?—almost forty. How can you say such a thing?"

"Because," Joe said slowly, "I wasn't there for Mike when he needed a real father. When Dan died, Mike was about the same age as you were when your dad passed away. I missed out on all those years. And I still marvel at how well Mike turned out. Maybe I owe Dan something, too."

Judith bit her lip. "You can't do this to me. Not after

all the agony I've been through and the guilt and the—"

Joe cut Judith off with a wave of his hand. "Stop. This isn't the time for a family crisis. You need to concentrate on getting well. Let me think it over." He stood up. "I don't know why the hell a preschooler needs a family tree. He'd be better off if I built him a tree house."

"Do it," Judith said, forcing a small smile. "That's what grandpas do. If you weren't around for Mike, you're here for Mac."

"Right." Joe's shoulders slumped. "Got to go. Hey, Bill—let's hit the pavement."

Bill, who had been plucking food particles from Renie's sling and other parts of her person, stood up. "Okay." He turned back to Renie. "Joe picked me up at the Toyota place downtown. I left Cammy there to have new windshield wipers put on, just in case it snows." Bill bent down to kiss his wife on the one spot on her face that wasn't covered with mayonnaise, butter, or bread crumbs.

The husbands, who seemed to exit at a rather brisk pace, hadn't been gone for more than five minutes when Judith glimpsed a patient being rolled down the hall.

"Who's that?" Renie asked, following her cousin's gaze.

Judith didn't answer right away, listening to see if she could hear anyone speak. "I couldn't see, but I wonder if it's Addison Kirby. I'm almost sure they took whoever it was into Bob Randall's private room."

"How can they?" Renie demanded. "Isn't that what you'd call a crime scene?"

"Not as far as the hospital officials are concerned,"

Judith said with a frown. "I don't get it. Nurse Appleby told us that the county has jurisdiction in a sudden hospital death. So why haven't we seen the sheriff and his men prowling around? The only real cop who showed up was Johnny Boxx, who looks as if he hasn't sprouted a beard yet."

"A beat cop at that," Renie remarked. "Not a detective."

"Exactly. Coz?" Judith leaned in Renie's direction and gestured toward the hallway with her thumb. "Could you?"

Renie finishing cleaning up from her picnic lunch. "Yeah, yeah, I can. I have to go to the bathroom anyway. I'll do that first."

"Good. See if you can hear anything through the wall," Judith urged.

Renie was in the bathroom for almost five minutes. When she emerged, she looked triumphant. "It's Addison Kirby, all right. I could hear a doctor talking to him. A very humble doctor, I might add."

"Which one?" Judith asked.

"I don't know. Shall I?" Renie moved toward the door.

"Please." Judith tried to sit up a little straighter as Renie peered out into the hall. "Anything?"

"Hold on." Renie waited for at least a full minute before turning back to Judith. "It's a damned parade, coming from the other direction. TV people, with cameras and sound equipment, in apparent pursuit of a woman in a sable coat."

"Sable?" Judith was impressed.

"And a gold turban," Renie noted. "*I'm* impressed." She turned to look at Judith. "It's Blanche Van Boeck. I recognize her from her photographs. They've stopped down by that alcove with the seats for visitors. It looks as if there's going to be a press conference."

"Is Mavis there from KINE-TV?" Judith asked, once again undergoing a bout of frustration.

"It isn't KINE, it's KLIP," Renie replied. "I don't know any of these people, do you?"

"No. Can you hear them?"

Again, Renie didn't answer right away. Finally, she stepped back into the room. "They're too far down the hall. I don't dare go any farther because Dr. Garnett just came out of Addison's room and he's standing about six feet from where I parked myself. He doesn't look very happy, I might add."

"It was Garnett next door, huh?" Anxiously, Judith pleated the sheet between her fingers. "Let me get this straight—Van Boeck is chief of staff, Mrs. Van Boeck is queen of the world. Peter Garnett, chief of surgery, is second in command to Van Boeck. Thus, Dr. Garnett has a stake in all this."

"You might say that," Renie conceded, glancing back into the hall.

"Any sign of Sister Jacqueline?" Judith inquired.

"Not that I can see," Renie replied. "She's tall, too. I should be able to spot her."

"Yoo-hoo," called Mr. Mummy from across the hall. "Don't we have excitement around here today?"

"Yes, Mr. Mummy," said Renie. "Have you heard anything about what happened to Mr. Randall?"

Mr. Mummy lowered his voice, and Judith could barely hear him. "I heard he took poison. Isn't that dreadful?"

"Yes," Renie agreed with a sad shake of her head and a rise in her own voice. "Taking poison is a bad way to kill yourself."

"It may not be true," Mr. Mummy said. "What do you think?"

"I think," Renie said slowly and clearly, "that too many healthy people die in this hospital."

"Exactly." Again Mr. Mummy's voice dropped, forcing Judith to lean far over to the side of the bed. "I don't believe a word of it. The poison, I mean. Where would he get it?"

"Where indeed?" Renie said a bit absently as she tried to keep track of what was going on down the hall.

"Can you move just a little closer?" Judith asked in a humble tone.

"Well . . . Dr. Garnett is wandering off toward the media," Renie said. "I'll try to sneak up behind him."

As her cousin disappeared, Judith propped herself up on the pillows and considered patience as a virtue. But there wasn't time to practice it. A moment later, Renie back-pedaled into the room with Heather Chinn right behind her.

"*Please,* Mrs. Jones!" the nurse admonished, shaking a slim finger. "How many times do I have to tell you to stay out of the way?"

"Sorry." Renie trudged back to bed. "I was curious, that's all. You can't blame me when the guy next door kills himself, another guy gets run over outside my window, and Mrs. Van Boeck holds a press conference just down the hall."

Heather grimaced. "Yes, it has been an eventful day. But you won't make a good recovery unless you rest more. Now let me take your vitals."

"This," said Renie, holding out her left arm, "is not a restful place. On TV I've seen war zones in Bosnia that were more peaceful. Speaking of TV, what's the interview down the hall all about?"

"I'm not sure," Heather answered a bit nervously. "I gather Mrs. Van Boeck has taken it upon herself to speak out on the hospital's behalf."

"In defense of Good Cheer, huh?" Renie said before the nurse popped the thermometer in her mouth.

"Something like that," Heather replied.

"Is Blanche Van Boeck on the hospital's board of directors?" Judith inquired.

"No," Heather responded. "Since Dr. Van Boeck is chief of staff, that would be a conflict of interest."

"How long has Dr. Van Boeck held that position?" Judith asked.

Heather cocked her head to one side. "Mmm . . . Nine years? I trained at this hospital, and he was chief of staff when I started seven years ago."

Raised voices could be heard in the hall. Heather turned toward the door, her forehead furrowed in apprehension.

". . . no right to speak out on this issue," an angry male voice shouted. "I'll take this before the board."

A woman's shrill laugh cut through the air like jagged glass. "Don't be silly, Peter. As a member of the city council, I have a right to speak out."

Judith's eyes widened as the backs of the sable coat and gold turban filled the door. Apparently, the confrontation was taking place just a few feet away.

Heather had removed the thermometer from Renie's mouth and started for the door. Grabbing the nurse's wrist with her good left hand, Renie shot her a warning look.

"Don't even think about closing that door," Renie ordered.

"Mrs. Jones, you mustn't use physical force," Heather reprimanded.

"Yes, I must," Renie declared. "Now shut up."

The nurse gave Renie a helpless look as the wrangling between Blanche Van Boeck and her unseen male opponent continued.

". . . that you're on TV?" Blanche said in her strident voice. "Don't be a fool, Peter. You're not irreplaceable."

"Garnett?" Judith mouthed at Heather.

The nurse gave a brief, single nod. The sound of a struggle followed next, then what sounded like something breaking. Renie let go of Heather and hurried as fast as she could to the door. She was nearly there when Blanche Van Boeck stumbled backwards into the cousins' room, almost colliding with Renie.

"You'll regret this, Peter," she shouted as she caught herself on Judith's visitor's chair and her turban fell off onto the commode. Blanche whirled on Renie. "You clumsy idiot, you almost killed me!"

"Gee," Renie said, eyes wide, "I must be a real failure by Good Cheer standards. Usually, you come to this place, you end up dead."

"How dare you!" Blanche slammed the door behind her, narrowly missing Dr. Garnett, who was standing on the threshold. "See here, you little twerp, you have no right to cast aspersions on this fine institution. Nurse, put this creature back to bed."

Heather placed a tentative hand on Renie's left arm. "Mrs. Jones, would you . . . ?"

"No, I wouldn't," Renie snapped, shaking off Heather's hand. "Listen, Mrs. Big Shot, are you trying to tell me that I can't criticize a hospital where perfectly healthy people die within twenty-four hours after surgery? Or some poor guy gets run down before my very eyes?"

"*You* saw that?" Blanche was taken aback. "Well, he's still alive, isn't he?" She snatched the turban from the commode and jammed it back on her platinum hair.

"Addison Kirby may still be alive," Renie shot back, "but his wife, Joan, isn't."

"That was tragic," Blanche allowed, regaining her composure. "Drugs are a terrible curse." She spun around toward the door. "As for Mr. Kirby, it's too bad his wife died instead of him. Nobody likes snoopy reporters. Or snoopy patients, either." With a hand on the doorknob, she threw one last warning glance at Renie and Judith. "I suggest you two keep your so-called suspicions to yourselves."

Blanche stormed out of the room as Renie glanced at Judith. "Was that a threat?" Renie asked.

Judith winced. "Yes. All things considered, maybe we should take Blanche seriously."

"I would," Heather said quietly.

The statement carried more weight than a loaded gun.

SEVEN

TEN MINUTES LATER, Dr. Garnett surprised the cousins with a professional visit. "Dr. Ming and Dr. Alfonso are in surgery this afternoon. They asked me to look in on you two."

Peter Garnett wasn't a true double for Ronald Colman, but he did have the film actor's distinguished air, along with silver hair, a neat mustache, and a debonair manner.

"I think," Judith said in her pleasantest voice, "we could get more rest if it wasn't so noisy around here. It's been a very hectic day."

Dr. Garnett was checking Judith's dressing. "Yes . . . that looks just fine. Can you stand up?"

"Not very well," Judith said.

"Let's try," Dr. Garnett said, smiling with encouragement. "Here, sit up and swing around to the edge of the bed, then take hold of me."

Painfully, Judith obeyed. The doctor eased her slowly into a sitting position. "Now just take some breaths," he said, still smiling. "Good. Here we go. Easy does it."

Awkwardly, agonizingly, and unsteadily, Judith found herself rising from the bed. At last, with Dr.

Garnett's firm grasp to support her, she managed to get on her feet. Briefly.

"Oh!" she exclaimed, swaying a bit before sitting down again. "I did it!"

"Of course." The doctor patted her arm. "You're very weak, you've lost a great deal of blood. Tomorrow we'll see if you can take a few steps."

"About that noise," Renie said as Dr. Garnett moved to her bedside, "what was that last to-do about with the KLIP-TV people?"

Dr. Garnett's smile evaporated. "Didn't I see you out in the hall earlier?"

"Probably," Renie said. "I'm the designated observer. What gives with the TV crew?"

The doctor frowned. "Such nonsense. A hospital ward is no place for the media. It should have been handled in the lobby. Unfortunately, Mrs. Van Boeck decided to act coy, so our patients and staff ended up in the middle of a disruptive situation."

"Isn't it strange," Judith queried, "for Mrs. Van Boeck to be speaking on the hospital's behalf?"

"Perhaps," Dr. Garnett responded as he studied Renie's incision. "However, I must admit that she was instrumental in getting the local hospitals to merge their specialty fields. Still, since her husband's in charge here at Good Cheer, it would have been better to let him do the interview."

"Oink, oink. Blanche Van Boeck is a publicity hog," Renie declared.

Dr. Garnett didn't respond to the comment. Instead, he reaffixed Renie's bandage and smiled rather grimly. "You're coming along, Mrs. Jones. You lost a lot of blood, too. You shouldn't be on your feet so much. I understand you'll start physical therapy Friday morning, before you're discharged."

"Oh?" Renie looked surprised. "I didn't know when they planned to release me."

Gently, Dr. Garnett flexed the fingers on Renie's right hand. "That's what Dr. Ming told me. This is Tuesday, you've only got two more full days to go."

"What about me?" Judith asked from her place on the pillows where she'd finally stopped quivering from exertion.

"You're another matter, Mrs. Flynn," Dr. Garnett said, his smile more genuine. "Saturday at the earliest, Monday if we think you need some extra time."

"Oh, dear." Judith made a face, then tried to smile. "Of course our house has a lot of stairs, so maybe it's just as well."

The doctor patted Judith's feet where they poked up under the covers. "We don't want to rush things. Besides, it's starting to snow."

Both Judith and Renie looked out the window. Big, fluffy flakes were sifting past in the gathering twilight.

"You girls behave yourselves," Dr. Garnett said, moving toward the door. "By the way, what did Mrs. Van Boeck say when she was in your room a while ago?"

Judith grimaced. "She was rather rude."

"She was a jerk," Renie put in. "She threatened us."

"Really?" Dr. Garnett's expression was ambiguous. "That's terrible. Mrs. Van Boeck has no right to intimidate patients. I must speak to Dr. Van Boeck and Sister Jacqueline about her behavior. You're certain it was a threat?"

Judith nodded. "She also said that it was too bad that Joan Fremont died instead of her husband, Addison

Kirby. Mrs. Van Boeck remarked that nobody liked snoopy reporters, especially her, I guess."

"Yes." Dr. Garnett seemed to be trying not to look pleased at the cousins' revelations. "I believe that Mr. Kirby has been covering city government for many years. He has been quite critical of Blanche Van Boeck in some of his articles."

"Maybe," Renie said, "that's where I got a poor impression of her."

"Perhaps," Dr. Garnett said in a noncommittal tone.

"Is she dangerous?" Judith asked, feeling rather foolish for asking such a melodramatic question.

But Dr. Garnett seemed to take Judith seriously. "Let's put it this way—Blanche Van Boeck is a very determined, ambitious woman. She has little patience with anyone who stands in her way."

The doctor's assessment didn't bring any comfort to the cousins.

Renie was on the phone with her mother. Somehow Aunt Deb, perhaps threatened by her grandchildren to have the telephone surgically removed from her ear, hadn't yet called her only daughter.

"Yes, Mom," Renie was saying after the first ten minutes, "I promise not to let the doctors take advantage of me when I'm in this helpless condition . . . No, I don't have the window open . . . Yes, I realize it's snowing . . . Of course it's warm in here . . . No, I'm not going to wear three pairs of bed socks. One's enough . . . Really? I'd no idea Mrs. Parker's brother-in-law got frostbite . . . *After* he was admitted to Norway General? That *is* unusual . . ."

Judith tried to turn a deaf ear, but the conversation painfully reminded her of not having talked to

Gertrude since she was admitted. Not that her mother would mind; she hated the telephone as much as her sister-in-law adored it. Still, Judith felt guilty for not having called. In her heart of hearts, she missed the old girl, and assumed that the feeling was mutual.

She was about to dial the number in the toolshed when the phone rang under her hand. To her surprise, the caller was Effie McMonigle.

"I don't much like paying these daytime long distance rates," Judith's mother-in-law declared in a cranky voice, "but I have to go out tonight to the Elks Club with Myron."

Myron was Effie's long-time companion, a weather-beaten old wrangler with a wooden leg. His tall tales of life in the saddle smacked of romance to Effie, but Judith had always wondered if the closest he'd ever gotten to a horse was taking his grandkids for a ride on the merry-go-round at the county fair.

"It's very sweet of you to call," Judith said. "How's Myron doing?"

"As best he can," Effie replied. "Which isn't all that good. Say, I got to thinking, how come you never had an autopsy performed on Dan? He was pretty darned young to pop off like that. I've always wondered."

"You have?" Judith made a face at Renie, but her cousin was absorbed in trying to explain to Aunt Deb why it wouldn't be a good idea for her to visit at the hospital. "Well, you know," Judith said in a strained voice, "Dan was quite a bit overweight and he hadn't been well for a long time."

"He looked fine to me the last I saw of him about six months before he died," Effie asserted. " 'Course he couldn't work, he was too delicate."

Delicate. Judith held her head. "Actually, Dan was—"

"So how come?" Effie barked.

"How come what?" Judith responded with a little jump.

"No autopsy." There was an ominous pause. "I used to be a nurse, remember? Autopsies are routine in such cases."

The truth was that Judith had been asked if she would like to have an autopsy performed on Dan. She had refused. What was the point? Dan was over four hundred pounds and lived on a diet of Ding-Dongs and grape juice laced with vodka, so it hadn't surprised her in the least when he had expired.

"I wanted to spare him that," Judith said, though her thoughts were more complicated: *I wanted to spare me that. I just wanted it all to be over. Nineteen years is a long time to be miserable.*

"Hunh," Effie snorted. "It's been on my mind."

"It shouldn't be," Judith said, trying not to sound annoyed. "It's been a long time. What good would it have done?"

"I was thinking about Mac and the one on the way," Effie said, suddenly subdued. "What if Dan had some hereditary disease? Shouldn't Mike and Krissy know about it?"

"Kristin," Judith corrected. Effie had a point, except in Dan's case, it didn't apply to Mike or little Mac. "It's too late now."

"Too bad," Effie said. "These pediatricians today can nip things in the bud."

"I don't think Dan had anything he could pass on," Judith said, sounding weary. "Really, it's pointless to fret over something that happened more than ten years ago."

"Easy for you to say," Effie shot back. "All I have to do is sit here and think."

"I thought you were going to the Elks Club with Myron," Judith said as Renie finally plunked the phone down in its cradle and rubbed her ear.

"Once a month, big thrill," Effie said with a sharp laugh. "I'm not like you, out running around all over the place and doing as I please."

"Effie, I'm in the hospital."

"What?" There was a pause. "Oh—so you are. Well, you know what I mean. Think about what I said, in case Dan had something hereditary. It'll help kill time. Thinking helps me keep occupied. I'd better hang up. This phone bill is going to put me in the poorhouse."

"Lord help me." Judith sighed, gazing at Renie, who was lying back on the pillows looking exhausted. "You, too?"

"At least I love my mother," Renie said in a wan voice, "but having seen you break out into a cold sweat indicated you were talking to Effie McMonigle."

"That's right," Judith said. "She wonders why I didn't have an autopsy done on Dan."

"Before he died? It might have been a smart idea. Maybe you could have figured out what made him tick."

"Sheesh." Judith rubbed her neck, trying to undo the kinks that had accumulated. "To think I was putting off calling Mother."

The door, which had been left ajar, was slowly pushed open. Jim Randall, dusted with snow and carrying a slightly incongruous spring bouquet, stepped into the room and stopped abruptly.

"Oh! Sorry." He pushed his thick glasses up higher on his nose. "Wrong room." He left.

"What was that all about?" Renie asked.

"I don't know," Judith replied, sitting up a bit.

But Jim reappeared a moment later, looking flustered. "There's someone in there," he said, gesturing at the room that had been occupied by his late brother. "How can that be?"

"It's Mr. Kirby," Judith said. "The hospital is very crowded. I guess they had to use your . . . the empty room."

"Oh." Jim looked in every direction, cradling the bouquet against his chest. Then, in a jerky motion, he thrust the flowers in Judith's direction. "Would you like these? I don't know what to do with them. I was going to put them on Bob's bed. You know, in remembrance."

"Ah . . ." Judith stared at the yellow tulips, the red carnations, the purple freesia, and the baby's breath. "They're very pretty. Wouldn't Mrs. Randall— Margie—like them?"

"Margie?" Jim's eyes looked enormous behind the thick lenses. "Yes, maybe that's a good idea. Where is she?" He peered around the room, as if the cousins might be hiding his sister-in-law in some darkened corner.

"We heard she'd collapsed," Judith replied. "They must have taken her home by now. The children, that is. They were here earlier."

Jim's face suddenly became almost stern. "How early?"

"Well . . . It was an hour or so after your brother . . . passed away," Judith said. "Noon, maybe? I really don't remember."

Jim's expression grew troubled. "Were they here before Bob was taken?"

"Taken where?" Renie broke in. "We heard he killed himself."

"Oh!" Jim recoiled in horror at Renie's blunt speech. "That's not true! He wouldn't! He couldn't! Oh!"

"Hospital gossip," Judith said soothingly. "Please, Mr. Randall, don't get upset."

"How can I not be upset?" Jim Randall was close to tears. "Bob was my twin. We were just like brothers. I mean, we *were* brothers, but even closer . . . Gosh, he saved my life when we were kids. I fell into a lake, I couldn't swim, but Bob was an excellent swimmer, and he rescued me. . . . If he didn't kill himself, what happened? I mean, I'd understand if he did. I've felt suicidal sometimes, too. There've been days when I wished Bob had never saved me from drowning. But Bob wasn't the type to take his own life. He had everything to live for, that is." Jim fought for composure. "Nancy . . . Bob Jr. . . . Did they . . . ?"

"Did they what?" Judith prodded.

"Never mind." Jim gave himself a good shake, shedding some of the moisture from his baggy raincoat. "I should have been here, with Bob. I should have kept watch over him. I'll never forgive myself."

"Where were you?" Renie asked, popping a piece of cantaloupe into her mouth.

Jim raised his right arm and used his sleeve to wipe off some melted snow from his forehead. "That's the irony. I was here, in this very hospital, having an MRI."

"Goodness," Judith remarked, "that's a shame. I mean, that both you and your brother had medical problems at the same time."

Flexing his left leg, Jim gave the cousins a self-deprecating smile. "It was to be expected. You see, Bob and I are—were—mirror twins. It's a fairly rare phenomenon.

We faced each other in the womb, so everything about us is opposite. Bob was right-handed, I'm left-handed; he was good at numbers, I'm not. And he's been lucky with his health over the years, except for the kinds of injuries athletes suffer in their playing days. Nothing serious, though. But unlike Bob, my constitution's not strong. I've had my share of medical problems. An MRI, a CAT scan, an ultrasound—you name it, I've had them all."

"That's a shame," Judith commiserated. "Nothing serious, I hope?"

"Not so far," Jim said, adjusting his glasses. "But then Bob's right knee went out, so my left one goes. That's part of the mirror-twin effect, you see. I planned to have my surgery after Bob got back on his feet. But now . . ." Jim's voice trailed away.

"You still need to think of yourself," Judith said gently. "Although I suppose Margie and perhaps her children will need your support for a while."

Jim hung his head. "I can't replace Bob," he said on a note of defeat.

"But you can lend them moral support," Judith said, her voice still gentle.

Clumsily, Jim Randall lowered himself into Judith's visitor's chair. He still held the bouquet, though his slack grip allowed the flowers to brush the floor. "I don't know about Nancy and Bob Jr. Young people, you know how they are. All caught up in their own little worlds. Margie, maybe, will need my help. She's kind of . . . high-strung. Well, not exactly. She's more low-strung—if you know what I mean."

"Depression?" Renie asked.

Jim nodded. "She's tried every kind of medication, several different therapists. The last one just about drove her over the edge."

"Hold it!" Renie yipped.

Judith threw her cousin a fierce warning glance. "Maybe Margie didn't give him enough time."

"No," Jim began, "that wasn't it. He was very hard on her, saying that maybe she didn't want to get well. I don't blame her for—"

"Maybe she doesn't," Renie interrupted, ignoring Judith's glare. "Maybe she likes the attention. Maybe sitting around on the sidelines for almost twenty years while Bob grabbed the headlines ticked her off. Maybe she's a spoiled brat."

"Wow." Jim spoke softly as he peered at Renie. "That's harsh."

"Maybe Bob killed himself because Margie was a big fat pain in the butt," Renie went on, despite the sliver of cantaloupe that dangled from her lower lip. "That's clinical talk, of course."

Jim looked dumbfounded. "It is? But it's not fair. Margie is a wonderful person."

"Then you'd better take her those flowers before you step on them," Renie said. Her tongue darted out like a lizard's as she retrieved the bit of cantaloupe.

"Oh!" Jim snatched up the flowers, which he'd managed to let fall to the floor. "Gosh, that was careless. You're right, I'd better try to find her."

"I understand your niece and nephew are dealing with some serious problems of their own," Judith said, still at her kindliest. "That must be very hard on Margie."

Briefly, Jim's pliant features turned hard. "She mustn't feel guilty about Nancy and Bob Jr. If there's blame for what's happened to them, you can look elsewhere."

"Oh?" Judith's gaze was fixed on Jim's face.

Jim dropped his head and shuffled his feet. "Sorry. I spoke out of turn. I'd better get going."

"Say," Judith said, not quite ready to relinquish their visitor, "you were outside this afternoon when Addison Kirby got hit by that car. Did you happen to see who was driving it?"

"That was Addison Kirby?" Jim had risen to his feet. "Gee, I didn't realize it was him. His wife died recently, didn't she?"

Judith nodded. "Yes, here in this same hospital."

"Gosh." Jim shook his head several times, then frowned. "What was he doing here?"

"He'd been talking to your weird niece and nephew," Renie put in. "I suspect he was trying to figure out if they felt their father had been murdered."

"Oh!" Jim dropped the flowers again. "No! That's worse than suicide!"

"Same result," Renie noted.

Judith was trying to shut her cousin up, but the glares and the gestures weren't working. "Now, Mr. Randall, I'm sure that Mrs. Jones doesn't mean . . ."

Tears were coursing down Jim Randall's gaunt cheeks. He snuffled several times, removed his glasses, and swiped at his eyes. "My brother didn't have an enemy in the world. He was one of the most beloved sports figures in America. And here, in this city, he was a god."

"Mr. Fumbles," Renie muttered. "I remember one headline after a big loss that read, 'Can Randall Get a Handle on the Ball?' Between interceptions and fumbles, he turned the ball over six times that day, leading to a total of twenty-four points for the other guys. His so-called eagle eye couldn't seem to tell who was wearing which uniform."

"He'd eaten bad beef!" Jim cried. "He was very ill, he was playing on courage alone."

"He should have played on the field," Renie retorted. "He should have sat down and let his backup take over. I don't know what the coach was thinking of, except that Randall was a big star and the second-stringer was a third-year man who was out of football by the next season."

"I can't stand it!" Jim bent down to pick up the bouquet and stormed out of the room.

"Coz . . ." Judith was exasperated.

"I'm sorry," Renie said, exhibiting absolutely no sense of remorse. "Bill and I were at that game, and it made me mad. Granted, it was probably the worst performance of Bob Randall's career, but we paid out over a hundred bucks for tickets and we saw a really rotten game. Furthermore, I don't like Margie Randall blaming Bill for her Sad Sack state. I'll bet I'm right, she enjoys being miserable."

"That's not the point," Judith said. "You were rude, even mean. The poor guy just lost his brother, he's got his own health problems, and now he's saddled with two very unfortunate young people and a sister-in-law who's an emotional wreck." Judith pointed to the statue of Mary and the baby Jesus. "You're in a Christian hospital. How about a little charity?"

Renie let out a big sigh. "Okay, okay. So I was kind of blunt with Jim. I suppose I'm feeling sorry for myself, for you, too, and wondering how many more of these procedures and surgeries and operations we'll have to have before they carry us out like Bob Randall. If, like Margie Randall, I were inclined to depression, I'd be in about a forty-foot hole by now."

Judith was quiet for a few moments, considering Renie's words. "You're right, this isn't one of our brightest moments. But we can still act like decent human beings, especially to people who are in a worse mess than we are."

"Yeah, right." Renie flipped open the top of a can of Pepsi. "I told you, even though I know Bob Randall was the best quarterback ever to play for the Sea Auks, I simply never saw him give one of his better performances. I guess I had that one lousy game all bottled up inside for the past twenty-odd years. And," she went on, gathering steam and wagging a finger, "I *still* don't know why the coach didn't pull Randall and put in his backup. Maybe Bob was sick, but if that had been the case, he should have come out of the game. No wonder the second-stringer quit football and went to medical school."

"He did?" Judith eyed Renie curiously. "Who was he?"

Renie shook her head. "I forget. It was a name like that quarterback from the Rams a million years ago." She took a big sip of Pepsi and choked.

"Coz," Judith said in alarm, "are you okay?"

Renie sputtered, coughed, and waved her arms. "Yeah, yeah, I'm fine. Give me a minute." Getting herself under control, she stared at Judith. "I *do* remember the guy's name. It was Jan Van Boeck. I guess," Renie said slowly, "I remembered Norm Van Brocklin, but I got him mixed up with Bill Van Bredakoff, who played basketball, not football. Anyway, Van Boeck's name suddenly came to me after all these years. I never made the connection before. He played so seldom for the Auks."

"I suppose I'm dreaming," Judith said, fingering her chin. "But what if Dr. Van Boeck has been jealous of Bob Randall all these years? What if he blamed him for ruining his chances at becoming a superstar?"

"Van Boeck would be delusional," Renie said. "If

he'd had any real talent, he could have gone to another team. I don't recall an era when any franchise had a plethora of outstanding quarterbacks."

"Maybe not," Judith admitted. "Still . . ."

"Besides," Renie noted, "Van Boeck *is* a superstar in the medical world."

"It's not the same," Judith pointed out. "Doctors don't do TV ads for Nike scrubs. Furthermore," she continued, sitting up as straight as she could manage, "all your harangues kept us from finding out if Jim Randall saw who was driving the car that hit Addison Kirby."

"Darn. Sorry." At last Renie looked genuinely contrite.

Judith smiled faintly. "That's okay. I don't think Jim Randall can see much of anything with those Coke-bottle glasses. Besides, it all happened so fast."

Dinner arrived, brought by the silent orderly. Judith was disappointed; she'd hoped that the garrulous Maya would be on duty. After the orderly had left the trays, the cousins dared to take a peek.

"Some kind of meat," Renie said.

"Some kind of greens," Judith said.

"Perhaps a potato on the side?" Renie suggested.

"I don't think so," Judith replied. "It might be a very pale squash."

"Turnip—or maybe parsnip?" Renie ventured as she picked up the phone and punched in a single digit. "Operator, can you connect me with Delphi Pizza?" She waited, meanwhile grinning at Judith. "We don't need this crap. We can get real food. Hello? This is Mrs. Jones at Good Cheer Hospital. I'd like to place an order for delivery. One extra-large pizza with . . . what? The snow? No, I haven't looked out lately. Really? Damn. But thanks anyway," she added hastily.

"What's wrong?" Judith asked.

Renie was getting out of bed and going to the window. "Good grief, it's really coming down. The driveway into the parking lot is covered. Oh—here comes a car now. Slowly. It looks like the driver's having trouble. I guess the children to whom I gave life have another excuse for not visiting their ailing mother."

"You were expecting them?" Judith asked.

"Sort of," Renie replied, still watching the snow. "So if we can't get a Delphi pizza delivered, will anybody else brave the storm?"

Judith poked at her meal with her fork. "I'm not really that hungry. And you have your Falstaff's stash to fall back on."

"But I wanted something hot," Renie said, her tone faintly querulous. "I need serious protein. Now that I think about it, a steak sounds good."

"Try one of your other sources, some place closer to the hospital," Judith suggested.

"I don't know this neighborhood," Renie complained. "What's close?"

"Bubba's Fried Chicken," Judith said. "Their flagship restaurant isn't too far from here."

Bubba's was legendary. Renie turned away from the window and licked her lips. "Um-um, good idea."

She'd just picked up the phone when Judith heard voices in the hall. The speechless orderly had left the door halfway open.

"Hold on," Judith said, cocking an ear. "Listen."

A hefty, mild-voiced man in a cashmere overcoat was speaking to a woman Judith couldn't see. But after a few words the woman's voice was recognizable as belonging to Sister Jacqueline.

". . . just as long as you don't upset Mr. Kirby," the

nun said. "He hasn't been out of the recovery room for very long."

"We had an appointment," the man said, still sounding mild, almost indolent. "Addison said it was urgent, though I can't think why. I mean, he's not a sports reporter."

"Tubby Turnbull," Renie said in a whisper.

"Ah." Judith tried to lean farther away from her pillow.

"Ten minutes," Sister Jacqueline said. "While you're with him, please keep reminding him to drink plenty of fluids. He hasn't been taking in as much liquid as he should, and he'll become dehydrated."

"Will do," Tubby replied, and disappeared from Judith's range of vision.

Judith looked at Renie. "Addison is going to blow this story all over the *Times*," Judith said. "He's certain that his wife, Somosa, and Randall were murdered. I don't think that his catastrophe out in front of the hospital was an accident."

Renie had picked up the phone again. "I don't either. Obviously, Addison wanted to meet with Tubby Turnbull to see how he and the rest of the Seafarers' front office felt about Joaquin Somosa's death."

"Comparing notes," Judith said as Renie asked the operator to put her through to Bubba's Fried Chicken. "Do you suppose the person who ran Addison down is the killer?"

Renie, however, gave a quick shake of her head, then spoke into the phone. "Are you delivering? . . . Within a one-mile radius? I think we qualify. Now here's what I'd like . . ."

After placing the large order, Renie beamed at Judith. "Bubba's has chained up their delivery vans. They'll be here in forty minutes. Oh, happy day!"

"For you, maybe," Judith said with a grim expression. "Not for some other people."

"Right." Renie didn't look particularly moved.

"Say," Judith said, "how are you going to get the fried chicken past the front desk this time? You didn't give any special instructions."

Renie slapped at her forehead. "Shoot! I forgot." She thought for a moment. "I'll go meet them at the door."

"You can't walk that far," Judith pointed out. "Even if you could, you can't carry that great big order with only one hand."

Resting her chin on her left fist, Renie thought hard. "I know," she said, brightening, "I'll ask Tubby Turnbull to meet the delivery guy and bring it up to us."

Judith cocked her head at Renie. "You're going to ask the general manager of a major league baseball team to deliver a box of fried chicken? Are you nuts?"

"No," Renie replied. "Wouldn't you like to talk to Tubby? Not that he'll say much. He's Mr. Ambiguous."

"Well . . . I suppose I can't miss the opportunity," Judith said. "I'll time his visit with Addison. Sister Jacqueline told Tubby to keep it to ten minutes."

"That'll be twenty," Renie put in. "Tubby talks and moves in low gear. That's why he never makes a trade deadline."

"Okay," Judith agreed. "I figure a little over five minutes have gone by."

Renie's phone rang. She picked up the receiver and smiled. "Hi, Bill. You're using the phone. What a nice surprise . . . Yes, I realize you can't come up tonight. It's snowing hard here, too . . . What?" Renie's face froze. "You're kidding! Did they call the cops? . . . Joe reported it? . . . Good . . . Yes, sure . . . Now don't get too riled . . . Okay, will . . . Love you."

Renie hung up and stared at Judith. "Joe took Bill to pick up Cammy at the Toyota dealership," Renie said, her face pale. "Cammy wasn't there. She'd been stolen."

EIGHT

"How," Judith demanded, "does a car that's in for service at a dealership get stolen?"

"That's what Bill and I would like to know," Renie said angrily. "We're a one-car family. We're stuck."

"Your kids each have a car," Judith pointed out, hoping to assuage her cousin's distress.

"Yes, but that doesn't mean they'll lend one to us," Renie said, still fuming.

"Nobody's going out in this snow anyway," Judith said, eyeing the young orderly, who had advanced into their room to mop the floor for the second time that day.

"That's not the point," Renie snapped. "Poor Cammy's out there in this blizzard, shivering and sobbing. Her little engine is probably freezing up."

"Don't you and Bill have antifreeze in the radiator?" Judith inquired.

"What?" Renie scowled. "Of course. It comes with the car these days. I meant metaphorically speaking."

"So Joe reported the car as stolen?" Judith asked, putting the dinner tray aside and smiling at the orderly as he made his exit.

Looking glum, Renie nodded. "Stolen cars won't be a high priority for a while. I'm sure there are too many accidents out there right now."

"Cheer up, coz," Judith said, still not surrendering in her efforts to make Renie feel better. "Nobody's taking your car anywhere in this storm. I guess I'll bite the bullet and call Mother."

"Go for it," Renie muttered, sinking back onto the pillows.

Predictably, Gertrude answered on the eleventh ring. "Well," she said in a deceptively affable voice, "so you pulled through. How come you didn't let your poor old mother know before this?"

"Joe told you I was okay," Judith replied. "I'm sure that Carl and Arlene mentioned it, too. Besides, you hate to talk on the phone."

Gertrude bridled. "I do? Says who?"

"Mother, you've always hated to talk on the phone," Judith said patiently. "How are you getting along?"

"Good," Gertrude said. "I just had supper. Liver and onions. Arlene makes the best. And she gets it to me on time, straight-up five o'clock. That's when supper ought to be served. Who cares about late meals and being fashionable?"

Judith glanced at her watch. It was a few minutes after six. Usually, Judith wasn't able to deliver her mother's dinner until almost six-thirty. The timing had nothing to do with fashion, and everything to do with Judith's busy late afternoons, greeting guests and preparing for the social hour. "Arlene's very thoughtful," Judith allowed. "What are you doing right now?"

"Making a family tree," Gertrude said. "Mike called. He wants to see who all's hanging on it for Little

Stinkers Preschool or whatever it's called. Dumb. Why can't kids stay home and play like they used to?"

"I don't entirely disagree with you," Judith said. "Today's parents seem in such a rush to get them to grow up. Maybe that's why when they hit twenty, they suddenly stop maturing until they're almost middle-aged. They're making up for all the lost years when they should have been carefree kids."

"Well." Gertrude chortled. "Maybe I haven't raised such a nitwit after all. When was the last time you agreed with me on anything?"

"Come on, Mother," Judith said. "I agree with you on many things. Um . . . Who are you putting on the family tree?"

"Family," Gertrude retorted. "Our side. The Grovers and the Hoffmans. You can do Lunkhead's."

Judith wasn't sure which husband Gertrude was referring to. Her mother referred to both Dan and Joe as Lunkhead. In fact, Judith had never been sure if Gertrude knew—or recognized—that Mike wasn't Dan's son. Over thirty years ago, a baby conceived out of wedlock was a shameful thing. At least by Gertrude's strict, old-fashioned standards. While Judith believed that her mother knew, deep down, she'd been in denial for the past three decades.

"That's good," Judith said, aware that her mother's memory, like those of most elderly people, recalled more from the distant past than the immediate present. "I mean, you can remember all those relatives who were dead before my time."

"You didn't miss much with some of 'em," Gertrude declared. "Take Uncle Kaspar. He thought he was a pencil. My grandmother was always pretending to sharpen him. The funny thing was, his head *did* come to a point."

"I never heard you mention him before," Judith said.

"Maybe I forgot till now," Gertrude said. "Then there was my father's cousin, Lotte. Big woman. Lotta Lotte, my papa used to say. She sat on his favorite mare once and the horse fell down, broke a leg."

"Did they have to shoot her?" Judith asked.

"Yep," Gertrude replied. "The mare was fine, though. Fixed her up good as new."

"Mother," Judith said severely, "you're not telling me they shot Lotte!"

Gertrude was chuckling. "Why not? It was the old country. They did a lot of queer things over there. Old-fashioned stuff, like wars and bombs and all that other goofy stuff."

"Mother," Judith said stiffly, "I don't want you making up information. It's important to Mike and Kristin. In fact, I'd like to know more about our family tree myself."

"Wait till I get to your father's side," Gertrude said in a low, insinuating voice. "Bet you never knew about Uncle Percy."

"Before my time?" Judith ventured.

"A bit."

"What about him?"

There was a long pause. "I forget. It'll come to me. Hey, toots, got to go. Arlene's here to let me teach her how to play gin rummy."

Gertrude hung up.

Judith looked at Renie, who was guzzling more Pepsi. "Did you ever hear of Uncle Percy on our fathers' side of the family?"

"No," Renie replied. "Did your mother invent him?"

"I think she's making up most of my side," Judith said. "It's not like she doesn't remember from way back. It's five minutes ago that eludes her. Have you made up your mind how to get dinner from the front door to our room?"

"I told you," Renie replied with a scowl, "I'm asking Tubby Turnbull. He should be about ready to leave. I'll go look."

Tubby, in fact, was sauntering out of Addison Kirby's room. Renie put out a stocking-covered foot, which caught him above the ankle. "Oof!" Tubby exclaimed in mild surprise. "Sorry. Did I step on you?"

"Mr. Turnbull," Renie said, turning on what meager charm she could manage, "I'm upset. Who are you getting to replace Joaquin Somosa?"

"Well . . . ," Tubby drawled, rubbing his prominent chin, "that's a darned good question. Who do you think we should get?"

"Me?" Renie pointed to herself. "I'm just a fan, a mere woman at that. How should I know?"

"Well . . ." Tubby scratched at the elaborate combover that covered his bald spot. "Sometimes player trade ideas come from the darnedest places. I got the inspiration for our closer, Ho Boy Pak, from a fortune cookie."

"Really," Renie breathed. "I'm not surprised. He sort of pitches like chop suey."

"Yes," Tubby agreed, "he can be kind of erratic. Now if you'll excuse me . . ."

Renie put out her good left hand. "Oh, please, Mr. Turnbull, could you step in for a minute and meet my cousin? She's a huge Seafarers fan."

Renie made the introductions. "What a pleasure," Judith enthused, studying Tubby more closely. He was definitely tubby, soft, and pliable. For a moment, Tubby seemed to be deciding whether to sit or stand. He eyed the visitors' chairs, the beds, even the commode. At last, he stayed put. Judith knew of his reputation for indecisiveness, and noticed that the socks under his galoshes and shoes didn't match. Judith wondered if he'd simply not been able to make up his mind when he got up that morning. "I've been rooting for the Seafarers ever since the franchise got here," she said as Tubby slowly released her hand. "I'm a big sports nut. Wasn't that terrible about Bob Randall?"

Tubby nodded. "Really terrible. Just like Juan. And that actress, Addison Kirby's wife. It makes you stop and think." Tubby stopped, apparently to think.

"It was nice of you to call on Mr. Kirby," Judith said. "My cousin here actually saw him get hit by that car."

"Really?" Tubby turned to gaze at Renie. "That's terrible, too. I guess you can't blame Addison for being kind of upset."

"That's true," Judith responded. "You know, we spoke to him before the accident. He told us he was on his way to meet you. I'll bet you wondered what happened to him when he didn't show up."

Tubby rubbed at the back of his head. "Did I? Yes, sure I did. I wondered a lot. Then the hospital called and told me what happened and that I'd better mosey on over to see him. So here I am."

"How thoughtful," Judith said. "We gathered that Addison had something very important on his mind. I hope he was feeling strong enough to tell you about it. It's so hard to be laid up and not able to get things off your chest."

"That's terrible," Tubby agreed, "being laid up like that and not able to . . . Yes, he got it off his chest. But I don't see how I can help him. I know very little."

Behind Tubby, Renie nodded emphatically.

"You know very little about . . . what?" Judith prompted.

"About . . ." Tubby scratched his triple chins. "About how Joaquin and Mrs. Kirby and Ramblin' Randall died so all of a sudden. But I told him—Addison—that it seems like a real coincidence to me."

"It does?" Judith said, trying not to sound incredulous.

"Well . . . sure," Tubby replied, holding out his chunky hands in a helpless gesture. "What else? I mean, I know it wasn't drugs with Joaquin. He never did drugs. He believed his body was like a . . . temple. Or something. And I suppose I have to believe what Addison said about his wife not taking drugs, either. He ought to know. But I can't say about Bob Randall. I hardly knew him, except to see him at sports banquets and such. I figure this drug talk is a smoke screen. The doctors just plain screwed up. It happens."

"Occasionally," Judith allowed, wondering if it was worthwhile to continue the conversation with Tubby Turnbull.

Renie apparently thought not. She put a hand on Tubby's elbow and steered him toward the door. "Thanks for coming by, Mr. Turnbull. You've given us a real . . . thrill. Good luck when spring training rolls around."

"What?" Tubby looked startled. "Oh—spring training. Yes, it's coming. At the end of winter, right? Bye now." He trundled off into the hallway, where he stopped, apparently undecided about which way to go.

"You didn't ask him to meet the dinner wagon," Judith remarked. "How come?"

"Because Tubby couldn't handle it," Renie said. "It'll take him half an hour to find the exit, and then he'll have to figure out if he's going in or going out.

I've got a better idea. Hey," Renie called from the doorway, "Maya?"

Judith heard a far-off voice tell Renie that Maya wasn't on duty. Renie leaned back into the room. "No Maya tonight. But I'm not without resources. Are you in there, Mr. Mummy?"

With great effort, Judith scooted farther down in the bed. She was just able to make out Mr. Mummy, who apparently had come out of his room and crossed the hall to Renie.

"How," Renie murmured, "do you feel about fried chicken, Mr. Mummy?"

Mr. Mummy's feelings about fried chicken, especially Bubba's, were extremely positive. He was in a walking cast, and could get down to the main entrance with no trouble.

"Can I fit the Bubba's box into my plastic carryall?" he inquired, his cheeks pink with excitement.

"Yes, you can," Renie said, handing over the check she'd already written. "Just be sure no one sees you make the transfer."

Mr. Mummy beamed at Renie. "It's like a spy story, isn't it? You know, where one man sits on the park bench and the other one comes along with a folded newspaper and he leaves it on the seat and the first man—"

"My, yes," Renie interrupted. "You'd better go, Mr. Mummy. The delivery may be arriving any minute."

Judith saw Mr. Mummy scoot off down the hall, the leg in the walking cast at an angle, and his sacklike hospital gown waving behind him like a rag tied to a large load on a pickup truck.

"He's sweet," Judith said as Renie headed back to bed. "I'll bet he has a crush on you."

"Probably," Renie said, a trifle glum. "Why couldn't Sean Connery have fallen off a ladder instead of Mr. Mummy?"

Heather Chinn appeared, taking more vital signs. "When will Maya be back?" Judith asked.

Heather concentrated on Judith's pulse. "Maya's not with us anymore."

Judith lurched forward, disrupting Heather's pulse count. "Literally? Figuratively?"

"Both, I suppose," Heather replied, slightly irritated. "Yesterday was her last day working for Good Cheer."

"Oh." The thermometer cut off further comment from Judith.

"Seeking new opportunities, huh?" Renie remarked.

"Yes," Heather said, still intent upon her tasks.

"What was in the autopsy report on Bob Randall?" Renie inquired.

"I don't know," Heather replied.

"Surely not suicide," Renie said.

"I don't know," Heather repeated, her pretty face set in stone.

"Yes, you do," Renie asserted. "Bob Randall was one of your patients. You would be informed if he'd taken his own life. Don't you think it would be prudent for you to tell other patients on this floor what really happened? Cover-ups never work, and then you're left with serious egg on your face."

Heather removed the thermometer from Judith's mouth and glared at Renie. "We've been told not to discuss Mr. Randall's death. The orders have come down from on high."

"Dr. Van Boeck or Queen Blanche?" Renie retorted.

"Dr. Van Boeck, of course," Heather said stiffly. "He's in charge here."

"That's not the impression I got this afternoon," Renie said. "Now let me think—Good Cheer is kind of conservative, old-fashioned. Which is good. I'm still here, and in any other hospital in the city, I'd have been sent home this morning, right? Keeping me longer may not suit the bottom line. So maybe the Van Boecks aren't merely fighting to keep Good Cheer's reputation spotless, but for the hospital's very survival. How am I doing, Nurse Chinn?"

Heather yanked the blood pressure cuff off Judith's arm with more force than was necessary. "All hospitals are fighting to stay alive," the nurse said grimly. "Over the years, the Sisters of Good Cheer have wisely managed this institution. They've refused to remodel for the sake of appearances, the plant budget is always used for necessities and equipment, and we rely on a heavy corps of volunteers."

Robbie the Robot could be heard beeping along the hallway. "Hi, I'm Robbie . . ." He moved on.

"Nonpaid personnel like him?" Renie said, pointing toward the door.

"In a way, yes," Heather replied. "He delivers things. He's programmed to take charts and other paperwork to various departments. Robbie can even use the elevators."

"Good," said Renie. "I'd hate to see him clank down a flight of stairs. You'd probably have to put his parts in a dustpan."

Somewhat warily, Heather moved over to Renie's bed, holding the thermometer as if it were a weapon. "So what are the problems Good Cheer is facing?" Judith asked.

"The same as every hospital," Heather replied, showing some enthusiasm for shoving the thermome-

ter in Renie's mouth. "The merger of medical specialties helped everyone. Hospitals spent far too much
money on duplicating equipment. It wasn't necessary
or feasible, especially in a city like this, where so many
of the hospitals are within a five-mile radius."

"The decline in religious orders must have hurt," Judith noted. "It certainly made a difference in the
schools when they had to hire lay teachers instead of
nuns."

"That's true," Heather said, then paused to take
Renie's pulse. "We only have five nuns on staff at
Good Cheer. There used to be dozens."

"So salaries have gone up dramatically," Judith
mused. "Malpractice insurance, too, I suppose."

Heather nodded. "It's terrible for the doctors. But
you can't practice medicine without it. Look at what's
happened . . ." She stopped abruptly and bit her lower
lip.

"Yes," Judith said kindly. "Have the suits been filed
yet in the instances of the Somosa and Fremont
deaths?"

"I can't say," Heather replied doggedly as she read
the thermometer.

"Yes, you can," Renie retorted. "It's a matter of public record."

But Heather refused to cooperate. "Whatever comes
next, it's not Good Cheer's fault," she insisted.

"Meaning?" Judith coaxed.

"We did nothing wrong," Heather said, her manner
heated. "Not the nurses, not the doctors, not anybody
employed by Good Cheer."

"You sound very certain," Judith remarked.

"Hey," Renie yipped, "aren't you putting that blood
pressure cuff on awfully tight?"

Judith grew silent, staring up at the cracks in the aging plaster, as if the wiggly lines provided some sort of map to The Truth. Except for a desultory word of farewell to Heather, she remained quiet for several moments after the nurse continued on her rounds.

"Maya got fired," Judith finally announced.

"I agree," said Renie. "She talked too much, at least to us. I hope we didn't get her into trouble."

"So do I," Judith said. "But Maya is the kind who can't stop talking. And what did Heather mean by that solemn statement about nobody at the hospital being at fault?"

"It would suggest," Renie said slowly, "that she knows more than she's telling. That is, she's aware that there were no medical mistakes."

"In other words," Judith said, hauling herself up on the pillows, "all three victims were murdered, possibly by outsiders."

Renie was skeptical. "*Three* outsiders?"

"It's unlikely," Judith said, "but you can't completely discount the notion. Of course the modus operandi is similar, as far as we can tell. Unless they're copy-cat killings."

"And just what *is* the MO?" Renie asked.

"It has to be something—the drugs that the victims supposedly ingested on their own—that was put into their IVs."

"We still haven't heard what Bob Randall's drug of choice was," Renie pointed out.

"No," Judith agreed. "But I'll bet it's something like the other two. A street drug, I'd guess."

"Not self-ingested?" said Renie.

"No." Judith grimaced as she tried to make herself more comfortable. "I don't know why I haven't asked Joe if the police are investigating. I think I'll call him."

Before she could pick up the phone, Mr. Mummy appeared in the doorway with a carton marked "Sutures." "Cluck, cluck," he said with a merry smile. "May I?"

"Of course," Judith said, and introduced herself. "Why don't you join us, Mr. Mummy? There's plenty for three."

"How kind," Mr. Mummy said as he helped Renie unload the carton. "The delivery wouldn't fit in my carryall so I found this box, which makes quite clever camouflage, don't you think?" He paused as Renie rewarded him with a big smile. "Maybe just a small piece," he said, sniffing the air that was now redolent with fried chicken. "I'm not terribly hungry. I did manage to eat my hospital tray."

"Was it better than the food?" Renie asked.

"What?" Mr. Mummy looked puzzled, then comprehension dawned. "Oh-ho! Very funny, Mrs. Jones. Yes, I must say, the meals here aren't very delectable. Still, I'm not a fussy eater."

Renie was filling the carton's lid with chicken, mashed potatoes, corn on the cob, coleslaw, and baking powder biscuits. "Here, Mr. Mummy, pass this to my cousin."

"Delighted," Mr. Mummy replied. "I thought it wise to put the chicken delivery box inside something that looked as if it belonged to the hospital. It worked out just fine."

"You're a genius," Renie said, offering a white box filled with chicken to Mr. Mummy. "Take some."

"Indeed, I will." Mr. Mummy beamed at Renie. "Sometimes I can hear you two from across the hall. It sounds quite lively in here. You've had a lot of guests."

"Not really," Judith said, munching on corn. "I

mean, only our husbands have been to see us. The others have sort of dropped in."

"I see," Mr. Mummy said. "Yes, even Mrs. Van Boeck was in here briefly, am I not right?"

"Briefly," Judith said with a nod.

"Such a spirited woman," Mr. Mummy remarked, biting into a juicy thigh. "Did you find her conversation invigorating?"

Judith hesitated. "Well . . . I suppose. She didn't stay long."

"I hear she may run for mayor," Mr. Mummy said. "Our current mayor has had his problems lately."

"Yes," Judith said. "The step up from the city council would be a natural for Blanche Van Boeck."

"I'm surprised she didn't do a little campaigning while she was in here," Mr. Mummy said with a sly look.

"Not really," Judith said, remembering Blanche's menacing attitude.

"It sounded to me," Mr. Mummy said with a twinkle, "as if Mrs. Van Boeck and Dr. Garnett had quite an argument. I don't suppose she mentioned it to you."

"She told him to buzz off," Renie said, glancing down at the particles of crisp chicken skin that had fallen onto her sling and hospital gown. "Or words to that effect. I gathered there was bad blood between them. You have to wonder how Dr. Garnett and Dr. Van Boeck get along."

"Well," said Mr. Mummy, giving Renie a "May I?" glance before taking a biscuit out of a box, "there must be a rather intense rivalry there. That is, all doctors have big egos, and I assume Dr. Garnett may sometimes resent Dr. Van Boeck's decision-making."

"So Dr. Garnett is ambitious?" Judith asked. "I mean, he'd like to run Good Cheer?"

Mr. Mummy stretched out his leg with its walking cast. "I have no idea. But he could be. I suspect he doesn't like what's been going on around here lately."

"You mean," Renie said, "the epidemic of death?"

"Yes." Mr. Mummy nodded slowly. "It's very unfortunate."

"So you've heard all about the previous deaths?" Judith remarked.

"Oh, yes," Mr. Mummy said. "We may live in a rural area, but we take the city newspapers. Not to mention TV. I find health issues very interesting, since they affect almost everyone in this country."

"What's surprised me," Renie said, buttering her second piece of corn, "is how little coverage there has been in the media. Considering that Somosa and Joan Fremont were very well-known popular figures—and now Bob Randall—you'd think the local reporters would be all over the stories."

Judith clapped a hand to her head. "Oh! We forgot to turn on the evening news."

Mr. Mummy waved a pink, pudgy hand. "You didn't miss much. I saw the news, and they merely said that Mr. Randall had died unexpectedly. They did advise that further details would be on the eleven o'clock news."

"Ah." Judith looked relieved.

"You two seem very aware of what goes on around you," Mr. Mummy said with admiring glances for both cousins. "You must pick up on a lot of scuttlebutt."

Judith's expression was modest. "We're interested in people. Besides, it helps pass the time when you're laid up."

"I think it's wonderful," Mr. Mummy said approvingly. "These days, so many people are completely wrapped up in themselves."

"Not us," Renie said through a mouthful of coleslaw. "Fwee lok to kwee abwes."

Judith smiled at Mr. Mummy's understandable perplexity. "My cousin said we like to keep abreast. I'm used to her speaking when she's eating. I can translate."

"Amazing," Mr. Mummy murmured as he stood up in an awkward manner. "I should be getting back to my room. Thank you for this delicious treat. If you hear anything interesting, do let me in on it. I'm a bit bored, since my wife and family live so far out in the country that it's hard for them to get into the city."

"Any time," Renie said. "And thanks for playing deliveryman."

Judith didn't speak until Mr. Mummy was out of earshot. "He seems quite caught up in what's happening at Good Cheer, don't you think?"

"That's not so very odd," Renie said, attacking yet another piece of chicken. "Mr. Mummy's right, you get bored lying around in the hospital."

"He never did say exactly where he lived, did he?"

"Mmm . . ." Renie swallowed the big bite of chicken and licked her lips. "No. But then I didn't ask."

Judith grew quiet for a few minutes. The only sounds in the room were Renie's chewing, the hum of the equipment, and the usual distant voices and footsteps in the hall. Judith leaned far enough forward to gaze out the window. It was still snowing, the flakes now smaller, and thus more likely to stick.

"I'm calling Joe," Judith announced at last. "I've got a question for him."

Renie brushed at the collection of crumbs on her front. "About our car?"

"No," Judith replied, dialing the number at Hillside

Manor. "There's nothing he can do about that. Nobody else can either until the snow stops." She paused, then a smile crossed her face. "Hi, Joe. How's everything going?"

"Oh, hi." Joe sounded disconcerted. "How're you doing?"

"Fine. What's wrong?"

"Um . . . Nothing. It's snowing."

"I know. Anything going on that I should know about?"

"No, not a thing," Joe said rather hastily. "Except that before it started to snow so hard, FedEx delivered a crate containing a hundred whoopee cushions. Where do you want me to store them?"

"Whoopee cushions?" Judith was perplexed. "I didn't order any. Why would I? It must be a mistake. Call them and have them returned when FedEx can get back up the hill, okay?"

"Sure," Joe said. "I wondered what they were for. I thought maybe a guest had ordered them to be sent here."

"How *are* the guests? Did they get in all right?"

"Yes. All the rooms are occupied."

"They are?" Judith was surprised. "We only had four reservations as of Monday morning."

"The airport's closed," Joe said. "Some people got stranded. Which, if the planes don't start flying tomorrow, means we'll be overbooked for Wednesday."

"Oh. That *is* a problem." Judith thought for a minute. "Arlene has the B&B association number. She can call them to help out."

"Okay."

"Nothing else to report?"

Joe hesitated. "Not really."

"You're a bad liar, Joe."

He sighed. "One of the couples who got stuck at the airport have a pet snake."

Judith gasped. "No! Pets aren't allowed. You know that; Arlene knows that."

"Nobody told Arlene about the snake," Joe replied, on the defensive. "I didn't know anything about it until they got here."

"What kind of snake?" Judith asked, still upset.

"A boa constrictor." Joe paused again. "I think."

"You *think?*" Judith threw a glance at Renie, whose ears had pricked up.

"I haven't seen it," Joe said. "Nobody has. I mean, not since the Pettigrews arrived."

"You mean *the snake is loose?*" Judith asked in horror.

"I'm afraid so. His name is Ernest," Joe added.

"Oh, good grief!" Judith twisted around so far in the bed that she felt a sharp pain course through her left side. "How are the other guests taking it?" she asked, trying to calm down.

"Not real well," Joe replied. "Of course they can't go anywhere else because of the snow. You know how impassable the hill is in this kind of weather. Anyway, the Pettigrews insist he isn't dangerous."

"They better be right," Judith said through gritted teeth. "Why couldn't the Pettigrews leave Ernest at the airport?"

"They say he has a very nervous disposition," Joe explained. "Ernest suffers from anxiety attacks. When he has one, they have to put a paper bag over his head. A small paper bag, of course."

"Of course." It was Judith's turn to heave a big sigh. "Okay, I guess I can't worry about it. But I will. I wanted to ask if you could find out from Woody what the police are doing about this situation with the three hospital deaths. Could you check in with him tomorrow?"

"I already did," Joe replied. "They're not doing anything."

"What?" Judith shot Renie an incredulous look.

"Woody said there's no official investigation," Joe said. "The county isn't doing much either, according to him."

"That's unbelievable," Judith declared.

"I agree," said Joe.

"It's also highly suspicious," Judith added.

"Yes." Joe suddenly became very serious. "I wouldn't get mixed up in this if I were you. I mean it."

Judith drew in a sharp breath. "Yes."

"Yes what?" Joe said.

"Get mixed up. In this." Judith winced.

"Something's not right," Joe said, "but it's not up to you to find out."

"No," said Judith.

"Okay?"

"Yes."

After Judith hung up the phone, she gazed at Renie. "We are in danger."

"Yes," said Renie, and took a big bite out of another biscuit. "Ith thapend befwo."

Judith nodded. She knew it had happened before, but the thought didn't make her feel any better.

NINE

"WHAT ELSE AM I supposed to do while I'm lying here like a big lump?" Judith demanded. "At least I can speculate."

"Which, being in a helpless condition, you figure is a harmless pastime," Renie replied, finally finishing her meal and starting to clean up the mess. "Meanwhile, I get to drag my battered body around doing all the grunt work."

Judith glared at Renie. "I thought you were encouraging me. What would you expect me to do with people dropping like flies and the police not investigating? Don't you find this whole situation highly suspicious?"

"I do," Renie admitted, shoving boxes and napkins and garbage into her now-overflowing wastebasket. As ever, Judith envied her cousin's metabolism, though sometimes she wondered—perhaps with a touch of malice—if Renie didn't have a tapeworm. "You know," Renie said with a scowl, "we're not in very good shape to defend ourselves."

"If somebody wanted us out of the way," Judith persisted, "we'd have been dead by now. We're past the deadline for early dismissal from Good Cheer.

Besides, what have we done except show a normal amount of curiosity?"

Renie gave a shake of her head. "Curiosity killed the you-know-what, and I don't mean Sweetums, who appears to be an indestructible force of nature."

"Do we look dangerous?" Judith shot back. "Here we are, a couple of middle-aged matrons swathed in bandages and looking like the you-know-what dragged us in the you-know-whose small door."

Renie climbed into bed. "There's no dissuading you, right?" She gave Judith a look of surrender.

"Let's think this through," Judith said, reaching for her purse and taking out a small notebook and pen. "Joaquin Somosa, Joan Fremont, Bob Randall. Except for being well-known, the only connection is that they all died in this hospital after routine surgery." She paused to finish writing down the trio of names. "All three died in less than a month."

"Maybe there *is* another connection," Renie put in, her umbrage evaporated. "What if they were all involved in some charitable cause or some other activity not directly tied to their professional careers?"

Judith tipped her head to one side, considering. "It's possible. But who goes around bumping off people involved in good works or other civic activities?"

Renie shrugged. "Just a thought."

"That's fine," Judith said. "Think all you want. It helps. Anyway, we've got two causes of death allegedly nailed down—Somosa and Fremont, both from illegal drugs. Randall may be the same, though I'm guessing it was something different from the other two, who were different from each other."

"A different source for drugs?" Renie suggested.

Judith nodded. "We weren't here so we don't know

the circumstances of the first two deaths. But Ecstasy and that—whatever the date-rape drug is called—provide different kinds of reactions. Street drugs are available to anybody who knows where to get them. It's a little trickier to put them in an IV."

Renie had placed the leftovers—such as they were—into one of the smaller boxes and slipped it into the drawer of her nightstand. "How do we know it was an IV?"

"We don't." Judith made another note, then glanced at her water carafe. "Everybody who has surgery is instructed to drink plenty of fluids. Not everybody likes water or even juice. Look at your Pepsi stash. What if Bill had slipped a little something into it?"

"He couldn't," Renie replied. "The cans are foolproof."

"I mean, more accessible beverages. Besides," Judith went on with a sly smile, "Bill could doctor your Pepsi after you'd opened it."

"He wouldn't dare!" Renie cried. "He knows better than to screw with my Pepsi."

"You know what I mean." Judith twirled the pen in her fingers. "The problem is, we don't know what the three victims were drinking at the time of their deaths. I wonder if the staff took the possibility of tampered beverages into account."

"Judging from the state of denial they're in," Renie said, waving her current can of Pepsi at Judith, "I doubt it. The party line seems to be that each victim was some kind of addict."

"Which brings us to motive," Judith said. "Hospital politics. Who benefits from ruining Good Cheer's reputation?"

"Dr. Garnett comes to mind," Renie said. "He wants to take over from Dr. Van Boeck."

Judith sighed. "Would a doctor really go to such extremes?"

"He'd know how to do it," Renie said.

"True. Still . . . I like Blanche as a suspect. She's such a self-serving pain."

"Why would she sabotage her own husband's hospital?" asked Renie.

"Maybe she doesn't like her husband," Judith suggested.

"Maybe Sister Jacqueline doesn't like either of them," Renie said.

"Are you considering a nun as a suspect?" Judith asked, aghast.

"Well . . . nuns are human. Maybe it's for the greater good. You know, all those moral theology questions. Is it a sin for a father to steal medicine to save his child's life? Et cetera."

"Don't go Jesuitical on me," Judith cautioned. "Okay, I'll admit you have a point. We can't rule anyone out."

"What about the victims' nearest and dearest?" Renie inquired. "Since when have you not considered them as prime suspects?"

Judith ran a hand through her short salt-and-pepper hair. "Since nonpersonal motives seem more obvious. Hospitals are big-bucks institutions. Not to mention the power involved in running them. Let's face it, we've got at least four high-profile people involved—Dr. Garnett, Dr. Van Boeck, Mrs. Van Boeck, and Sister Jacqueline."

"Agreed," said Renie. "But you can't rule out the lesser players." She rolled over as far as she could on her right side. "Look at it from this point of view—maybe only one of the three victims needed to die. But in order to throw suspicion off, all three get killed so it looks like a serial kind of thing. What if a rival player on the Seafarers team wanted to get rid of Joaquin Somosa? Better yet, a rival actress at Le Repertoire who felt Joan Fremont was standing in her way? Or something even more basic, such as Margie Randall being sick and tired of Ramblin' Robert?"

Judith reflected for a few moments. "All of them could have some kind of enemies, I suppose. That is, in a personal and professional sense. The trouble is, we don't know much about their private lives."

"Exactly," Renie said, lying back on the pillows.

"I'd rule out Addison Kirby, though," Judith mused. "I can't help but think that the killer was the one who ran him down this afternoon."

"It could have been an accident," Renie pointed out.

"Do you really think so?" Judith asked with a frown.

"No. That is, I can't be sure. People drive like such nuts these days." Renie plucked at her blankets. "Not to mention taking cars that don't belong to them."

"I figure that Addison's on to something," Judith said, remembering to drink her water and taking a big swallow. "Maybe not who the killer is, but related to the motive."

"Why Cammy?" Renie said. "Our Toyota is exactly like thousands of cars out there in the city. It's one of the most popular brands in America. Why not steal a Mercedes or a Cadillac or a Beamer?"

"Addison has been covering city hall," Judith went on, "which means he's probably got the inside dope on Blanche Van Boeck. But if it's something ruinous, why not kill him instead of his wife? Why kill Somosa and Randall? Or, given Blanche's clout, why not get Addison fired?"

"What," Renie demanded, "were those morons at the Toyota place thinking of? They're usually so reliable. Why wasn't somebody watching Cammy? Why did they leave the keys in the car?" She stopped and made one of her typical futile attempts to snap her fingers. "Because they'd finished their work and sometimes they tuck the keys under the floor mat on the driver's side." She hung her head. "Oh, my God, until my shoulder heals, I won't be able to drive Cammy for months! Maybe we won't ever ride in her again! What if she's been driven over a cliff?"

Judith sat up straight and glared at Renie. "Will you *shut up?*"

"Huh?" Renie swerved around to face Judith. "What's wrong?"

"I thought," Judith said in an irritated voice, "we were trying to sleuth."

Renie stifled a yawn. "We were. We were trying to figure out what happened to Cammy."

"No, we weren't," Judith argued. "We were speculating about methods and motives."

"*You* were," Renie shot back. "You can afford to do that, you have two cars, your Subaru and Joe's MG. Bill and I are now demoted to taking *the bus.*"

"Don't be ridiculous," Judith sniffed. "You have insurance, you can rent a car until Cammy turns up. And if she—I mean, *it*—doesn't, you can buy another one."

"Easy for you to say," Renie snapped. "Go ahead, feel all smug. See if I care." She reached out with her good arm and pulled the curtain between them.

Again, the room was silent. Someone was paging a doctor over the intercom. A glimpse of hospital equipment could be seen rolling down the hall. Somewhere, female voices laughed. Judith sat up in bed, her arms folded across her chest, her lower lip thrust out.

It was she who broke the silence. "Coz. We never fight. What's wrong with us?"

Judith heard Renie sigh. "We're tired, we hurt, we've been through major surgery, and we got a room next to a corpse. My car's been stolen, you're stuck with a major life decision about telling Mike who's who on his family tree. What else could be wrong?"

"You're right," Judith said. "We're a mess."

"Justifiably so," said Renie, pulling the curtain back. "It's going on nine o'clock and we need a nap. I'm shutting off the light."

"Go for it," murmured Judith, clicking off her own bedside lamp. "Frankly, I'm exhausted."

"We should be," Renie said. "G'night."

"Mmm," said Judith.

Five minutes later, the night nurse, whose name was Trudy and who wasn't given to idle chatter, came in to take the cousins' vital signs and replenish their supply of pain medication. Ten minutes later, a workman in overalls arrived to check the thermostat.

"Kinda cold tonight, huh?" he said, fiddling with the dial.

Judith and Renie didn't respond.

"Still snowing," he said, pounding on the radiator with his fist. "Must be close to six inches out there."

The cousins remained silent.

"Lots of accidents out there," the workman said. "Damned fools don't know how to drive in this weather. All those folks who move up here from California."

Judith buried her head in the pillow; Renie chewed on her blanket and swore under her breath.

"Warm enough now?" the workman asked after yet another bang on the radiator, which wheezed like a dying asthmatic.

"Fine," Judith bit off.

"Okey-dokey," he said. "I'll come back to check on it later."

"Don't," Renie said, "or I'll have to kill you."

"Har, har," said the workman, who finally left.

Seven minutes later, Trudy returned. Judith knew it was exactly seven minutes because she was now wide awake and had been staring at her watch with its glow-in-the-dark dial.

"You need to use the bedpan, Mrs. Flynn," Trudy announced. "You haven't voided for almost two hours. Are you sure you're drinking enough fluids?"

"Yes. No. I'm trying to sleep," Judith said, sounding cross.

"Plenty of time for that," Trudy said. "It's only a little after nine. Come, come, try to lift those hips."

"Good Lord," muttered Renie in a mutinous voice.

After the usual painful effort to move on and off the bedpan, Judith mumbled her thanks to Trudy and closed her eyes.

The radiator clanged and clanked, whistled and hissed. After two minutes of what sounded like a one-man band, Renie pressed her buzzer.

"We can't sleep with that damned thing making such a racket," she complained. "It was fine until Stoopnagle came in to supposedly fix it."

Almost ten minutes passed before a male nurse peeked in. Judith explained the problem. The nurse said he'd see what he could do about it. The radiator continued its atonal cacophony.

"I'm wide awake," Renie declared, sitting up and turning her light back on. "Damn."

"I am, too," Judith grumbled. "It's no joke about not being able to get any rest in a hospital."

"I'm hungry again," Renie said. "I wonder if there's a microwave around here. Don't the nurses usually have one? I think I smelled popcorn earlier in the evening."

"Why do you need a microwave?" Judith asked.

"To heat the leftover chicken," Renie responded. "I don't care much for cold chicken, unless it's in a sandwich or a salad."

"Go ask," Judith said.

"They won't tell me," Renie replied, getting out of bed. "I'll take the chicken with me and see what I can find. There's a biscuit left over, too, and one piece of corn. I might as well bring them along."

"Good luck," said Judith in a tired voice.

Renie was gone so long that Judith had almost fallen asleep when her cousin returned.

"Pssst!" Renie called from the doorway.

"Huh?" Judith raised her head from the pillow and tried to focus on Renie. "What?"

Renie gestured with her bag of food. "Mr. Mummy. Sister Jacqueline just went in there and closed the door."

Struggling to sit up, Judith gave herself a shake. "So?"

"Isn't this a little late for a visit from the hospital administrator?" Renie asked, half in and half out of the room.

"Maybe," Judith allowed. "But is it suspicious?"

Renie stepped all the way inside, keeping her eye on the closed door across the hall. "I think so. It's pretty quiet out here right now. I was sneaking out of the staff room, where I found a microwave, and I turned the corner just in time to see Sister Jacqueline outside Mr. Mummy's room, looking very furtive. I ducked back where she couldn't see me, and when I peeked around the corner again, she slipped inside."

"Hunh. That *is* odd," Judith conceded, finally wide awake.

Renie sat down on the end of Judith's bed, where she could keep an eye on the hall. "I think there's something peculiar about Mr. Mummy."

"I agree," Judith said. "He's very vague about his family and where he lives. I can't think of any reason why, with a broken leg, his doctor would send him all the way into the city to recuperate. It seems downright fishy."

After offering the leftovers to Judith, who insisted she was still full, Renie was gnawing on a chicken wing when the workman returned.

"So Clarabelle's acting up tonight, is she?" The workman chuckled. "Temperamental, that's our Clarabelle. But then so's Jo-Jo and Winnie and Dino."

"Those would be radiators?" Renie asked. "You name them?"

"Yep." The workman, who Judith had noticed bore the name of Curly embroidered on his overalls, chuckled some more. "After almost twenty years, you get to know these things pretty well. Every radiator has its own personality. Come on, Clarabelle, settle down." Curly whacked the radiator with a wrench. "Take Rin-Tin-Tin next door. Last night, Rinty acted up something terrible. That football player, Bob Randall, thought it was funny. He said it sounded like his old Sea Auks coach on a bad Sunday. Too bad he passed on this morning." Using the wrench, Curly turned something on Clarabelle that let out a big stream of vapor.

"Mr. Randall seemed all right last night, I take it," Judith said.

"What? Oh—yep, he seemed real chipper." Curly gave the radiator another whack. "That oughtta do it." He grinned at the cousins. " 'Course, I'd be chipper, too, if I had a pint of Wild Turkey under the covers."

"He had booze stashed away?" Renie said in mild surprise.

"Sure," Curly replied, adjusting the radiator one last time. "You'd be surprised what people smuggle in here." Renie's overflowing wastebasket with its telltale Bubba's chicken boxes caught his eye. "Then again, maybe you wouldn't."

"Do the patients bring these illicit items in," Judith inquired, "or do other people sneak them past the front door?"

"Both," Curly answered, moving toward the door. "A couple of months ago, one guy brought in his barbecue grill. Damned near set the place on fire. Smoke everywhere, all the alarms went off, everybody in a panic. A shame, really, he burned up some mighty fine-looking T-bones."

"Terrible," Judith remarked. "I don't suppose Mr. Randall mentioned who brought him the liquor."

"That was the funny part," Curly said, swinging his wrench like a baton. "He swore he didn't know where it came from. A Good Samaritan, he insisted. *I* should know such good guys. Wild Turkey's the best. I feel real bad about him dying. He was a swell guy, and not just as a ballplayer. He even offered me a swig out of his bottle."

Judith's eyes narrowed. "Did you accept?"

Curly shook his head, which, in fact, was adorned with a crown of gray curls. "Nope. I was on duty. The good sisters here, they got rules."

"I can see why you want to abide by them," Judith said with a smile. "Your job must be a challenge. Everything in this hospital is so old, and I understand that they'd rather fix it than replace it. Besides, you get to meet some fascinating patients. Did you happen to get acquainted with Joan Fremont or Joaquin Somosa before they . . . ah . . . departed?"

Curly scratched his neck. "That actress? No, can't say that I did. No problems with her room. But Somosa's TV got unplugged somehow, so I went in there to get it going for him. Nice guy, great arm. But his English wasn't all that hot. He seemed kind of agitated and kept saying something about a bear. I guess he'd seen it on TV before the set got unplugged. Anyway, I tried the nature channels, but no bears. Poor fella—I heard he died not more than twenty minutes after I fixed the set and left."

"Goodness," Judith murmured. "That's terrible."

Curly shrugged. "It happens in hospitals. You get kinda used to it. But it's a damned—excuse my language—shame when people go before their time. The Seafarers will miss him in the rotation this season."

"The team will have to trade for a new ace," Renie said. "Not that I have much faith in Tubby Turnbull. He'll end up giving two hot minor league prospects away for a first aid kit and a case of wienies."

"Har, har," laughed Curly. "Ain't that the truth? You gotta wonder why the Seafarers don't fire his ass—excuse my language. But maybe he's got pictures. If you know what I mean." Curly winked, waved the wrench, and left the room.

"A bear?" said Judith.

"The drugs," Renie responded. "They were probably taking effect. Poor Joaquin must have been hallucinating."

"It's really awful," Judith said, taking another sip of water. "Here these three people were, helpless and trusting."

"Like us," Renie noted. "Helpless, anyway," she amended.

Judith looked askance. "Yes. It's something to ponder."

"Let's not," Renie said. "Let's go to sleep."

Judith agreed that that was a good idea.

But she fretted for some time, wondering if, in fact, they hadn't put themselves in danger by asking too many questions. The killer was faceless, unidentifiable. Anyone they talked to—Curly, Heather, Torchy, the doctors, the rest of the nurses, even the orderlies—could be hiding behind a deadly mask.

Judith slept, but not deeply or securely. Indeed, she had never felt quite so helpless. Her dreams were not filled with homicidal maniacs, however, but with family. Dan. Mike. Joe. Gertrude. Effie. Kristin. Little Mac. The faces floated through her unconscious, but only one spoke: It was Mike, and he kept saying, "Who am I?"

Judith tried to answer, but the words wouldn't come out. She felt as if she had no breath, and awoke to find that she'd been crying.

TEN

ON WEDNESDAY MORNING, breakfast was again palatable. Dr. Ming and Dr. Alfonso made early rounds, assuring both patients that they were making progress. Judith would take a few steps later in the day, said Dr. Alfonso. Renie could try flexing her right wrist a few times, according to Dr. Ming.

"You need to keep from getting too weak," Dr. Alfonso said to Judith.

"You don't want to tighten up," Dr. Ming said to Renie.

After their surgeons had left and Corinne Appleby had taken their vitals and added more pain medication to the IVs, the cousins looked at each other.

"Are we atrophying?" Renie asked.

"Probably," Judith responded, glancing at the morning paper, which had been delivered along with breakfast. "Guess what, we didn't stay up late enough last night to see the news."

"You're right," Renie said, making an attempt to brush her short chestnut hair, which went off in several uncharted directions. "Do you see anything in the paper about Addison's accident or Blanche's impromptu press conference?"

Judith studied the front page, which was full of national and international news, all of it bad. "No, I don't even see a story about Bob Randall's death. I'll check the local news."

"Toss me the sports and the business sections," Renie requested, reaching out with her good arm.

Judith complied. "Here," she said, "on page one of the second section—'Former Star Quarterback Dies Following Knee Surgery.' There's not more than two inches of copy, along with a small picture of Bob that was taken in his playing days."

"What?" Renie gaped at Judith. "That's it?"

"The article only says that the surgery was pronounced successful, his death was unexpected, and he had been in good health otherwise. There's a brief recap of his career, lifetime stats, and how he once saved two children from a house fire and received an official commendation from the governor."

"What about Blanche?" Renie asked.

"I'm looking. I . . ." Judith's head swiveled away from the paper as Margie Randall, wearing her blue volunteer's jacket, tapped tentatively on the door frame.

"Hello. May I come in?" Margie inquired in an uncertain voice. Her pale blonde pageboy was limp, and her delicate features seemed to have sharpened with grief.

"Of course," Judith responded. "Mrs. Randall? We're very sorry for your loss."

Margie slid her hands up her sleeves and hugged herself. "Oh, so am I! How will I manage without darling Bob?"

"I was widowed when I was about your age," Judith said kindly. *My grief was only for the waste that had been Dan's life, not for me.* "Somehow I managed." *Much better, after he was gone.* "I had to learn to stand on my own two feet." *Instead of letting Dan's four hundred plus pounds lean on me until I was about to collapse from worry and exhaustion.*

"Easy to say." Margie sighed, taking small, unsteady steps into the room. "I feel as if my whole world has fallen apart."

"You're working today?" Renie asked, her tone slightly incredulous.

Slowly, Margie turned to look at Renie, who hadn't quite managed to tame her wayward hair. Several strands were standing up, out, and every which way. She looked like a doll that had been in a cedar chest too long.

"Yes," Margie replied softly. "We couldn't make the funeral arrangements until this afternoon because of the autopsy, so I felt obligated to come in today. I can't let my patients and their families down. So many need cheering. How are you feeling? I wasn't able to visit with you yesterday because of . . ." She burst into tears and struggled to find a Kleenex in her jacket pockets.

"We're okay," Renie said in a chipper voice.

"Is there anything we can do for you?" Judith inquired with concern.

Margie shook her head. "N-n-no. I'll be fine." She dabbed at her eyes and blew her nose. "Please tell me if you're comfortable, if there's anything you need." She gazed at Judith with red-rimmed eyes. "Hip replacement surgery, I believe? Oh, dear, that can be so dangerous! I can't tell you how many patients dislocate within a short time of being sent home. It's terribly painful, worse than childbirth."

"Really?" Judith's dark eyes were wide.

Margie turned back to Renie. "Shoulder?" She nodded several times. "You never really recover from rotator cuff surgery. Oh, they tell you, ninety, even ninety-five percent, but it's nowhere near that high, especially if you're past a Certain Age. You'll be fortunate if you can ever raise your arm past your waist."

"Gee, thanks," said Renie in a bleak voice. "I feel so much better since you came to see us."

"Good," Margie said, dabbing again at her eyes. "Anything I can do to cheer you, just let me—" She stopped and turned as two young people stood at the door. "Oh! My children! How sad!"

Mother, daughter, and son embraced in a three-way wallowing of hugs. Margie's tears ran afresh. "Let me introduce you," she blubbered to the cousins. "This is Nancy, and this is Bob Jr., my poor semiorphans!"

Nancy Randall was a pale, gaunt younger version of her mother except that her hair hung below her shoulders. Bob Jr. was thin, with rimless glasses, scanty blond hair, and sunken cheeks. They both waved listlessly at Judith and Renie, who waved back. Neither of the Randall offspring spoke.

"They're numb with grief," Margie lamented, a hand on each of her children's arms. "Come, darlings, let me get you some nice Moonbeam's coffee from the staff room. Then we can talk about the funeral. We'll make some wonderful plans." With a surprisingly energetic wave, Margie Randall left the cousins in peace.

"Jeez," Renie shuddered, "she's a real crepe pants, as my mother would say."

"Those poor kids," Judith said. "They look awful. It can't be just grief—they look like they've been drawn through a knothole—as *my* mother would say."

Renie nodded. "Bill was right. Something's wrong

with them. I mean, really wrong." She got out of bed and gazed through the window. "It's stopped snowing. I'll bet we got at least a foot. It's beautiful out there."

"Maybe I can walk far enough to look outside later today," Judith said, digging into her purse. "Maybe I won't pass out if I try."

"What're you doing?" Renie asked as Judith began dumping items onto the bed.

"I'm looking for something bigger than my little notebook to start putting together the family tree. I don't suppose—you being an artist and all—you'd have any drawing paper with you?"

"I do, actually," Renie replied, going to the coat closet. "I've got a pad tucked away in the side of my suitcase. Hang on."

A moment later, Renie produced the drawing pad, but wore a puzzled expression. "That's odd. I could have sworn I closed this suitcase. I mean, I know I did, or the lid would have opened and everything would've fallen out."

"Has somebody been snooping?" Judith asked in apprehension.

Renie was going through the small suitcase. "I guess so. My makeup bag's unzipped. I always close it when I'm finished." She turned around to stare at Judith. "Who? When? Why?"

Judith gave a faint shake of her head. "While we were asleep, I suppose. That's when. But who and why are blanks I can't fill in."

"Nothing's been taken," Renie said, going through the few belongings she'd brought along. "Of course there's always the problem of thievery in a hospital. None of them are sacred."

Judith agreed. "Some people, especially borderline poverty types, can't resist temptation."

"How about just plain crooks?" Renie said, now angry. She slammed the lid shut and closed the clasps with a sharp snap. "I suppose that's who it was. It's a damned good thing I didn't have anything valuable in there except for a twenty-five-dollar lipstick that the would-be thief probably figured was from Woolworth's. Let me check your train case."

"I locked it," Judith said. "It's just a habit. I used to hide any extra money I earned from tips at the Meat & Mingle in there. If I hadn't, Dan would have spent it on Twinkies and booze."

Renie checked the train case to make sure. "It looks okay." She stood up and handed over the drawing pad.

Judith offered her cousin a grateful smile and then sighed. "I feel as if I'm about to sign my life away."

"Put it down on paper and see how it looks," Renie suggested, glancing up from the newspaper. "That's what I do with my work. If it seems okay, then it's right, then it's Truth."

"Uh-huh," Judith responded without enthusiasm. She started with Mac and a question mark for the baby to come, then put in Mike and Kristin. Next, she wrote in her own name, Judith Anne Grover McMonigle Flynn. Then she stopped. "Here I go," she said, and incisively lettered in Joseph Patrick Flynn above Mike's name. "It's official. Joe is down here in black and white as Mike's real father."

"I'll be damned," Renie said in amazement.

"Did you think I was a complete coward?" Judith retorted with a faintly hostile glance.

"What?" Renie turned away from the newspaper. "I'm not talking about you. I'm referring to this brief and almost-buried article in the business section. Listen: 'Restoration Heartware of North America yesterday reiterated its intention to expand its medical facilities beyond cardiac care. The Cleveland-based firm has shown interest in a half-dozen orthopedic facilities in the United States, including Good Cheer Hospital, which is currently owned and operated by the Sisters of Good Cheer. A spokesperson for Good Cheer stated that the religious order is not interested in any kind of merger or buyout at this time.' Is that spokesperson Blanche Van Boeck?"

Intrigued, Judith leaned on one elbow to face her cousin. "Who's asking the question?"

"Me," Renie replied. "The article doesn't identify the spokesperson. Maybe that's because Blanche isn't official. Why didn't Dr. Van Boeck or Sister Jacqueline meet with the press? How come Blanche barged in instead? The morning paper must have gotten this from the TV news story, since KLIP seemed to be the only one asking questions out here in the hall yesterday."

Judith was also puzzled. "You know a lot more about the business world than I do, coz. What do you make of all this?"

With her disheveled hair standing on end, the big bandage on her shoulder, the blue sling on her arm, and the baggy hospital gown sagging around her figure, Renie's boardroom face looked more like it belonged in the bathroom. Still, she approached the question with her customary professionalism.

"There's a conspiracy of silence about Good Cheer," she said. "It's not necessarily malevolent or mysterious. Any institution or business enterprise deplores speculative publicity and rumors. If a company is ripe for a takeover or a merger, they feel vulnerable, like a wounded animal. It's a sign of weakness, particularly when stockholders are involved. The top brass go to ground to wait for the worst to blow over."

"Are you saying," Judith inquired, "that Good Cheer is in financial trouble?"

"Many hospitals are in financial trouble," Renie answered. "In the past few years, I've done brochures and letterheads and other design projects for at least three hospitals, including our own HMO. All of them were very bottom-line conscious, and all of them expressed serious concerns about keeping afloat."

Judith nodded. "I understand that modern medicine is a mess, but it seems impossible in a country as rich and supposedly smart as the United States that we could have gotten into such a fix. No wonder Mother keeps ranting about how Harry Truman tried to get universal medical coverage legislation through Congress over fifty years ago, and how if he couldn't do it, nobody could. And nobody has."

"Very sad, very shortsighted," Renie agreed. "But in the case of Good Cheer, I get the impression that they're simply trying to survive. Certainly the nuns would hate to give up the hospital. There may be a shortage of vocations, but certainly nursing—and administrative skills—are worthwhile in a religious community. Not to mention that they're drawing cards for women who are contemplating a vocation. If the Sisters of Good Cheer don't have a hospital to run and patients to care for, what will they do? Medicine is their tradition of service."

"It's sad," Judith sighed. "If it's true." She gazed up at the statue of Mary with the infant Jesus. The plaster was a bit cracked and the paint a trifle chipped, but the

Virgin's expression was easy to read: She looked worried, and Judith couldn't blame her.

"It's the whole bigger-is-better mentality," Renie said in disgust. "By the time our kids are our age, about four people will own everything in the world. It'll be stifling, stupid, and I'll be damned glad to be either dead or gaga."

"Don't say that, coz," Judith said in mild reproach. "And don't get off on a tangent. You still haven't explained why you think there's a cover-up."

"Do I need to?" Renie snapped. "There are tons of reasons for a cover-up. Good Cheer may be losing money hand over fist. They're certainly losing patients in a most terrible way. The hospital and the religious order have their reputations on the line. So do individuals, like Dr. Van Boeck, Dr. Garnett, Sister Jacqueline. With Blanche in their corner—or at least in the hospital's corner—there's enough clout to muzzle the media. Except, of course, for a rogue reporter like Addison Kirby, who's not only something of a star in his own right, but who has a personal stake in all this because of what happened to his wife."

Judith paused as the mop brigade arrived. Two middle-aged women, one Pakistani and the other Southeast Asian, silently and efficiently began cleaning Judith's half of the room. When they reached the other side where Renie had trashed her sector, they looked at each other in dismay. In her native tongue, the Pakistani rattled off a string of what, in any language, sounded like complaints. The Southeast Asian looked mystified, but responded with her own invective, jabbing a finger at Renie and scowling.

"Hey, what did I do? I'm crippled," Renie said, holding up her good hand. "I can't help myself."

Both women directed their unintelligible, if vitriolic, comments to Renie. The Pakistani shook her finger; the Southeast Asian stamped her foot. Renie looked dazed.

"Hey, girlfriends," she finally said, raising her voice to be heard, "knock it off. You're giving me a relapse."

The women didn't stop. In fact, the Southeast Asian pointed to the wastebasket and glared at Renie in a warning manner. The Pakistani waved her arms at all the clutter on the nightstand, narrowing her eyes at Archie the doll, who grinned back in his eternally cheerful manner.

"Touch Archie and prepare to be the next patient in the OR with a broken arm," Renie warned.

The cleaning women looked at Renie, again at Archie, and then at each other. They shook their heads. Then they shook their fingers at Renie.

"That's it," Renie said. "I'm dead." She closed her eyes and disappeared under the covers.

The cleaning women simply stared at the mound in the bed and shook their heads. Then they resumed their work and began chattering to each other, though it was clear to Judith that neither of them understood what the other was saying. A few minutes later, they left, and Renie came up for air.

"Finally," she gasped. "I feel like I've been smothered."

"You can't really blame the cleaning women," Judith chided. "You do make a terrible mess."

"Nonsense," Renie scoffed, tearing open a pack of gum and tossing the wrapper on the floor. "You know I'm a decent housekeeper."

"In your own house," Judith noted, then gave her cousin a coy smile. "I wonder if Addison Kirby would like a visitor this morning."

"Meaning me," Renie grumbled. "I'll be glad when I can dump you in a wheelchair and send you off on your own."

"So will I," Judith retorted. "Do you think I like lying around like a bump on a log?"

Renie was getting out of bed. "I'm going to go wash my hair and take a shower," she said, unhooking the IV bag and carrying it in her good hand. "I'll visit Mr. Kirby on the way back when I'm clean and beautiful."

After watching her cousin traipse off to the shower area, Judith returned to the family tree with an air of resignation. Joe's mother was already dead by the time Judith had met the family. His father, known as Jack, but named John, had been a bombastic man with a barrel chest and a booming voice. He drank too much, he worked only when he felt like it, and after his wife died, he'd let their four sons fend for themselves. That all of them had achieved a certain measure of success in life was due, Judith felt, to their own ambition and determination, along with a debt they felt they owed their mother, who had put up with a great deal before dying of cancer two days before her fortieth birthday.

Mary Margaret Flynn had been a redhead, like Joe. Like Effie McMonigle, too. Judith considered Effie. If she found out that Dan wasn't Mike's father, that she wasn't his grandmother or Little Mac's great-grandmother—the pen dropped from Judith's hand. It was too cruel. Effie was a selfish woman, but not without reason. Her husband, Dan's father, had left her for another woman. She had become bitter and very protective of herself and her only child. Judith had always felt sorry for her mother-in-law. Maybe Effie would never find out the truth. Judith looked up at the statue of the Madonna and child again, and said a little prayer for her mother-in-law. Then she looked at the statue of the Sacred Heart and said a prayer for herself. Having created a monstrous deception, there seemed to be no way out of it without the risk of hurting someone. Judith wished she weren't such a convincing liar.

A pale blonde head edged around the doorway. "Ma'am?" said a pitiful voice.

Judith turned away from the statues. "Yes?" she responded, then saw Nancy Randall hesitate before moving into the room.

"Excuse me," Nancy said. "Did my mother leave her worry beads in here?"

"Her worry beads?" Judith responded, then added without thinking: "Does she really need them?"

"I beg your pardon?" Nancy's china blue eyes were wide. "Yes, they're a great comfort to her. She used to say the rosary, but she got too depressed when she recited the five Sorrowful Mysteries."

"She should have concentrated on the Joyous and Glorious Mysteries," Judith said before guilt tripped up her tongue. "I'm sorry, that was flippant. Do come in and look around. If your mother dropped her beads, I didn't see them. But lying here in bed, I'm at a disadvantage."

"Yes," Nancy said slowly, bending down to search the floor. "I don't see them, either. Mother is at a disadvantage, too. She can't plan my father's funeral without those worry beads."

"Surely you and your brother can help her," Judith said in a kindly voice. "What about your uncle Jim? Is he here, too?"

"Not today," Nancy replied, kneeling by Renie's bed. "He's very upset. And he's not well, either."

"What's wrong?" Judith inquired.

Nancy, looking frustrated, stood up. "They aren't sure. He's had all sorts of tests. A CAT scan, an MRI, ultrasounds. Uncle Jim has never been in good health. He's just the opposite of my father. They were mirror twins, you see."

"Yes," Judith said. "Your uncle mentioned that. I'd never heard of it before."

"It's fairly unusual," Nancy said, her eyes drifting around the room. "Bobby—my brother—and I are twins, too, but not identical."

"Yes," Judith replied, "I can see that."

"Thank you," Nancy said, and wandered out of the room.

"Vague," Judith thought, "very vague."

She returned to the family tree, reluctantly omitting Effie McMonigle. The phone rang as she was trying to remember Kristin's mother's first name.

"Jude-girl," said Joe, sounding chipper. "We found Ernest."

"Ernest?" Judith frowned into the receiver. "Oh! The snake. Good. Dare I ask where he was?"

"Well . . . Ha-ha!" Joe's laugh was unnatural. "How about around your mother's neck?"

"That's not funny, Joe," Judith said in a warning voice. "Where was this horrible boa constrictor who should never have been permitted inside the B&B in the first place?"

Joe's tone grew serious, if not remorseful. "He was in the garbage can under the kitchen sink."

"Oh, dear. Who found him?"

"Arlene," Joe replied. "This morning, while she was making French toast for the guests."

"What . . . did . . . Arlene . . . do?" Judith asked with trepidation.

"She grabbed the snake and turned the clothes basket upside down on him," Joe explained. "Then she went back to fixing French toast."

Judith had a feeling that the story wasn't over. "What about Ernest's owners, the Pettigrews?"

"Well . . . They were worried, of course." Joe paused. "But they were waiting for breakfast and I guess Arlene sort of forgot to tell them about Ernest. Phyliss Rackley showed up about then, and the first thing she did was—Hold it." Joe went away from the phone, and Judith heard voices in the background. She could barely make out her husband's words but she caught fragments that sounded like ". . . can't make it . . . let the medics walk . . . only five blocks . . . chains? Oh, good."

"Joe?" Judith called into the phone. "Joe!"

"What?"

"What's going on, Joe?" Judith demanded. "Did something happen to Phyliss? I can't afford to lose my cleaning woman when I'm laid up like this."

"Well . . . It seems that Phyliss grabbed the laundry basket to take upstairs so she could strip the beds, and as you might imagine, the snake got loose, and—" Joe stopped speaking as Judith heard the cleaning woman shriek in the background:

"Lucifer! Satan! Beelzebub! He's on the loose, tempting sinners! Look out, Lord, he may be coming after me! Keep him away, Lord! I don't want to wear scanty underwear and dance to suggestive music!"

"You hear that?" Joe asked. "Phyliss passed out cold when she saw the snake, but she's come to now."

"Oh, good grief!" Judith cried, raking her fingers over her scalp. "Is she okay?"

"Not exactly," Joe replied calmly as voices continued to sound in the background. "She came to, but she swears she's having a heart attack. Arlene says it's just gas, but you know Phyliss, she's kind of a hypochondriac."

Phyliss Rackley was indeed a hypochondriac as well as a religious zealot. But she was also a terrific cleaning woman. Judith hung her head. "What's happening now? Did you say 'medics'?"

"Yes, yes, I did," Joe replied, still keeping his voice calm. "Phyliss insisted we call an ambulance. But the medics were having trouble getting up the hill with all this snow. Even with chains, they had trouble, but they think they can make it if they give it another try."

"Where *is* Phyliss?" Judith asked, aware that a global-sized headache was setting in.

"On the sofa in the living room," Joe said. "Really, she seems okay. I wish Arlene wasn't trying to get her to take all that Gas-X, though. That can produce some pretty revolting results with somebody like Phyliss."

"What about the damned snake?"

"The snake?" Joe hesitated. "A good question. I'm not sure."

"Joe . . ."

"I'll check. Right away. Hey, I really called to see how you were feeling this morning."

"How do you think I feel?" Judith retorted. "I feel absolutely awful. I'm hanging up now so you can straighten out this horrible mess. I'm not even going to ask how the rest of the guests are managing. Goodbye." Judith slammed down the phone with a big bang.

Bob Randall Jr. stood in the doorway. "Excuse me," he said in a diffident voice, "have you seen my sister, Nancy?"

"Yes," Judith said in a testy voice. "She was here

and then she left. She couldn't find your mother's worry beads."

"Oh." Bob Jr. looked forlorn. "Darn."

Judith regretted her sharp tone. It wasn't Bob Jr.'s fault that she was in a bad mood. "I imagine Nancy went off to search wherever else your mother had been after she'd called on us."

But Bob Jr. shook his head. "Mom wasn't anywhere else after we met her in this room. We went straight down to the staff lounge."

"What about before your mother came in here?" Judith asked, making an effort to be helpful.

Bob Jr. had moved closer to the bed, and appeared as if he'd like to sit down. "Do you mind?" he asked, pointing to the chair and panting a bit.

"Not at all," Judith replied. "Do you feel ill?"

"Sometimes." Bob Jr. sat down with a heavy sigh. "I think Mom called on Mr. Kirby before she came to see you and that other lady. I'll check in there as soon as I catch my breath. He's close by, right?"

Judith nodded. "Next door."

Bob Jr. also nodded, but didn't speak.

"Have you been hurrying?" Judith asked, still feeling a need to make up for her previous curt manner.

Bob Jr. shook his head. "No. It's my condition."

"Oh?" Judith put on her most sympathetic expression. "Would it be rude to ask what that might be?"

"Yes." The young man took a deep breath, then got to his feet.

"I'm sorry," Judith apologized. "I won't pry anymore." She paused, hoping that Bob Jr. might give her a hint. But he just stood there, looking desolate. "How is your mother doing with the funeral plans? It must be very hard for her."

"It is," Bob Jr. said, very solemn. "Sometimes she feels like she's responsible for all these deaths."

"Why is that?" Judith inquired.

"Because," Bob Jr. said, "she thinks she was the vessel." Anxiously, he looked over his shoulder, toward the hallway. "I'll check with Mr. Kirby now. I should have done that first before coming in here. I know how anxious my mother was to see him."

Bob Randall Jr. made his exit, leaving Judith puzzled. And very curious.

ELEVEN

BOB JR. HAD scarcely been gone more than a few seconds when Renie returned. "In the nick of time," she said. "I just met Bob Jr. going into Addison Kirby's room as I was leaving." Renie stopped at the end of Judith's bed and peered at her cousin. "What's wrong? You look miffed."

"I *am* miffed," Judith declared. "My replacements are running amok."

Renie tipped her head and gazed at Judith's left hip. "I thought you only had one."

"I don't mean that," Judith said with a wave of her arm. "I mean, my replacements at the B&B. It's that damned snake they let in."

"Enough with the snakes!" Renie cried, yanking the blanket from Judith's bed and putting it over her head. "You know I hate snakes. I don't want to hear another word about that creepy thing."

Judith, however, prevailed, her attitude conveying just how sorry she felt for herself and how little sympathy she had for Renie. As for Hillside Manor's reputation, Judith was certain that it was hopelessly tarnished.

When Judith had finished her tale of woe, Renie peeked out from under the blanket. "Phyliss," she declared, "is not having a heart attack or whatever she claims. She's merely trying to get attention."

"That's the least of my worries. Marooned guests, reptiles on the loose, whoopee cushions, emergency vehicles in the cul-de-sac—why can't I be allowed an unencumbered recovery?" Judith reached for her water glass, took a big swallow, and choked.

Renie replaced the blanket, doing her best to tuck in the corners. "Are you okay?"

Between splutters, Judith nodded. "Yes," she gasped. "I'm just frustrated. For about a hundred reasons. Tell me about Addison Kirby and I'll tell you about the younger Randall twins."

"Twins?" Renie looked intrigued.

"Yes, but not identical," Judith deadpanned.

"No, I guess not." Renie shifted around on the bed, trying to make herself more comfortable while not disturbing Judith's leg and hip. "Addison's in pretty good shape this morning. Or, as he put it, he's still alive, which I gather sort of surprised him."

"I can imagine," Judith said. "He may have thought he'd end up like his wife, Joan."

"Right. Anyway, he was reluctant to talk at first, not that I blame him. He doesn't know me, I could be a maniacal killer." Renie stopped as her phone rang. "Drat. Let's hope it's not my mother." She managed to grab the receiver on the fourth ring. "Hi!" she said with a big smile, propping the phone between her chin and shoulder. "Yes, I'm feeling better . . . Don't feel bad about not being able to come see me, Tom . . . No, I realize you can't go to work. Oh? . . . Then ask your dad . . . He's *what?*" Renie's jaw had dropped and she was staring at Judith.

"To what purpose?" Renie said into the phone as

her good hand clawed at her hair. "Why? Where?
Don't you dare let them near Clarence! . . . What?
How much smaller? What are they, rats or dogs? Oh,
good night!"

There was a long pause as her son apparently of
fered some sort of explanation. At last Renie spoke
again. "If you find out, let me know. Or call for the
men with the white coats and the butterfly net. Meanwhile, I don't know why you need money—you can't
go anywhere . . . Oh, good grief! If you can ski down
Heraldsgate Hill, you could get to work. Really, you're
thirty-one years old and it's about time you got a serious job instead of making tacos at Miguel's
Muncheria. Good-bye, my son. I'm having a relapse."
With a weary expression, Renie replaced the receiver.
"Bill found two Chihuahuas, lost in the snow up at the
park by our house. He's taken them in and has dressed
one in a tuxedo and the other in University of Wisconsin sweats."

It was Judith's turn to stare. "What?"

"I don't know why," Renie responded, holding her
head. "My husband's a psychologist. Therefore, he
can't possibly be crazy. Can he?"

"Dare I ask where he got a tuxedo that would fit a
Chihuahua?"

Renie glanced at Archie the doll. "It's Archie's formal wear. The dogs are very small, not as big as
Clarence," she added, referring to the Joneses' lop-
eared rabbit. "In fact, the sweats belong to Clarence,
but he never wears them. The last time we dressed him
in them, he ate the Badger logo off the front." She
paused, holding her head. "I should never leave Bill
alone for too long, especially now that he's retired."

Judith didn't feel up to making sense out of her

cousin's report. Renie and Bill had a strange menagerie of creatures, both living and stuffed. Sometimes it was best not to ask too many questions. "Could we go back to Addison Kirby?" Judith pleaded. "You'd begun to get something useful out of him."

"I had?" Renie pulled the covers up to her neck. "Brrr . . . it's cold in here. I don't think Clarabelle is working full-time, either." She glanced at the radiator, which was emitting asthmatic hissing sounds. "Yes, Addison definitely thinks that his wife, Somosa, and Randall were murdered. However, he has absolutely no idea who did it."

Judith frowned. "Was he going to write up his suspicions for the paper?"

"He can't," Renie said. "He has to have facts, evidence, just like a cop. That's what he was trying to gather when he got hit by the car. He'd talked to the Randall kids, but they weren't much help. He'd interviewed Somosa's widow in the Dominican Republic via long distance a couple of days ago, before Bob Randall died. Addison said she wasn't much help. Her English is almost nonexistent and she seemed inclined to blame her husband's death on God's will. Addison doesn't agree, and neither do I. It'd be more likely that the teams in the rest of our division did Somosa in. But that's not realistic, either."

"What about Tubby Turnbull?" Judith asked. "Did Addison find him helpful?"

Renie gave Judith a sardonic look. "Has Tubby ever been helpful to anyone? After hemming and hawing and trying to figure out if he'd put his pants on backwards, Tubby insisted he couldn't think of anyone connected to the team who'd want Joaquin out of the way. He was popular with the other players, the press liked him, management considered him a huge part of the franchise, and even his agent is a good guy—as sports agents go. Anyway, the agent works out of New York. He hasn't been out this way since the end of last season."

Judith gave a faint nod. "Nothing there, as far as we can tell." She pondered the matter of Joaquin Somosa for a few moments. "The bear," she said suddenly. "What did he mean by saying 'a bear' and pointing to the TV?"

Renie frowned at Judith. "I told you, he must have been hallucinating. Why else would he keep saying 'a bear, a bear, a bear'?" Renie's scowl faded as she clapped her hand to her head. "A bear—in Spanish, that would be *aver*, to see. Maybe he couldn't see—the TV or anything else. The drugs might have been taking effect. Doesn't Ecstasy blind you?"

"I'm not sure," Judith said, "but it would fit. All I really know is that it does terrible things, including making you crazy. Joaquin must have ingested it just before the repairman, Curly, got to his room. I wonder who'd been there ahead of him?"

"We don't know," Renie responded with a helpless look.

"That's the trouble," Judith said. "We weren't around when these other deaths occurred and it's almost impossible to get any concrete information out of the staff. I sure wish Maya was still here." She sighed and rearranged herself on the pillows. "What about Joan Fremont? Did she and Addison sound like a happy couple?"

"Yes," Renie responded, delving into her goodies stash and hauling out some cheese and crackers. "Want some?"

"No, thanks."

"Addison didn't make a big deal of it," Renie continued, "which indicated to me that the marriage must have been solid. You know, if he'd gone on and on about how devoted they were and all that junk, I'd have figured him for a phony."

"What about their kids?" inquired Judith.

Renie shrugged and chewed on her crackers. "They haven't been in town since Thanksgiving, which, alas, was the last time they saw their mother alive. I mean, they came for the funeral. But I got the impression they were a close family, emotionally, if not geographically."

"What about Joan's colleagues at Le Repertoire?"

Renie shrugged again. "By and large, she got along with most of them. Addison indicated that she wasn't happy with the direction the theater was going—too much emphasis on social issues, rather than good drama. But he didn't know of any big rift. As for so-called rivals, he said that there were always some of those. The theater is full of big egos. But Joan knew how to handle them. She was a veteran, a real pro."

"Gosh," Judith said in a bleak voice, "it sounds as if the community has lost more than just talent. Both Joan and Joaquin sound like decent, upstanding human beings. Did Addison say anything about Bob Randall? We know he was brave both on and off the field. Bob saved some lives, as well as games."

"Addison hadn't had time to do more than speak with Nancy and Bob Jr.," Renie responded after she'd devoured two crackers and another chunk of cheese. "As you might guess from the looks of them, they weren't a lot of help. Like their mother, they seem ineffectual and unable to cope with the rest of the world.

I sure wish Bill would open the vault on his blasted patient confidentiality and let us know what's going on."

"Tell me," Judith said, making yet another attempt to get comfortable in the bed, "does Addison know why there isn't a full-fledged homicide investigation going on around here?"

Renie shook her head. "That's where he sort of clammed up. I suspect he knows more about that than he's saying."

"But does he agree that the police aren't involved?" Judith persisted.

"He told me he'd gotten nowhere going to his usual sources at city hall, including the police department." Renie shot Judith a cryptic glance. "Think about it— Addison Kirby has been covering city hall for ten, fifteen years. He must have cultivated all sorts of people who can help him. But not this time. Why? Could it be Blanche Van Boeck on the city council? She who would be mayor?"

"Drat," said Judith. "That woman has clout."

Judith had opened her mouth to tell Renie about the Randall twins' visits when Corinne Appleby entered the room, looking determined and pushing a wheelchair. "You're getting up today, Mrs. Flynn. We're going to put you in this swift little number."

"That's good—I think," Judith responded.

But she was not without trepidation, especially when Corinne didn't request any help with the lifting process.

"Just take your time," Corinne said, exuding more confidence than Judith felt. "I'm used to doing this. My mother is very crippled with arthritis and can't stand without assistance."

"My mother also has arthritis," Judith said, sitting

up and struggling to swing her legs over the side of the bed. "Unfortunately, it's often just part of old age."

"My mother's not quite sixty," Corinne said, her freckled face clouding over. "She developed arthritis in her early twenties. It was terrible. She'd planned to become a concert pianist."

"Oh, that *is* awful!" Renie exclaimed. "We had a dear family friend, we called her Auntie May, who played beautifully, but she had arthritis, too, and all her professional dreams were dashed at a very young age. Can your mother play at all?"

Corinne shook her head as she put her arms under Judith's. "No. She hasn't played in almost thirty years. We sold the piano when I was still a child. Mummy couldn't bear to have it in the house."

"That's very sad," Judith said, gritting her teeth. "Oooh . . . I don't know if I . . ."

"You're doing fine," Corinne said. "Just keep coming up. Be thankful that eventually you'll be mobile again. Not everyone is so lucky. There. You're on your feet. Don't move for a few seconds. Steady . . ."

Judith wasn't steady. In fact, she was swaying. But after focusing her eyes on the bathroom doorknob, she began to get her bearings.

"Good," Corinne said, slowly letting go of Judith. "Now try to take a step toward me. Don't worry—if you fall, I'll catch you."

Judith inched her way forward on her good leg, though most of her weight was against the bed. Then, closing her eyes and taking a deep breath, she tried to move her left leg. It hurt, but not as much as she'd feared. Corinne gave her a nod of encouragement. Judith gently tested putting weight on the hip replacement. She felt unsure of herself and gritted her teeth.

"Go ahead," urged Corinne. "It'll hold you up."

To Judith's amazement, it did.

"Hooray for modern medicine!" Renie cried, grinning at her cousin. "Go, girl, go."

Judith didn't go very far, but she did manage another step before she felt on the verge of collapsing.

"Hold it right there," Corinne said, angling the wheelchair so that Judith could sit down. "That was very good. Now you can visit the rest of the world."

Uttering a feeble laugh, Judith gratefully eased herself into the chair. The nurse pushed her to the doorway. Judith, who had thought that Corinne's remark about the "rest of the world" was merely an attempt at hospital humor, realized that for two days she hadn't seen anything outside the four walls of her room. The hallway, with its ebb and flow of staff, the nurses' station, the doors leading to other patient rooms, the flowers on desks, and even Robbie the Robot, who was heading her way, were indeed a brave new world. Until now, Judith had relied on Renie's eyes to see beyond the small space outside their ward. Finally Judith was on her own and felt a strange surge of independence. Jauntily, she waved at Robbie as he swerved and beeped past her.

"Wow," Judith said under her breath. "People. Places. Things."

"We'll go down to the end of the hall," Corinne said. "There's a big window there where you can see out. It's not snowing, but it's very cold, down around twenty, I heard. Almost all of the staff has been staying in the nurses' former residence halls. Unless you have chains and know how to drive in this stuff, it's much safer to stay put."

Judith glanced into Mr. Mummy's room across the

hall, but he wasn't there. Then she looked into Addison Kirby's room. He was there, but was on the phone, looking frustrated. She passed three more patient rooms, each of which contained four beds. On her left, she saw the small area set into an alcove where Blanche Van Boeck had held her press conference with KLIP-TV. Then there were supply rooms and six more patient wards, and finally the staff lounge and what might have been a small kitchen, judging from the aromas that wafted out into the hall.

The snowscape made Judith catch her breath. "It's gorgeous," she said to Corinne. "I haven't even been able to look out the window in our room."

Judith wasn't exaggerating. The trees, the shrubs, the sweeping lawn were covered in a pristine blanket of snow. The driveway to the entrance had been shoveled, but there were only a few tire tracks and footprints in the main parking lot off to the right. Beyond, the rooftops of the surrounding residential neighborhoods looked like a Christmas card, with smoke spiraling out of chimneys and soft lights behind windows warding off the winter gloom.

"This is lovely," Judith said. "It's the first real snow of the season. Last year we didn't get more than a couple of dustings."

"It cuts down on our visitors," said Renie, who had followed Judith and Corinne down the hall. "Which is good. I don't like playing hostess when I'm recovering from surgery."

The door to the staff lounge opened and a red-faced Dr. Van Boeck came storming out. When he spotted the cousins and Corinne Appleby, he stopped in his tracks, adjusted his white coat, and forced a smile.

"Enjoying the weather?" he remarked in his deep

voice. "Very nice, as long as you're inside." Van Boeck nodded and continued on his way.

"Is he upset?" Judith asked of Corinne.

"I couldn't say," Corinne answered, her freckled face masking any emotion. "Doctors are always under such stress, especially these days."

Judith didn't comment, but resumed looking out the window. As far as she could tell, there were at least a dozen or more cars in the parking lot, almost all of them buried under several inches of snow, except for an SUV that probably had four-wheel drive.

"We should head back," Corinne said. "You don't want to sit up for too long the first time out. I'm going off duty now, but Heather will get you up again this afternoon."

"Okay," Judith said, feeling proud of herself for making progress. "By the way—have you had a problem with theft at Good Cheer?"

"Theft?" Corinne looked mystified. "No. The sisters are very, very careful about the people they hire. Plus, they pay better wages to the nonprofessional staff than most hospitals do. Why do you ask?"

"Oh—just curious," Judith replied. "You hear stories about hospitals and nursing homes having problems with stealing. Plus, we were told not to bring any valuables to Good Cheer."

"That's for insurance purposes," Corinne responded as she turned the wheelchair around. "The only thing that goes missing around here are lunches from the staff refrigerators, occasional boxes of Band-Aids, and, lately, some of the surgical instruments. They started disappearing before Christmas, and Dr. Van Boeck said that maybe somebody wanted to use them to carve the Christmas goose."

At that moment, Dr. Garnett came out of the staff lounge. He looked tense, Judith thought, and wondered if he and Van Boeck had had a row.

"Good morning, Doctor," Judith said with a big smile. "How are you?"

Peter Garnett straightened his shoulders and regained his usual urbane expression. "Very well, thank you. It appears as if Dr. Alfonso has done his usual outstanding job. I see you're out and about today."

"Yes," Judith responded, "I'm very grateful to him. In fact, I appreciate everyone on the staff here at Good Cheer. When I get home, I'm going to write a thank-you letter to the board."

Dr. Garnett's trim mustache twitched slightly. "You are? That's very kind. Now if you'll excuse me, I must return to my office."

"My," Judith said as Corinne rolled her down the hall, "Dr. Garnett seemed sort of surprised that I'd write a letter of appreciation. Don't patients do that once in a while?"

"I believe they do," Corinne replied in her noncommittal way.

"Maybe I shouldn't send it to the board," Judith mused. "Maybe I should send it to Dr. Alfonso directly. Would it be passed on to the rest of you?"

"It might," Corinne said, steering Judith past the luncheon carts, which had just arrived on the floor. Renie paused to examine the carts, but the sliding doors were locked.

"I'll have to think about the addressee," Judith said. "What would you do, Nurse Appleby?"

"About what?" Corinne asked as they reached Judith and Renie's ward.

"The letter," Judith said. "Who would you send it to?"

"That depends," Corinne said. "Here, let's get you lined up with the bed."

Judith figured it was useless to press the nurse with further questions. Corinne was a clam. Or, Judith considered charitably, very discreet.

Feeling more confident, if not actually stronger, she was able to get back into bed without much difficulty. Judith was surprised, however, to discover that her excursion down the hall had tired her out.

"I can't believe how weak I am," she sighed as Corinne adjusted the IV drip.

"That's natural," Corinne said. "That's why you have to go at it slowly but steadily."

Ten minutes later, after Corinne had taken the cousins' vitals and gone on her way, Judith and Renie went back to their speculations.

"I thought Bob Jr.'s remark about his mother being 'the vessel' was very interesting," Judith said. "What do you think he meant?"

"Whatever his goofy mother meant when she told him that," Renie replied. "I kind of think Margie Randall might enjoy being an Angel of Death."

"I think she meant something else," Judith countered. "I mean, what if Margie was the one who . . ." She stopped, her forehead furrowed in thought. "What if she was the one who had unwittingly delivered the drugs that killed Somosa and Fremont and maybe her own husband?"

Renie frowned at Judith. "You mean in Randall's Wild Turkey or something that one of the other two had brought in from outside?"

Judith nodded. "Somebody—maybe it was Heather—mentioned that other patients besides us had had food or beverages smuggled into the hospital.

Whoever got them for the patients may have conned Margie into delivering the stuff. Maybe that's where the drugs were administered, rather than in the IVs."

"Creepy," Renie remarked as their luncheon trays arrived. *"Creepy,"* she repeated, lifting lids and taking sniffs. "What now, plastics?"

Judith, however, usually enjoyed what looked like chicken-fried steak. She liked green noodles, too, and lima beans. "I can eat it," she said, taking a bite of the chicken. "It's not bad."

Renie's response was to heave her lunch, tray and all, into the wastebasket. "Berfle," she said in disgust. "Where's Mr. Mummy?"

"Coz," Judith said with a scowl, "you're not going to order out again, are you?"

"Why not?" Renie said, picking up the phone. "Lots of places are probably delivering today. They've chained up."

But Renie's attempts proved futile. Even Bubba's Fried Chicken had decided to close for the duration.

"This town is full of scaredy-cats," Renie declared. "They're too cowardly to go out in a little bit of snow."

"You won't drive in it," Judith noted. "You never do. Why should other people risk it?"

"Because they have hamburgers and french fries and malted milks to deliver, that's why," Renie declared.

"Forget it," Judith said, scooping up lima beans. "You're getting on my nerves."

"So what am I going to eat for lunch?" Renie demanded.

"Dig some of it out of the wastebasket," Judith said with a shrug. "It's clean."

"I can't eat that swill," Renie said, pouting.

"Then get something out of your goodies bag," Judith shot back. "Just put something in your mouth so you'll stop complaining."

Renie rang her buzzer. In the five minutes that she waited for a response, she didn't say a word. Instead, she drummed her fingernails on the side of the metal bed and almost drove Judith nuts.

Heather Chinn showed up before Judith could threaten to throttle Renie. "What can we do for you?" she asked in her pert voice.

" 'We'?" Renie retorted. "I don't see anybody but you. And *you* can get me a big ham sandwich, preferably with Havarti cheese and maybe a nice sweet pickle. I don't care much for dills. They're too sour, except for the ones my sister-in-law makes."

"Excuse me?" said Heather, her almond eyes wide. "What became of your lunch?"

Renie tapped a finger against her cheek. "What *became* of my lunch? Let me think. It *came*, but it didn't *be* a lunch. That is, it was not edible." She pointed to the small grinning doll that rested next to the Kleenex box on the nightstand. "I wouldn't feed that swill to Archie."

"That's a shame," Heather said with a tilt of her head. "I see Mrs. Flynn found it edible. She's almost finished. How was the lime Jell-O, Mrs. Flynn?"

"Um . . ." Judith gazed at the small green puddle that was left on her plate. Lime was not her favorite flavor, but that wasn't the hospital's fault. "It was . . . fine."

"Jell-O, huh?" said Renie. "I thought it was a dead frog."

"I'm afraid you'll have to wait for the evening meal, Mrs. Jones," Heather said, at her most pleasant. "I don't think you'll starve. Aren't you just a teensy bit squirrel-like?"

"Are you referring to my *teeth?*" Renie asked, looking outraged. "Are you making fun of my overbite because my parents couldn't afford braces?"

Heather's eyes grew even wider. "Goodness, no. I'd never do such a thing. You have very nice teeth. They're just . . . sizable. I meant your little stash of treats in that rather large grocery bag on the other side of the bed."

"Oh, that." Renie attempted to look innocent.

But Judith seized the moment. "Don't be too hard on my cousin," she said. "She's always had a lot of allergies and is used to providing her own food. I suspect that many patients do that."

"Well," Heather said, "some, of course. But your cousin—all of our patients—are asked to put down any allergies when they fill out the admitting forms. That's so the dieticians can avoid foods that may cause an allergic reaction. I'm sure you both filled out those sections." Heather cast a sly glance in Renie's direction. Renie was still pouting.

"I understand," Judith said. "But it's a funny thing about illness. You get certain cravings. One time after I'd had the flu, I couldn't eat anything for two days except scrambled-egg sandwiches."

Heather nodded. "That's because your system is depleted. You've lost certain vitamins and minerals."

"One of my husband's nieces ate all the paint off her bed after she had bronchitis," Renie said, still looking annoyed.

"That's a bit unusual," Heather remarked, her fine eyebrows lifting.

"I assume," Judith said before Renie could go on about Bill's nieces and nephews, who numbered more than a dozen, "that you don't really come down too hard on patients who insist they have to have a certain item. I imagine some of them are rather amusing."

Heather dimpled. "Oh, yes. We had an elderly man last year who insisted on eating chocolate-covered grasshoppers. I gather they're quite a delicacy in some cocktail party circles."

"That's very different," Judith agreed with a big smile. "Most, I suppose, are more ordinary."

"That's true," Heather said. "Milk shakes are very popular. So is chocolate and steak. Now while protein is necessary, post-op patients shouldn't eat steak because it's difficult to digest. Quite frankly, a hamburger is more acceptable."

"It would be to me," Renie said.

Judith ignored her cousin. "I heard," she said with a straight face, "that Joan Fremont had a fondness for peppermint stick candy."

Heather frowned. "I don't recall that. I believe she preferred Italian sodas. The ones with the vanilla syrup in the cream and club soda."

"Was she able to sneak one in?" Judith asked innocently.

"She did," Heather said. "I wasn't on duty, but Corinne told me about it. At least one of them was brought to the main desk by a funny little man wearing polka-dot pants and a yellow rain slicker. Sister Julia, our receptionist, got such a kick out of him. Ms. Fremont—Mrs. Kirby—actually had two of them brought in, and first thing in the morning. It was very naughty of her."

"Really," Judith said. "Was Mr. Kirby with her then?"

"No," Heather responded. "Mr. Kirby had a deadline

to meet, so he didn't come in that morning until . . ." The nurse paused, her face falling. "He didn't come in until after his wife had expired."

"Poor man!" Judith said with feeling. "Had he been told that Joan died before he reached the hospital?"

"I don't think so," Heather said. "He'd come directly from the newspaper."

"What a shock," Judith murmured. "Mr. Kirby must have been overcome."

"The truth is," Heather said, "Mrs. Kirby wasn't one of my patients. I heard all this secondhand from Dr. Garnett."

"Oh," Judith said, remembering what Heather had told her earlier. "But you were on duty when Mr. Somosa died, right?"

"Yes." Heather nodded solemnly. "I was the one who found him. That is, I saw his monitor flat-line, and immediately started the emergency procedures."

Judith wore her most wistful expression. "I hope he got to have his favorite thing, like Joan Fremont—Mrs. Kirby—had with her Italian sodas."

A spot of color showed on each of Heather's flawless cheeks. "He did, actually, even though I tried to dissuade him. Somebody had brought him a special juice drink, the kind he always drank before he pitched. I saw Mrs. Randall bring it in to him, and she said it smelled delicious."

"So someone brought it to the front desk?" Judith asked.

"I suppose," Heather said, then frowned at Judith. "You're interrogating me, aren't you? Why?"

Judith's smile was, she hoped, guileless. "Curiosity. What else is there to do but lie here and try to work out a puzzle? Surely you see that the three deaths—I'm including Bob Randall's—were peculiar?"

"It happens," Heather said, looking away. "It's part of nursing, to have patients, seemingly healthy, who don't recover from even a minor surgery. I must say, I've never gotten used to it, but it's part of the job."

"I suppose," Judith said, without conviction. "Still, I'd think you or the other nurses wouldn't have allowed Mr. Randall to drink Wild Turkey so soon after his operation."

Heather appeared flustered. "Wild Turkey? Isn't that some kind of whiskey?"

"Very strong whiskey," Judith said. "Did you know he had a bottle in bed with him?"

"No," Heather replied in a worried voice. "I wasn't on duty Tuesday morning. Corinne Appleby had her usual morning shift. That's odd—she didn't mention finding a whiskey bottle in Mr. Randall's room. It's the kind of thing you usually mention, especially after a . . . death."

"Did the night nurse notice, I wonder?" Judith said.

"Not that I heard," Heather replied, still looking concerned. "It would have been Emily Dore. You may not know her. I believe you have Avery Almquist and Trudy Womack on the night shift."

"Yes," Judith said, recalling the young male nurse who made his rounds silently and efficiently. "I really haven't had much chance to talk to him. I'm always half asleep when he comes in."

"He's very professional," Heather said, moving toward the door. "Are you certain about that whiskey?"

"Yes," Judith said. "You can check with your repairman, Curly. He's the one who told me."

"I will," Heather said. "I'll check with Emily and Trudy, too, when they come on for the night shift."

"Hey," Renie called out as Heather started into the hall, "what about me? I'm famished."

"That's too bad," Heather said. She looked apologetic, but kept on moving into the hall and out of sight.

"Great," Renie said in disgust. "I can't believe they don't have a lousy ham sandwich."

"You have about ten pounds of food over there," Judith said. "You won't starve."

"I wanted some meat," Renie said. "I don't have any meat."

"You'll live," Judith said, "which is more than I can say for some of the other patients. At least we found out that Margie Randall brought that juice to Joaquin Somosa. The next question is, who brought it to the hospital?"

Renie scowled at Judith. "I thought the next question would be, what was in the juice?"

Judith stared at her cousin. "You're right. That should be the next question. Why weren't those vessels, as Margie might call them, tested for drugs? Joan Fremont's Italian sodas, Joaquin Somosa's juice, Bob Randall's Wild Turkey—why weren't the residues checked?"

Renie shrugged. "How do you know they weren't?"

Judith stared even harder. "You're right. We don't. Maybe they were, maybe that's how those reports about illicit drugs came about." Briefly, she chewed on her lower lip. "Then again, maybe the residues weren't there to test."

"You're not making sense," Renie remarked.

Judith gave her cousin an ironic look. "Nothing about this case makes sense."

Renie nodded faintly. "I know. That's what scares me."

Judith said nothing. But of course she agreed.

TWELVE

UNFORTUNATELY, BOTH JUDITH and Renie began to suffer considerable pain as the afternoon wore on. Renie pressed the buzzer again, summoning Heather, who explained to the cousins that they were both hurting more because their anesthetic had almost worn off.

"It stays in your system for twelve to thirty-six hours," Heather said. "I'll get some pain medication to make you more comfortable."

"Thanks," Judith said as she tried to move around in the bed to find a less bothersome position. "My back aches more than my hip."

Heather nodded and left the ward. Judith's phone rang a moment later. It was Joe, and he sounded brusque.

"I'm going to try to get out this afternoon," he said, "so maybe I can stop by the hospital later on."

"You're going out?" Judith said in surprise. "How come?"

"Just business," he said. "I put the chains on your Subaru. I don't like to chain up the MG."

"Where are you going on business?" Judith asked, concern surfacing.

"Just routine," Joe replied.

Judith knew when to quit pushing her husband for answers. Instead, she switched to a different sort of question. "How's Phyliss?"

"Fine." Joe's tone lightened a bit. "The medics hung around for a while to make sure she was all right. I think she converted one of them."

"What about Ernest?"

"Ernest? Oh—the snake."

"Yes?"

"I'm sure Ernest is fine."

"*Where* is Ernest?" Judith asked in a stern voice.

"Somewhere," Joe answered, far too breezily. "Got to run or I'll be late for my appointment."

Judith stared into the receiver as Joe rang off. "He's keeping something from me," she declared.

"Like what?" Renie inquired, her face a mask of misery. "A cache of opium?"

"I don't know," Judith said. "But whatever it is, it's important enough to get him to chain up the Subaru and go out in this snow."

Wincing, Renie looked out the window, which was partly frosted over. "It's not snowing now, hasn't been all morning. Joe's like Bill. They know how to drive in it."

"True," Judith conceded as Heather returned with their pain medication.

"No ham sandwich?" Renie asked hopefully. "It'd make a nice chaser for the painkiller."

But Heather had only Demerol, which provided some relief. But not much. Half an hour later, Renie buzzed again for the nurse.

"This stuff's not as good as Excedrin," Renie complained. "Or are you giving it to us with an eye-dropper?"

"Well . . ." Heather studied the charts. "I could boost it slightly."

"Boost away," Renie ordered.

Judith waved a hand. "I could use some more, too. Really, I'm not a baby. I've had plenty of pain these last few weeks while I was waiting for my surgery."

Heather complied. As she was leaving, the cousins heard a loud voice out in the hall.

". . . and your sports reporters stink, too! They always have and they always will." Jan Van Boeck strode past the door, still red in the face.

"What was that all about?" Judith asked of Renie.

"Van Boeck must have been talking to Addison Kirby," she replied. "The good doctor seems to be in a really foul mood today."

At that moment, Mr. Mummy showed up at the door. "Knock-knock," he said in his cheerful voice, "may I come in?"

"Sure," Renie replied. "Where've you been? We haven't seen you all day."

"Physical therapy," Mr. Mummy said, moving awkwardly with his walking cast. "I had to wait there for some time and then it was quite a long session. How are my favorite lady patients doing today?"

"Stinko," Renie said. "They're certainly cheap about giving pain medication. It must be priced like caviar, so much per ounce. In fact, it probably is—those pharmaceutical companies are greedy."

"Medical professionals don't want patients to get addicted," Mr. Mummy said, angling himself into Judith's visitor's chair. "You know what kind of problems that can cause."

"Of course," Renie responded, eyeing the IV bag with displeasure. "But isn't pain medication supposed to relieve pain? And so these medical morons really believe that middle-aged women such as my cousin and me are going to succumb to a sudden addiction? That's ridiculous. And it's not good medicine."

"Dear me," said Mr. Mummy, pushing his glasses farther up on his nose. "You're quite upset, Mrs. Jones. Have you expressed your feelings to your doctor?"

"I haven't seen Dr. Ming since he came by this morning, before I started to hurt this much," Renie said, becoming crabbier by the minute. "I think I'll start screaming soon if this pain doesn't ease up. How about you, coz?"

"Not so hot," Judith replied, lifting her head to look at their visitor. "How do you feel, Mr. Mummy? Is pain a problem for you?"

"Ah . . . Not too much," he said, looking down at his cast. "It wasn't a terribly bad break."

"I thought it was fractured in several places," Renie said.

"Well . . . yes, it was," Mr. Mummy agreed, giving the cousins a diffident smile. "But they weren't *severe* fractures. Tell me, did you speak with Mr. Randall's children this morning?"

Judith noted the swift change of subject, but let it go. "Yes, Nancy and Bob Jr. stopped by. Have you met them?"

"Not exactly," Mr. Mummy answered. "I'd like to, to convey my condolences. Their mother seems a trifle . . . ineffective. I hope the young people are more able to cope."

"Dubious," said Renie.

Mr. Mummy nodded slowly. "Yes. I suppose they're like the children of many successful parents—spoiled, lacking incentive or ambition of their own."

"Something like that," said Renie. "Okay, I'm going to scream now."

She did, loud, piercing shrieks that alarmed Mr. Mummy and annoyed Judith. At the same time, Renie banged the buzzer against the bed to make the light outside in the hall flash on and off.

"Dear me," said Mr. Mummy, leaning closer to Judith so he could be heard, "is she really in that much pain?"

"Maybe," Judith allowed. "I know I feel pretty rotten. It's impossible to get comfortable."

Heather arrived looking disconcerted. Jan Van Boeck was right behind her, frowning deeply.

"What's this?" he demanded, his bass voice bouncing off the walls.

Renie stopped screaming. "It's suffering. Recognize it?"

Dr. Van Boeck's face reddened with anger. "You're exaggerating. No one in real pain could make such a noise."

"Wrong." Renie glared at the chief of staff. "I can. I'll do it again, to prove the point." She let out a mighty yelp.

"Close that door!" Dr. Van Boeck commanded Heather. "See here, Mrs. . . ." He faltered, and Renie stopped yelling.

"Jones, Serena Jones," Renie retorted. "And don't you forget it, buster."

Judith thought Dr. Van Boeck looked as if he might explode. It was all she could do to not cower under the blankets and pretend she'd never seen Renie before in her life. Instead, she summoned up her courage, and, as usual, attempted to act as peacemaker.

"Dr. Van Boeck," she said in a not-quite-steady

voice, "please excuse my cousin. She really does feel awful, and I don't feel much better myself. The staff here seems very chary with the pain medicine."

Dr. Van Boeck scowled at Judith. "Are you questioning our medical expertise?" he asked in a gruff tone.

"She's questioning your common sense," Renie broke in, "of which you people seem to have very little. What the hell is the point of allowing patients to feel miserable? How can we sleep? How can we assume the proper attitude toward recovery? If you want to keep up your little charade about your concern for patients, why don't you just shoot us after we come out of surgery and be done with it? Or," Renie went on, her eyes narrowing, "is that more or less what happened with Somosa, Fremont, and Randall?"

Dr. Van Boeck's face had turned purple. Apparently, the commotion had attracted the attention of other staff members. The silent orderly, a nurse Judith didn't recognize, and Peter Garnett crowded in the doorway.

"You miserable creature!" Dr. Van Boeck shouted at Renie, and then choked. He grabbed his throat and staggered, bumping into Mr. Mummy in the visitor's chair.

"What is this?" Dr. Garnett demanded, rushing into the room. "Jan, what's wrong?"

Dr. Van Boeck turned to look at Garnett, tried to speak, clutched his right arm, and crashed to the floor.

"Good lord!" Garnett cried, and kneeled beside his colleague. "Quick, get help! I think he's had a stroke!"

Heather and the other nurse ran off. Mr. Mummy, looking pale, put a hand to his chest. The silent orderly stood like a statue, watching the little scene on the floor.

"Oh, dear," said Renie in dismay.

"Are you okay?" Judith whispered to Mr. Mummy.

He nodded. "Yes. Yes, but this is . . . terrible." Clumsily, he got out of the chair. "I'd better leave." He bustled out of the room.

Despite all the confusion, Judith noticed that Mr. Mummy wasn't limping.

Five minutes later, Jan Van Boeck had been removed from the room. Judith hadn't been able to tell exactly what kind of emergency measures the frantic staff members had applied, but another doctor, Father McConnaught, and Sister Jacqueline had also shown up. Few words were exchanged, except for terse directions from Dr. Garnett. Then everyone was gone and the cousins were left staring at each other.

"I feel awful," Renie said, shrinking back into the pillows.

"Well . . ." Judith was at a loss for words. "I guess you should. Maybe."

"Maybe?" Renie brightened a bit.

"I really doubt if your little horror show caused Dr. Van Boeck's collapse," Judith said carefully. "A perfectly ordinary man wouldn't have gotten that upset. He'd have just blown you off or walked out. But he must have been on the edge in the first place. You can't be the first patient who ever had a tantrum at Good Cheer. Just think of all the genuinely crazy people who must have been in and out of this hospital over the years."

Renie looked perturbed. "Are you saying I'm not genuine?"

Judith grinned at her cousin. "You know what I mean. But you definitely hit a nerve with Van Boeck.

Remember, he was yelling at somebody out in the hall, probably Addison Kirby, and he certainly didn't look very happy when he came out of the staff lounge a while ago. I still think he had a row with Dr. Garnett."

"They don't seem to get along," Renie noted. "It's a wonder Garnett tried to save Van Boeck."

"He has to," Judith said, wishing the effort to converse didn't exacerbate the pain. "The Hippocratic Oath."

"Uh-huh," Renie said in a thoughtful voice. "So maybe I just sort of gave him a little nudge. I still feel terrible about it. Besides, we never got our pain medication. I don't hurt any less just because Van Boeck had a fit."

"True enough," Judith sighed. "Neither do I. In fact, I feel worse. By the way, did you notice that Mr. Mummy wasn't limping when he left?"

"I couldn't see him with all those people blocking my view." Renie gave Judith a curious look. "No limp, huh? Interesting. I wonder what he's doing here."

"So do I," Judith said as Heather came into the room.

"I've brought your pain medication," she said in a voice that was chilly with disapproval. "Maybe it will settle you down." She gave Renie a hard look.

"Thanks," Renie said meekly. "How's Dr. Van Boeck?"

"I don't know," Heather replied, her mouth in a straight line. "He's in the OR."

"Goodness." Renie lay very still.

"His wife has been sent for," Heather added. Her tone seemed to indicate that Renie should feel even guiltier for alarming the illustrious Blanche Van Boeck.

Renie, however, remained silent. Heather moved on
to Judith's IV. "You're certain you need more Demerol?" the nurse asked.

"I am," Judith said. "If anything, I hurt worse right
now than I did an hour ago."

Heather gave a little sniff, but added another dose.
"That ought to do it for both of you," she said, sounding stern.

"I'll bet," Renie said after the nurse had left, "that
the little twit has never had more than a headache. I
don't get it. Medical practitioners don't seem to give a
hoot for the patient's comfort. Do they really prefer to
listen to us gripe?"

"I suspect a lot of people don't gripe," Judith said.
"They suffer in silence, they're too shy to ask, they're
intimidated by the staff, especially the doctors."

"Phooey," said Renie, digging into her grocery bag.
"Snack?"

"No, thanks." Judith looked askance at her cousin,
who apparently didn't feel sufficient guilt to have lost
her appetite.

For a few minutes, Judith lay back against the pillows, hoping the Demerol would start to work. Little by
little, the worst of the pain seemed to ebb. At last she
picked up the family tree and sighed.

"I think I'll call Mother," she said.

"You're procrastinating," Renie accused, smearing
Brie on a water wafer.

"No, I'm not. I mean, I can't do much about
Kristin's family because I don't know all their names."
Judith shot Renie a self-righteous look and dialed
Gertrude's number.

For once, the old lady answered on the third ring.
"Who *is* this?" she growled. "You selling something?"

"It's me, Mother," Judith said wearily. "How are you?"

" '*Mother*'? I don't have any kids," Gertrude snapped. "Is this some kind of joke?"

"Please," Judith begged, "don't tease me. I'm not feeling real good right now."

"So who is? You want a list of my ailments? Is that what you're peddling? Home remedies? I'll take a half-dozen. You want me to pay for it with my credit card?"

"You don't have a credit card, Mother," Judith said. "You don't believe in them."

"I have one now," Gertrude declared. "I've bought a bunch of stuff the last couple of days, right off the TV. They sell all kinds of doodads and whatnots. '*Act now,*' they said, so I did."

Judith was puzzled. Until she suddenly became worried. "Where did you get that credit card?"

"I don't remember," Gertrude said, her voice an octave higher than usual. "Maybe I found it."

"Have you got it there on your card table?" Judith asked, sounding stern.

"Maybe. Maybe not. I'm old. I forget."

"That's *my* credit card," Judith asserted. "I left it on the kitchen counter Sunday night because I remembered to pay the cable bill by phone before I went into the hospital. I was distracted, I didn't put it away. Mother, promise you won't use the card again?"

" '*Act now,*' " said Gertrude. "That's what they say on TV."

"Mother . . ."

"What did you say you were selling? Elixirs? Snake oil?"

"I didn't say . . ."

"Speaking of which, I'm seeing snakes. One just ate my sandwich. Where did he go? He's kind of cute. Oof!" It sounded as if Gertrude had dropped the phone.

"Are you there, Mother?" Judith asked, growing anxious.

There was a rustling noise before Gertrude spoke again. "I'm here. Not all there, maybe, but I'm here. Now where'd that snake go? He'd better not eat my custard pudding. I'm hanging up now."

Gertrude did just that.

"Honestly," Judith groaned, "I don't know when Mother is putting me on and when she really doesn't know what's going on. You wouldn't figure she'd fool around when I'm laid up in the hospital, would you?"

"Sure I would," Renie said. "She's jealous. You're too young to be in the hospital, that's how she thinks. Or she's into denial. If anything happens to you, your mother is sunk."

"If I stick around here long enough, I'm going to end up as depressed as Margie Randall," Judith asserted. "How many more days? Three, four, even more?"

"For you, maybe," Renie responded, using a Kleenex to wipe off her hands. "I'm out of here day after tomorrow."

"Don't remind me," Judith said. "When you leave, I'll be in despair."

"Despair?" Father McConnaught was standing in the door, his old face evincing disbelief. "Not that, my child. 'Tis a sin. Our dear Lord came to give us hope, even in death."

Judith forced a smile. "It was a turn of phrase, Father. I'm usually an optimistic person."

Clasping his hands behind his back, the old priest shuffled into the room. "Despair—they often call it depression, these modern folk, and hand out pretty pink tablets—is the spiritual cancer of our age. Not all the electric lights and neon signs can dispel the gloom. Such a waste." He shook his head, but his eyes twinkled. It occurred to Judith that the old priest didn't seem quite so vague this afternoon. "Such a pity," he added, the wisps of hair standing straight up on his head.

"All I want is a ham sandwich," Renie said.

Judith winced at her cousin's remark, but Father McConnaught smiled. "A simple pleasure. But the getting of things—even a ham sandwich—isn't as grand as the giving. Giving up, letting go, surrendering. There's the beauty of it." His gaze wandered around the room with its plaster cracks, its peeling paint, its scarred wood. His eyes lingered briefly over the holy statues, but finally they came to rest on Archie the doll. "See that little fellow? He's happy. He has nothing but that big smile."

"He has a suitcase," Renie said, pointing to the small brown box on the nightstand.

Father McConnaught's face evinced curiosity. "And what might be in that little case?"

Renie smiled at the priest. "It's empty."

"Ah. Of course." Father McConnaught turned around, his gnarled fingers twisting behind his back. "They won't listen, these sad, empty souls. That's why Dr. Van Boeck made himself ill."

"Oh?" Judith sat up straighter. The Demerol seemed to be working. Or maybe it was Father McConnaught's presence.

The priest nodded. "He can't let go. None of them can. Not even Sister Jacqueline."

"Let go?" Judith echoed. "Of what?"

Father McConnaught spread his hands. "Of this. The hospital. Their life's work. A hundred years of the order's dedication. The sisters think it's wasted. But it's not, and even so, nothing is forever in this life. We own nothing, we belong nowhere. Except to God."

"Then Good Cheer is . . . doomed?" Judith wrinkled her nose at the melodramatic word.

"Not precisely," Father McConnaught replied. "That is, it won't be torn down or turned into a hotel." He smiled again at the cousins, but his blue eyes had lost their twinkle. "I don't understand it, I don't wish to, don't you see. But it's all very upsetting for those who work here, and it should not be so. It's all transitory, isn't it?"

As if to prove his point, Father McConnaught shuffled off into the hall.

"Goodness," Judith said. "That sounds bad. If the old guy knows what he's talking about."

"I think he does," Renie said slowly. "Most of the time. Restoration Heartware, remember?"

"A takeover?" Judith sighed. "That's really a shame. For all of Father's spiritual advice—not that he's wrong—it's still hard for the people involved. Even a stuffed shirt like Jan Van Boeck. I wonder if he's going to be okay?"

The question was answered in a surprising way. Five minutes later, Blanche Van Boeck stormed into the cousins' room. "You!" she shouted, pointing at Renie. "You almost killed my husband!"

"Oh, boy," Renie muttered. "Almost? As in, he's not really dead?"

Blanche, who was swathed in fox and wearing a silver turban, advanced on Renie. "Listen, you little pest,

I can have you thrown out of this hospital, right into a snowbank. What do you think of that?"

"I think you wouldn't dare," Renie shot back, looking pugnacious. "There's a reporter in the next room who'd plaster that all over page one of the next edition."

"He wouldn't dare!" Blanche shouted, waving a kid-glove-encased fist. "He's incommunicado."

"What do you mean?" Renie demanded. "I saw him on the phone this morning."

A nasty smile played at Blanche's crimson lips. "He was *trying* to talk on the phone," she said, "but his line's been shut off. Do you think we'd allow a viper in our midst?"

"I thought Mr. Kirby was a patient," Judith remarked in an unassuming voice.

Standing next to Renie's bed, Blanche ignored Judith. "I should sue you for almost killing my husband. He's not out of the woods yet."

"The woods?" Renie was round-eyed. "Is that where they take patients around here? No wonder so many of them croak."

Trying to signal Renie to keep her mouth shut, Judith was fighting a losing battle. Blanche's large form and even larger fur coat blocked Renie's view of her cousin.

"You haven't heard the last of this," Blanche warned, her arm pumping up and down. "I'm personally seeing to it that you're discharged as soon as possible. Then expect to hear from my attorneys." She turned on her high-heeled boots and started to leave the room.

"Wait," Judith said plaintively. "Please."

"What?" Blanche snapped.

"What did happen with Dr. Van Boeck? Was it a stroke?" Judith asked, hoping she exhibited sympathy.

"Not precisely," Blanche replied, finally lowering her voice. "He was . . . overcome. They took him to the OR merely as a precaution. My husband suffers from high blood pressure. His medication needs adjusting. But," she went on, whirling around to look at Renie again, "it was a very near thing. That doesn't let you off the hook."

Blanche Van Boeck stalked out.

"Dammit," Renie cried, "that woman *will* sue me. She's just that ornery."

"She won't win," Judith said. "She admitted that Dr. Van Boeck has a preexisting condition."

"Bill and I don't need the aggravation," Renie declared, then frowned. "I can't stop thinking about Bill and those Chihuahuas. What do you think he's doing?"

"Call him, ask," Judith suggested.

Renie shook her head. "You know how Bill hates to talk on the phone. He doesn't answer it most of the time. I'll wait until he calls me."

"He's probably just amusing himself," Judith said. "He's housebound, you're not around, the kids may be getting on his nerves."

"Maybe." Renie, however, was still frowning. "When I went to see Addison Kirby this morning, he didn't mention that he couldn't use his phone."

"He may have just thought the system was fouled up," Judith said. "You know, the weather and all."

"Yes," Renie said absently as Mr. Mummy again poked his head in the door.

"I thought I'd see if you two were all right," he said, looking worried. "You've had a lot of commotion in the last hour. I saw Mrs. Van Boeck. Did she say how her husband was doing?"

"Tolerably," Renie replied as Mr. Mummy limped into the room on his cast. "As near as I can tell, he blew a gasket."

Mr. Mummy seemed mystified, but smiled. "Mrs. Van Boeck appeared quite disturbed. Was she upset about her husband?"

"She was upset with me," Renie said. "She's going to sue me for causing her husband to have a fit. But it really wasn't my fault."

"Of course not," Mr. Mummy soothed, approaching the foot of Renie's bed. "I'm sure Dr. Van Boeck is under a great deal of stress. Why, just running such a large institution would take its toll on anyone."

"Or being married to Blanche Van Boeck," Renie muttered. "I wonder how he stands her."

"An interesting question," Mr. Mummy said, tipping his head to one side. "Yes, she must sometimes be a trial. Now which would you think would be worse? A rather overbearing woman such as Blanche Van Boeck or a helpless, dispirited creature like Margie Randall?"

"Goodness," Judith said, "that *is* a conundrum."

"Mere observation," Mr. Mummy responded. "I've seen them both, and I wonder which is more difficult for the husband. Of course, in Mr. Randall's situation, he's beyond all that. Then again, perhaps Mrs. Van Boeck spoke kindly of her spouse when she was here a few minutes ago?"

"Kindly?" Renie made a face. "She was mostly mad at me, for—allegedly—making him foam at the mouth or whatever."

"At you, eh?" Mr. Mummy beamed at Renie. "Dear Mrs. Jones, I don't see how you could ever annoy anyone." Apparently, Mr. Mummy didn't notice Judith choking on her water, for he continued. "Are you certain she didn't blame . . . someone else?"

"Quite certain," Renie replied firmly. "I'm the villain."

"Oh" Mr. Mummy looked vaguely disappointed, perhaps in Mrs. Van Boeck's judgment. He made a little bow. "I should be going on my way. You've had a tiring afternoon. Perhaps I'll call on Mr. Kirby. The days here are so long when you can't be particularly active."

Their visitor began his laborious exit, but before he could get out the door, Judith had a question:

"What do you do for a living when you're not laid up, Mr. Mummy?"

He turned slightly, though his gaze didn't quite meet Judith's. "I'm a beekeeper," he said, then chuckled. "Buzz, buzz."

"A beekeeper, huh?" Renie said after Mr. Mummy had disappeared. "Do you believe that?"

"It's so unusual that maybe I do," Judith said. "He would definitely have to live out in the country to raise bees."

Renie's phone rang, and this time it was her mother. Judith was trying to tune out the conversation when a hulking physical therapist named Henry arrived and announced that he was going to teach her to walk.

"I thought Heather was going to let me sit in the wheelchair again," Judith protested. "I really don't think—"

On the phone, Renie was trying to get a word in edgewise. "There really isn't a draft through the windows, Mom. I couldn't put a coat on over my sling if I had . . ."

Henry snapped his fingers. "You don't need to think. It's better that you don't."

"Truly, none of the doctors have gotten fresh," Renie was insisting. "No, I haven't seen any white slavers . . ."

"But," Judith began, involuntarily shrinking back among the pillows, "it's only been two days since—"

"That's the point, ma'am," Henry said, beckoning to Judith. "Come on, sit up, let's get you moving."

"Who did you say impersonated a doctor?" Renie sounded incredulous. "Well, sometimes a veterinarian knows more about medicine than . . . Yes, I know there's a difference between a man and a squirrel. Usually."

"No, there isn't any difference," Henry said with a solemn expression. "They both have nuts. Come on, Mrs. Flynn, be brave."

Renie shot Henry a withering glance. Judith shut her eyes tight, then attempted to sit up and swing her legs over the side of the bed. Henry held on to her forearms. It occurred to Judith that she didn't feel dizzy this time, only weak. She took a step. Two. Three. Henry slowly released her. Judith took a final step on her own.

"Oh!" she exclaimed. "I did it!"

"Two more," Henry urged. "Then you can go for a nice ride." He pulled the wheelchair just out of her reach.

Judith expected to wilt, but she didn't. Hesitantly, cautiously, she took the extra steps, then sank into the chair. "I'll be darned," she breathed.

"You know how to run this thing?" Henry inquired.

Judith nodded. "I was confined to a wheelchair for some time before I had the surgery."

"Good." He released the brake. "Hit the road, Mrs. Flynn. You're on your own. Come back before it gets dark."

Judith eyed the hallway as if it were the open road. *Freedom,* she thought. Sort of.

But she didn't go far. Mr. Mummy blocked her way as he came racing out of Addison Kirby's room.

"If I ever see you again," Addison was shouting, "I'll kill you! So help me God!"

Trying to avoid Mr. Mummy, Judith steered the wheelchair to the left, but Robbie the Robot was heading straight toward her. She reversed, bumped into a laundry cart, and spun out of control.

"Help!" Judith cried.

But the only response was from Robbie the Robot.

"Beep, beep," he uttered, and kept on going.

THIRTEEN

THE WHEELCHAIR SAILED into Addison Kirby's room and bumped up against his visitor's chair. The journalist, whose broken leg was in traction, looked apoplectic.

"What the hell . . . ?" Addison shouted. "Get out, get out!"

"I can't," Judith shouted. "I've lost control." Having come to a stop, she braced herself, trying to determine if the mishap had done any damage to the hip replacement. To her relief, there was no new pain. She offered Addison a piteous look. "I'm so sorry. This wheelchair must be broken."

Addison's features softened a bit. "I didn't recognize you right away. You're Judith Flynn from next door, right?"

Collecting herself, Judith nodded. "Yes." She paused to take some deep breaths. "It was my cousin, Mrs. Jones, who saw the car that hit you. Do you have any idea who was driving it?"

Addison grimaced. "Unfortunately, no. I barely saw the car. It was one of those mid-sized models, kind of beige or tan. It all happened so fast. Has your cousin given a formal statement yet?" Addison inquired.

"Not in writing," Judith said, finally managing to get the wheelchair into a more convenient position.

Addison snorted. "I'm not surprised."

Judith looked at the journalist with shrewd eyes. "Part of the cover-up?"

"Is that what you call it?" Addison looked at her, a quirky expression on his face.

"I'm beginning to think so," Judith replied. "You think so, too. Does it have something to do with Restoration Hcartware's attempt at a takeover?"

Addison uttered a sharp little laugh. "You're no slouch when it comes to figuring things out, are you, Mrs. Flynn?"

"Call me Judith. Figuring things out is about all I can do while I'm lying around in bed," she asserted.

Addison's dark eyes narrowed slightly. "Do you own a B&B on Heraldsgate Hill?"

"Ohmigod." Judith, who knew what was coming next, felt the color rise in her cheeks.

"You got some publicity on TV a while ago," Addison said. "There was a murder at an old apartment house not far from where you live. But if I remember correctly, it wasn't the first time you'd been involved in crime-solving."

"That's true," Judith said, "but it was an accident. They were all accidents. I mean," she went on, getting flustered, "I don't seek out homicide cases. I just sort of stumble into them. I guess it has something to do with my work. I meet so many people, and some of them aren't very nice."

The understatement didn't seem to convince Addison. "The buzz around city hall was that you had an uncanny knack for fingering killers. I've read about detectives, both real and fictitious, who could pick out a murderer just from the way they looked. How do you do it? Shape of the head? Look in the eyes? Manner of speaking?"

"Nothing like that," Judith said modestly. "I'm interested in people. They talk to me. I listen. And often, they make some tiny slip that gives them away." She shrugged. "It's not a talent. It's just . . . paying attention."

Again, Addison seemed to regard Judith with skepticism. "Your husband's a cop, isn't he? Joe Flynn, very sharp. I remember him from my beat at city hall. Hasn't he retired?"

"Yes," Judith answered. "He's a private investigator now."

Addison merely smiled. Judith decided to change the subject. "Why were you so angry with Mr. Mummy just now? He seems like a harmless little guy."

"Does he?" Addison shifted his shoulders, apparently trying to get more comfortable. "You don't find him . . . suspicious?"

"Ah . . ." Judith wondered how candid she could be with Addison Kirby. "I have to admit, I've wondered why he was transferred into Good Cheer. His fractures don't seem very severe."

"Exactly." Addison suddenly seemed to grow distant. Perhaps he had doubts of his own about confiding in Judith. "He's a real snoop."

"Curiosity," Judith said. "He's bored, too. Did he tell you he's a beekeeper by trade?"

"No." Addison stroked his beard. "Interesting."

"Different," Judith allowed.

"Yes," Addison said quickly, "that's what I meant."

Judith gave Addison a questioning look, but he didn't amplify his comment. "You've had a rather rigorous day so far," she finally said. "I happened to hear Dr. Van Boeck shouting by your door. I hope he didn't upset you."

"He didn't." Addison looked pleased with himself. "He's one of those professional types who hates the media. Most doctors don't like criticism—the godlike ego and all that tripe. Doctors and lawyers are the worst. CEOs are up there, too, except most of them are too dumb to understand the news stories. That's why they hire PR types—to translate for them."

"Does Dr. Van Boeck have a specific gripe?" Judith inquired.

Addison chuckled. "Dozens of them, going back to his football playing days. He actually played pro ball, for the Sea Auks."

"I know," Judith said. "He backed up Bob Randall for a season or two before he washed out of football."

Addison cast Judith an admiring glance. "So you know about that? Well, Van Boeck has never forgiven the sportswriters for criticizing his ineptitude. He might have good hands for a surgeon, but he sure as hell didn't have them for handling the ball. The irony, of course, is that Mrs. Van Boeck uses the media to great effect."

"And tries to manipulate it as well?" Judith put in.

"That, too," Addison said, looking grim.

The conversation was interrupted by the arrival of Jim Randall, who walked straight into the coat closet's sliding doors.

"Ooof!" he cried, staggering. "Sorry. Am I interrupting?" He peered first at Addison, then at Judith. "You have a guest. I can't quite see who . . ."

Judith hastily identified herself. "From next door, remember?"

"Oh." Jim nodded as he carefully moved closer. "Yes, we spoke. I just came to let Mr. Kirby know when the funeral for my brother will be held. He's going to put it in the newspaper for me."

"Since I can't call from here, I'll have a nurse phone it into the obit and sports desks," Addison said. "Have you written it out?"

Jim fumbled at an inside pocket in his overcoat. "It was a group effort. Margie, Nancy, Bob Jr., and me. Here." He handed several sheets of paper to Addison.

The handwriting was difficult to decipher. Addison was forced to read the verbiage aloud to make sure that everything was accurate. "You've hit the highlights of Bob's football career," he said to Jim, "except for the stats. One of the football reporters can fill those in for the sports page."

"Very illustrious," Judith remarked. "I'd forgotten how good Bob Randall really was."

Addison began reading the official obituary. " 'Robert Alfred Randall Sr., born Topeka, Kansas . . .' " He hurried through the factual information, then slowed down as he read the more personal copy written by the family members: " 'Bob, nicknamed Ramblin' Randall, and not just for his rushing feats on the football field . . .' " Addison frowned at Jim. "I don't get that part."

Through thick lenses that made his eyes look like oversized coat buttons, Jim peered at Addison. "What do you mean?"

"Okay," Addison said sharply, "this sounds like you're talking about your brother's off-the-field exploits. In particular, his love life."

Jim nodded once. "That's right."

Addison stared at Jim. "You can't do that. Nobody

ever criticizes the deceased in an obit. Upon occasion, they'll make excuses, especially if it's a suicide. But criticism—never."

Jim took umbrage. "I thought you dealt in facts. Isn't that what you told me the other day when we spoke? That's a fact—my brother was a philanderer. Margie had to put up with a lot. Read the rest of it."

"No." Addison's bearded jaw set stubbornly.

Judith leaned forward in the wheelchair, and before the journalist could realize what she was doing, she plucked the sheets of paper out of his hand.

"If it means so much to you, Jim," she said, looking sympathetic, "I'll go over it with you. During the years, I've helped write several obituaries for relatives."

"Hey!" Addison cried, attempting to retrieve the pages. "Don't do that!"

But Judith had managed to move herself just beyond Addison's reach. "Please, we must see what can be salvaged here, or the family will have to do it all over again."

Jim was hovering over Judith's shoulder. "Do you see the part where we said he drove Margie to depression? And ruined his children's lives?"

Judith did, and despite Addison's professional reservations, she read the sentences aloud:

" 'Bob Sr. was so selfish and self-absorbed that he could offer his wife of twenty-five years no sympathy or understanding, even when her emotional problems threatened to undermine her physical as well as her mental health. His legacy to his children is not that of a loving, caring father, but a cold, conceited athlete who demanded excellence from Nancy and Bob Jr. but who never gave them the slightest word of encouragement, much less any sign of real love. He will be missed by some of his cronies from the sports world, but not by his family.' " Judith was appalled, and could hardly blame Addison for looking outraged. But she'd had to know what was in the scurrilous obituary. "Here," she said, handing the sheets of paper back to Addison. "I agree. That's not printable."

"Then don't give that crap to me," Addison cried, batting at Judith's hand. "It belongs to Jim—or in the trash."

"But it's all true," Jim declared, sounding offended. "How could we lie about my brother? He was a wretched man."

"I thought," Judith said, frowning, "that you mentioned how Margie and the kids couldn't get along without him."

"They can't," Jim replied with a helpless shrug as he took the obituary from Judith. "Bob made good money as a football consultant. Now all they'll have is what he left in the bank."

"Which," Addison sneered, "is considerable, I'd bet."

Jim shrugged again. "It's fairly substantial. But Bob didn't play in the era of million-dollar contracts. And he tended to spend much of what he made. On himself, of course. He had it all, in more ways than one. As if," Jim added, tearing the obituary into small pieces that fluttered to the floor, "he didn't have enough to begin with. All that talent and a fine physique and good looks besides." Defiantly, he flung the final pieces of paper onto the floor.

"Frankly," Judith asserted, "he sounds like a pitiful sort of person. I can't imagine he was truly happy."

"Oh, he was very happy," Jim said bitterly. "I never

knew a man who was as happy as he was. As long as he got his way, which he usually did."

"Look," Addison said, his aggravation spent, "I'm sorry I can't send on that obit. Why don't you write another draft with just the facts? Plenty of people don't tack on personal notes. Remember, on the obituary page you're paying for it by the word."

"I am? I mean, we are?" Jim fingered his chin. "I'll tell Margie. I don't think she knows that." He started for the door.

"Say," Judith called after him, "may I ask you a question?"

Jim looked apprehensive. "Yes?"

"Your nephew, Bob Jr., mentioned that his mother—Margie—felt like 'the vessel' in terms of bringing on the deaths of your brother, Mr. Kirby's wife, and Joaquin Somosa. Do you have any idea what Bob Jr. was talking about?"

Jim blinked several times and his hands twitched. "No. No idea. Whatsoever. Margie—as usual—is being hard on herself. Poor Margie." He sketched a little bow and dashed out of the room, narrowly missing a collision with Dr. Garnett.

"I have some good news for you," the doctor said to Jim as both men proceeded down the hall and out of hearing range.

Judith turned to Addison. "I'm sorry I had to bring that up about Margie being a vessel. Did you know that your wife had two Italian sodas the morning that she passed away?"

"No." Addison's voice was hushed. "Are you sure? They were her favorites, but no one told me about it."

"No one tells anyone about anything around here, right?"

"Right." Addison looked sour. "How did she get them?"

"I have no idea," Judith admitted, "other than that apparently Margie Randall took them to her. I just happened to hear a chance remark from one of the nurses."

Addison nodded. "Otherwise, a wall of silence. Do you know what happened today? Dr. Van Boeck informed the front desk I wasn't to have any visitors. That's because they must be afraid one of my colleagues in the media will try to see me. I can't call out on my phone, either. That's why I couldn't call in the obit myself." He gestured toward the floor on the other side of the bed. "You probably can't see it from your wheelchair, but at least four people have tried to visit me today, including my editor. All they could do was leave me their get-well gifts and go home. Imagine, after going to the trouble of coming out in this snow."

Judith made an extra effort to steer the wheelchair around the end of Addison's bed without bumping him. His position in traction temporarily made her stop feeling sorry for herself.

"Oh," she said, making the final maneuver without mishap, "I see. That's all very nice. Lovely chocolates, a crossword puzzle magazine, a couple of other books I can't make out, and a bag of black jelly beans."

"I love black jelly beans," Addison declared. "I won't eat any of the other kinds. Do you think you could reach them? I'm not much of a chocolate fan, though. I'd give that box to the nurses, but the whole damned staff makes me angry. Do you want them?"

Judith tried to edge closer to the stack of presents. "I'll take the chocolates, but are you sure you want to eat those jelly beans?"

Addison gave a small shrug, which was all his posture permitted. "Why not?"

Judith didn't dare bend down far enough to pick up the cellophane bag with its bright blue and yellow ribbons. "Well , , what if they've been . . . interfered with?"

"My God." Addison breathed. "So that's how you think Joan and the others died? My money was on the IVs."

"It's possible," Judith said, just managing to pick up the chocolate box, which was on top of the books. "Using an IV to administer some kind of deadly dose would be trickier, unless the killer is a medical professional. Which is also possible, of course."

"If you believe in the poisoned-present theory, why are you taking that candy?" he asked, looking suspicious.

"I don't intend to eat it," Judith said. "I'm going to have my husband get it analyzed. He's a retired cop, remember?"

"Hunh." Addison's gaze turned shrewd. "Good idea. Take the jelly beans, too."

"I can't reach them," Judith admitted. "I have to be very careful about bending with this hip replacement. If I lean or reach, it could dislocate without warning." She stopped speaking to examine the cellophane bag. "The jelly beans look okay, they seemed tightly sealed. Maybe you can get them to me later. But if they're one of your favorite things and somebody knows that, I wouldn't take any chances."

"I won't," Addison responded, looking grim. "Maybe I *will* offer those to the staff. If anybody turns me down, I might get an inkling of the culprit's identity."

"You might also poison some innocent people," Judith warned.

"I might." Addison's brown eyes were hard. "Frankly, it'd be worth it if I could find out who killed my wife. I'm not in a merciful mood."

"Chocolates!" Renie exclaimed after Judith had related the details of her visit next door. "Yum!"

"Forget it," Judith said, placing both hands on the gold-foil box. "This little present for Addison Kirby just might prove fatal." Cautiously wheeling herself to the bedside stand, she slipped the chocolates into the drawer, then explained the situation to Renie.

"What if our night thief comes back and swipes the candy box?" Renie inquired when Judith had finished her account of the visit with Addison and Jim Randall.

"Let's face it," Judith said, wondering if she could get back in bed by herself, "we don't know if that was a homicidal thief—or just a thief."

"True." Renie said. "Hey—you need some help?"

"Could you buzz?" Judith asked. "I don't want to undo anything."

"You can lean on me," Renie said, getting out of bed. "Haven't we each done quite a bit of leaning on each other for the past fifty-odd years?"

Judith smiled fondly at her cousin. "Closer than sisters," she murmured.

Renie stumbled over the commode. "Oops!" she cried, then swore.

"Are you okay, coz?" Judith asked in alarm.

"Yeah, yeah, I didn't really need ten toes. Here, I'll steady the wheelchair with my right hip and you lean on my left side."

To Judith's surprise, the tactic worked. Judith inched

her way onto the bed, sat on the edge to get her breath, then let Renie help her swing her legs onto the mattress. Lying back on the pillows, Judith closed her eyes and sighed.

"I can't believe how glad I was to get out of bed and go down the hall," she said with a feeble smile. "Now I can't believe how glad I am to get back into bed. I'm exhausted."

"I know," Renie said, heading back to her own bed. "These surgeries take a lot out of us. And, sorry to say, we aren't spring chickens anymore."

"I forgot to look out at the weather," Judith said. "What's it doing?"

"Nothing," Renie replied. "Dr. Ming stopped by while you were gone to tell me I could start PT tomorrow. He said the temperature had dropped down to eighteen degrees by four-thirty, but there was no snow in the forecast for tonight. There's black ice on the streets, and, as usual, our city's snow-removal crew—you know, the two guys with the truck, the buckets, and the shovels—hasn't been able to sand any streets except for the major thoroughfares."

Judith nodded faintly. "We get snow so seldom, sometimes not at all, that I guess the city doesn't feel it should spend money on something that might not be needed for a couple of years at a time." She looked at her watch. "I didn't realize how late it is. It's after five. I guess Joe wasn't able to make it to the hospital after all."

"At least you spoke with him," Renie said, irked. "I haven't heard a peep out of Bill all day. I know he hates the phone, but it wouldn't kill him to call and check in."

"Maybe he got involved in trying to find your car," Judith suggested.

"What's he doing?" Renie retorted. "Conducting a street-by-street search? Or is he too caught up with those damned Chihuahuas?"

Judith tried not to smile as she envisioned Bill teaching the dogs to dance. Or fetch. Or make his lunch.

"The phones might be out of order in some parts of town," Judith said, trying to soothe Renie. "If there's ice, the lines could be down. In fact, if Blanche Van Boeck wants to do something helpful for the city, she should advocate better weather preparedness. Do you really think she's going to run for mayor?"

Renie had turned listless. "Who knows? Who cares? Where's dinner? What *is* dinner? My Falstaff bag's getting low."

"Want to watch the news?" Judith asked in her most cheerful voice.

"No. I hate television news. Why can't we get an evening paper?"

"They may not be able to deliver it," Judith said, clicking on the TV. "Look, there's Mavis Lean-Brodie again."

"Why do we get only four channels on this stupid set? Why can't we get ESPN or Fox Sports so we could watch basketball?"

"Mavis looks like she's changed her hair color. It's much lighter. I like it."

"How can I find out who's heading for the NCAA tournament? What about our own drippy pro basketball team? Why don't I like hockey?"

"What's the other anchor's name? Tim Something-or-Other?"

"I like the violence in hockey. I just don't understand the game. And I never learned to ice-skate. I have weak ankles."

"They don't seem to be showing anything but the weather. Goodness, the city really is paralyzed."

"Without ESPN and Fox Sports, I can't even keep up with the Hot Stove League. How do I know which baseball players have been traded in the off-season? I might as well be in never-never land."

"Look at all the event cancellations. Oh, here come the school closures. Goodness, the entire public school district and the private schools are shut down for the duration."

Dinner arrived, courtesy of the silent orderly. Judith optimistically uncovered her entrée. It looked like some kind of cutlet.

Renie turned her back on the orderly and buried her head in the pillow. "Take it away. I can't eat things that look like high school science experiments."

The orderly set the tray on the nightstand and wordlessly walked out.

"This isn't bad," Judith said, tasting her entrée. "It's pork."

Renie didn't look up until her phone rang. "Now what?" she grumbled, yanking the receiver off the hook. "Bill!" she cried in surprise. "I thought you'd forgotten me. What's going on with Cammy?"

Her sudden pleasure turned to consternation. "Oh? That's rotten luck. But it can't be helped with all the snow, I guess . . . Yes, I'm sure they'll find the car eventually . . . I'm doing okay, I'm just sore and hungry . . . Because it's inedible, that's why. Say, what about those Chihuahuas?"

Judith watched her cousin closely, but Renie's face revealed only perplexity. "Well, you're the psychologist, so I guess you know what you're doing, but it sounds kind of loony to me. Don't you think the dogs'

owners would like them back? . . . Yes, I know, the
weather . . ." Renie heaved a big sigh. "The weather is
putting a crimp in everything, from finding our car to
seeing you and the kids . . . Friday, unless they throw
me out, which Blanche Van Boeck has threatened to
do . . . Never mind, it's a long story . . . You're *what?*"
Renie pulled a face, cradled the phone against her
shoulder, and made circular "he's nuts" motions with
her finger by her ear. "Anne can't sew any better than
I can. How could she and Tony make the damned dog
a Sea Auks uniform? Forget the dogs, how's everything else going?"

This time, Renie's face fell. She stared at Judith,
then turned away. "Really? That's not good." Her voice
sounded unnatural; she grew silent, listening intently.
"Yes . . . Yes . . . Yes . . . No. I wouldn't dream of it.
Let me know what happens. Love you. Bye." Renie
hung up and disappeared under the covers.

"What was that all about?" Judith asked. "At the
end, I mean."

"Nothing," Renie said in a muffled voice.

Judith, who had turned down the sound on the TV,
now turned off the set. "Is everything all right?"

"It's fine," Renie replied.

Judith stared at the mound that was her cousin.
"Look at me," she demanded.

"I don't feel good," Renie said. "Leave me alone."

"Coz." Judith's tone was stern, almost imperious.
"Get out from under there and talk to me. We don't
keep secrets from each other."

The mound didn't move. Judith set down her fork
and folded her arms across her breast. "This cutlet is
quite good. I thought you were starving."

"I'm not hungry," Renie mumbled.

Judith's sense of apprehension mounted. "Coz, this isn't funny. Talk to me or I'll . . ." She stopped, aware that there wasn't anything she could do to Renie except get angry or sulk.

At last Renie's head appeared from under the bedclothes. She propped herself up and regarded Judith with a pale, drawn face. "Please don't insist."

Judith felt something sink in the bottom of her stomach, and it wasn't the pork cutlet. "Out with it. I can't sit here and look at you look at me like that. You know it's impossible."

Shuddering, Renie faced Judith head-on. "You know Bill—how he has to build up to bad news in his careful, deliberate fashion. Finally, he told me Joe's been stabbed. He's been taken to the hospital, and his chances are fifty-fifty."

Judith passed out cold.

FOURTEEN

HEATHER CHINN CAME running. It wasn't Renie's insistent buzzer or even her horrified shrieks, but the sudden change in status on Judith's monitor at the nurses' station.

"What happened?" Heather asked in alarm, seeing Judith's unconscious figure and ashen face.

"She got some bad news," Renie replied. "She fainted."

Heather began chafing Judith's wrists and speaking to her in low, encouraging tones. Sister Jacqueline entered the room, followed by Dr. Garnett and another nurse, who wheeled in some sort of equipment. Renie clung to the edge of her bed, eyes wide, breathless.

"I didn't want to . . ." she moaned, but was ignored.

Judith's eyelids flickered open. "Ohhh . . ." She tried to recognize the pretty face with the almond-shaped eyes. It was someone she knew. Wearing white, with a cap. A nurse. She must have fainted during her labor. "The baby," she gasped. "Is he okay?"

Apparently, doctor, nurse, and nun weren't unfamiliar with Judith's type of reaction.

"Everything is fine, Mrs. Flynn," Dr. Garnett said in a soft but authoritative voice. "You've had hip surgery, remember?"

"Hip?" Judith was mystified. "What do you mean 'hip surgery'?"

Dr. Garnett signaled for the nurse to back off with the resuscitation equipment. "You had a hip replacement. What year is it, Mrs. Flynn?"

Judith looked down at the big dressing on her hip. "Then I didn't go into labor?"

"No," Dr. Garnett replied. "Dr. Alfonso replaced your right hip."

At last, Judith grasped the present and tried to sit bolt upright. But she fell back at once. "Joe!" she cried in a thin, reedy tone. "What happened to Joe?"

Dr. Garnett, who was wearing surgical scrubs, took in the puzzled looks of his colleagues.

"It's her husband," Renie said, some of the color returning to her ashen face. "He's had a very bad accident. Mrs. Flynn just found out about it. That's what made her faint."

All eyes were now on Renie. "If you don't mind, I'd rather not discuss it in front of everybody," she said firmly.

Sister Jacqueline was not put off, however. "Where is Mr. Flynn? Was he in a car accident?"

Renie was looking mulish, but Judith intervened. "For God's sake, coz, tell me. I don't care who knows what."

Renie flung out her good hand in a gesture of surrender. "Okay, okay. Joe found out this morning that another homeless man was murdered yesterday. He couldn't start investigating because of the weather, but he managed to get out this afternoon after he chained up your car."

Though Judith's gaze was riveted on Renie, she sensed that the two nurses and Sister Jacqueline were going into various states of shocked surprise. Renie never took her eyes off Judith, and continued speaking in her most businesslike voice: "Bill didn't know the details, but Joe headed out for a park two or three blocks from here, which was where the homeless people moved when it started snowing so hard. I guess many of them had abandoned that place under the freeway along with some of their other usual haunts. The city had opened up some of the public buildings because of the bad weather. Anyway, he was trying to question witnesses when somebody stabbed him in the back. He was able to stagger out of the park and get the attention of a man who was shoveling his walk. The guy called 911."

Tears stung Judith's eyes. "I knew he was keeping something from me. I should have guessed . . . Oh, my God, will he be okay?"

"They notified Bill because both you and Joe have our phone numbers for emergencies," Renie said. "Bill was told that his chances were even. But that's not bad odds, coz," she added, her voice suddenly breaking as she got out of bed and put her good arm around her cousin.

Judith fought for control. Despite the tears, she managed to choke out a question. "Where is he?"

It was Dr. Garnett rather than Renie who answered. "Mr. Flynn is here," he said. "He's in the intensive care unit. I just finished operating on him."

Peter Garnett explained that he had just been on his way up to inform Judith about her husband's stabbing.

He hadn't wanted to alarm her until the surgery was completed. Because of the weather, all the other hospitals were full. Joe had been rushed to Good Cheer, which was closest to the park where he was stabbed.

"What do you really think, Doctor?" Judith inquired, dabbing at her eyes with a tissue.

"I think," Dr. Garnett responded carefully, "that we'll have to wait and see. The blade went very deep, and there was quite a loss of blood before he reached the hospital. The good part is that the weapon missed his vital organs." He tried to give Judith a smile of comfort, but his attempt seemed forced. "Nurse Chinn will get you a sedative," he said, nodding at Heather. "I know this has been a terrible shock."

Sister Jacqueline moved closer to the bed. "I'm very sorry about all this. I didn't realize until just now that Mr. Flynn was your husband. I didn't see him when he was brought in. I do know that Father McConnaught has administered the Sacrament of the Sick. I'm sure that will help in your husband's recovery."

The Sacrament of the Sick, Judith thought, and felt sick at heart. It used to be Extreme Unction or the Last Rites, but had been renamed, and in some theological feat that defied her understanding, revamped as an encouragement to heal rather than as a signal of impending death. On the other hand, she had asked to be anointed before her own surgery. Maybe Father McConnaught's efforts wouldn't be wasted on Joe. She mustn't lose hope. That, Judith understood, was what the sacrament was all about.

Moving away from Judith, Renie eyed Dr. Garnett. "I assume they haven't caught whoever stabbed Joe? My husband didn't mention it, and I couldn't quiz him closely because I didn't want to frighten Judith."

"I don't know any of the details," Dr. Garnett said. "I'd just come from attending to Dr. Van Boeck and had to scrub up immediately to operate on Mr. Flynn." The surgeon, who looked so weary that his mustache seemed to droop, started for the door.

As beset as she was with her own troubles, Judith managed to take in the wider world. "How is Dr. Van Boeck?"

"He'll be fine," Dr. Garnett said without turning around. "Unfortunately."

"He doesn't like his boss much, does he?" Renie said, directing the remark to Sister Jacqueline after Dr. Garnett had left.

The nun's fine features puckered slightly. "They have differing philosophies on some issues. It's common among medical professionals."

"You'll keep me posted on Joe?" Judith asked Sister Jacqueline as Heather returned with the sedative.

"Of course." Sister Jacqueline's smile seemed tense. "Once he's out of intensive care, I'm not sure what floor he'll go to. We're terribly crowded here, too. Maybe tomorrow we can release some of the patients who are ready to go home. Right now, we can't take chances since our patients are all orthopedic post-op. A spill on the ice or an out-of-control vehicle could be disastrous."

"Blanche Van Boeck wants to throw me out into the snow," Renie said. "Do you think she's serious?"

Sister Jacqueline cocked her head to one side. "I doubt it. That would be up to Dr. Ming. She'd have to convince him that you're ready to be discharged."

"She could do it, though," Renie said. "She has the influence."

Sister Jacqueline's nod was curt. "That's true. But

she'll be too busy tomorrow to worry about you. Blanche Van Boeck is announcing her candidacy for mayor."

The Valium helped relax Judith, but it didn't erase her fears for Joe. For an hour, she fussed and fretted. She also repeated over and over how she wished she could see him.

Renie was remarkably patient. But as seven o'clock rolled around, she finally called a halt. "You're literally going to make yourself sick," she told Judith. "If you don't stop stewing, I'll ask somebody to give you another dose of Valium."

"Okay," Judith said, "but you know you'd worry like this if it were Bill."

"I'm already worried about Bill," Renie responded. "It isn't normal—even for a shrink—to dress up Chihuahuas."

"That's nothing compared to what happened to Joe," Judith pointed out.

"It could be if Bill's gone nuts," Renie argued. "Do you think I look forward to visiting him in some institution where he's wearing a waffle on his head and talking to the begonias?"

"You're just trying to make me stop fussing," Judith declared. "Okay, so tell me what Bill said about the Chihuahuas. What was that about a Sea Auks uniform?"

"I'm not sure," Renie admitted. "Between the doggy concept, the car, and his news about Joe, I couldn't figure out what he was talking about. Maybe Bill should analyze himself."

"I gather you didn't get a chance to ask him about Nancy and Bob Jr.," Judith said, though her mind was mostly in the ICU with Joe.

"No," Renie replied. "I could tell from the start that something was wrong. I knew he'd get to it in his own good time, but I didn't want to put any detours in the way." She glanced out the window, where night had settled in over the snow-covered city. "I still can't believe that obit the Randall family put together. Jim and Margie are both kind of weird, but I didn't think they were stupid."

Judith didn't respond immediately. "You're right. Maybe they simply wanted to vent. The odd thing is that when we spoke with him right after Bob died, Jim acted as if he was fond of his brother. And, in fact, there was no mention of his relationship to Bob in the write-up. Does that mean Bob and Jim really did get along?"

"I don't know," Renie said, delving into her Falstaff's bag. "It's a good thing I'm not hungry anymore. All I have left is an apple and a small chunk of Gouda. I'll be a bag of bones by the time I leave this place. We could use some good news around here. Then maybe my appetite will come back."

Judith eyed Renie curiously. "That's funny, now that you mention it—when Jim Randall left Addison Kirby's room this afternoon, Dr. Garnett met him in the hall. He said he had some good news for Jim. I wonder what he meant?"

"Didn't Jim have some tests done the other day?" Renie responded. "Maybe the results came back."

Judith snapped her fingers. "That must be it. I'd forgotten." She gazed at the phone. "I think I'll call ICU."

"They'll let you know when they have anything to report," Renie said, munching on her apple.

"I should call Mike," Judith said. "I should have done that sooner. Why didn't I?" She picked up the phone.

"Because you don't know anything for sure and you don't want to scare the wits out of Mike until you do. Hold off," Renie urged.

"I can't," Judith declared. "It wouldn't be fair." She used her long distance calling card to get an outside line, then waited as the phone rang a dozen times up at the mountain summit. "Nobody's answering," she said, finally clicking off. "Where could they go in this weather?"

"Maybe the phone lines are down," Renie suggested. "Or maybe Mike's got his other line tied up. He could be busy."

"True," Judith allowed, but redialed in case she'd made a mistake the first time. The result was the same. Nobody picked up the phone.

"Doesn't he have an answering machine?" Renie asked.

"Not on his private phone," Judith said. "Kristin feels it's bad enough to have the forest service lines ring in the house. She's not much for gadgetry. My daughter-in-law is strictly a no-nonsense person."

"I know," Renie acknowledged. "Kristin's a natural phenomenon, like a giant redwood." Renie did not add, as she might have, that Kristin was damned near as big.

Judith tensed as Sister Jacqueline quietly entered the room. "Mrs. Flynn?"

"Yes?" Judith flinched, her voice hoarse.

"I wanted to thank both you and your husband for being organ donors," the nun said, approaching Judith's bed. "We're very big proponents of the program, and I'm sure you know what a wonderful thing it is."

Judith barely heard what Sister Jacqueline was saying. "What about Joe?"

"He's still in the ICU," Sister Jacqueline replied.

"The last I heard, he was holding his own. He's officially listed as in critical condition."

"Is that the worst?" Judith asked in an anguished voice.

The nun shook her head. "No. Please don't fuss. We'll let you know as soon as there's any change in your husband's condition. I simply wanted to mention our gratitude for your participation in the organ donor program, and," she went on, moving over to Renie's bed, "to encourage you to sign up, Mrs. Jones. Your husband might be interested, too."

"My husband could give you a couple of over-dressed Chihuahuas," Renie replied, "but I'm not sure he wants to surrender his body parts."

A faint smile touched the nun's mouth. "We don't take them while you're still alive, Mrs. Jones. People say miracles don't occur in the modern age. But they do, in ways that we can understand and that are made possible by people whose generosity saves lives every day. Heart, kidneys, liver, eyes—they make many miracles. What, for instance could be a better gift? For example, Mr. Randall's corneas went to an aspiring artist who had lost his sight in a tragic accident. Now that young man will be able to see again and fulfill his dream."

"That's sweet," Renie allowed. "But who'd want my eyes? I'm not exactly a kid anymore."

"Neither was Mr. Randall," Sister Jacqueline declared. "Of course, he had excellent vision, which I'm told was one of his greatest assets on the football field. But even slightly impaired eyesight is better than none."

Renie gave a slight nod. "Yes, I realize that. Bill and I'll talk it over when he gets out of the doghouse. So to speak."

Sister Jacqueline looked pleased, if vaguely puzzled. "That's wonderful. I'll pray that you make the right decision."

A voice erupted sharply from the hallway. "Sister! Come at once! We need your help!" Blanche Van Boeck stepped inside the door, beckoning with an imperious finger.

"What is it?" Sister Jacqueline inquired.

"We have decisions to make," Blanche declared. "With Jan not feeling well, you're going to have to help with this crisis. After all, you *are* the hospital administrator."

"Crisis?" The nun quickly crossed herself. "Of course." She nodded vaguely at the cousins. "Good night, God bless."

"Wait!" Judith cried. "Does this have anything to do with my husband, Joe Flynn?"

Blanche scowled at Judith. "Not unless he's the CEO of Restoration Heartware," she snapped.

As the two women left the room, Judith sighed with relief. "That scared me. I thought something had happened to Joe."

"If it had," Renie said dryly, "they wouldn't have called in Blanche and the hospital administrator. There must be some new word out of Cleveland about a possible takeover."

"At this time of night?" Judith asked. "It must be going on eleven o'clock back there."

"Big business never stops working," Renie said. "In fact, I think the late-night sessions are strategic. They wait to make decisions until everybody's so exhausted that they give in just so they can go home."

Judith didn't comment immediately, and when she finally spoke, it was of a different, if related, matter.

"Who benefits from unexpected deaths in a hospital? I mean, in a business sense? I assume that the mortality rate is important when it comes to rating a hospital."

"Of course," Renie replied. "Reputation is vital. Admit it, weren't we nervous about coming here after Joaquin Somosa and Joan Fremont died?"

"Yes," Judith said. "I certainly was. If Bob Randall had died before I was admitted, I might have changed my mind. Or at least postponed the surgery. But what would be the point of indiscriminately killing off patients?"

Renie thought for a moment. "I understand they all had different doctors, so it can't be that somebody's out to get just one surgeon. Still, the ultimate responsibility rests with Dr. Garnett as head of surgery, and of course with Dr. Van Boeck as chief of staff. So I suppose it's possible that someone may be after one of them. But I can't imagine who'd benefit."

"Garnett, wanting Van Boeck's job?" Judith suggested.

"That's a possibility," Renie allowed. "Or Van Boeck trying to ruin Garnett to eliminate a potential rival."

"That doesn't wash," Judith countered, "not as long as Blanche Van Boeck wields so much clout. Anyway, what's the point of any of it if the hospital's about to be absorbed by some big company from the East? Aren't they likely to put in their own people?"

"That depends," Renie said. "Sometimes corporations like to leave the locals in charge. It's good public relations, and it's good business if the people in place are already doing a satisfactory job for a particular company. Then there's the tactic where the headquarters' chieftains move slowly, not wanting to upset the apple cart. Changes are made, but the powers that be take their time doing it."

Judith grew thoughtful. "I don't see how dead patients can be to anyone's advantage. Unless," she added slowly, "it's someone trying to scare off Restoration Heartware from making the merger."

"That," Renie said, "would be the current owners, who happen to be a religious order. Can you picture Sister Jacqueline cold-bloodedly killing helpless people?"

"No," Judith admitted, "but as you said earlier, nuns are human, too. Hasn't this order been around the Pacific Northwest for well over a hundred and fifty years? Weren't they the first women in the territory? Pride is a sin, but they have a right to be proud of their heritage. They were pioneers, especially in medicine. All those years that the sisters dedicated themselves to their hospital work is down the drain in this city if they lose control of Good Cheer."

Renie shivered. "I hate to even consider such an idea."

"Me, too," Judith agreed as Mr. Mummy appeared in the doorway.

"Just dropped by to wish you a restful night," he said in his cheerful voice. "By the way, I assume that the man who was stabbed is no relation to you, Mrs. Flynn."

"He's my husband," Judith said tersely.

"Oh!" Mr. Mummy slapped at his bald head. "I'm so sorry! I thought the name was just a coincidence. Whatever happened?"

"Someone attacked him," Judith said. "The assailant hasn't been caught, as far as I know."

"My, my!" Mr. Mummy was agog. "Do you know what provoked the attack?"

"No," Judith said, unwilling to elaborate.

Mr. Mummy appealed to Renie. "Mrs. Jones, surely you have some ideas on the matter? A clever guess, perhaps."

Renie shrugged. "Not a clue. There are plenty of loonies out there. Most of them don't need any provocation to harm an innocent person."

"That's so," Mr. Mummy remarked, looking puzzled. "Still . . . Have you spoken with the police?"

The question caught Judith off guard. "What? No, I . . . ah . . . I guess I was too focused on my husband's condition to think of it."

"You can hardly be blamed for the oversight," Mr. Mummy allowed. "You mustn't fret too much and make yourself ill. I'm sure Mr. Flynn is getting the best of care."

"It's very kind of you to look in on us," Judith said, trying to smile. "We hope you have a good night, too."

The obvious, if tactful, dismissal seemed to hurt Mr. Mummy's feelings. "Really, I didn't mean to intrude. Or to upset you. I had no idea that the Mr. Flynn who was—"

"Forget it," Renie said with a wave of her hand. "See you in the morning."

Mr. Mummy, with a rueful expression on his round face, nodded and left. Judith turned to Renie. "He was right about contacting the police. I should have done that right away. But I've been too worried about Joe to think logically."

"You probably won't learn much even if you call," Renie pointed out. "Unless, of course, you could talk to Woody."

"Woody." Judith pressed her palms together, as if in prayer. "Of course. I'll call him at home." She reached for the phone.

Sondra Price answered right away. "Judith?" she said in surprise. "How are you? How's Joe? I've been afraid to call the hospital."

"You know?" Judith asked, giving Renie a high sign.

"Yes," Sondra replied. "When Woody heard what happened, he demanded to be assigned to the case. Do you want to talk to him?"

"Of course," Judith said. "I'm so relieved that Woody's involved."

"How are *you*?" Sondra inquired. "I tried to send flowers yesterday, but nobody's delivering until the streets are clear."

Judith informed Sondra that she was doing all right. Sondra, sensing Judith's urgency, put Woody on the line.

"I don't know much," Joe's former partner admitted in his mellow baritone. "Joe had talked to me about the previous homicides involving homeless people, but there wasn't much I could tell him. I hadn't worked either of those cases, so all I could do was look over the reports the other detectives had filed." He paused, then his voice turned apologetic. "Joe may have mentioned that, as a rule, indigent murders don't get a high priority. It's a terrible shame, but with such a shortage of personnel these days, that's the way it is."

"Were there any leads at all?" Judith asked.

"Not really," Woody answered. "When the first one occurred a month or so ago, one of the other homeless persons told the detectives that he'd seen a guy in a raincoat hanging around late that evening. Two of the killings took place at night, you see, when everybody was asleep. Have you heard anything new on Joe?"

"No," Judith admitted. "I keep waiting for word. To

be honest, I'm scared. Someone meant to kill Joe, I'm convinced. What if they try again? Plus, Renie and I think someone searched our room last night. It's occurred to me that we might be in danger, too."

Woody didn't answer at once. "Well," he finally said, "maybe I can get a patrol officer to watch out for you folks. Though if Joe was stabbed in a homeless camp, I doubt very much that his assailant would show up at the hospital. Whoever it was probably wouldn't know where he'd been taken. Not to mention that the attacker may assume Joe is already . . . ah . . . dead."

Judith winced at the word, but Woody continued: "As for you and Serena, I wouldn't worry too much. Was anything stolen?"

"No," Judith admitted.

"Then," Woody said, "whoever searched your room—and he or she might have been just a compulsive snoop—did you no harm. It's doubtful that this person would come back."

"You may be right," Judith allowed, though her concern ebbed only a jot. "I guess it's just that my anxiety over Joe makes me more sensitive to potential peril. The uncertainty about whether Joe will recover may have addled my brain."

"Joe'll be fine," Woody said, and Judith hoped that he had a good reason for the confidence in his voice. "When he comes to, he may be able to give some sort of description."

"They said he was stabbed in the back," Judith said, having difficulty getting the words out. "I have a feeling he never saw his assailant."

"That's possible," Woody said. "But Joe might have seen someone suspicious before the attack. I imagine that the members of FOPP will be very concerned about this. They wouldn't have hired Joe if they weren't serious about making the homeless camps safer."

"It's a worthy cause," Judith said, though when it came to Joe's welfare, FOPP's anxieties couldn't possibly be as serious as her own. "Who are these people, anyway?"

Woody chuckled faintly. "Are you thinking of suing them?"

"It crossed my mind," Judith confessed. "But Joe took on the job, and thus assumed the liability. I doubt that we'd have a case."

"That I can't say," Woody responded, his tone solemn. "But FOPP's members mean well. And they're building political momentum."

"How is that?" Judith asked, not particularly interested. She suddenly felt as if she should get off the phone, just in case she was tying up the line and making it impossible for Joe's caregivers to contact her.

"FOPP's president is one of the city's biggest movers and shakers," Woody replied. "In fact, you may know who she is. Does the name Blanche Van Boeck ring a bell?"

FIFTEEN

"SO," RENIE SAID after Judith had finished speaking to Woody Price, "Blanche hired Joe?"

"Blanche or one of her minions," Judith replied. "She certainly does have a finger in every pie around this town."

"And now she's going to try to run it," Renie mused. "As mayor, I mean."

"Yes," Judith said absently, then after a pause turned to face Renie. "What if some political rival is trying to discredit Blanche because she's on the hospital board and her husband is chief of staff?"

"That's a stretch," Renie said, still thoughtful. "On the other hand, if the current administration and the board are so good at running this place, why does Good Cheer have to be absorbed by Restoration Heartware?"

"Good point," Judith responded. "Except that so many hospitals can't go it alone these days. Good Cheer is owned by a religious order. If Dr. Van Boeck has been ineffective, why not just fire him?"

"Maybe the Sisters of Good Cheer are too kind-hearted," Renie said.

"The Sisters of Good Cheer are very sensible businesswomen," Judith asserted. "If they weren't, they wouldn't have been around for so long. It's not their fault that medical care in this country has gone down the drain."

Dr. Garnett entered the room so quietly that the cousins didn't notice him until he was at Judith's bedside. "Mrs. Flynn?" he said as Judith gave a start. "I've just come from the ICU."

Judith tensed. "Yes?"

The bedside lamps left Dr. Garnett's face in shadow. "I thought that you and Mrs. Jones would want to know that Dr. Van Boeck has been moved out of the ICU and is spending the night in a private suite. He ought to be able to—"

"What about Joe?" Judith interrupted.

". . . return to the job in a few days." Dr. Garnett looked at Renie. "I didn't want you to think you'd caused any real harm to our chief of staff."

"Thanks," Renie said in a bleak voice. "But what about Joe?"

"No change," Dr. Garnett said with a shake of his head before looking again at Judith. "You'll make sure you discourage all visitors to your husband, won't you, Mrs. Flynn?"

"Of course," Judith said, trying to overcome her distress. "I doubt that anyone would try to come out to see him in this weather."

"We've already had at least one inquiry," Dr. Garnett said with a frown. "Most insistent, I understand. It's very important that Mr. Flynn is kept absolutely quiet."

"Yes," Judith agreed, trying to concentrate on the matter at hand. "Who wanted to see him?"

"I don't know," Dr. Garnett responded. "I believe someone at the main switchboard took the call. Whoever this person was, I understand that he or she was difficult to put off. You'd think people would know better. That's what happens when these incidents get on the news."

"Joe's stabbing was on the news?" Judith gaped at the surgeon. "Oh, dear! I didn't see that. I turned off the news when dinner arrived."

"Perhaps that was just as well," Dr. Garnett said, his expression sympathetic. "You shouldn't become overly upset so soon after surgery."

"Upset?" Judith felt as if her eyes were bugging out. "How can I not be upset when my husband is hovering between life and death?"

"I meant," Dr. Garnett said carefully, "that sometimes learning bad news through the media can be far more disturbing than hearing about it from a friend or relative."

Judith glanced at Renie. "I still passed out," Judith said.

"Yes, so you did." Dr. Garnett put a cold, dry hand on Judith's. "But you seem to be doing much better now. I'll see to it that the night nurse brings you some more Valium so you can sleep." He withdrew his hand and headed for the door. "Please don't distress yourself, Mrs. Flynn. You'll hear immediately when we have any news about your husband."

"Wow," Renie said in a dejected voice, "I'm racking up some big scores around here when it comes to upsetting people, you included."

"That's not your fault," Judith countered. "Somebody had to tell me about Joe. I'd much rather it was you."

The male night nurse, whose name was Avery, arrived with the Valium. Judith eyed the small yellow tablet and told the nurse she'd take it a little later. It was too early to try to go to sleep.

After Avery had left, Renie gave Judith a suspicious look. "Every so often, I can tell when you're lying. What's up, coz?"

"Nothing," Judith replied. "Nothing concrete."

Renie looked at her watch, which said that it was eight-thirty. "Shouldn't you let Carl and Arlene know what's happened to Joe?"

Judith shook her head. "It's hard for me to pass the news on. I'm actually glad I couldn't reach Mike."

"I'll call the Rankerses," Renie volunteered. "If they haven't seen it on TV, they'll begin to wonder when Joe doesn't come home." She picked up the phone and dialed.

Just as Renie greeted Arlene, Judith's phone rang. She grabbed the receiver and almost dropped it in her eagerness to hear if there was news of Joe.

"Mrs. Flynn?" said a familiar voice that Judith couldn't quite identify. "I just heard about your husband's stabbing. Can you give me any details?"

"Who is this?" Judith inquired.

"Addison Kirby, your next-door neighbor. Excuse my butting in, but you have to understand that it's almost impossible for a reporter to lie here helpless and not know what's going on."

"Oh." Judith relaxed a little, then gave Addison the bare bones of the incident.

"You say he was working for FOPP?" Addison said. "As in Blanche Van Boeck's do-good group?"

"That's right," Judith responded, trying to listen in on Renie's conversation with Arlene. "Do you think Blanche is sincere?" Judith asked of Addison.

"Blanche is sincere about Blanche," Addison said. "Look, if some project polishes her image, she'll take it on. But I don't think she gives a hoot about the homeless or any other category—unless she can convince them to vote for her."

"You may be right," Judith said, again glancing at her cousin.

"Honestly, we don't know the details," Renie was saying on the phone. "Of course Judith's upset. That's why she didn't call you herself . . ."

"In the past few weeks, I heard some rumors around city hall," Addison said. "The first two homeless victims had just made some money. They bragged about it, and that same night they were killed."

"So call Herself if you want to," Renie was saying to Arlene. "Yes, she has a right to know, even if she is sunning her body down in Florida . . ."

Judith stared at Renie. The mention of Joe's first wife's name distracted her, and a sudden feeling of resentment roiled up in the pit of her stomach. The emotion was more from habit than any real threat posed by Vivian Flynn. But Arlene was right; Herself should be informed. She was the mother of Joe's daughter, Caitlin. In fact, Judith realized, Caitlin should also be notified at her home in Switzerland where she worked for an international banking firm. Herself could make the call. Judith didn't have Caitlin's number with her.

Getting back on track with Addison, Judith asked if he thought the men had been murdered for the money they'd acquired.

"That was the weird part," Addison replied. "According to what I heard, at least one of the victims still had the money on him. Damn, if only I could get out of bed and use a different phone. I could do some checking myself."

"You're using your phone now," Judith pointed out.

"I can only make calls inside Good Cheer," Addison grumbled. "I can't get an outside line. And of course you can't use a cell phone in a hospital. They won't work and they can screw up the high tech equipment."

"Yes, that's true," Judith said. "Where did those homeless men get the money? That's very strange. I wonder if this most recent man who got killed also had cash on him."

"I've no idea," Addison replied. "I only heard about your husband through the grapevine here. I won't watch TV news. Those so-called pretty-faced reporters and anchors don't know their heads from their hind ends."

"I appreciate your feelings," Judith said as Renie suddenly gave a start, apparently at something unexpected from Arlene.

"Judith doesn't know anything about it," Renie said, wincing. "Are you sure?"

The comment rattled Judith, who decided she'd better terminate the conversation with Addison. "I'll let you know when I hear anything about Joe," she said into the receiver. "Thanks for calling."

"That doesn't make sense," Renie said to Arlene. "We'll let you know when we hear anything about Joe. Bye."

"What was that all about?" Judith inquired.

Renie gave herself a little shake. "Arlene sometimes gets things mixed up, but she's certain about this one. She got a call at the B&B today saying that Federal Express couldn't make deliveries to Heraldsgate Hill with all the snow, but they were holding two pot-bellied pigs for you in their warehouse."

"*Pot-bellied pigs?*" Judith was incredulous.

"That's what Arlene said," Renie responded, looking

bewildered. "They're in cages. Or kennels. Or something."

"Maybe FedEx has the wrong address," Judith said hopefully.

"They can't deliver the pigs—if they *are* pigs—until the streets are clear," Renie pointed out. "Don't fuss about it."

"I can't," Judith responded in a weary voice. "I'm already fussing too much about Joe. Who do you suppose wanted to see him? If it had been Woody, he or Sondra would have told me."

But Renie couldn't even guess. Instead, she called home, hoping that one of her children would answer. Luckily, Tony Jones picked up the phone.

"You mean it?" Renie said, brightening at her son's words on the other end of the line. "Oh." Her face fell. "Then hide that Uzbekistani cookbook from your father. You can't live on millet until I get back in the kitchen. Tell me," she inquired of her son, "what's he doing with those damned Chihuahuas?"

Judith ignored Renie's anxious probing on the phone and dialed zero and asked to be connected to the ICU. Whatever Bill Jones was doing with a couple of dogs wasn't nearly as urgent as Joe fighting for his life.

It took some time for Judith to be connected to the intensive care unit. Meanwhile, she imagined that the problem reaching a nurse was because Joe had taken a sudden turn for the worse. She'd seen it happen with Bob Randall, with people shouting, running, and rushing equipment down the hall. She could visualize the same frantic movements being performed on Joe's behalf.

Finally, a tired-voiced female answered. Judith felt momentarily strangled by anxiety, but she managed to give her name and ask how Mr. Flynn was doing.

"Flynn . . . Flynn . . . Joseph Flynn," the nurse said in a voice that dragged. "He's listed in critical condition."

Judith flinched. "No change from earlier this evening?"

"That's correct."

"Officially, you mean," Judith said. "But can't you tell whether he's a little bit better or . . . not?"

"There's been no change," the nurse replied and yawned in Judith's ear.

Judith and Renie hung up at the same time, then stared at each other.

"Well?" Renie inquired.

Judith's features sagged with disappointment. "No change."

"I told you they'd let you know as soon as anything happened," Renie said. "Take it as a good sign. Wouldn't you think that if Joe wasn't going to pull through, he would have gotten worse by now? It's almost ten o'clock."

Judith flopped back on the pillows. "Maybe."

Renie waited a few moments before speaking again. "Tony says Bill has the Chihuahuas in his workroom in the basement. He sits down there watching them. Then the dogs watch Bill. And he watches them watch him."

"Maybe it's better than watching what's on TV," Judith said without much interest.

"Bill doesn't usually conduct those kinds of experiments," Renie fretted as Avery, the night nurse, came in for the relentless vital signs routine.

"Maybe," Judith suggested after submitting herself to the procedures, "he did that kind of thing while he was still teaching at the university. You just never knew about it."

"Dubious," Renie replied before the thermometer was stuck in her mouth.

Judith bided her time, drumming her fingernails on the bedclothes. After the nurse left, she turned to Renie.

"I can't stand it," Judith announced. "I'm getting out of here."

Renie sighed. "I should have known. That's why you didn't take your Valium a while ago."

"Yes." Judith signaled for Renie to be quiet. A full five minutes passed as she listened for the voices to die down and the patter of feet to fade. "They're settling in for the night. Help me get into the wheelchair."

"No." Renie glared at Judith. "You'll do yourself some harm. Besides, we'll get caught."

"We won't," Judith asserted, laboriously starting to get out of bed. "Come on, give me a hand."

"That's all I've got," Renie shot back. But, seeing that Judith was determined, she got out of bed. "I really don't want to do this, coz. Where are we going? As if I couldn't guess."

"You can," Judith replied. "The ICU, of course."

"Of course." Renie shoved the wheelchair next to the bed, then used her good arm to help Judith stand. "Didn't you tell Woody you thought we were in danger? Isn't this trip a trifle risky?"

"It's also necessary," Judith declared.

Renie sighed again as she helped her cousin prepare to sit down in the wheelchair. "Are you okay?"

Judith waited to make sure she didn't feel dizzy. "I'm fine." She let Renie help ease her into place and put a blanket across her lap. "Let's roll."

Just down the hall, an older nun sat at the nurses' station. She looked up and eyed the cousins curiously.

"Excuse me," she said with a faint lisp, "where are you going this time of night?"

"The chapel," Judith replied. "My husband is in the ICU. Perhaps you've heard. He was stabbed earlier today. I want to pray for him."

"I see," the nun replied with a benevolent smile. "You know where the chapel is? The second floor."

"Thank you," Judith replied as Renie leaned into the wheelchair to aid her cousin's progress.

The elevator was empty. "Blasphemy," Renie muttered. "What next?"

"I really would like to go to the chapel," Judith said. "Luckily, it's on the same floor as the ICU."

"That makes sense," Renie said as the elevator stopped on two. "Gosh," she remarked, giving Judith a shove into the hallway, "it's dark around here. Which way, I wonder?"

Metal light fixtures with three bulbs hung from the ceiling at twenty-foot intervals. The somber dark green walls were relieved only by the tan linoleum floor. A wooden sign with flaking gold letters and arrows directed the visitor to the operating rooms, the intensive care unit, the isolation unit, the waiting room, and the chapel.

"To the left," Judith said, steering herself. "Everything but the ORs are that way."

Heavy glass-and-steel double doors bore a sign that read "No Admittance—Staff Only." Perplexed, Judith paused. "Now what?" she asked.

"There's some kind of buzzer system on the wall to punch in what must be a code," Renie replied. "As you may have guessed, we don't know what it is."

"Drat." Judith gripped the arms of the wheelchair and peered through the glass. She could see nothing except for a short hallway and another set of doors about ten yards away. "Double drat."

Behind them, they heard the elevator doors open and close, followed by a beeping sound. "Robbie!" Renie exclaimed. "He's headed this way."

The robot cruised down the hall, swerving to avoid the cousins. The double doors swung open at his approach. Hurriedly, Renie pushed Judith inside. Instead of going straight ahead, Robbie swung to the right where a single wood-frame door said "Keep Out." Again, Robbie was given access and disappeared as the door swung shut behind him.

"What's that, I wonder?" Judith murmured.

"How should I know?" Renie replied. "Hey, this second set of double doors doesn't have a code system. Shall we?"

The cousins passed through, using the wheelchair for leverage to open the heavy doors. Almost immediately they came upon a nurses' station that looked out through glass at the patients in the ICU.

"Oh!" Judith gasped. "Joe must be in there. Where is he?"

A middle-aged nurse with a jutting jaw stared at the cousins. "What are you doing here?" she demanded, whipping off her glasses.

"Where's Joe Flynn?" Judith asked, refusing to be put off by the nurse's fierce countenance.

"You don't belong in this area," the nurse retorted. "This is off-limits to anyone but medical staff. Please leave at once."

"Where's Joe Flynn?" Judith persisted as Renie tried to angle the wheelchair so that they could see into the dimly lighted ward that lay behind the glass windows. Some half-dozen patients lay in small cubicles with elaborate lighted monitors that looked as if they belonged in the cockpit of a jumbo jet.

"If you don't get out," the nurse growled, "I'm calling Security."

"Look," Renie said in the voice she reserved for dealing with dimwitted CEOs and obstinate public relations directors, "this is Mrs. Flynn, and the least you can do is point her husband out to her."

"That does it!" the nurse cried, and reached under the desk. A soft but persistent alarm sounded, making Judith jump.

"Come on, you old crone," Renie railed at the nurse. "Give this poor woman a break! She's just had hip surgery and her husband may be at death's—"

Torchy Magee appeared as if from nowhere, huffing and puffing through the near set of double doors. "What's up?" he wheezed, practically falling against the desk.

"Get these two out of here," the nurse ordered. "They've broken into the ICU without permission."

If Torchy had still had his eyebrows, he probably would have raised them. Instead, he merely stared at the cousins. "I know you two. Aren't you from the third floor?"

"Y-e-s," Judith said, as something moving in the shadows of the ICU caught her eye. Probably a busy nurse, prompting Judith to worry that Joe was in there, requiring immediate medical attention.

Torchy shook his head. "Now, now, you should know better than to come into an area like this. It's staff only. Didn't you see the sign?"

"Yes," Judith began, "but—"

"In fact," Torchy said, scratching his bald head, "how *did* you get in here?" He gave the nurse a questioning look.

"*I* didn't let them in," the nurse snapped. "They must have tripped the code somehow and opened the outer doors."

"Is that what happened?" Torchy asked, looking stumped.

"Something like that," Renie answered. "Look, as long as we're here, couldn't Hatchet-Face at least point out to Mrs. Flynn where her husband is in the ICU?"

The nurse fingered her glasses, scowled at Torchy, then looked down at her charts. "If I do, will you leave right away?"

"Yes," Judith promised. "Just point him out and tell me how he's doing."

The nurse turned to her computer screen. "What was the name again?"

"Joe Flynn," Judith said with emphasis.

There was a long pause. The nurse scrolled the screen up and then down. She slowly shuffled through the charts on her desk. "Sorry," she said with an expression of supreme satisfaction, "you must be mistaken. There's no Joe Flynn here."

SIXTEEN

JUDITH WILLED HERSELF not to faint twice in one day, but she definitely felt light-headed. She couldn't find her voice. The words formed in her brain but wouldn't come out.

"You're crazy," Renie yelled at the nurse, banging her left fist on the desk. "Joe Flynn had surgery this afternoon and was moved to the intensive care unit. Dr. Garnett operated on him. Look again."

"Look for yourself," the nurse smirked, turning the computer monitor so that Renie could view the screen. "Do you see any Flynn?"

"No," Renie gulped after carefully eyeballing the patient list, which included a Kyota, a Fairbanks, a Diaz, a Gustafson, a Littlejohn, and a McNamara—but no Flynn. "When did you come on duty?" she demanded with a lowering stare.

"Tonight." The nurse still seemed smug. "Ten o'clock."

"You mean you just got here?" Renie asked.

"That's right," the nurse replied. "About fifteen minutes before you two showed up." She leaned past Renie to look at Torchy Magee. "Can you get these pests out of here? I've got patients to monitor."

"I'll see these ladies home," Torchy said with a

chuckle. "Come on, let's head back to the old corral." He grasped the wheelchair firmly and steered Judith through the double doors.

She regained her speech only when they got to the elevator. "Mr. Magee," she said, sounding weak, "can you check this whole thing out for me? I swear to you, my husband was in ICU until . . . until whenever he was moved."

"I'll try," Torchy replied as the elevator doors opened, "but I'm the only one on duty tonight. My backup couldn't get here in this snow."

"Please." Judith sounded pitiful. Then, summoning up all her courage, she asked the question that had been uppermost on her mind: "If something happened—that is, if my husband didn't make it— wouldn't they tell me right away?"

"Oh, sure," Torchy replied breezily, hitting the button for the third floor. "Say," he said, looking around the car, "where's the other one?"

Judith gave a start. For the first time, she realized that Renie wasn't with them. "I don't know. Wasn't she right behind us?"

"If she was, she didn't get in the elevator," Torchy said as the car began its ascent. "I hope she's not still down in the ICU, giving Bertha heat. Bertha's pretty tough."

"So's my cousin," Judith said. But her worries rose right along with the elevator.

"I'll check on Mrs. Jones after I get you to your room," Torchy said as they exited into the hall. "Maybe she didn't make it into the car before the door closed. She'll probably show up in a few minutes."

When Judith and Torchy passed the third-floor nurses' station, the nun at the desk looked up. "Your mind must be at rest after going to the chapel," she said with a smile. "Prayerful moments with our Lord before bedtime are much better than any sedatives."

Judith uttered a response that was supposed to come out as "My, yes," but sounded more like "Mess." Which, Judith thought dismally, was more appropriate to her situation.

"Please," she begged after the security guard had gotten her back into bed, "can you find out what happened to my husband?"

"I'll give it a try," Torchy said. "What about your cousin?"

"She'll be all right," Judith said, though not with complete conviction. "For now, I'm more worried about Joe."

Torchy nodded half-heartedly. "Okay, I'm off."

It was impossible for Judith to get comfortable. She called the main desk and asked for Sister Jacqueline, but the nun was unavailable. Then she dialed Woody's number at home.

Woody sounded half asleep when he answered. Judith briefly apologized before explaining that Joe had gone missing.

"How can he be missing?" Woody asked, sounding confused.

"Maybe that's the wrong word," Judith said as she heard Sondra's sleepy mumbling in the background. "But I don't know where he is. Which makes him missing as far as I'm concerned."

"I'll see what I can do," Woody said. "Frankly, I think it's just a mix-up. Try to calm down. It isn't good for you to get yourself so upset after surgery."

Judith had confidence in Woody, but realized that the most he could do at the moment was try to send a couple of patrol officers to the hospital. They might get the runaround, too. She cudgeled her brain to think who else she might contact for help. Feeling impotent and distraught, Judith considered taking the Valium to settle her nerves. But it might fuddle her brain, so she set aside the yellow pill in its tiny pleated cup. It was almost eleven o'clock; she considered turning on the late-night news. She might see the story on Joe. But, she decided, that would only upset her.

For a quarter of an hour, she twisted, tossed, and turned—at least as much as she could without disturbing the artificial hip. She was about to ring the front desk again when Renie staggered into the room.

"Coz!" Judith cried. "Where have you been? Did you find Joe?"

Dragging herself to her bed, Renie shook her head. "No. But he's not dead. I finally got that much out of Bertha down there in the ICU. They moved him to a private room on the fourth floor."

Judith clutched the bedsheet to her breast. "Does that mean he's better?"

"It may," Renie replied, collapsing onto the mattress. "Bertha wouldn't give me any details. The only way I got any information was to grab the power cord to her computer with my good hand and threaten to unplug her. To tell the truth, I don't think she knew anything else. Remember, she just came on duty. Joe was moved before she got there."

Judith grabbed the phone. "I'm calling the nurses' station on four."

A man with a foreign accent answered. "Very sorry," he said after Judith stated her request for information. "We cannot give out any word on that patient."

"But I'm his wife," Judith protested. "I'm next of kin."

"Very sorry," the man repeated. "We must follow strict orders."

"Tell me this much," she persisted. "Would they have moved him if he'd still been on the critical list?"

"No word on that patient. Good-bye." The man hung up.

"Damn!" Judith cried. "Is this some kind of conspiracy?"

"I don't know," Renie said in an exhausted voice. "But at least you found out Joe's still in one piece."

"That's not a great deal of comfort," Judith moaned. "And why move him at all?"

"It gets zanier," Renie declared. "Didn't you wonder how Torchy Magee arrived so fast after Bertha hit the alarm button?"

"No," Judith admitted. "I didn't even think about it. I was too upset about Joe."

"Torchy may run hard, but he doesn't run fast," Renie pointed out. "He's too bulky. Anyway, I figured that the only place he could have come from in that short period of time was the room we saw Robbie the Robot enter. After giving Bertha the third degree, I peeked inside the door. Robbie was still there, all beeped out. The room is where they keep some of their records, and it has a paper shredder that had been left on. I figured that Torchy was in there shredding documents, maybe some that Robbie had delivered. Sure enough, Torchy had left a couple of undamaged pages next to the shredder." Renie looked hard at Judith. "They bore the name 'Joe Flynn.' "

At first, Judith was baffled. According to Renie, the two sheets appeared to be only the standard admitting forms. Except for Joe's identification, the date, the time, the type of injury, and the signature of the hospital staff member who had signed him in, there was nothing of interest.

"That's why I didn't swipe them," Renie explained. "As long as they didn't tell us anything we didn't already know, I thought that stealing the two pages would cause more trouble than it was worth."

Judith frowned. "I wonder how many records from this place have gone through that shredder in the past month or so?"

"You mean like Joaquin Somosa's and Joan Fremont's and Bob Randall's?" Renie suggested.

"Exactly." Judith was silent for a few moments, then turned to Renie again. "There *is* a cover-up, but I'm beginning to think it doesn't have anything to do with the hospital's reputation per se."

"What do you mean?" Renie asked.

Judith shook her head. "I'm not sure. I just have this feeling that maybe it's more personal than professional." She saw that Renie looked confused. "I have to think it through, really, I do. By the way, did you notice someone moving around in the ICU while we were there?"

Renie made a face. "I don't think so. Why? Did you?"

Judith hesitated. "I did, and my first reaction was that it was a nurse, but there was something not quite right about whoever it was. Except for all those monitors with their red, green, and yellow lights, it was completely dark. I could only make out a form. But now that I think about it, the person wasn't wearing a nurse's cap or scrubs."

"It could have been a male nurse," Renie said. "They don't wear caps. It might even have been a doctor."

Judith shook her head. "No. The doctors here wear either white coats or scrubs. Ditto for the male nurses. I don't think this person was dressed like that. But it's only an impression."

"Hunh." Renie stared up at the ceiling. "Maybe it was an orderly or the cleaning crew."

"Maybe," Judith said, but wasn't convinced. She remained silent for a few moments, then announced, "It's eleven o'clock."

"Yes." Renie was trying to get comfortable. "So what?"

"I want to go to the fourth floor."

"N-o-o-o," Renie groaned, pulling the sheet over her head. "Not tonight. Please, I'm worn out."

"I'll go without you," Judith said with an obstinate set to her jaw.

"Don't," Renie shot back as she emerged from under the sheet. "You're as tired as I am. You'll do yourself some serious harm. The killer may be loose, and out to get you. Knock it off. *Please.*"

"I can't go to sleep until I find out more about Joe's condition," Judith declared, then pointed a finger at Renie. "I don't think Torchy's going to be any help. Would you go ask Mr. Mummy to check on Joe?"

"Mr. Mummy?" Renie looked startled. "I thought you didn't trust him."

"I'm not sure I do," Judith said, "but I can't see any danger in asking him to peek in on Joe."

"Other than that Mr. Mummy's probably asleep," Renie responded. "It's not fair."

"I'll bet he wouldn't mind," Judith asserted. "He's always nosing around, and this would make him feel useful. Can you ask him?"

"No," Renie replied, "I'm utterly beat. Dial his room

number. If he doesn't answer, one of the nurses will pick up the line and wake him. But," she added in a disapproving tone, "I think it's a bad idea."

Judith ignored her cousin and punched in Mr. Mummy's number. It rang six times before a woman answered.

"Excuse me," Judith said, trying not to notice Renie's critical expression, "is Mr. Mummy in Room 322 sleeping?"

"I don't think so," the nurse replied. "When I looked in on him five minutes ago, he wasn't there."

"What is this?" Judith railed after hanging up the phone. "Musical beds? First Joe, now Mr. Mummy."

"The nurse didn't say that Mr. Mummy was moved, did she?" Renie said in a reasonable tone. "Maybe he's just wandering around, trying to settle down for the night."

"On a broken leg?" Judith shot back. "No, coz. Mr. Mummy may be doing some snooping of his own."

"To what purpose?" Renie responded.

Judith was brooding. "I don't know. I wish I'd asked Woody to check out Mr. Mummy."

"You think he's a crook?" Renie asked, stifling a yawn.

"I don't know what to think," Judith replied, "except that he's a phony."

Renie's eyes were half closed. "At this point, I don't care if Mr. Mummy is really Fidel Castro. Take that damned Valium and knock yourself out. I'm going to sleep." She turned off the bedside lamp.

For several minutes, Judith lay with arms folded across her chest, face set in a stubborn line, and worrisome thoughts racing through her brain like mice in a maze. But though her mind was active, her body betrayed her. Weariness tugged at every muscle, every sinew, and, finally, at her eyelids. She reached for the little cup with its little pill, but her hand failed. Judith fell asleep with the light still burning by her bed.

The sounds and smells of the morning routine were becoming all too familiar to Judith. The food arriving in the big steel carts, the cleaning crew's disinfectant, the clatter of breakfast trays, the soft padding of the nurses in the hallway, the incessant announcements over the PA system—all had piqued Judith's curiosity at first. But on this Thursday, the fourth day at Good Cheer, they were nothing more than a tiresome reminder of her confinement and concerns. Her first thought was of Joe. She fumbled for the phone as Renie got out of bed and went over to the window.

"The sun's out," Renie announced. "Maybe it's warming up enough that the snow will start melting."

Judith ignored the remark as she dialed the fourth-floor nurses' station. To her dismay, the line was busy.

"It's a cruel plot," Judith declared, "just to make me crazy. Furthermore," she went on, taking her frustration out on Renie, "I don't see how you seem so awake this early when you're in the hospital. The rest of the time, you don't get up until almost ten, and even then you're not exactly bright-eyed."

"At home, I don't have thirty people running around outside my bedroom door," Renie replied. "Nor am I usually in pain. Not to mention that until recently, I could sleep in more than just one position. Hospitals are not conducive to sleeping in."

Judith barely heard the rest of her cousin's explanation. She dialed the fourth floor again; the line was still engaged.

Corinne Appleby appeared, going through the usual check on the cousins' conditions. Renie asked the nurse if the weather was getting warmer. Corinne didn't know, and seemed unusually glum.

"What's wrong?" Judith inquired, hoping to ingratiate herself so that the nurse might prove useful in the quest for Joe. "Has being stuck over in the residence hall gotten you down?"

"In a way," Corinne replied without looking up from Judith's chart. "My mother's not feeling at all well, and I can't be home with her."

"Is she alone?" Judith asked.

Corinne made some notations before responding. "We're lucky to have a neighbor who can look in on her. Stay with her, too, when I'm on duty. But this is the longest time in years that I've been away. It's very hard on Mother."

"And on you, I imagine," Judith said with sympathy. "You must worry so. I know I do when I'm away from my mother, though we have wonderful neighbors who help out."

"You're fortunate," Corinne replied, fine lines appearing on her forehead. "Is your mother able to get around on her own?"

"She uses a walker," Judith replied, then glanced at Renie. "My cousin's mother is pretty much confined to a wheelchair, but she has very kind neighbors, too. Of course our mothers are both very elderly."

Corinne gave a brief nod. "Yes. My mother isn't much older than you are. You're really blessed that you'll be able to come out of this surgery and be independent. So many people don't appreciate the good health they've been given. I can't help but take offense at that. But of course I see so many patients who complain about the least little infirmity. They don't understand real suffering and helplessness."

Judith gave Corinne a compassionate smile. "That's true. I feel so helpless now, but I know I'll get over it. I'm grateful for that. Meanwhile, though—are you aware that my husband is on the fourth floor as a result of a severe stab wound?"

Corinne gave a start. "That was your husband? No. I didn't realize . . . I'm so sorry."

"They moved him from the ICU to the fourth floor last night," Judith explained. "I can't get through on the phone this morning. Would it be an imposition to ask you to check on him for me? I'm very worried."

"I'll try," Corinne said, though she sounded dubious. "I must finish my rounds first, though."

"I'd certainly appreciate it," Judith said. "Of course I'll keep calling up there."

Breakfast arrived while Corinne was taking Renie's vitals. "Say," Renie said to the nurse, "you don't happen to have an extra tray this morning, do you? I got cheated on dinner last night, and I'm famished."

"I'll see what I can do," Corinne replied, then turned back to Judith. "We're going to try to get you in the shower today. I imagine you're tired of sponge baths."

Judith made a noncommittal noise. The sponge baths were dreary, but she was frightened by the thought of standing in a shower. Before starting to eat her breakfast, she tried to call the fourth floor again. The line was still busy.

Corinne went off on the rest of her rounds. Judith nibbled on toast and a soft-boiled egg. Renie, meanwhile, was devouring oatmeal mush, grapefruit, toast, eggs, and bacon.

"If you don't want all of yours, I'll eat it," Renie volunteered.

"I'm not hungry," Judith admitted. "I'm too worried about Joe."

Renie started to say something, but stopped when she saw Margie Randall enter the room. The recent widow wore her volunteer's blue smock and a surprisingly cheerful expression.

"Nurse Appleby told me you had an errand," Margie said, smiling at Judith. "I understand it involves your husband."

"It does," Judith said, and explained the situation.

Though Margie didn't seem particularly moved by Judith's plight, she shook her head in commiseration. "That's terrible. Those homeless people are dangerous, not only to themselves, but to others. I hope they catch whoever did it. Was Mr. Flynn robbed?"

"No," Judith replied. "What makes you ask?"

"Well . . ." Margie blinked several times. "It seems like a motive for such an attack, doesn't it?"

"I suppose," Judith said. "Did you hear about the other homeless people who were also victims of stabbings?"

Margie shoved her hands in the pockets of her smock and avoided Judith's gaze. "Did I? Yes, I suppose I did. On the news. Or in the paper. I forget exactly." She back-pedaled out of the room. "I'll go up to the fourth floor right now and see what I can find out about your husband."

"Weird," Renie remarked, wiping egg yolk off her chin.

"Yes," Judith agreed. "Everything about Margie

seems weird. When is the funeral for Bob Randall being held?"

"Saturday, I think," Renie said, unfolding the morning paper, which had arrived just minutes earlier. "Let's see if there's anything in here about Joe."

Judith leaned closer, her nerves tingling at the mere thought of hearing the account of her husband's attack in cold black type.

"It's pretty brief," Renie said. "There's about two inches in the local news roundup in the second section. Shall I read it out loud?"

"Yes," Judith said, steeling herself for the worst. "Please."

" 'A Heraldsgate Hill man was stabbed yesterday at Viewpoint Park,' " Renie read. " 'According to police, Joseph Flynn was allegedly attacked by one of the homeless persons who have set up a temporary camp in the park. Flynn, who apparently wandered onto the site without realizing that it was occupied, was taken to Good Cheer Hospital, where he is listed in critical condition. Two days ago, a homeless man was stabbed to death in the same vicinity. No suspects have been found in either attack.' "

Judith shuddered. "How odd. They give Joe's name, but not his previous or current occupation."

"The police don't want to broadcast Joe's activities," Renie said.

"Maybe," Judith allowed, deep in thought.

"Addison Kirby might be able to read between the lines," Renie suggested as her phone rang. Once again, she smiled broadly as she heard Bill's voice on the other end.

Judith started to listen to her cousin's half of the conversation, but was interrupted by the arrival of Dr.

Alfonso. He was upbeat about her progress, and assured her that she'd be able to manage a shower.

"Just don't stay in there too long singing Broadway hits," he advised. "We'll see about getting you on a walker tomorrow. It looks as if you'll be able to go home Saturday if you keep improving at this rate."

Judith started to ask the doctor if he knew anything about Joe, but his beeper went off, and he made a hasty, if apologetic, exit. Renie had just hung up the phone and was looking disconcerted.

"Bill just spoke with Jeff Bauer, the manager at the Toyota dealership," she said. "It seems that some scruffy-looking guy was hanging around the lot and they figured he must have stolen it. Cammy still hasn't turned up."

"Why didn't they keep an eye on him?" Judith asked.

"They were really busy," Renie replied. "Bill wasn't the only customer who'd come in to have work done before the snow started. The salesman who noticed the scruffy guy was with some long-winded customer who wanted to look at a used car on the other side of the lot. Bill figures that Cammy was taken while the salesman and the customer were looking at the other car."

"Scruffy, huh?" Judith murmured.

"It figures," Renie said, looking angry. "Who else but some impecunious jerk would steal a car?"

"Good question," Judith said with an odd expression on her face.

"What are you thinking?" Renie asked, narrowing her eyes at her cousin.

"Well . . . Nothing much, really, except that . . ." Judith's voice trailed off as she avoided Renie's gaze.

"Fine," Renie snapped. "If you're going to keep secrets, I won't tell you what Bill said about the Randall kids."

Judith jerked to attention. "What?"

"My husband's mind works in convoluted ways," Renie said cryptically. "After thirty-five years, more or less, I still have trouble figuring out what lies behind his rationale for doing things. That's one of the many reasons Bill never bores me."

"Good grief," Judith cried, "you sound like Bill. Just tell me what he said about the Randall kids. And don't give me your usual parroting of your husband's psychobabble."

"Okay." Renie's expression was bland. "Bill broke his confidence because you need a distraction. That's how I figure it, anyway."

"What?" Judith stared blankly at her cousin.

"Because you're so worried about Joe," Renie said. "Besides, Margie Randall isn't Bill's patient anymore. Not to mention the fact that Margie's husband has been murdered."

"Get on with it," Judith said between clenched teeth.

"According to Margie, Bob had been an extremely stern, demanding father," Renie said. "The obituary the family put together wasn't too far off the mark. In consequence, the kids rebelled. Nancy has been fighting a drug addiction and Bob Jr., who is gay, was tested for HIV."

"Good Lord!" Judith cried. "Those poor kids! And poor Margie!"

Renie nodded. "It's awful. But Bill didn't know what the results of the HIV test were because Margie quit seeing him about that time. It seems that Bob Sr. left quite a legacy—and it's not in dollars and cents."

"Not in common sense, either," Judith murmured.

"He doesn't seem to have been a very good father. I guess he wasn't much of a husband, either. Of course you can't blame him for everything. That is, children can make choices. But to rebel, they often choose the—" Judith stopped speaking as Margie Randall all but pranced into the room.

"No matter what happens," she said in a chipper voice, "we don't want to be glum, do we?"

"What?" Judith gasped.

"Life can be hard, so it's not always easy to endure what fate has in store for us," Margie said, all smiles.

"Just tell me about Joe," Judith said as apprehension overcame her.

"I will," Margie replied. "If you think you can take it."

Judith swallowed hard, and said she could.

SEVENTEEN

"I FOUND MR. FLYNN," Margie Randall announced with a triumphant expression.

"Oh!" Judith clenched her hands. "How is he?"

Margie simpered a bit. "Doing rather well," she said in a tone that indicated she was taking some of the credit. "He's expected to recover."

Judith sagged against the pillows. "I'm so relieved! When can I see him?"

"Well . . ." Margie frowned, chin on hand, fingers tapping her cheek. "That's a different matter. He's not allowed visitors."

"But," Judith protested, "I'm not a visitor, I'm his wife!"

Margie shook her head. "That doesn't matter. Dr. Van Boeck is back at work today, and he makes the rules. I'm sure it's all for your husband's good. He mustn't be disturbed."

"Can I call his room?" Judith asked.

"No," Margie replied. "There's no phone. Tomorrow, perhaps. Time is the best healer." Again, her expression changed, radiating joy. "I must dash. My brother-in-law has just gotten the most amazing news. I must be with him."

Margie fairly flew out of the room.

"Damn!" Judith breathed. "I know I should be elated that Joe's better, but I wanted so much to see him. I wonder if Margie's right about the no-visitors rule?"

"It makes sense, in a way," Renie said. "After all, he's just turned the corner and he probably has to stay completely quiet."

"I guess." Judith heaved a big sigh, then turned to Renie. "Goodness, I hadn't thought about it until now, but how are Joe and I going to manage when we both get discharged? Neither of us will be in any shape to help the other, let alone take charge of the B&B. I can't expect the Rankerses to keep pitching in."

"Don't get ahead of yourself," Renie cautioned. "If things get really desperate, won't the state B&B association help you out?"

"Yes," Judith answered slowly, "they have backup personnel. But I'd hate to avail myself of it. Besides, I'd go nuts watching somebody else run Hillside Manor."

"Relax," Rene urged. "We've got other things to worry about. Like our recovery. And Joe's. Not to mention Bill's mental state."

"Did he mention the Chihuahuas this morning?" Judith inquired, trying to stop fussing.

"No," Renie said. "He was too involved with the car disaster and the Randall kids." She paused, gazing out the window. "Hey—the icicles are dripping. Maybe it's finally beginning to thaw."

"It's certainly sunny enough," Judith said, then gave a start as a loud whirring noise could be heard from somewhere. "What's that? I don't recognize it as a routine hospital sound."

The whirring grew louder, making Renie wince. "I don't know. I think it's coming from outside," she said, her voice rising to be heard over the noise as she got out of bed and went to the window. "Good grief!" she cried. "It's a helicopter! It looks as if it's going to land on the roof!"

"An emergency, I'll bet," Judith shouted. "Someone has been flown in from an outlying site."

"What?" Renie watched as the copter disappeared from her view. The whirring died down a bit. "Did you say an emergency?"

"What else?" Judith said. "An accident, I suppose."

The whirring resumed almost at once. Renie gaped as the helicopter reappeared and began ascending over the parking area. "It's leaving. What did they do, throw the patient onto the roof?"

Judith frowned. "I suppose they can make the transfer really fast," she said. "But that was *really* fast."

"*Too* fast," Renie muttered, heading back to bed. She'd just gotten back under the covers when Dr. Ming appeared.

"I hear you've been a very active patient," the surgeon remarked with an off-center grin. "You aren't wearing yourself out, are you, Mrs. Jones?"

"Me?" Renie gave the doctor a sickly smile. "I don't want to get weak."

"You won't," Dr. Ming assured her. "What's making you run all around the hospital?"

"Oh—this and that," Renie replied vaguely. "For example—what was with that helicopter just now?"

Dr. Ming was examining Renie's shoulder. "That's coming along just fine. Your busy little ways haven't done any visible damage." He paused, moving Renie's wrist this way and that. "Helicopter? Oh, that was a transplant delivery. We don't usually get them here since we do only orthopedic work. But with the snow, this week has been different. We've had to take on some exceptional cases."

"Transplant?" Renie said. "What kind?"

"I'm not sure," Dr. Ming replied. "Does this hurt?" he inquired, bending Renie's arm toward her body.

"Not much," she answered. "Heart, maybe?"

"Heart?" Dr. Ming frowned. "Oh—the transplant. I don't think so. We couldn't do that here at all. What I suspect is that the organ was flown in along with the surgeon. None of our doctors could handle a transplant. We aren't trained for that kind of specialty." He patted Renie's lower arm. "You're coming along just fine. Want to visit the physical therapist and then go home tomorrow?"

"You mean Blanche Van Boeck isn't evicting me today?" Renie asked, faintly surprised.

Dr. Ming laughed as he backed away from the bed. "No, she's too busy." He glanced at his watch. "In fact, in about twenty minutes, Blanche is going to hold a press conference just down the hall. If you're not doing anything else, Mrs. Jones, you might want to listen in. I'm sure she'll have some words of wisdom for us all."

Renie sneered, but said nothing until Dr. Ming had left. "Why is Blanche holding her damned press conference out in the hall? Why not the foyer? Or the auditorium? I assume they have one. Teaching hospitals always do."

"Don't ask me," Judith responded without enthusiasm. She couldn't take her mind off Joe, though something else was niggling at her brain. Not that it had anything to do with her husband. Or did it? Judith was afraid that the anesthetic had dulled her usually logical mind. "Blanche held that other press conference out in the hall," she pointed out. "Maybe she likes the intimacy."

Renie had gotten out of bed again. The icicles were definitely thawing, in big, heavy drips. "Hey," Renie said, excited, "there are some workmen out in the parking lot. It looks as if they're clearing off the cars that have been stuck there."

"Good." Judith shifted positions, trying to get more comfortable. The sound of happy voices in the hallway distracted her. "Who's out there?" she asked Renie.

"Huh?" Renie turned toward the door. "I can't see . . . Oh, it's the Randall kids. Jeez, they're practically skipping down the hall." She moved as quickly as she could to watch their progress, which halted at the elevator. "They're high-fiving," she said. "What's going on with this family? Whatever happened to proper respect and bereavement?"

Judith's interest perked up. "They're glad he's dead," she declared. "That's the only possible explanation."

As the brother and sister disappeared inside the elevator, Renie stared at her cousin. "Do you think they killed Bob Randall?"

Judith shook her head. "No. I can't imagine an entire family plotting to murder another relative. I mean, I *can,* but it seems unlikely."

"Hold it," Renie said, sitting down in Judith's visitor's chair. "What are the three guidelines Joe uses when it comes to homicide? Motive, means, and opportunity, right?"

"Right." Judith was looking dubious. "Okay, so Margie had all three, assuming she really hated Bob. In fact, she indicated that she may have delivered something lethal to each of the victims."

Renie raised a hand in protest. "Who told you she admitted being the so-called vessel? It was Bob Jr., not Margie. How do we know Margie ever said such a thing?"

"Good point. But either way, it assumes that Margie—or her son—knew what was in Joan's Italian soda, Joaquin's juice, and Bob's booze. Why would Margie admit such a thing to anyone?"

"Because she's a total ditz?" Renie offered.

"I don't think she's as much of a ditz as she pretends," Judith said. "I think Margie—if she really said it in the first place—was speaking metaphorically. Why would she go to all that trouble to kill Joan and Joaquin before finally getting to Bob? And why kill him here, in the hospital? She could have slipped him a little something at home."

"What about the others? Bob Jr. and Nancy and even Jim?" Renie asked. "Could one of them have used Margie?"

"As 'the vessel'?" Judith gave her cousin an ironic smile. "Maybe. But why kill the other two? We haven't seen any connection between Joaquin Somosa and Joan Fremont and Bob Randall Sr.—except that they were all well-known, successful individuals."

Renie looked thoughtful. "I know that Margie and Jim both evinced a certain amount of sadness at the time of Bob's death. But then they let loose, and the funeral hasn't even taken place yet. What do you think? Denial? Relief? Hysteria?"

Slowly Judith shook her head. "It's impossible to figure out because we don't know them. You have to consider who benefits from any or all of the three deaths. Apparently, not the Randalls. Bob Sr. was worth more to them alive. Stage actresses in repertory theaters don't earn that much. Of course you have to consider insurance policies, but would Joan or Bob have had huge amounts? That means expensive premiums. Bob was probably insured to the max when in his playing days, but the team, not Margie, probably was the beneficiary. And he didn't really play ball in the era of million-dollar quarterbacks."

"Somosa might have had a big personal policy, since he did play in the era of million-dollar pitchers," Renie pointed out. "But Mrs. Somosa was in the Dominican Republic when Joan and Bob died. That bursts that balloon."

Judith looked startled. "What?"

"I said, that bursts that . . ."

"Balloons," Judith broke in. "What about the guy who delivered the balloons and the cardboard cutout to Bob's room after he came back from surgery? Did you get a good look at him?"

"No," Renie confessed. "He went by too fast. And I was still sort of groggy. The only thing I really remember besides what he was carrying was that his shoes didn't match."

"Interesting." Judith paused for a moment. "What if he also delivered the Wild Turkey? They must know at the desk who came in."

"Probably," Renie said, then stopped as a chattering stream of people began to filter down the hall, accompanied by TV equipment and snaking cables.

"It must be the newshounds arriving for Blanche's announcement," Judith said. "Help me get into the wheelchair. I want to hear this."

It was a bit of a struggle, but the cousins managed it. Judith, who was becoming accustomed to the wheelchair's vagaries, was able to propel herself into the doorway, where she sat with Renie standing next to her. At least thirty people had filled the corridor. Sister Jacqueline was one of them, and she didn't look happy.

While the reporters and cameramen positioned themselves, Dr. Van Boeck and Dr. Garnett appeared, coming from different directions. Judith noted that Dr. Van Boeck didn't look much the worse for his collapse the previous day, though both physicians seemed grim.

At last, the elevator doors opened and the star of the show made her entrance. Blanche Van Boeck had shed her furs, revealing what Renie whispered was a gray Armani suit. Knee-high boots and a black turban completed the ensemble. "Big bucks," Renie noted as Blanche passed by on her way to the alcove down the hall.

Judith gestured at the empty doorway across the hall. "No Mr. Mummy," she murmured. "Where do you suppose he is?"

Renie shrugged as Sister Jacqueline found herself being pushed back in the cousins' direction.

"Excuse me," the nun apologized, bumping into Judith's wheelchair. "This is quite a mob. I wish Mrs. Van Boeck hadn't chosen this place for her announcement."

"It does seem like an odd venue," Judith remarked. "Does she have a reason?"

"Does she need a reason?" Sister Jacqueline retorted, then gave herself a little shake. "Sorry. That was unkind, especially given that Mrs. Van Boeck has always been such a big supporter of Good Cheer. The truth is, the auditorium is being painted. The workers just got started Monday, and then weren't able to come back after it began snowing. And it's too cold and draughty to hold the press conference in the foyer."

"Not to mention," Renie put in, "that I suspect Blanche enjoys the cozy atmosphere of a more intimate setting."

"A more neutral setting as well," Sister Jacqueline said, then again looked rueful. "The foyer, the auditorium, so many other places in the hospital feature religious symbols. If Mrs. Van Boeck is going to run for mayor, she has to appeal to a broad range of voters, the majority of whom aren't Catholic."

"So she's going to announce her candidacy today, right?" Renie whispered as, down in the alcove, Blanche raised her hands for silence.

Sister Jacqueline shot Renie a swift, puzzled glance. "I'm not certain. Maybe she'll do that later, downtown."

Judith gave the nun a puzzled look, but there was no opportunity for further questions. Blanche was beginning to speak, her strong, sharp voice carrying easily without a microphone.

"I'll keep my remarks brief," Blanche said, her expression somber. "I appreciate your efforts in coming out in this winter weather. I know it wasn't easy getting here." She paused, her gaze resting on her husband, who stood a little apart from the rest of the crowd. "As of February first of this year, Good Cheer Hospital will be taken over by Restoration Heartware of Cleveland, Ohio."

A gasp went up from the crowd in the hallway. Hardened journalists they might be, but Blanche's statement wasn't what they'd expected. Judith gasped right along with them, then turned to Sister Jacqueline.

"Did you know this was coming?" she asked of the nun.

"Yes." Sister Jacqueline kept staring straight ahead, in Blanche's direction.

"This," Blanche continued, "is a very difficult time for those of us who have been associated with Good Cheer. We are all very grateful to the sisters who founded this hospital almost a century ago. Their dedication to physical, emotional, and spiritual health has been unparalleled in this region. Fortunately, the order still has hospitals in other cities, and will continue to administer Good Cheer's retirement and nursing homes."

Blanche drew in a deep breath. "This is a sad day for us, but we are not without hope. The state of medicine in this country is pitiful, and universal health care has been only a dream for the past fifty-odd years. It's time to stop talking about it, and act. Therefore, I intend to run for Congress in the upcoming election. Health care will be the issue—my *only* issue. Thank you very much."

Blanche stepped down amid more gasps from her audience. She moved quickly through the crowd to her husband's side. A few yards away, Dr. Garnett glared at the couple. Sister Jacqueline had bowed her head and appeared to be praying.

"Well." Renie was fingering her chin and observing the reporters who were pressing in on the Van Boecks. Dr. Garnett had turned away and was coming down the hall toward the cousins. He stopped when he spotted Sister Jacqueline.

"Courage," he said, touching the nun's arm. "You know that you and the other sisters share no blame in this disaster." He nodded in the direction of the Van Boecks, who were trying to escape the media. "If there are villains other than governmental ineptitude, there they are."

Sister Jacqueline gave Dr. Garnett a bleak look. "What's the use of blame? It's over."

Dr. Garnett said nothing. He merely patted Sister Jacqueline's hand, offered her a small, tight smile, and walked away.

"Courage?" the nun echoed bitterly. "What good is courage? You can't fight the Devil when you can't see him."

As Sister Jacqueline started to turn away, Judith called her name. "My condolences," she said. "There are many of us in the community who will be sorry to see the Order of Good Cheer relinquish the hospital."

"Thank you," Sister Jacqueline replied, her voice devoid of life.

"A question," Judith went on. "A very minor question. Do you know who brought Bob Randall the balloons and cutout of him in his playing days?"

"No," the nun replied without interest. "Sister Julia at the front desk would know. She was on duty Monday night. Why do you ask?"

An embarrassed expression flitted across Judith's face. "Oh—ah, my cousin thought she recognized him as one of her children's old high school chums. How do I get in touch with Sister Julia?"

"You don't," Sister Jacqueline replied. "She started making a private retreat in the convent Tuesday morning. Sister can't be reached until Sunday afternoon. It's a shame, since I wish I could tell her that not all of her prayers were answered." Shoulders slumped, the nun left the cousins and headed for the stairwell.

As the Van Boecks disappeared around the corner at the far end of the hall, Renie reversed Judith's wheelchair and pushed her cousin back into their room. "Did Sister Julia volunteer for the retreat or did somebody give her an order—excuse the pun."

"I think your imagination may be running away with

you," Judith said. "I'm sure the retreat was Sister Julia's idea, but her isolation is inconvenient. And what did Sister Jacqueline mean by fighting the Devil?"

"Restoration Heartware?" Renie suggested as Corinne Appleby came into the room. "Or a certain individual?"

"Time for your shower," Corinne announced with forced cheer. "Good, you're ready to go," she added, indicating the wheelchair. "Shall we?"

Judith had no choice. Renie volunteered to go along and take her own shower. As they reentered the hall, the journalists were dispersing. Snatches of conversation could be heard as they passed down the hall toward the elevators.

". . . Funny stuff going on around here . . ." ". . . Hey, I intend to keep my job . . ." "Congress, huh? Why not, she's no bigger windbag than they already . . ."

At the rear of the group, Judith spotted Mavis Lean-Brodie. She was standing outside Addison Kirby's room. "Kirby!" Judith heard Mavis exclaim as the KINE-TV anchorwoman saw the newspaper reporter's name posted by the door. Mavis galloped across the threshold and disappeared.

"What's going on?" Judith heard Mavis demand as Corinne pushed the wheelchair down the hall. "Are you a prisoner in this place or what?"

Judith hit the brake, catching Corinne off balance. The nurse almost fell over the top of the wheelchair. "Sorry," Judith apologized, looking shamefaced. "Could we back up a bit?"

"What for?" Corinne asked, catching her breath.

"I just saw an old friend," Judith said with a lame little smile. "I wanted to say hello."

"If your friend has come to visit, whoever it is will

wait," Corinne declared. "I have to keep to a schedule.
I don't want to lose my job when this Cleveland bunch
takes over. I have a mother to support, remember?"

Judith felt the wheelchair move forward at what
seemed to be headlong speed. Unfortunately, Renie
was up ahead. If she had seen Mavis, she hadn't bothered to stop. But Renie and Mavis didn't always get
along. Maybe, Judith thought, her cousin had chosen
to ignore the TV anchorwoman.

Once they reached the shower area, Corinne struck
a more amiable attitude. "I'm sorry if I was rude," she
said as she helped Judith take off her hospital gown,
"but this has been a very difficult day, what with this
takeover and all. Plus, we've had some problems with
the showers the last couple of days. Curly, our mainte-
nance man, thinks one or two of the pipes may have
frozen. In fact, the shower area has been off-limits
until just a little while ago."

"That's fine," Judith murmured. "It's just that I'm so
worried about my husband, and when I saw Mavis . . .
my old friend . . . I thought she might be able to help
me find out what's going on."

"There's nothing to fret about," Corinne said glibly as
she turned on the taps and helped Judith into the shower.
"I'll stand right outside. If you need help, just call."

Judith regarded the steady stream of water with
trepidation. "Are you sure this waterproof cover on the
dressing will keep my wound dry?"

Corinne nodded. "That's why it's there. Just don't
do anything to dislodge it."

"Where's my cousin?" Judith asked, looking around
at the other stalls as if she were searching for a lifeline.

A stream of curses exploded out of a shower stall
across the aisle, answering Judith's question.

"My cousin hates showers," Judith explained to a startled Corinne. "She never can manage the taps."

"She manages quite well with her mouth," Corinne noted with disapproval.

"Uh . . . yes," Judith replied, maneuvering her way under the showerhead. Though she was unsteady, the rush of warm water felt wonderful. For a brief time, she submitted her body to a sense of total cleansing, as if her anxieties were flowing right down the drain. Confidence as well as strength seemed to grow within her. She vaguely heard Corinne say something about having to step outside for a moment. Then Judith found the shampoo and began to wash her hair.

"I'm done," Renie announced grimly. "Are you okay?"

Judith peeked around the curtain. "Yes, I'm almost finished."

Renie finished putting on her gown and robe. "I'll get Corinne to help you come out."

Judith rinsed the shampoo out of her hair, then fumbled with the taps. She wasn't quite sure which way to turn them, but eventually figured it out before scalding herself. She shook herself as vigorously as possible, then reached for the towel that Corinne had left on a peg just outside the stall. Judith was awkwardly drying off when she heard a noise nearby.

"Coz?" she called, wielding the towel. "Coz?"

Renie didn't answer. Nor was there any response from Corinne. Puzzled, Judith rubbed at her wet hair, then wiped away the moisture that had gotten into her eyes. When she finished, she blinked several times to bring her vision into focus.

Then she screamed.

A man's hand appeared from the other side of the shower curtain and was reaching out to grab her.

As strong masculine fingers wrapped around her wrist, Judith screamed again.

EIGHTEEN

"MOM! WHAT'S WRONG?"

Judith's mouth hung open as she gaped at her son. "Mike?" she gasped, squeaking out his name as if she were more mouse than mother.

"Didn't you hear me call to you from outside?" Mike asked, gallantly trying to avoid peering into the shower stall.

"Ah . . . No." Judith swallowed hard, then did her best to wind the towel around her body. "The water was running."

"Hang on to me," Mike said, looking sheepish. "I'll help you out. Gee, I didn't mean to scare you."

Judith gingerly stepped out of the stall. Her knees wobbled and she had to lean against her son. "Give me a minute to collect myself. This is the first time I've been able to take a—" She stopped, her heart suddenly in her mouth as she realized what Mike's arrival could portend. "Joe . . ." she said with difficulty. "Is he . . . ?"

"He's doing okay," Mike said. "I talked to him a few minutes ago."

"Oh!" Relief swept over Judith. "You're sure? He really seemed to be on the mend?"

Before Mike could answer, Renie reappeared. "I

see you got your mother out in one piece," Renie said. "It's a good thing—Corinne was called off to help some post-op patient."

Judith stared at her cousin. "You knew Mike was here?"

Renie nodded. "I met him when I went to get Corinne. Aren't you tickled to see him?"

Judith started to laugh, a gust of relieved tension that verged on hysteria. Renie put an arm around her cousin. "Take it easy, I'll help you get dressed. Then we can talk."

Ten minutes later, Judith was back in their room, where she gratefully let Mike help her get settled. "Now," she said, finding the least painful position in the bed, "tell me about Joe and how you got here."

"I saw the story on the news," Mike explained after pulling Renie's visitor's chair over by Judith's bed so that both he and his aunt could sit down. "The snow had stopped up at the summit around midnight, and the highway crew started clearing the pass not long afterward. I'd called the hospital to ask about Joe, but they wouldn't tell me anything, even when I tried to get tough with them. What really bugged me was that they wouldn't put me through to you. They said it was too late. I guess it was, maybe twelve-thirty."

"I can understand why they don't want to disturb patients that late," Judith said, "but I'm sorry I didn't get to talk to you."

Mike shrugged his broad shoulders. "Not talking to you made up my mind—as soon as the roads were clear, I headed for the city. I've got four-wheel drive, chains, everything except skis on my forest service vehicle. When I arrived at the hospital, they wouldn't let me come up to the third floor. No visitors, they said at

the front desk, because of some dumb press conference. So," Mike continued, lifting his hands, "I went to
the fourth floor, to see how the other Flynn was doing."

Judith smiled fondly at her son. "I'm so glad. I
haven't seen Joe since they brought him in here. It's
been terrible. How did he look?"

Mike laughed ruefully. "Like hell. And bitching like
crazy. I guess he was in a pretty bad way, but the surgeon who worked on him was some kind of wizard."

"Dr. Garnett?" Judith put in.

Mike shrugged. "Whoever. Anyway, they moved
him out of intensive care last night."

"We know," Renie said dryly. "We thought he'd
been kidnapped. Or worse."

"What else did he say?" Judith asked eagerly. "Does
he know who stabbed him?"

Mike shook his head. "I didn't want to wear him out,
so we didn't talk much." He paused, his gaze wandering around the room. Maybe, Judith thought, Mike was
aware that since her marriage, he and Joe didn't ever
talk much.

'So," Mike went on, "I left and came down to this
floor. Whatever they were doing here was over by then,
and I was able to see you. But you weren't in your
room, and somebody told me they thought you'd gone
to the shower." He shrugged again. "That's where I
went, and found Aunt Renie. I feel bad that I scared
you."

"It's been a scary kind of hospital stay," Renie said.
"You don't know the half of it."

Mike looked unsettled. "Do I want to?"

"Probably not," Judith said with an ironic smile.
"It's a long story, and really doesn't have anything to
do with us. I don't think."

Mike eyed both Judith and Renie curiously. "What does *that* mean?" Mike asked.

Judith winced. "Nothing. Have you had lunch? It's almost noon. How are Kristin and little Mac? Will you take me to see Joe?"

Mike grinned at the onslaught of queries. "Kristin and Mac are great. I'll get some lunch in the cafeteria. I didn't have much breakfast this morning because I wanted to get an early start." He hesitated and grew serious. "I don't know if I can take you to see Joe. I had to sort of sneak in to see him myself."

"Why?" Judith demanded. "Is his condition still critical?"

"No," Mike responded, "it's not that. It was more like a question of security or something. In fact, there was a cop outside the room. Officer Boxx, I think his name was."

"Woody!" Judith grinned. "That must have been his doing, thank goodness. But Officer Boxx let you in when you identified yourself?"

"Not at first," Mike replied. "I had to prove we were related, and having different last names didn't help, so I—"

Torchy Magee appeared in the doorway. "Mrs. Jones? I got a crazy question for you." He glanced at Judith and Mike. "Sorry to interrupt."

"What kind of crazy question?" Renie asked.

Torchy laughed. "I know Jones is a real common name, but all the same . . . This sounds stupid, but . . ."

"But what?" Renie was impatient.

"We've been clearing off the cars in the parking lot this morning," Torchy explained. "We can't get into most of them, so we don't know who they all belong to. But this one car, a beige Toyota Camry, had a work order from the dealership on the front seat that had the name Jones, William on it. Any relation?"

Renie was speechless.

After Renie got her keys out of her suitcase, she insisted that Torchy Magee take her to the parking lot. The security man wasn't happy with the idea.

"I want to make sure it's our car," Renie insisted.

"Too risky," Torchy argued. "The lot's real slippery. You might fall and hurt yourself. Let me take the keys. I can check the registration."

"But is Cammy okay?" Renie demanded.

Torchy looked puzzled. "Cammy?"

"That's what we call our car, dammit," Renie barked. "Has Cammy suffered any damage?"

"Not that I can see," Torchy replied, bemused. "Come on, let me go check and save you a nasty accident."

Renie relented. As soon as Torchy had left, she went to the phone and called Bill. Judith and Mike kept quiet while Renie spoke with one of her children.

"What do you mean, Anne? Your father went *where?*"

There was a long silence, then Renie shook her head. "I don't believe it. He'll freeze. He'll wear himself out. It must be four or five miles from our house to the hospital." She paused, apparently for Anne to reply. "Okay, I'll try not to have a nervous breakdown. Thanks, and let me know if you hear from your father."

Replacing the receiver, Renie stared at Judith and Mike. "Bill took off for the hospital about an hour or more ago. He decided to come in person to try to find out what was going on with Joe."

"He's walking?" Judith said, incredulous.

Renie nodded. "The buses haven't started running again, and you know how Bill likes to walk. But it's a long, long trek and it's cold and the streets are slippery and . . ." She fell back against the pillows.

"Maybe," Mike offered, "I could take my vehicle and try to figure out what route Uncle Bill would follow. Then I could meet him and give him a ride the rest of the way."

"That's sweet, Mike," Renie said, "but not very practical. I imagine a lot of the streets are still closed to traffic. Bill can walk anywhere he wants, but you'd never get through to collect him."

Unusual noises in the hallway distracted the trio. Mike got up to find out what was happening.

"They're moving somebody into the room across the hall," Mike said. "It looks as if whoever it is has just come from surgery."

The cousins exchanged puzzled glances. "Mr. Mummy?" they chorused.

Mike moved farther into the hall. "Is that his real name?" he called over his shoulder.

"Yes," Judith replied. "Don't you see it posted next to the door?"

Mike disappeared briefly. When he came back into the room, he shrugged. "There's nobody named Mummy—what a goofy name—listed outside the room. It's some other person—Randall, James. Does that sound familiar?"

Judith and Renie were dumbfounded. "What," Judith asked, "happened to Jim Randall that he required surgery? I thought we heard somebody tell him he'd gotten good news. And where is Mr. Mummy?"

Renie simply shook her head. "This place keeps getting crazier. How the hell did our car end up in the parking lot at Good Cheer?"

Judith shot Renie a sharp look. "That may not be as crazy as it sounds."

"What do you mean?" Renie demanded.

"Let me think," Judith said, frowning. "I wish my brain wasn't still addled from that blasted anesthetic. If I could just put everything in logical order, I might be able to figure this out."

"Figure what out, Mom?" Mike asked, looking bewildered. "Say, wasn't that football player who died named Randall, too?"

"Oh, Mike." Judith's expression was pitying. "There's so much you don't know, that you don't need to know . . . Except," she went on, suddenly looking panicked, "if Joe's in real danger. Can you go upstairs and stay with him?"

Mike was clearly perplexed. "Isn't that Officer Boxx's job?"

"Officer Boxx may have to go to the bathroom, get some lunch, whatever," Judith said, still speaking rapidly. "I want you to go up to the fourth floor now and make sure Joe is okay. Will you do that?"

"Sure." Mike stood up and gave his mother an off-center smile. "Why wouldn't I? After all, he's—"

Corinne Appleby entered the room, looking harried. "Sorry about the shower," she said to Judith, then noticed Mike. "Oh—I didn't realize you had company."

"I'm just leaving," Mike said with a wave for Judith. "Relax, Mom. I've got it under control."

Corinne's gaze followed Mike out of the room. "Is that your son?"

"Yes," Judith said. "He's a forest ranger."

"He's a nice-looking young man," the nurse remarked. "I admire the color of his hair." Corinne twirled one of her own red locks. "He must get it from his father."

"Yes," Judith said in a weak voice. *"Yes."* She spoke emphatically the second time. "He gets his red hair from his father, Joe." Judith shot a quick, exultant glance at Renie. "There," she murmured as Corinne left the room, "I said it."

"So you did," Renie nodded with a smile. "But how does Corinne know about Joe's hair?"

Judith sucked in a startled breath. "You're right—when did she see Joe? More to the point, *why* did she see Joe? There may be a logical explanation, but my logic seems to have stalled since the surgery."

"Which means you can't figure out why Jim Randall is across the hall," Renie noted as she got out of bed. "I'm going to take a peek."

It was a temptation for Judith to join her cousin, but she decided it would take too long to get into the wheelchair by herself. Almost five minutes passed before Renie returned.

"I was getting worried about you," Judith said. "What's up with Jim Randall?"

"That's what I was finding out," Renie replied, looking a bit rattled. "That helicopter—it was for Jim, bringing him new corneas for a transplant."

"Oh!" Judith was astounded. "But . . . that's wonderful!"

"For him," Renie replied, sitting down in the wheelchair. "I guess you don't have to be stone blind to receive a transplant."

"What happened to Mr. Mummy?" Judith asked. "Did they move him to another room?"

"No," Renie answered slowly. "Mr. Mummy was officially discharged late last night."

Judith didn't say anything for at least a full minute. "I wish I could figure out what Mr. Mummy was doing here. I'm convinced he wasn't a real patient. And why did Sister Jacqueline have that late-night closed-door meeting with him?"

"He certainly was snoopy," Renie remarked.

"Yes." Judith's voice held a curious note. "He seemed driven to find out every little thing that went on in this hospital. Remember how he interrogated us—politely—about Blanche stopping by our room and some of the other seemingly small incidents. He tried to do the same thing with Addison Kirby. Mr. Mummy didn't want to miss a trick. To what end, I wonder?"

"A spy?" Renie suggested.

Judith frowned. "Maybe. Industrial espionage."

Renie uttered an ironic laugh. "They call it keeping abreast. And it wouldn't be industrial espionage in this situation. That is, nobody wants to steal trade secrets from Good Cheer. Hospitals aren't creative institutions, like chemical or munitions companies."

"Maybe," Judith said, "Mr. Mummy was spying for Restoration Heartware."

"He might have been spying for Good Cheer," Renie offered. "He had to have the approval of the hospital administration. How else could he get himself in here with a fake injury?"

Judith was pondering the question when the phone rang. It was Arlene, and she was highly agitated. "I hope there's room for me in that hospital when I have a nervous breakdown in the next ten minutes," she announced in a voice that shook. "Do you have any idea how worried I've been about Joe?"

Judith hung her head. "I'm *so* sorry. But I didn't know myself if he was going to . . . It's only in the last few minutes that I got good news from Mike."

"He'll live?" Arlene asked in a breathless voice.

"Yes," Judith replied. "He's improved enought to complain. How's everything at your end?"

"Fine," Arlene replied, the tremor no longer in her voice. "By the way, I got another call from FedEx this morning. I canceled the pigs, but now they have a fifty-pound case of Granny Goodness chocolates awaiting delivery. They wanted to let us know that if the snow melts enough, they may be able to bring it to the B&B by late afternoon."

Judith was astounded. "I never ordered any . . ." The light dawned. *"Mother,"* she said under her breath, glancing again at Renie.

"You ordered them for your mother," Arlene broke in. "That's lovely, Judith. So thoughtful of you to give her a little treat while you're not able to be with her. Let's hope that the streets are passable in a few hours. Oops!" she cried. "I must run. There goes Ernest. Now how did he manage to get up *there?* He could fall in my minestrone soup!"

Arlene hung up.

"Is there no end to my troubles?" Judith wailed, holding her head. "I finally get some encouraging news about Joe, but now I realize that Mother has been using my credit card to order all those weird items. Only she would put me in debt for fifty pounds of Granny Goodness chocolates."

"Oh, dear," Renie said, obviously trying not to laugh. "That's awful."

"And Ernest is still on the loose," Judith lamented. "Damn this weather—I want those Pettigrew people to leave my B&B and take their stupid snake with them."

"Maybe they will today," Renie said. "The airport closing must have screwed up their travel plans."

"I don't care," Judith groaned. "They never should have brought the snake into Hillside Manor."

"If they'd delivered the pigs, they might have eaten Ernest," Renie said brightly.

Judith gave Renie a dirty look. "It's not funny. And how am I supposed to make a speedy recovery if I'm beset with all these horrible problems? My health is probably beginning a downhill descent into my early demise."

"Speaking of which," Renie said, "I'm curious. I thought only really healthy people could get cornea transplants."

As the silent orderly came in with the cousins' lunches, Judith gave Renie a puzzled look. "What are you talking about?"

Renie withheld her answer until the orderly had gone. "Jim Randall," she said, scrutinizing the food on her tray. "I may be wrong, and of course I have no idea what the demand is for cornea transplants, but if he's as big a mess as everybody claims, how did he get so high on the recipient list?"

"I don't know how to answer that," Judith admitted, also staring at the three mounds of multicolored food on her plate. "I think these are salads, by the way."

"Like Donner & Blitzen Department Store has in their tearoom?" Renie said. "Those salads are really good. My favorite is the one with shrimp."

Judith sampled a bite from the mound that was primarily white. "This *could* be potato salad."

Renie followed her cousin's lead. "It could also be library paste. Oddly, I used to like library paste when I was a kid. Sometimes I'd ask to be kept in for recess just so I could be alone and eat the paste."

"You also ate erasers, as I recall," Judith said, trying the mostly green salad next. "If you could eat stuff that really wasn't edible, why can't you eat hospital food?" She swallowed the mouthful of green and let out a startled cry. "Mrrff! That's not very good." Judith choked twice before she could get whatever it was down into her digestive tract.

"I refuse to try the red stuff," Renie declared. "I'm sure it has tomato aspic in it. I hate tomato aspic. These so-called salads should be taken out and shot. Maybe they're wholesome, possibly even nutritious, but to me, they're an insult. I'm personally offended by being forced to consider this ersatz meal as food."

Judith gazed inquiringly at Renie. "For once, I almost wish you'd say all that nonsense again."

"Huh?" Renie looked surprised.

"I think," Judith said deliberately, "you may have just enlightened me as to the killer's identity."

NINETEEN

RENIE WAS AMAZED by Judith's theory. She was even more astonished by the alleged motive. "What," she asked in an awestruck voice, "are you going to do about it? You have absolutely no evidence."

"That's the problem," Judith said, looking worried. "Not to mention that the whole thing's so crazy I can't be absolutely sure. If only Joe had seen who attacked him."

"DNA," Renie put in. "There's got to be some trace of the killer in our car."

"That doesn't prove that person was the killer," Judith pointed out.

"You're right." Renie scowled at the salad mounds on her plate, then dumped them in the wastebasket. "I'm thinking, honest."

Judith set the luncheon tray aside and picked up the phone. "I'm not going to eat this slop, so I'll call Woody instead."

Woody was about to leave for the hospital to see Joe. Although he tried to sound enthusiastic about Judith's idea, a note of skepticism lingered in his mellow voice. "I'll certainly have the Joneses' Camry checked out. Don't let Bill drive it anywhere until we've finished."

Judith passed the message along to Renie. "That's fine," Renie said in a doleful tone. "Bill's probably frozen into a grape-flavored Popsicle by now anyway."

"It's above freezing," Judith pointed out, "or it wouldn't be thawing so much."

The silent orderly came in to remove the cousins' trays. As usual, he made no comment, not even when he saw that Judith's lunch was virtually untouched and Renie's was lying in the wastebasket. For the first time, Judith noticed that his name tag read "Pearson." Assuming it was his surname, she called out to him as he started to leave.

"Mr. Pearson?"

Even though he wasn't through the door, the orderly didn't stop.

"That's rude," Judith declared as Heather Chinn entered the room, seeking vital signs. "Say," she addressed the nurse, "why won't that orderly, Mr. Pearson, talk to me? Does he disapprove of us?"

Heather gave Judith a gentle smile. "Pearson is his first name, and he's a deaf-mute."

"Oh!" Judith reddened with embarrassment. "I feel terrible!"

"Don't," Heather said, applying the blood pressure cuff. "You couldn't know."

"I'd still like to talk to him," Judith said. "I mean, exchange written notes. To let him know we appreciate his work. Could you ask him to drop by when he has the time?"

Heather looked wary, but agreed. "I know how to sign," she offered. "Would you like to have me join you?"

Judith started to accept, then politely declined. "I don't want to take up your valuable time. I also wanted to ask him a couple of questions about . . . how we might be able to get some other kind of food. My cousin hasn't been able to eat some of the last few meals."

"Oh." Heather looked dubious. "I'm not sure Pearson could help you. That's something that should be taken up with the dietician."

"Let Mrs. Flynn do it her way," Renie broke in. "I trust her. She knows my needs."

Apparently, Heather wished to avoid arguing with the cousins. "All right," she said, putting the thermometer in Judith's mouth.

A quarter of an hour passed before Pearson reappeared. He wore a curious expression and tugged at the ear that bore the gold stud.

Judith had already written her questions on a piece of paper. Giving Pearson a big smile, she handed him the single page. "No rush." She formed the words as emphatically as possible.

Pearson sat down in the visitor's chair, carefully reading the questions. He scratched his shaved head and frowned. Judith handed him a ballpoint pen. With a quizzical glance, Pearson began to write down his answers.

1. Were you on duty when any of these persons died—Joaquin Somosa, Joan Fremont, Bob Randall? *Yes.*
2. Which ones, if any? *All of them.*
3. If you were, do you recall seeing such items as a take-out juice cup in Somosa's room, one or two plastic Italian soda glasses in Fremont's room, and a pint of Wild Turkey in Randall's room? *Yes, all of them, vaguely.*
4. If so, what happened to the containers?

At the fourth and last question, Pearson looked flummoxed. He started to give Judith a palms-up signal, but stopped abruptly.

"Nurse Appleby removed S's and F's drink containers," he wrote, and gave Judith a diffident grin. Then he formed a single word: *"Why?"*

Judith wasn't sure what he meant. "Why do I ask?" she wrote. Pearson nodded. "Because I'm trying to help my husband, who has been stabbed." Pearson looked bewildered. Judith added another note. "His stabbing may be connected with the deaths of S, F, and R." The orderly grimaced. Judith scribbled another question.

"What about R's liquor bottle?"

Pearson shook his head and shrugged.

Judith held up one finger to indicate she had yet another query. "What did Appleby do with the juice and soda containers?"

Pearson pointed to Judith's wastebasket, then held up two fingers.

"Both?" Judith formed the word carefully.

Pearson nodded again.

Judith put out her hand. "Thank you," she mouthed, and gave the orderly a grateful smile.

Pearson stood up and smiled back, then nodded at Renie and left.

"Let's see those questions," Renie said, getting out of bed.

"What do you think?" Judith asked after her cousin had finished reading.

Renie's face screwed up in concentration. "Corinne threw out the containers belonging to Somosa and Fremont. So what?"

"Let's call on Addison Kirby," Judith said, attempting to sit up on her own. To her astonishment, she managed it. "Hey, look at me! I'm just like a real person!"

"So you are," Renie said with an encouraging smile. "Don't get too frisky. I'll help you into the chair."

A few minutes later, the cousins were at Addison's door. He turned and grinned, apparently glad to see them.

"I'm so bored I could start tweezing my beard with ice tongs," he told them as they moved to the bedside. "Since I don't watch much TV except sports, all I can do is read, and it seems the hospital library is woefully lacking in sex-and-violence thrillers."

"That's probably because the nuns are reading them," Renie said, only half joking.

Addison chuckled, then turned a more serious face to Judith. "I guess you never had a chance to ask your husband about those chocolates. I heard he got himself stabbed. How's he doing?"

"Better," Judith replied, "though I still haven't seen him. My—*our*—son is with him right now. As soon as I hear from Mike—our son—I'll try to see Joe. Right now, I've got a couple of questions for you. They may be painful." She hesitated, then continued. "After Joan's death, when and where did you first see the body?"

Addison looked surprised. "In her room. They wouldn't move her until I'd gotten here. I'd been covering a story downtown, and only found out she was dead when I got here. I suppose it was at least an hour after she . . . died."

"Think hard," Judith urged. "Was her wastebasket empty?"

Addison Kirby gave Judith an odd glance, then slowly nodded. "I know what you're getting at. I remember, because my first, crazy reaction was that Joan wasn't wearing her wedding band. She never took it off, not even onstage." He held up his left hand, revealing an intricately carved gold ring that caught the sunlight coming through the window. "We had these specially made. The masks of tragedy and comedy are entwined with a pen, to symbolize both our professions. My first thought was that the ring had been stolen, but somehow that seemed unlikely at Good Cheer. Then I wondered if it had fallen off and was on the floor or under the wastebasket. I looked around and saw that the wastebasket was empty. And then I remembered that Joan had left the ring at home, on the hospital's advice." Addison's face clouded over at the memory.

"Empty," Judith echoed. "That makes sense. Can you tell me the exact date that your wife died? I want to be very sure about this."

"January sixth," Addison replied promptly. "How could I forget? We had the funeral last Saturday."

Exuding sympathy, Judith nodded. "Do you remember exactly when Joaquin Somosa died?"

Addison gave Judith a crooked little smile. "Actually, I do. It was on my late father's birthday, December nineteenth."

"Good," Judith said. "I mean, it's good that you remember."

Addison was eyeing her curiously. "You're on to something, aren't you, Mrs. Flynn? Or should I call you Miss Marple?"

Judith assumed a modest expression. "I don't want to elaborate because my theory is so far out that, along with my hip, Dr. Alfonso may have replaced my brain with a battery—a faulty one at that. And unlike Miss

Marple with her St. Mary Mead village eccentrics, I don't know anyone on Heraldsgate Hill who reminds me of the possible suspect."

Addison looked disappointed. "So I can't ask who it is?"

"Don't feel bad," Renie put in. "Sometimes, when she really gets whacked out, she won't even tell *me* who she suspects."

Addison grinned. "You aren't going to tell me who I should be wary of? Remember, I almost got killed out there in front of the hospital."

Coincidentally, Torchy Magee poked his head in the door. "Mrs. Jones? That's your Camry, all right. At least it is if you live at this address I copied down." He recited the house and street number from a slip of paper. "That yours?"

"It sure is," Renie said with a big smile. "Thanks. I'm relieved that the car is safe."

Suddenly angry, Addison was staring at Renie. "*Your* car was the one that hit me?"

"I'm afraid so," Renie said. "Our Toyota Camry was stolen from the dealership. I didn't recognize it when I saw it hit you because it looks like every other mid-sized sedan these days. Besides, I'm not used to looking down on it unless I'm on a ferry boat's upper deck."

Addison was frowning. "I don't get it—somebody stole *your* car and then hit *me*. Was it deliberate?"

Renie glanced at her cousin, who shrugged.

"Who?" Addison asked, still frowning.

"I'm not sure what his name is," Judith replied, "but he may be dead."

As Judith rolled out of the room with Renie behind her, Addison made a request.

"Hey—you never told me who I should watch out for."

"I told you," Judith said, over her shoulder. "The man who hit you might be dead."

"He was the man who killed my wife? For God's sake, I have to know that."

"No," Judith responded. "He didn't kill your wife. He didn't kill anybody. I'm not entirely convinced that your accident wasn't just that—an accident."

Addison wasn't finished. "Am I in danger?"

"I don't think so," Judith said, "but it's always prudent to trust absolutely nobody in this kind of situation."

"Not even you two?" Addison shot back.

"Not even us," Judith replied. But she smiled.

Judith was intent on talking to Sister Jacqueline. Heather Chinn thought that the hospital administrator was in a meeting, probably something to do with the Restoration Heartware takeover. But she promised to convey the message to Sister Jacqueline.

"Meanwhile," Judith said, "I'm going to see Joe."

Renie made a face. "Are you sure you're up to it? That shower must have taken a lot out of you."

"Of course I'm up to it," Judith asserted, once again sitting up on her own. This time she managed to swing her legs around to the side of the bed, put her feet on the floor, and start to stand up. "See? I can . . . Oops!" Judith started to topple forward and caught herself on the wheelchair.

"Good grief," Renie muttered, hurrying as fast as she could to help her cousin, "I warned you about being too rash."

"Okay, okay," Judith grumbled, "let's get out of here."

The cousins paused briefly outside the door to what had been Mr. Mummy's room and now was tenanted by Jim Randall. Two nurses and a doctor Judith didn't recognize were hovering over Jim's bed.

"He must have been almost blind," Judith remarked. "Otherwise, he might not have gotten a cornea transplant."

The lunch carts had been removed from the hallway; the Pakistani woman was polishing the floor with an electric cleaner; the two nurses at the station, one of whom was a nun, were consulting over charts. No one stopped Judith and Renie as they proceeded to the elevator.

But they were stopped anyway. An OUT OF ORDER sign was on the door of the car.

"Damn!" Judith cursed under her breath. "Where's the freight elevator?"

Renie didn't know. "It's probably down this hall," she said, pointing to their right. "It's the only place I haven't been yet."

Judith was about to suggest that they try it when Sister Jacqueline appeared from the stairwell. "You wanted to see me?" she inquired.

"Yes," Judith said, then added, "when will this elevator be fixed?"

"Curly's working on it now," Sister Jacqueline replied. "Our elevators are not only too few, but too old. I imagine Restoration Heartware will install new ones. Among other things," she concluded on a baleful note.

The three women returned to the cousins' room, where Sister Jacqueline tentatively seated herself in Judith's visitor's chair. The nun looked as if she either expected to be ejected from the chair by force, or else didn't want to be there in the first place. *A real hot seat,* Judith thought as she got back into bed.

"You're probably going to think I'm nuts." Judith said with a self-deprecating smile, "but would it be possible for you to find these dates for me?" She handed the nun a slip of paper on which she'd already written her request.

Sister Jacqueline looked startled. "That would be a breach of patient confidentiality," she said. "Why on earth do you want this answered in the first place?"

"Sister," Judith said earnestly, "would you believe me if I told you it was a matter of life and death?"

It hadn't been easy, but Judith had finally convinced Sister Jacqueline that it was imperative to provide the information. Mike returned shortly after the nun left.

"Did you know the elevator's broken?" he said upon entering the room.

"Yes," Judith retorted, "we know. We tried to get up to the fourth floor to see Joe. How is he?"

"Good," Mike replied, taking the chair that Sister Jacqueline had just vacated. "He seemed better than when I saw him earlier. Woody Price is with him. Gosh, it was great to see Woody after all this time."

"Did Joe see who stabbed him?" Judith asked anxiously.

"That's what Woody was asking," Mike replied. "Joe told him that he thinks he saw the attacker before it happened. At least he saw some guy who was acting suspicious. Joe has an instinct for that sort of thing, being a cop for so many years."

Judith could barely contain her excitement. "Who was it?"

Mike gave his mother and his aunt an ironic smile.

"That's the weird thing. He didn't look like most of the homeless types."

Judith nodded. "I'm not surprised."

"Huh?" Mike looked puzzled. "What do you mean?"

Maybe, Judith thought, it was only fair to enlighten her son. But before she could say anything, Bill Jones came through the door, panting mightily.

"Bill!" Renie cried. "You're alive!"

Bill leaned one thermal-gloved hand against the door frame and panted some more. "Huhuhuhuhuhu," he uttered.

"Did you bring me some snacks?" Renie asked, smiling widely.

Bill, his tongue hanging out, shook his head. "Uhuhuh."

Renie's face fell. "Oooh . . ."

"Why don't you smack her, Uncle Bill?" Mike asked, half serious.

Bill finally caught his breath. "The crowns in heaven that await me . . . ," he murmured, coming all the way into the room and kissing his wife.

Renie appeared contrite. "Are you all right? Are you cold? Are you tired?"

Bill nodded emphatically at each question, then slumped into Renie's visitor's chair and removed his snap-brim cap. "I came to find out how Joe was doing, but the elevator's broken. I couldn't make it all the way to the fourth floor on the stairs. What's happening?"

"Joe's much better," Judith said happily. "Mike's seen him, but I haven't yet. Because of the elevator."

Bill nodded again. "You two seem to be doing okay."

"We are," Renie replied, patting Bill's arm. "Are you sure you don't have frostbite?"

This time, Bill shook his head. "It's actually beautiful out there, with the sun shining and all the snow that's still left. I didn't mind the walk at all."

"Good," Renie said, then turned serious. "Tell me, what on earth are you doing with those blasted Chihuahuas? I was beginning to think you'd gone over the edge."

"Oh." Bill chuckled. "This may sound whimsical, but an occasional nonscientific experiment can prove interesting, if not entirely valid. This was one I'd had in mind for a long time. I became curious about animal versus human behavior several years ago and—"

"Bill," Renie interrupted, "spare us the background, okay?"

"What?" Bill frowned at his wife. "Okay, okay. Anyway, you must realize that this wasn't a controlled situation. But recently I'd read an abstract in one of my psychology journals by Dr. Friedbert Von Schimmelheimer in Vienna, who had some fascinating ideas on the subject, though his experiments involved—"

"Bill . . ." Renie broke in.

"What? Oh, all right, never mind. If you understand the problems with replication, then you'll appreciate how—"

"Bill!" Renie looked fierce. "Layman's language, *please.*"

Bill glared at his wife. "*Okay, I'll cut to the chase.* I would have preferred to do it with monkey siblings, but then we found the dogs. Anyway, you know how Oscar is about experimenting with apes."

Renie nodded while Judith gazed at the ceiling and Mike looked puzzled. Oscar was the Joneses' stuffed ape and was treated like a member of the family.

"So how did it turn out?" Renie asked, her patience restored.

"Fascinating," Bill replied. "I called them John and Paul. For the pope. John's the one wearing Archie's tuxedo." He paused to look at the doll on his wife's nightstand. "Hi, Archie. How are you doing? You look really cheerful." Judith and Mike exchanged amused glances. "Anyway," Bill continued, "Paul has on those Wisconsin sweats, the ones that Clarence ate most of the badger symbol off. John got the expensive dog food, Paul got the cheaper kind. I made a bed for John in the bottom drawer of my desk. I put Paul in a cardboard box. John drank Evian water; Paul had to make do with water from the tap. Sure enough, after twenty-four hours, John started to become spoiled, while Paul sulked. Then, this morning, when I gave John a leftover rib-steak bone, Paul pounced on him. The experiment proved what I thought would be true. Even nonhuman siblings can suffer resentment and lack of self-esteem when one of them gets preferred treatment over the other. They can also exhibit hostility and aggression."

Judith stared at Renie. "What do you think?"

Renie glanced at Bill. "I think my husband's right. As usual."

Judith turned to Mike. "Go upstairs and get Woody. The time has come to call in a consulting police detective."

Sister Jacqueline telephoned a few minutes later. The nun still sounded dubious about revealing the information Judith had requested, but when she finally did, another piece of the puzzle fell into place. Feeling as if she had a solid grip on the solution to the murders, Judith smiled grimly.

Mike and Woody had their own way of making Judith smile. When they entered the ward fifteen minutes later, they were pushing a wheelchair. Joe Flynn offered his wife a feeble, though fond, grin.

"Joe!" Judith cried. In her excitement, she instinctively leaned forward to touch him, then screamed and doubled over in pain. "Oh, my God!" she cried through her misery. "I think I've dislocated my hip!"

TWENTY

JUDITH LET OUT a terrible cry of anguish. Joe tried to reach out to help his wife, but weakness overcame him. It was Mike who rushed to his mother's side as she moaned in pain.

"Mom!" He attempted to move her into a sitting position, but she resisted.

"I can't move!" she gasped through tears. "Get a nurse! A doctor!"

Corinne Appleby and Heather Chinn both showed up almost immediately. Then, in a haze of agony, Judith saw Pearson, the orderly, arrive with a gurney. Though the slightest movement was agonizing, she endured being moved onto the gurney, rushed down the hall and into the elevator, which obviously had been repaired, and hustled to a room with bright lights. Staff members she'd never seen before were at the ready.

Despite a fresh dose of painkillers, the next half hour was a nightmare. At last, after X rays had been taken and Dr. Alfonso had arrived, her self-diagnosis was confirmed: She had indeed dislocated the new hip. It would take only a couple of minutes to put it back, but Judith would have to be virtually unconscious during the procedure. She welcomed the oblivion.

An hour later, Judith awoke in her own bed on the third floor. Through a haze, she saw the same people who had been there when disaster had struck.

"Joe   " she murmured.

"I'm here, Jude-girl," he said, taking her hand.

"So cunning, so cruel . . ." she mumbled.

Joe looked at Renie, who was sitting in Judith's visitor's chair. "Does that mean *me?*" he asked with a worried expression.

Renie, however, shook her head.

"Threes . . ." Judith murmured, squeezing her eyes shut against the bright, setting sun. "Everything in threes . . . Three lives saved . . . three patients dead . . . three homeless men stabbed . . . three inedible salads . . ."

"Salads?" Joe looked at Bill.

Bill shrugged.

"Is she delirious?" Woody whispered.

"Must be," Joe muttered. "My poor little girl."

"Planned in advance . . . Surgical instruments stolen . . . Should have guessed . . . to kill homeless . . . Poor souls, set up with bribes to provide iron-clad alibis and drive car . . . Bill and Renie's car . . . stolen because the snow starting, couldn't get to usual vehicle . . ."

Renie glanced at Bill. "Poor Cammy," she sighed.

Joe shot both the Joneses a quizzical look. "Your Toyota?"

Bill nodded.

"Who's Cammy?" Woody asked.

"Uncle Bill and Aunt Renie's car," Mike said under his breath.

Woody looked befuddled.

"So sad, those homeless men . . ." Judith made a feeble attempt to squeeze Joe's hand. He made a feeble attempt to squeeze back. "Had to die, couldn't be trusted not to tell . . . Only organ donors need apply . . ."

"What?" Joe leaned closer to his wife. "Jude-girl, what the hell are you talking about?"

"Definitely delirious," Woody murmured. "Maybe I should come back later."

"No, please . . ." Judith opened her eyes and gazed compellingly at Woody.

Woody stayed.

"So many odd little things . . ." Judith tried to sit up, failed, and pointed to the water container on the nightstand. Mike filled a glass and handed it to her. "Thirsty," she said with a small smile of thanks. "After surgery, fluids so important . . . Everybody must drink, drink, drink . . . Why not put street drugs into IVs? Simple, if you know how . . . not so simple if you don't . . . Everybody must drink, any fluids, all fluids . . . exotic juice, Italian sodas, booze . . . Just keep pouring it down . . ." She paused to take another sip of water. "The Chihuahuas, one in a tuxedo, one in a sweatsuit . . . They clinched it."

"I'm afraid," Joe said, a note of alarm in his voice, "that whatever they gave her when they put her hip back in has fried her brain. Do you think we should send for a psychologist?"

"I *am* a psychologist," Bill reminded Joe. "She's not crazy. I think I know what she's trying to say."

Joe glanced at Archie, cheerfully smiling on Renie's nightstand, then gave both the Joneses a look that indicated he wasn't convinced of their sanity, either. "O-o-o-kay," he said under his breath.

"All those years of being the opposite," Judith said, her eyes wide open and almost in focus, "of feeling inferior, of being a mirror twin, of suffering near blindness . . . That's why Jim Randall killed his brother, and several innocent victims along the way."

The golden light from the fading winter sun bathed the room in a tattered antique splendor. With the dark wood, the wavery window glass, and the religious statues, Judith could almost believe she was in a nineteenth-century hospital, where only gaslights and candles provided illumination. The Demerol was working, and so was her brain. A wondrous calm came over her as she saw some of the people she loved most standing or sitting around her bed. Then her gaze traveled from Joe to Mike, and a surge of panic filled her. But she had made her resolution to tell the truth. Not quite yet, but later, maybe when she was home again.

"Jim Randall!" Woody exclaimed, his usual quiet demeanor shattered. "You mean Bob's brother?"

"His mirror twin," Judith replied after drinking more water. "They faced each other in the womb, they're exactly opposite. Bob once saved Jim's life, and I'm not entirely sure Jim was grateful. Even as a child, he must have sensed his physical inferiority. Then, when Jim started to lose his sight—or maybe he never had full vision—he brooded. Finally he got on a list for cornea recipients. Even there, he knew that he probably wasn't high on the list, and in some twisted, deranged way, decided to speed up the process. He found out—probably from Margie, his sister-in-law—where he stood on that list and which patients were organ donors at Good Cheer. Obsessed with the concept of finally being able to see clearly, he began to eliminate patients. Not just any patients, but successful ones, the type of person he could never be. Yes, those victims

were all órgan donors, though he didn't necessarily expect to get their corneas."

Judith paused to pick up the notes she'd taken down
from Sister Jacqueline. "On each of the dates that Somosa and Fremont died, Jim had scheduled medical
tests, right up to Tuesday when Bob Randall had his
surgery. Jim didn't strike me as a healthy person,
though he may also have been a hypochondriac. I suspect he faked that faint to allay suspicion. Anyway, he
talked his doctors into a CAT scan, an ultrasound, and
an MRI. But he never took those tests, he had a homeless person do it for him. Renie told me after she had
her MRI for her shoulder that all she had to do when
she went to the place where they did the test was hand
them some information in a folder she'd gotten from
the reception desk."

"Judith's right," Renie chimed in. "I thought it was
odd at the time, and even asked the people giving the
test how they knew it was really me. They said they
didn't, I could be anybody as long as I was female and
of a certain age."

"This deception not only gave Jim an alibi," Judith
went on, "but allowed him to get the homeless men to
drop off the special treats for his victims. Jim couldn't
risk doing it himself, and he certainly never could have
put the drugs into the IVs. He couldn't see well enough."

"Hold on," Woody interrupted. "How could Jim
know what special drinks Joaquin Somosa and Joan
Fremont wanted?"

"Margie," Judith said simply. "She'd hardly be suspicious of such an innocent question. Even though she
may have delivered the drinks—though not her husband's booze—it wouldn't dawn on her that Jim had
purchased the stuff."

"Still," Renie put in, "it must have occurred to Margie that the lethal drugs were in those drinks. That's why she referred to herself as 'the vessel.' "

Joe was still looking skeptical. "How," he asked, "could Jim ensure that he'd actually get corneas if he wasn't at the top of the list?"

"He couldn't," Judith said. "First of all, he may not have been down as far as you'd think. Even if the medical tests showed that something was wrong, it wasn't really him undergoing the tests. If one of the homeless men turned up with a problem, Jim could simply ask to retake the test and claim a medical mistake. But another key was the weather. Organs are flown in from all over the country. When we first met Jim, he mentioned that he knew there was a big storm coming in. That usually means the airport is closed—and it was—so that if a local donor died, the corneas could only be delivered by helicopter. And, having maneuvered himself to the top of the city's list, he knew he'd be here to receive them. Even if he wasn't number one, he was at the hospital. Another recipient might not have been able to reach a hospital in this weather."

"Taylor," Renie murmured. "I overheard Bob Randall talking to someone named Taylor. Addison Kirby said that was the name of his wife's eye doctor. Maybe he was Jim's doctor, too, and Bob was thanking him for good news, like Jim being near the top of the recipient list."

"That would make sense," Judith said.

Joe sucked in his breath, an effort that obviously cost him pain. "So a cold-blooded killer with new eyes is lying across the hall from us?"

Judith nodded. "I'm afraid he is."

Woody shook his head. "I've never heard of such a strange homicide case. All those innocent victims."

"Three in the hospital," Judith said. "The number three was symbolic to Jim. His brother had saved three lives—Jim's, and two children who were rescued by Bob from a house fire. It was as if Jim had to do just the opposite—take three successful lives, including that of the mirror twin who had saved him from drowning. The three homeless men may have—perhaps subconsciously—symbolized his own inferiority. Jim felt like them—a loser."

"I wonder," Renie said, "if Bob was really as big a jerk as Jim and the rest of the family indicated."

"I'll bet he was," Judith replied. "Big sports stars can be very hard to live with."

"What," Joe inquired, "about Addison Kirby getting run down? Was that an accident or something Jim cooked up?"

"I'm not sure," Judith admitted. "I'm not even certain who was driving. It might have been Jim after he got the homeless man to steal the Camry from the dealership. He might have told the guy to run over Addison, or at that point Jim himself may have been driving. If so, he may not even have seen Addison Kirby. We'll know when Woody checks for hairs and fibers."

"Good Lord!" Renie cried. "Jim may have driven our car? It's a wonder we didn't find it in pieces!"

"He wouldn't have driven it far," Judith said dryly. "Jim had used the homeless to help him get around, no doubt stealing cars and returning them, perhaps before the owners knew they were gone. This time, he had to leave Bill and Renie's Camry because of the bad weather. Plus, the last homeless victim was staying closer to the hospital because the camp had been moved from under the freeway. The snowstorm worked both for and against Jim Randall. And of course he couldn't take a chance of being seen with his stooge."

"Say," Renie put in, "was Jim Randall the one who got into my suitcase? And who was it you glimpsed in the ICU?"

"I still don't know who was in the ICU," Judith replied, "but I'm sure it wasn't Jim. It was dark, he couldn't see well, and I can't think of any reason why he'd be interested in us." She gave Woody a shrewd look. "Why don't you tell us who the intruder in our room was? Could it be the same person I saw in the ICU?"

"Ah . . ." Woody looked embarrassed. "I'm not supposed to say . . ."

"Come on, Woody," Judith coaxed. "Tell us."

Woody glanced at Joe. "She exerts a certain irresistible power, doesn't she?"

"In more ways than one," Joe murmured, the gold flecks flashing in his green eyes.

"I guess it's all right to reveal the truth," Woody said, though he cast a wary gaze on the closed door. "The intruder in your room was Harold Abernethy."

"Who?" Judith and Renie chorused.

Woody bestowed his engaging grin on the cousins. "I knew you wouldn't know who he was. Well," he amended with a quick glance at Judith, "I sort of thought you *might* have found out his real name."

"Mr. Mummy!" Judith exclaimed. "His name wasn't really Mumford Needles?"

"No," Woody replied, looking faintly amused. "That was his working alias. Blanche Van Boeck hired him to try to solve the murders before Restoration Heartware changed its mind and decided to withdraw its takeover attempt."

"But," Renie put in, "I thought Blanche actually sounded sincere when she expressed regret about the takeover."

"She probably was," Woody responded. "But it was the only way Good Cheer could survive. It was either that, or turn the place into condominiums. Dr. Garnett blamed Dr. Van Boeck for the hospital's problems. That was probably professional jealousy. Sister Jacqueline and Van Boeck were fighting an uphill battle, like so many other chiefs of staff and administrators."

"So," Renie murmured, "that's why Mr. Mummy— I mean, Harold Abernethy—checked out last night. The takeover had happened, his job was ended. No wonder he was so snoopy. But why was he interested in us?"

"Harold was interested in everybody," Woody said. "He probably went through your things to make sure you were what you appeared to be. Of course we knew about his investigation, which was why we agreed, along with county law enforcement, to keep the lid on everything, including the media. Blanche, Dr. Van Boeck, Sister Jacqueline, even Dr. Garnett all agreed that it was the best way to handle the situation. Given that Good Cheer is the only orthopedic hospital inside the city, they felt that publicity should be kept to a minimum. The main fear, aside from the damage to Good Cheer's reputation, was that people who really needed surgery would be put off and possibly cause themselves serious harm."

"But," Judith asked, "did Harold ever learn the killer's identity?"

Woody shook his head. "No. He felt like a big failure. He's been a private detective for over thirty years, and he insisted that he'd never come across such a baffling crime."

Joe shot Judith a rueful look. "The cunning killer never dreamed he'd come across my dear wife."

"Now, Joe . . ." Judith began, then turned to Woody. "What are you going to do about Jim Randall? I know he's probably not in any condition to be arrested right now, but later when he . . ."

Woody was looking remorseful. "Judith, I'm sorry. The truth is, we have no evidence. Even what's been collected before now doesn't prove Jim Randall was the killer."

"What was collected?" Renie asked.

"The containers," Woody said. "Sister Jacqueline saved all the containers, including the whiskey bottle. The fingerprints were smudged, but Sister had the dregs analyzed. You're right, the drugs were in the juice and the soda and the liquor. But what did that prove? It was impossible to pin down who had delivered them to the hospital, and in the first two instances, Margie Randall had brought the items to Joaquin Somosa and Joan Fremont. No one paid any special attention to the homeless men being at Good Cheer because the nuns offer them free medical care."

"But," Renie argued, "now you can have the technicians who gave those medical tests testify that they didn't give them to Jim Randall."

"That's possible," Woody allowed.

"You can do better than that," Judith declared.

Woody seemed skeptical. "How?"

Judith turned to Joe. "Could you ID the suspicious-looking man you saw in the park?"

Joe grimaced. "Maybe. It was pretty dark."

Judith nodded. "I'll bet you can when you see Jim Randall. But there's another way." She looked at Woody. "If you check Jim's clothes, I'll bet you'll find a surgical instrument or two among his belongings. He hasn't been able to go home because of the snow, and he wouldn't risk throwing them away. He couldn't be sure that there might not be some residual evidence implicating him. Nor would he have had time to get rid of them before he went into surgery. I'm told that with transplants, everything happens very fast. Anyway, the medical examiner should be able to match the wounds to the kind of weapon that killed those poor men."

Woody winced. "He already has. At least he indicated that surgical instruments might have caused the deaths. And of course he examined Joe."

Judith swung around to stare at her husband. "He did?"

Joe shrugged.

"That's why," Woody explained, "there was such secrecy surrounding Joe's hospitalization. In fact, Blanche hired Joe in the first place because she had an inkling that there might be some oddball connection between the hospital slayings and the homeless murders. It didn't seem like a coincidence that in each instance, the first two pairs of Good Cheer homicides, and the first two killings in the homeless camp, had occurred within twenty-four hours of each other. Say what you will about Blanche Van Boeck, she is one very sharp woman."

Judith looked at Joe. "Did you know Blanche thought there was a connection?"

Joe shook his head. "She never mentioned it. All she told me was that FOPP was concerned about the homeless homicides."

"So," Woody continued, "the ME was here last night in the ICU before Joe was moved upstairs. We'd begun to put together some theories of our own."

"*That's* who I saw in the ICU?" Judith cried. "The ME?"

"Probably," Joe said. "He couldn't get here until late, and I had to stay down there until he showed up. Bringing him to a ward would have raised a lot of questions. Or so Sister Jacqueline felt."

"Is that why some of Joe's medical records were shredded?" Judith asked. "For security reasons?"

Woody nodded. "Apparently Mrs. Van Boeck felt it was necessary to keep Joe's real condition a secret. Maybe—and I'm guessing—she had a hunch the murderer was on the premises, or at least in the immediate area. If Joe's life was already in jeopardy, Jim Randall—or whoever—might not bother to finish him off. Remember, Jim had undoubtedly seen Joe around the hospital. Jim may have learned he was a former detective and now a private investigator. Apparently, Jim never did figure out that Harold Abernethy—Mr. Mummy—was also on the case, but from a different angle."

"Wait a minute," Judith said, narrowing her eyes at Joe. "Are you trying to tell me you weren't at death's door?"

"Well . . ." Joe began, but avoided his wife's incensed gaze. "I *wanted* to tell that redheaded nurse I saw in the elevator because she was getting off on your floor . . ."

"Corinne," Judith breathed, and glanced at Renie. "That's where she saw Joe. Couldn't she tell me he wasn't in extremis?"

"He wasn't in good shape," Woody put in. "Really."

"But not fifty-fifty?" Judith demanded. "Not critical?"

"More like seventy-thirty," Joe said, grinning weakly. "And 'critical' covers a broad range these days."

"Joe." Judith folded her arms across her breast. "You can't imagine how upset I was."

"It couldn't be helped," Joe said, wincing a bit. "Honest."

"I don't care," Judith asserted. "I'm mad at you." She turned to Woody. "Well? Are you going to check Jim Randall's clothes or sit here and watch me ream your ex-partner?"

Woody appeared more than willing to do Judith's bidding. "I really should be going. Great to see you all again. Get well, ladies, Joe. Nice work with the dogs, Bill. Take care of your mother, Mike. Bye."

"Maybe," Bill said, more to himself than to the others, "I should try more random, unscientific experiments. Those Chihuahuas seem to have done . . . something or other."

"You're brilliant," Renie declared, with a loving look for her husband. "Haven't I always said that?"

"Well—" Bill began.

But Renie cut him off. "Are you *sure* you didn't bring me some snacks?"

The lethal surgical instruments had indeed been found in Jim Randall's clothing. The arrest was made shortly after five o'clock. Woody reported that Jim had laughed in his face. He didn't care if he went to prison, he didn't even care if he got the death penalty. He could *see,* and that was all that mattered. The case was closed.

Addison Kirby was impressed, as were members of the hospital staff. Now that the murders were solved, Addison had a big exclusive for the newspaper. He vowed to write it up in such a way that he'd be a shoe-in for a Pulitzer Prize. That would scarcely make up for losing his wife, though Addison said he'd dedicate the award to Joan's memory.

His candy gifts had been tested, though not scientifically. The night nurses had managed to swipe the jelly beans from Addison's room as well as the chocolates that Judith had claimed earlier. They had been devoured; no one died. Addison discovered that they had been sent by his fellow journalists. He also vowed to describe the night staff as pigs in his Pulitzer Prize-winning story.

Mike returned to his mountain cabin early that evening. Renie went home Friday, as scheduled. Joe was released the next day. But Judith, having dislocated the artificial hip, was told by Dr. Alfonso that she'd have to remain in the hospital until Monday. She protested mightily, but in vain. Meanwhile, she was treated like a queen by the staff. Even Blanche Van Boeck sent her four dozen roses, in magnificent red, white, yellow, and pink hues.

The roses, which had arrived Friday, were still fresh when Judith was ready to leave. She was checking through her belongings to make sure she hadn't left anything behind when Father McConnaught came to see her.

"Now would you be that glad to be going home?" the priest asked with a smile.

"Oh, yes, Father," she replied with an answering smile, "that I would. I mean, *I would*. That is . . ."

Father McConnaught nodded sagely. "Bless you, my child, for your great help in seeking justice. Poor Mr. Jim, I'm afraid he must be daft."

"I'm sure he is," Judith replied, growing solemn.

"We'll pray for the poor man," the priest said. "I'll pray for you, too. Is there anything I can do before you leave us?"

"Yes," Judith said. "I'd like you to hear my confession. I couldn't go before Christmas because I was laid up with my hip. Would you mind?"

"I'd be delighted," the priest replied, reaching into his pocket and taking out the purple stole he wore for the Sacrament of Penance.

Judith bowed her head and blessed herself, then recited a brief list of venial sins before she got to the crux of the matter. As briefly as she could, she told Father McConnaught about Joe and Dan and the deception surrounding Mike's paternity. She had resolved to end the web of lies. But was it fair to Dan's memory and his conscientiousness as a father to Mike? This was the sticking point, and had been since Dan died.

"Well now," Father McConnaught said, "you take Good Cheer and the blessed sisters who've run it all these long years. Soon this place will be taken from them, and they'll be left with only memories. But no one can take away what they did, how they served, how much love they offered in the name of our blessed Lord. Can we say less for your late husband, rest his soul? No matter what his faults or failures, he lived, he loved, he made his mark. Glory be to God, eh?"

Through glistening tears, Judith smiled at Father McConnaught. "You're right. Thank you so much. I feel better. It's just that it'll be so hard to finally tell Mike."

"God will guide you," the priest said, and gave Judith absolution.

Robbie the Robot, apparently swerving to avoid someone in the hall, briefly faced into the room. "Beep-beep," he said.

Still smiling, Judith beeped right back.

Shortly before eleven, Joe and Mike showed up in her hospital room. Judith was sitting with the release form, checking off the detailed information and list of instructions for posthospital care. Joe was wearing a big bandage under his jacket, but definitely seemed on the mend.

"Kristin and Little Mac are at the house," Mike said. "They rode down with me this morning. Mac wants to see Ga-ga."

Judith flinched as she always did when she heard Mac's name for her. She sometimes wondered if he couldn't pronounce "grandma" or if he was describing her. Maybe he really was a Little Einstein.

"Everything's fine at the B&B," Joe assured Judith, taking her reaction as concern about Hillside Manor. "All the odious guests are gone, and the Rankerses can go home because Mike and Kristin are staying through the week."

"Oh, Mike!" Judith beamed at her son as Joe went off to the nurse's station to check Judith out. "You don't have to . . ."

"It's cool," Mike asserted. "We want to. Kristin thinks it'll be fun. She's even got some ideas about how you could run the place more efficiently."

"Oh. Good." Judith swallowed hard. "Mike, I have something to tell you—"

"Hey," Mike said, holding up a hand. "Kristin won't

get in your face. She just wants to help. If you don't like some of her ideas, tell her."

"No, it's not that," Judith insisted. "It's about Joe. When you came down here to see him in all that bad weather, I felt then that I should have spoken to you about what a risk you took and that—"

Mike put his hand up again. "No problem. Why wouldn't I do that?" Suddenly Mike's expression grew uncharacteristically sober. "After all, he's my father."

Judith's jaw dropped. "You *know?*"

Mike's eyes were level with Judith's as he took her hand. "I've known for a long time. I just didn't know if you wanted me to know. Are you okay with it?"

"Oh, Mike!" Judith burst into tears.

Joe reappeared in the doorway. "We're all set. Hey, what's wrong?"

"N-n-nothing," Judith blubbered. "I'm just so happy!"

Joe stared at Mike. "This is *happy?*"

"It sure is. *Pops,*" Mike added. He grinned at Joe, then shoved the hospital form at his mother. "Here, sign this so we can go home."

With trembling fingers, Judith signed the form. She fought for control and handed the sheet of paper to Joe. "That's right. I'm very happy." Judith took a deep breath. "I've finally gotten my release."

There's always an upcoming vacancy at Mary Daheim's delightful Bed-and-Breakfast series. And the next one can be found in

SILVER SCREAM

available Summer 2002 in hardcover from William Morrow.

Just as the summer's waning, things are heating up at Hillside Manor, where rejuvenated innkeeper Judith McMonigle Flynn is out of the hospital and back in business. But when a host of Hollywood hooligans descends on the B&B, that bedside bottle of aspirin may not do the trick.

Read on, and get a glimpse of how Judith and Renie take on Tinseltown in

SILVER SCREAM

JUDITH McMONIGLE FLYNN twitched in the kitchen chair, jumped up, paced the floor, and leaned her head against the open cupboard. Desperately, she tried reason, argument, and, finally, bad grammar in an attempt to foist off Ingrid Heffelman from the State Bed & Breakfast Association.

"I don't want none of those crazy people at Hillside Manor," she shouted into the phone. "I mean, *any* of them. They're Hollywood types, and they're nuts."

"Just because they make movies doesn't mean they're crazy," Ingrid huffed. "Look, I know this is a big favor. But you've only got two other reservations besides the producer, Bruno Zepf, for the last weekend of October. I can put those non-movie people up somewhere else to make room for the rest of Mr. Zepf's crew."

Since Bruno Zepf had made his reservation two weeks earlier, Judith knew she was stuck with him. Like many Hollywood big-shots, he was as superstitious as he was successful. Ten years earlier, his career as an independent producer had been launched at a film festival in the Midwest. At the time, Zepf couldn't afford a hotel; he'd had to stay in a Bed & Breakfast. The movie had been a huge success, and ever since, he had stayed at B&Bs before premiering a new production. But now it seemed that other members of his company wanted to stay in the same B&B to ensure that Bruno's good luck would rub off on them.

"Please, Ingrid," Judith pleaded, moving away from the cupboard door and trying to shut it tight, "I know I'm stuck with Mr. Zepf, but I've had my fill of so-called 'beautiful people', from opera singers to gossip columnists to TV media types. I've had gangsters and psychos and . . ."

"I know," Ingrid interrupted, her tone suddenly cold. "That's one of the reasons you're going to accept this deal. You've managed to have some very big problems at Hillside Manor, and while they don't seem to have hurt your business, they give the rest of the B&Bs a black eye. Look at what happened a year or so ago—your establishment was included in a sight-seeing tour of murder sites, and you ended up on TV with a dead body."

"The body wasn't at Hillside Manor," Judith retorted, giving the stubborn cupboard door an angry slam. "And it certainly wasn't my fault. Besides, I got the tour group to take Hillside Manor off the sight-seeing itinerary, didn't I?"

"You still looked like an idiot on that television interview they did where they called you Nancy Drew or Miss Marple or some damned thing," Ingrid countered. "It was an embarrassment for inn-keepers all over the state. You owe me—and all the rest of the good people who run B&Bs around here."

"That was the editing," Judith protested. "I certainly didn't ask to be on TV. I begged them not to do the piece. I hardly consider myself a sleuth. I run a B&B, period. I can't help it if all sorts of weird people come here. Look, now you're the one who's setting me up. Will you blame yourself if something happens while all these movie nut cases are staying at Hillside Manor?"

There was no response. The line was dead. Ingrid had hung up on her.

"Damn," Judith breathed. "Ingrid's a mule."

"She always was," Gertrude Grover responded. "Fast, too. She wore her skirts way too short in high school. No wonder she got into trouble."

Judith stared at her mother. "This is a different Ingrid. She runs the state B&B association. She's my age, not yours."

Gertrude's small eyes narrowed. "You just think she is. Ingrid Sack's been dying her hair for years. Had a face-lift, too. More than once I heard."

"Mother," Judith said patiently, "Ingrid Sack—I believe her married name was Grissom—has been dead for ten years."

Now it was Gertrude's turn to stare. "No kidding? I wonder how she looked in her casket. All tarted up, I bet. Funny I didn't hear about it at the time."

There was no point in telling Gertrude that she'd undoubtedly read Ingrid's obituary in the newspaper. Read it with glee, as the old lady always did when she discovered she'd outlived yet another contemporary. Judith was used to her mother's patchy memory.

"I'm stuck," Judith announced, sitting down at the kitchen table across from her mother. "Come October, we're going to be invaded by Hollywood."

Gertrude pulled a rumpled Kleenex from the pocket of her baggy orange cardigan. "Hollywood?" she echoed before lustily blowing her nose. "You mean like the Gish Sisters and Tom Mix and Mary Pickford?"

"Uh . . . like that," Judith agreed. "A famous producer is premiering his new movie here in town because it was filmed in the area. He's bringing his entourage—at least some of it—to Hillside Manor."

"Entourage?" Gertrude looked puzzled. "I thought you didn't allow pets."

"I don't," Judith replied. "I meant his associates. Speaking of pets," she said sharply to Sweetums as the cat leaped onto the kitchen table, "beat it. You don't prowl the furniture."

Sweetums was batting at the lid of the sheep-shaped cookie jar. The cat did not take kindly to Judith's efforts to pick him up and set him down.

"Feisty," Gertrude remarked as Sweetums broke free and ran off in a blur of orange and white fur. "You got to admit it, Toots, that cat has spunk."

Judith gave her mother an ironic smile. "So do you. You're kindred spirits."

"He gets around better than I do," Gertrude said, turning stiffly to watch Sweetums disappear with a bang of the screen door.

Deciding that it was best not to open that can of worms, Judith said, "I ought to call in person to cancel the reservations of the guests who are being displaced by the movie people." She scrolled down the screen on her computer monitor. "Let's see—the Kidds from Wisconsin and the Izards from Iowa."

"Those are guests? They sound like innards to me." Gertrude was struggling to get out of her chair.

Judith reached out to give her mother a hand and escort her to the back door.

They had reached the porch steps when Joe Flynn pulled into the driveway in his cherished antique MG, top down, red paint gleaming in the late afternoon sun.

"Ladies," he called, getting out of the car with his cotton jacket slung over one shoulder. "You're a vision."

"You mean a sight for sore eyes," Gertrude shot back.

"Do I?" Gold flecks danced in Joe's green eyes as he kissed his wife's cheek, then attempted to brush his mother-in-law's forehead with his lips.

Gertrude jerked away, almost throwing Judith off-balance. "Baloney!" the old girl cried. "You just want to get my goat. As usual." She plunked the walker on the ground and shook off Judith's hand. "I'm heading for my earthly coffin. Send my supper on time, which is five, not six or six-thirty." Gertrude clumped off toward the converted toolshed, her self-imposed exile since she had long ago declared she wouldn't live under the same roof as Joe Flynn.

"Ah," Joe said, a hand under Judith's elbow, "your mother seems in fine spirits today."

"I can't tell the difference," Judith muttered. "She's always mean to you."

"It keeps her going," Joe said, hanging his jacket on a peg in the hall. "Beer would do the same for me. Have we got any of that Harp left or did Mike drink it all?"

"He didn't drink as much as Kristin did," Judith replied, going to the fridge. "But I think there are a couple of bottles left. Kristin, being of Amazonian proportions, has a much greater capacity than other mortals." She glanced up at the old schoolroom clock which showed ten minutes to five. "You're early. How come?"

"I found Sir Francis Bacon," Joe responded, sitting down in the chair that Gertrude had vacated. "How the hell can you lose an English sheep dog? They're huge."

"Where was he?" Judith asked, handing Joe a bottle of Harp's.

"In their basement," Joe said after taking a long swallow of beer. "He was trying to keep cool, and in the process, managed to get into the freezer. He found some USDA prime cuts and ate about a half-dozen which gave him a tummy ache. Then he went behind the furnace and passed out. He was there for two days."

"Sir Francis is okay?" Judith inquired after pouring herself a glass of lemonade.

"He will be," Joe said. "They trotted him off to the vet. I hate these damned lost pet cases, but the family's loaded, it took only a couple of hours to find the dog, and they paid me a grand." He patted the pocket of his cotton shirt. "Nice work, huh?"

"Very nice," Judith said with a big smile. "All your private detective cases should be so easy. And profitable. Maybe we can use some of that money to have Skjoval Tolvang make some more repairs around here."

"How old is that guy anyway?" Joe asked with a bemused expression on his round, florid face.

"Eighties, I'd guess," Judith replied, "but strong as an ox. You know how hearty those Scandinavians are."

"Like our daughter-in-law, Kristin," Joe acknowledged, opening the evening paper which Judith had retrieved earlier from the front porch.

"Yes," Judith said in a wondering voice. Kristin was not only big and beautiful, but so infuriatingly competent that her mother-in-law was occasionally intimidated. "Yes," she repeated. "Formidable, too. What is she not?"

The front door bell rang, making Judith jump. "The guests! They're all part of a tour, here for two nights. I didn't think they'd arrive until five-thirty." She dashed out through the swinging doors between the kitchen and the dining room to greet the newcomers.

The tour group, consisting of a dozen retirees from Eastern Canada, were on the last leg of a trip that had started in Toronto. Some of them looked as if they were on their last legs, too. Judith escorted them to their rooms, made sure everything was in order, and informed them that the social hour began at six. To a man—and woman—they begged off, insisting that they simply wanted to rest for an hour or two before heading out to dinner.

Cancellation of the social hour meant that she, too, could take it easy. Following hip replacement surgery in January, Judith still tired easily. But before taking a respite, she had to call the Kidds and the Izards to inform them that their reservations were being changed due to unforeseen circumstances.

Joe had just opened his second Harp when Judith returned to the kitchen. She observed the top of his head behind the sports section and smiled to herself. There was more gray in his red hair, and in truth, there was less of either color. But to Judith, Joe Flynn was still the most attractive man on earth. She had waited almost a quarter of a century to become his wife, but the years in between seemed to have faded into an Irish mist. On the way to the computer, she paused to kiss the top of his head.

"What's this rash outbreak of affection?" Joe asked without glancing up.

"Just remembering that I love you," Judith said lightly.

"Do you need reminding?"

"No."

"She noted the Kidds' number in Appleton, Wisconsin and dialed. They were repeat customers, having come to Hillside Manor six years earlier. Judith hated to cancel them.

Alice Kidd answered the phone on the second ring. Judith relayed the doleful news and apologized most humbly. "You'll be put up at a really lovely B&B which will be convenient to everything. Ms. Heffelman will contact you in a day or two with the specifics."

"Well, darn it all anyway," Mrs. Kidd said with a Midwestern twang. "We so enjoyed your place. How is your mother? Edgar and I thought she was a real doll."

A Voodoo doll perhaps, Judith thought. "Mother's fine," she said aloud.

"You're certain we'll be staying in as nice a B&B as yours?"

"Definitely," Judith declared. "Maybe even nicer."

"I doubt that," Mrs. Kidd said as if she meant it.

"You're very kind," Judith responded. "We'll be in touch."

Next she dialed the number of Walt and Meg Izard in Riceville, Iowa. A frazzled-sounding woman answered the phone.

"Mrs. Izard?" Judith inquired.

"Yeah, right. Who is this? We're watching TV."

"I'm sorry," Judith said, then identified herself as the owner of Hillside Manor.

"What's that?" Mrs. Izard snapped. "A rest home? Walt and I aren't ready for that yet. Call back in twenty years."

"Wait!" Judith cried, certain that Meg Izard was about to slam down the receiver. "I own the Bed-and-Breakfast you're staying at in October. The nights of the twenty-ninth and the thirtieth. I'm afraid there's been a change, and I won't be able to accommodate you that weekend."

She then informed Mrs. Izard that they would be hearing from Ingrid Heffelman who would make sure they were put up in a very nice inn.

"Heffelman?" Mrs. Izard echoed. "Are you calling from Milwaukee? Don't you have anybody out there who isn't a German?"

"My name is Flynn," Judith said primly, though in fact she was part German on her mother's side. "What does that tell you?"

"Irish," Meg muttered. "Not much better, if you ask me. Okay, we'll stay tuned. But this Heffelbump woman better call soon. October's not that far away."

It was two months away, Judith thought, but didn't want to argue. She was beginning to feel grateful that the Izards wouldn't be staying at Hillside Manor. Trying to remain gracious, Judith rung off, hoping now that the waning summer and the early fall would be relatively uneventful.

It was typical of Judith that, as Cousin Renie would say, she would bury her head in the sand. On that warm August evening, Judith dug deep and tried to blot out some of life's less pleasant incidents.

One of them was Skjoval Tolvang. The tall, sinewy old handyman with his stubborn nature and unshakable convictions had already made some improvements to Hillside Manor. He had repaired the sagging front steps, replaced the ones in back, re-built both chimneys which had been damaged in an earthquake, inspected all the electrical wiring, and put in what he called a "Super-Duper Door Spring" to keep the cupboard in the kitchen from opening by itself. What was left involved hanging a new door to the bathroom on the first floor and checking out the plumbing in the toolshed.

Judith came a cropper with the bathroom repair. On the first day of September, Mr. Tolvang showed up very early. It was not yet six o'clock when he banged on the back door. Joe was in the shower and Judith had just finished getting dressed. The noise was loud enough to be heard in the third-floor family quarters, and thus even louder for the sleeping guests on the second floor.

"Damn!" Judith breathed, taking the back stairs to the main floor as fast as she could without risking a fall.

"By early," she said, yanking open the back door, "I thought you meant seven or eight."

"Early is early," the handyman replied. "Isn't this early, pygolly?"

"It's too early for me to have made coffee," Judith asserted. "You'll have to wait a few minutes."

But Skjoval Tolvang reached into his big tool box and removed a tall blue Thermos. "I got my medicine to get me going. I was up at four."

Coffee fueled the handyman the way that gasoline propelled cars. He never ate on the job, putting in long, arduous days with only his seemingly bottomless Thermos to keep him going.

"I'm a little worried," Judith said, pouring coffee into both the big urn she used for guests and the family coffee-maker. "Having a bathroom just off the entry hall may no longer be up to city code."

"Code!" Skjoval coughed up the word as if he'd swallowed a spider. "To hell with the city! Vat do they know, that bunch of crackpot politicians? They be lucky to find the bathroom, let alone know where to put it!"

"It was only a thought " Judith said meekly.

"You vorry too much," Skjoval declared, putting the Thermos back into his tool box. "I don't need no hassles. I quit."

It wasn't the first time, nor would it be the last, that the handyman had quit over some quibble. Skjoval never lacked for work. He was good and he was cheap. But he was also temperamental.

Judith knew the drill, though it wasn't easy to repeat at six-ten in the morning. She pleaded, groveled, cajoled, and used all of her considerable charm to get Skjoval to change his mind. Ultimately, he did, but it took another ten minutes.

Luckily, the rest of the week and the Labor Day weekend went smoothly. It was only the following Friday, when Skjoval was finishing up in the toolshed, that another fracas ensued.

"That mother of yours," Skjoval complained, wiping sweat from his brow as he stood on the back porch. "She is Lucifer's daughter. I hang the bathroom door yust fine, but vy vill she not let me fix the toilet?"

"I don't know," Judith replied. Indeed, she had been afraid that Gertrude and Mr. Tolvang would get into it before the job was done. Given their natures, it seemed inevitable. "Did she give you a reason?"

"Hell, no," the handyman shot back, "except that she be sitting on the damned thing."

"Oh." Judith frowned in the direction of the toolshed. "I'll go talk to her."

"Don't bother," Skjoval snapped. "I quit."

"Please, Mr. Tolvang," Judith begged, "let me ask . . ."

But the handyman made a sharp dismissive gesture. "Never you mind. I don't vant to see that old bat no more. She give me a bad time all veek. Let her sit on the damned toilet until her backside falls off." Skjoval yanked the painter's cap from his head and waved it in a threatening manner. "I go now, you call me if she ever acts like a human being and not a vitch." He stomped off down the drive to his pick-up truck which was piled with ladders, scaffolding and all manner of tools.

Judith gritted her teeth and headed out under the golden September sun. Surely her mother would recant. The toilet needed to be plunged, since Gertrude threw all sorts of things into it, including Sweetums. It was either Skjoval Tolvang for the job or a hundred bucks to Roto-Rooter.

Gertrude wasn't on the toilet when Judith reached the toolshed. Instead, she was sitting in her old mohair armchair, playing solitaire on the cluttered card table.

"Hi, toots," Gertrude said in a cheerful voice. "What's up, besides that old fart's dander?"

"Why wouldn't you let Mr. Tolvang plunge the toilet?" Judith demanded.

"Because I was using it, that's why." Gertrude scooped up the cards and had just put them in her automatic shuffler, when Skjoval Tolvang burst into the toolshed.

"You got spies," he declared, banging the door behind him. "Building inspectors, ya sure, you betcha."

Judith's dark eyes widened. "Really? Where?"

"By them bushes," the handyman answered nodding at the azaleas, rhododendrons and roses that flanked the west side of the house. "Making trouble, mark my words."

"I wonder," Judith murmured, heading down the driveway.

There was, however, nobody to be seen. She moved on to the front of the house. An unfamiliar white car was parked in the cul-de-sac. There were no markings on it. Judith continued to the other side of the house.

A tall man in a dark suit and hat stood between the house and the hedge that divided Judith and Joe Flynn's property from their neighbors, Carl and Arlene Rankers. He had his back to Judith and appeared to be looking up under the eaves.

"Sir!" Judith spoke sharply. "May I help you?"

The man whirled around. "What?" He had a beard and wore rimless spectacles. There was such an old-fashioned air about him that Judith was reminded of a character out of a late nineteenth-century novel.

"Are you looking for someone?" Judith inquired, moving closer to the stranger.

He hesitated, one hand brushing nervously against his trouser leg. "Well, yes," he finally replied. "I am. A Mr. Terwilliger. I was told he lived in this cul-de-sac."

Judith shook her head. "There's no one by that name around here. Unless," she added, "he intends to stay at my B&B." She made an expansive gesture toward the old three-story Edwardian house. "I run this place. It's called Hillside Manor. There's a sign out front."

The man, who had been slowly but deliberately back-pedaling from Judith, ducked his head. "I must have missed it. Sorry." He turned and all but ran around the rear of the house.

Judith's hip replacement didn't permit her to move much faster than a brisk walk. Puzzled, she watched the man disappear, then returned to the front yard. He was coming down the driveway on the other side of the house, still at a gallop. A moment later, he got into the car parked at the curb and pulled away with a burst of the engine.

"Local plates," she murmured. But from where Judith stood some ten yards away, she hadn't been able to read the license numbers. With a shrug, she headed back to the toolshed. She'd mention the stranger's appearance to Joe when he got home. If she remembered.

Three hours later, when Joe arrived cursing the dead-end he'd come up against in a missing antique clock case, Judith forgot all about the man who'd shown up at Hillside Manor.

It would be two months before she'd remember, and by that time, it was almost too late.

Murder Is on the Menu
at the Hillside Manor Inn
Bed-and-Breakfast Mysteries by
MARY DAHEIM
featuring Judith McMonigle Flynn

Discover Murder and Mayhem with
～ Southern Sisters Mysteries ～
by
ANNE GEORGE

MURDER ON A GIRLS' NIGHT OUT
0-380-78086-0/$6.50 US/$8.99 Can
Agatha Award winner for Best First Mystery Novel

MURDER ON A BAD HAIR DAY
0-380-78087-9/$6.50 US/$8.99 Can

MURDER RUNS IN THE FAMILY
0-380-78449-1/$6.50 US/$8.99 Can

MURDER MAKES WAVES
0-380-78450-5/$6.50 US/$8.99 Can

MURDER GETS A LIFE
0-380-79366-0/$6.50 US/$8.99 Can

MURDER SHOOTS THE BULL
0-380-80149-3/$6.50 US/$8.99 Can

MURDER CARRIES A TORCH
0-380-80938-9/$6.50 US/$8.99 Can